The

Daedalus

Directive

A Novel

By

Doug

Dahlgren

RH
Publishing

ISBN : 978-0-9833767-7-4

LCCN : Pending

Printed in the United States of America

Ridge House Publishing

Decatur, Georgia

Cover Design

Erica Robb

Yoni Art and Design

yoniartanddesign.com

Dedication

We shared a name and a middle initial though I am not a junior.

His "E" stood for "Eric," while mine is for "Edwin."

He served in the Philippines in World War II, U.S. Army Air Corps, and went back to school went he came home.

A mechanical engineer by education, he wore many hats in his professional life. By trade he was also, a railway equipment design engineer, an aeronautical engineer, a heavy farm equipment design engineer, and a chemical engineer. He was a smart and versatile man.

He loved his family; his kids and his grandchildren especially. He loved to go to their sports events or anything else they were doing.

He loved the Braves, the Falcons, "The Edge of Night" soap opera, and many thirty minute comedy shows on TV.

He also loved to read. He read Sidney Sheldon, John LeCarre', Robert Ludlum, Fredrick Forsyth, and others of that day. I recall his fascination with John Jakes' series on the American Revolutionary period and how he got my wife interested in those. He read a bunch... but he never thought that his son would ever write a book.

My father passed away in March of 1988. He was sixty-seven years old.

I'd like to think he would love my stories, because he was my dad, sure, but for other reasons as well. I'll ask him about them someday.

In the meantime, I dedicate this novel and the entire series to him :

My father

Douglas Eric Dahlgren

Acknowledgments

Many thanks... to my volunteer group of proof readers and editors who make these stories readable.

They come from varying backgrounds and work experiences and I am very fortunate to have their support and assistance.

David Butler

Neil Lesser

Chuck McCorvey Sr.

Dr. Blane Woodfin

Patty Duke

Donna Dahlgren

Thank you all !

The
Daedalus
Directive

Book Six of
The Son

a conclusion.......

Prologue

Arriving at his modest home a bit later than some mornings, Warren Dawes took the delay in stride. Rain was at fault and that couldn't be helped. He drove as a substitute for the local school system, and rainy days were a sure thing for him. Regular drivers would call-in sick for fear of dealing with the screaming kids and the weather. A wreck could mean the loss of the job and worse. The two didn't bother this man. He had patience if nothing else.

Sliding down from the seat of his pick-up truck, the man fought off the urge to grab at his stiff and sore lower back. It was just over ten years since the accident. The injury he sustained prevented any work other than his part-time job of driving a school bus.

A slow and deliberate step up to his backdoor led to the warm interior of the house. He threw his keys on the kitchen table and noticed the red blinking light on his phone. Caller ID showed an odd number for the incoming call. It read 1-800-555-1115. The voice message was only one word, "Jamie."

Without reaction to the message, the man made a pot of coffee and took four aspirins from a large bottle in the cabinet. Washing them down with a handful of tap water, he leaned against the sink and watched the brewer do its work. When it was finished, he sat at a small, round table and stared at the phone as he drank two cups. Then he checked his watch. It was 10:45 A.M.

The number on the caller ID was really the message. In code, that number told him another call would come in on a burner cell, one of several he stored in a box on the shelf in his hall closet. The serial number of the correct one would end in 331.

Shifting through the box he found the correct phone and put a battery in it. Then laying it on the kitchen table, he poured yet more coffee, sat down with it, and waited.

At 11:15 A.M. the cell phone rang.

"Welcome to Oxford," the warden had said to her. He then leaned back in his large leather chair and smirked uncontrollably.

Natalie Barrett stood before the desk in her orange jump suit, hands shackled. She raised them as high as she could.

"I must admit," she glared at the warden. "I didn't expect this."

"Not sure what you expected, Miss Barrett. But this isn't a spa. You screwed that up for yourself."

The prisoner said nothing in response. She did react to the guard pushing a chair up behind her.

"Sit," the warden suggested.

"I'm fine," she muttered.

"You won't think so in a few days," he shot back. "This is Wisconsin, lady. Martha Stewart didn't come here."

He motioned for the guard to leave and leaned forward, both arms on the desk top. "Why did you screw up your stay at Alderson?"

"Didn't like being a sitting duck," she smiled.

"Somebody after you?"

"Everybody has somebody after them," her eyes dropped to the floor.

"If you felt you were in danger you could have just said so....you didn't have to set fire to your mattress and endanger others around you."

Again, she had no response.

"Your old boss wouldn't be pleased," he said with a tease.

Barrett looked up into his eyes and glared at the man for what seemed a long time.

"You think he is my boss?" she laughed. "He's nobody; we're finished with him like everyone else." Her eyes became stone as she paused. "He's not my boss..." rolled from her in a growl, "and he's not who the guy is after."

"You're a smart woman, Barrett," the warden said like it was difficult for him. "Who do you think is after you?"

Natalie Barrett rocked her head and tilted it to one side.

"We'll see," she said softly.

"Nobody can get to you in here, Miss Barrett...nobody."

~

The instrument chirped and danced around on the table top for nearly a full minute. He'd watched it bounce around from his leaned back position in the wooden chair. Finally reaching out, Warren Dawes put his coffee cup down. The part time bus driver then picked up the vibrating cell phone and answered it.

"Jamie?" he asked curtly.

"This is Jamie," the voice responded. "Is this Warren?"

"You know it is," Dawes said picking his cup up again. "What can I do for you?"

"You still into wet work?" the caller asked in a matter-of-fact tone.

"That depends, my friend," Dawes answered calmly. "Who do you represent?"

"You worked with us before...in Arkansas in '14."

"Okay," the man responded. The strange voice and name meant nothing to him, but that date sure did. "How deep is this job?" he asked.

"We need one individual sanctioned."

"One?"

"Yeah...just one. But getting to him will be your challenge."

The man turned his cup up and finished it off. He twisted his neck as though loosening up and spoke again.

"Particulars to box 826 and then call me in a week," he told this voice calling itself Jamie. "We'll talk then."

Prisoner number 37624-88 responded to a knock on the wall of his cell in the maximum security wing of Oxford, Wisconsin's Federal Correctional Facility. A wrinkled note appeared through the crack near his wall- mounted bunk. Propelled by a soft draft of air, blown through a plastic straw, the folded paper jutted out through the broken concrete.

Reaching up, the prisoner pulled the paper from the wall. He unfolded it and read the simple note several times.

"Your release possible," it read in miniscule type, "your talents needed for job."

At the very bottom were two other words, typed in separate locations, "interested" on one side... and "no" on the other.

Jackson Terrell stood and walked to his far wall, some four feet away. Leaning his head against the cold, rough surface the thought process didn't take too long.

He still had seven years before any consideration of parole. He tore the word, "interested" loose from the small paper and folded it. Wadding the rest into a tiny ball, he swallowed it whole and stepped back to the crack in the wall. The folded one word response was slipped back into the crack. He pulled his own plastic straw from a cup on the sink and blew the paper deeper into the wall. Then he tapped the wall with his fist.

Prisoner 37624-88 lay down on his bunk and smiled at the ceiling.

Whatever they want is better than rotting in here, he thought quietly.

Doug Dahlgren

"The battle, Sir, is not to the strong alone; it is to the vigilant, the active, the brave...There is no retreat but in submission and slavery!"

Patrick Henry

1

"So...you're just gonna let me do all the talking, huh?" The cowboy had been glad to hear from his friend, but expected a conversation about his concern. Instead, he got a silent listener on the other end of a phone call.

"I've told you before," Murray Bilstock went on. "I think I've earned the right to be more than just an outsider that you call in from time to time."

"You are not an outsider, Murray," the other voice said deliberately.

"Oh...really? Who am I talking to anyway, Jon or Silas? I can never tell anymore."

The silence after that outburst was deafening. Both sides waited for the other to speak. Jon finally gathered his patience.

"Murray...I've tried to explain this to you. I understand how you feel and I care about that. You are my friend...you're one of my closest friends," he corrected himself. "And you are a faithful and trusted brother-in-arms."

The pause that followed wasn't for effect. Jon measured his next words carefully before he continued.

"I don't want to lose either of those, Murray...and I really don't want to lose both. But this is the way it is...the way it has to be... and the way it will be. I will share with you everything you need to know about what I do. What I leave out is for our protection. Not just yours...but both of us."

He waited a few seconds for the cowboy to lash out, but that didn't happen this time.

"So it's Silas I've got on the line," Murray cracked.

The welcome display of his friend's sense of humor eased Jon's mind.

"Yeah...I guess so," he said back in a softer tone than before. "You know more than anyone, except Ben. You know more than Marsha. Think about that when you feel left out, will ya?"

"They've moved her, you know?" Murray had changed the subject which meant the former discussion was over.

"Moved who?"

"That Barrett woman."

"How do know that?" Jon asked.

"Tim heard before he left."

"Left?" Jon was surprised. "It's only been two weeks."

"Yeah, well...he has a whole NCIS team to protect him in New Orleans. He left several days ago, actually."

"So it's common knowledge about the move," Jon went back.

"In certain circles," Murray added. "I haven't seen it mentioned on TV yet."

"What do you believe happened?"

"She set fire to her room at Alderson. Damnedest thing I ever heard of, looks like she wanted to be moved."

"That's in line with what Ben has found out," Jon said thoughtfully. "Why would she do that?"

"She's more afraid of you than you are her."

Jon became quiet again, but only for a few moments.

"You think she knows we're on to her?"

"Oh... hell yeah."

"That complicates things."

"Well...you and Ben will figure it out," Murray said in an odd tone.

"Are Phil and Sara still with you?"

"Actually, they're packed up. I'm taking them back to Shreveport this afternoon."

Jon took a deep breath. "Westy and Rita left here yesterday," he admitted. "Harold took them back to Sault Ste. Marie. Looks like I may have been too cautious this time."

"Buddy," Murray said using a name he never had with Jon before, "You are never too cautious...Is Daniel still there?"

"Yeah, he's running things with Ben and Cheryl."

"Cheryl? Westy's girl stayed?"

Jon caught himself smiling. "We have a budding romance on our hands. Marsha is keeping an eye on it."

"How 'bout that? Good fer Ben," the cowboy grinned. "Speaking of...what has he found on this Barrett woman?"

"Another lawyer, by education," Jon told him. "Worked around her former boss for years and came up with him. The story is she wasn't pleased with taking all the blame, but did anyway."

"Lawyer, huh?" Murray said seriously. "We may need another tiger."

Jon grunted to hold back a laugh, "I get the feeling there's more to her than we or anyone knows."

"Can you get to her old boss?"

"That's my problem with her. I don't think her boss is who everyone believes it is."

~

Cody Arnold was happy to be back in Alabama. The former SEAL and Development Group Operator was healing nicely from his injuries. The encounter with Clifford Wyckoff at Nag's Head had been brutal. His left arm was still wrapped thickly and immobilized and the cuts across the young man's chest had ceased oozing. The doctors said that was a great sign.

Will, his friend, mentor and owner of the exotic animal preserve, wheeled Cody down to see Boris on day one. The chair was an aggravation to Cody but necessary to keep him from over-exertion.

"Hey big fella," Cody said, reaching for the first fence layer with his good hand.

Boris, a slightly undersized yet feisty lion, raised his eyes and then slowly brought his head up from its resting place. He stared at the man with confusion and shifted his eyes to Will for a second before looking back at his old friend.

"What's wrong, old boy? You don't know it's me?"

Boris rolled his huge head, sampling the scent in the air and focusing in more on the man in the strange chair. Antiseptics and other medicinal rubs had all but masked his identifying odor, but as the big cat concentrated, he realized it was indeed his friend.

Launching himself toward the fence, Boris rubbed at the chain link and uttered a low growl that both Cody and Will recognized.

"I'll leave you two alone for a bit," Will smiled and walked away.

NCIS Agent Leonard Monroe sat at his desk in the Jacksonville, Florida, field office staring into space. This was not his usual activity.

His partner, Jake Hansard, watched his friend for several minutes before disturbing him.

"What's on your mind?" he challenged.

Monroe shook his head before turning to his friend.

"Huh?" he answered and suddenly looked for a pen on his desk.

"You've been in deep thought over there since lunch," Hansard exaggerated with a grin. "It's not like you...not to share."

Monroe, having found the elusive pen, dropped it into a holder and leaned back before he spoke.

His thoughts were of the case he and Hansard had worked a few short weeks ago. Starting in the Okefenokee Swamp, they had assisted in tracking down a killer. One who had stalked members of a SEAL Team mission. The death of the murderer at an exclusive beach house brought the case to a close, but Monroe was not completely satisfied.

"Do you think that mess is over?"

Hansard knew what mess he was referring to instantly.

"I don't know," he said. "Obviously, you don't."

"There's a current running under it all," Monroe tried to explain. "I don't think that crazy guy, Wyckoff, was working with anyone else. But I still feel there's more to this thing."

Hansard closed a file he'd been half way studying and spun his chair toward Monroe.

"You talked to anyone about this?"

"Hell, no. Who would that be anyway?"

The senior agent took a more patronizing tone. "Me, for one," he said flatly.

"Alright then," Monroe took a deep breath. "You heard about Beale, right?"

Ted Beale, a congressman from Connecticut had been killed in his high-rise condo during the SEAL case.

"The congressman that got blown to pieces?"

"Yeah...him. I looked into that a bit, through some friends in D.C.."

"Really?" Hansard wrinkled his brow. "Why?"

"The timing of it all got me wondering if there was a connection."

"To Wyckoff?"

"Well, not directly," Monroe became a bit more animated. "But that mission was screwed from the get-go... six ways from Sunday."

Still listening, Hansard nodded but remained silent.

"It wasn't widely known, but Beale was the head of a secret committee that selected the team members for the NSWDG missions."

"No shit?" Hansard spit out.

"None...I doubt Wyckoff ever heard of Beale, but there's something going on that somebody didn't want that team to find out about."

Hansard leaned back himself and both men were quiet for a few minutes. Sitting up sharply, he looked straight at Monroe.

"My gut agrees with you," he spit out.

"Your what?"

"My gut! You've never had a gut reaction to something?"

"Well, yeah," Monroe laugh. "Back when I was a kid. I haven't heard that term in years."

"How long have we worked together?" Hansard demanded.

"I don't know...seven years?"

"Exactly...I've learned to have faith in your judgment, Lenny."

"In your gut, huh?" Monroe smiled. "I remember what you told me about North Carolina.

"You want my help or not?"

Monroe's face became serious again, "Yeah, I really do."

"I'll call that guy in Washington, the NCIS Director, see if there's any leads or "gut" feelings they have we can follow up on."

Monroe smiled.

"Thanks, Jake. I feel really strongly about this. I appreciate your back."

Hansard nodded profusely and grabbed at his desk phone.

2

A side trip on the way home from Shreveport was called for. It had been some time since Murray Bilstock had visited his mother and sister, Charlene, back in Dallas.

Stephen can keep an eye on the ranch, he told himself. The cousin, known by the nickname Slick, had become much more settled and dependable in the last year. His brush with death, at the hands of the biker gang, had changed him.

It was Murray's third day in Dallas, after spending three days with Phil and Sara at their lake house, he had flown directly there.

"Murray," Charlene called to him. "Is your phone not working?"

Feeling around at each pocket, Murray first said, "Its fine." But not finding it, he realized he'd left it in the helicopter. "I'm sure it is, wherever I left it," he corrected himself with a chuckle.

"Slick is on the phone," Charlene said seriously, "sounds like he's concerned about something."

Taking the phone, Murray's expression changed as he spoke into it.

"Hey, everything alright over there?"

"Man...I've been trying to call you since yesterday," Stephen was nearly stammering as he talked. "I went to town yesterday, passed two black pick-up trucks just sitting still out on the highway."

Murray remained quiet, letting his cousin concentrate on the story he was trying to relay.

"When I got back a couple hours later," Slick went on, "they were gone... but I checked the surveillance cameras on the grounds."

"Did they go inside?" Murray asked, assuming the cameras had shown intruders.

"No," Stephen continued, "just looked around. The hangar door was open, and they didn't go in there either."

"Any license plates or names on the trucks?"

"Naw...nothing. The trucks didn't carry plates."

"I'm assuming you scanned for any devices they may have left."

"Oh yeah," the cousin said. "We're clean, but those guys were up to something."

"Stay down in the safe room," Murray ordered with a tone in his voice. "I'll be there in the morning."

"That's where I've been, man. The house is locked up and I'm down here watching the monitors."

"Is Lucy okay?" her worried owner asked.

"She's below as well," Stephen smiled while explaining. "That new system you put in works like a champ."

Murray's Sikorski was a terrific bird, but his first love was still the Bell 407, his beloved "Lucy." With some of the bequeath from Jon, Murray had another dugout area built in the last six months. Lucy's concrete pad now sat on a hydraulic lift unit that could lower the Bell helicopter below ground and then slide a thin veneer of concrete in place of the actual pad.

When the operation was done at night, it would appear Lucy was out on a mission once daylight returned to the ranch.

"Good..." the cowboy pilot thanked him. "I'll see you tomorrow then." Murray put down his sister's phone and rubbed his jaw. *Jon may have been right after all*, he thought in silence.

Charlene had figured something was up. She also knew he wouldn't tell her unless she needed to know.

"You're leaving, huh?" she asked in lieu of anything else.

Her brother nodded, "In the morning, yeah." He leaned in and kissed her forehead, but offered no explanation.

"Let's not tell Mom right now, okay?"

~

Jerome Grimes answered on the first ring. He was standing behind his desk, about to go to a meeting in MTAC.

"Yeah?" he barked into the receiver.

"Director, this is Special Agent Jake Hansard out of the Jacksonville office."

Grimes smiled and sat back down. He paused for only a moment then spoke in his recognizable forceful tone.

"Yes, Agent Hansard. How are you?"

"I'm well, sir. Thank you," the agent told him. "I was wondering if I might ask a question of a rather sensitive nature?"

Grimes rocked back in his chair.

"You can ask...Might be as far as it goes," he cautioned.

"Is your office handling the investigation into what happened with Congressman Beale?"

"Why do you ask that, Special Agent?"

Hansard could tell the conversation had become quite official.

"My partner and I have a theory...more of a hunch really, that Beale was involved somehow with the SEAL killings."

"The death of the congressman...that investigation... is being handled at another level," Grimes stated. "Any involvement on our part is classified and we don't discuss those things, you know that, Agent Hansard."

"All due respect, sir, yes, I do understand. We're just trying to be of help."

"Then stick to what you know, agent. Not what you feel."

"Sir...remember, I was in that house...the beach house. I saw the man in the black suit and the other guy he helped get away from there."

Grimes stayed quiet.

"I've never heard anything more about either of them, sir," Hansard went on. "The guy in the suit flew a chopper, a dang slick Sikorsky. One like I've never seen before. He told me his black suit came with the job."

"I feel a question in there somewhere," Grimes muttered.

"What job, sir? Who is that guy...and his friend?"

"I'll try to find that out for you," the director shot back.

"You see, sir," Hansard went on. "We know Beale had a hand in the SEAL mission, most likely a bad hand."

A knock at his door distracted the NCIS Director for a second, but the word "theory" had been replaced with "know" and his agent was serious.

"Hold on," he hollered at the door with a hand over the phone.

"Look, Hansard," he said while standing. "I'll make a call this afternoon. You and your partner come up here...my guests. I'll arrange it through your superiors. We do need to talk."

Hansard tried to thank him but the line went dead.

~

Silence followed Phil Stone as he walked the short dock on Cross Lake.

Am I paranoid or just careful? He asked himself. *Or is there a difference?*

With his Smith and Wesson 40 caliber firmly in hand, this walk had become a daily ritual since he and Sara returned from Murray's place. Their home on Cross Lake was fairly remote. Due west of Shreveport, Phil and Sara had chosen a spot away from the main subdivisions closer to town. The closest neighbor was a hundred yards away, across the small cove on an unnamed access road.

Phil's dock reached out forty feet into the water and stood only thirty inches above the water line. He tied off his jon-boat and a 28 foot v-hull outboard on either side. All appeared normal until Phil turned back toward the house and started to holster his weapon. Sunlight caught and highlighted a new scuff mark along the wooden walkway.

Kneeling down, Phil could see faint traces of green paint beside the bare wood that had been rubbed raw. Any thoughts of it having been there and simply missed in his searches were cast aside by the obviously fresh wood the impact had exposed. Less than an inch in length and no deeper than a fingernail is thick, the mark would be obscured by the weather before dark that day. This was new and barely hours old.

"We've had company," retired Captain Phillip Stone said aloud.

3

Long sleeves were a good idea. His trails were overgrown and narrower now. The changes to the woods behind his small house were considerable in the nearly six weeks since Nags Head, as was the weather. The briars and other brambles on the running path had grown significantly while he'd been away. The dogs cared not about the thorns, the briars, or the chill. They were simply glad to see him, the silent man who ran with them again. Three of the four he remembered gleefully joined him for each run. New obstructions littered the path as several additional trees had fallen. Two of the dogs would scramble ahead on every lap to each new hurtle, jumping high over it while looking back as though pointing it out to their human companion.

His stamina was not as he remembered. The battle with Wyckoff was still in his head. He worked hard to regain and even surpass the strength and agility he once had and had taken for granted.

Other things had changed as well.

Weston and Rita were back in Michigan. They did decide to stay closer to Sault Ste. Marie for a while. The farm felt a bit too remote to be safe. Westy made day trips to Kinross, Michigan, setting up security systems and cameras. But for now the couple would remain patient.

Cheryl was still in Dalton. She and Ben had become nearly inseparable, and they worked well together. Their current task appeared to unearth no secret answers. Their prey, a former chief of staff to an impeached president, was now transparent. Her only new mark was a small fire set in her room at the West Virginia facility... which earned the move to a more secure federal prison.

Phil and Sara Stone had left Murray's weeks ago. They had gone back to Louisiana. Jon's concerns of an attack appeared to be without merit. No incidents had been reported in Dalton, Caddo Mills or in Washington, D.C.

Only Natalie Barrett had produced any commotion. The action causing her to be relocated seemed to say she was more concerned about their access to her than anything else.

Harold Foster was back into his daily routine caring for the Gulfstream Five. Things were beginning to look and feel like normal.

Jon had opted from the beginning to stay at the little house in town. Marsha joined him after the first two weeks and as his ribs healed he began to work out again. The experience with Wyckoff had an effect on Jon. One that Silas would not tolerate going through again. Jon worked with his weights in the basement and ran the woods with the dogs.

The onset of fall brought out the thorns, or so he thought. It was more the loss of greenery that had acted as a cushion, but either way he had come in with severely scratched arms. Marsha suggested the long sleeve Henley shirts for his runs.

~

Bourbon Street Café was beginning to get busy. The small shop on the second level of Westfield Town shopping mall was a gathering place for mall store employees at lunch time. Wheaton, Maryland, sat only five miles north of the D.C. area. This was a good spot for meetings, close, yet out of the way.

Sitting at a table in the corner, looking out over the mall walkway he waited. The man he was to meet approached carrying a tan brief case. After buying a small diet coke, he walked to a table behind the first man and sat with his back to him. The brief case was placed on the floor, at the window.

"Amber thickens," the second man muttered softly.

"Only to protect," answered the first, neither looking toward the other.

The second man sipped at his drink and then rubbed his forehead as though it ached. The hand slid down covering his mouth as he spoke again. "How many have been contacted?" he asked.

"Sixteen," came the quiet response.

"Acceptance?"

"All but four."

The second man stood, adjusted his jacket, and looked briefly at the first man's back. "That should do, fine," he said and then asked, "They know who to contact now?"

"Yes," the first man answered as he stared out the glass, "they have the code, and were told in two weeks."

"Excellent," the second man smiled and walked out the door leaving his case on the floor.

After several minutes the first man picked up the case and laid it across the table in front of him. He started to open it but realized that its contents, his fifty thousand dollar fee for services, could bring unwanted attention. Instead, he patted the case and stood. Leaving a five dollar tip, he then took the case by the handle and left the shop.

At his car, he drove around to a secluded area of the mall parking lot. A nearly empty section on the side of a Sears store offered him privacy. He parked and pulled the case closer on the front seat. As his thumbs pressed the latches on the case, his car erupted into a ball of flames.

4

Brushing himself off at the rear door, Jon realized she wasn't standing there to greet him. The feeling wasn't narcissistic. He didn't expect her to do so. She simply always had.

Today Marsha was in the kitchen at the small table. Her fingers rubbing the side of her coffee cup as she stared at the doorway.

"Hey," Jon smiled as he entered the room. "What's going on?" he asked. "You're still working that coffee cup?"

Marsha raised the cup to her lips. The coffee was cold but that didn't matter. It gave her another few seconds to think.

"I had a call from Charlotte," she heard herself say.

"Yeah?" Jon didn't flinch. "How's everybody over there?"

The question wasn't serious and she knew it. He was just moving the discussion along.

"It's been over a year, Jon," she said while putting the cup down and looking primarily at it. "They want me back."

Any reaction he may have had went unnoticed. Facing the cabinets, Jon took a glass and poured himself some iced tea. He turned, still holding the carafe, and asked, "Ready to switch to this?"

Marsha looked up at him.

"Did you hear me?" Her frustration was thick.

Jon smiled and looked over his shoulder at her.

"Of course I heard you," he nodded. "I'm not surprised and neither should you be. You're a good cop." His eyes turned to his glass as he lifted it to his lips. She waited, knowing what would come next.

As the vessel was lowered his smile went with it.

"But you're happy here now, right?" he threw out without looking in her direction.

Marsha expected that response and calmly asked, "Can I use that line on you, next time you're called away?"

Jon turned to her as though he'd been hit but before he could speak, she continued, "Don't you even try..." her words were firm and strong, "to tell me it's different."

Jon stepped to the table, pulled out a chair, and sat. Leaning against the wooden back he raised his glass and emptied it... trying to think of what to say next. Her logic had him.

"So...you've made up your mind, then?" he offered.

"I haven't heard the entire offer yet, so...no," she asserted. "The Chief and the Captain want to meet with me tomorrow."

"Who will chaperon Cheryl?" he asked, more as a thought than an argument.

"Doris and George will still be there for a while," she answered. "He plans to start the remodel on their house. I guess they figured they would be welcome at the mansion."

Jon nodded without speaking and Marsha went on, "Besides that, I'm here with you more than I'm there anyway."

Standing slowly, Jon walked to her and forced his best smile.

"I'll have Harold fly you over there," he told her.

"The department can send a plane for me," she countered. "They want to handle it."

Jon stood and moved to the counter. He grabbed the pitcher but simply stood where he was.

She's serious, he thought, *not much I can do.*

~

Hansard and Monroe arrived at Andrews on an FBI Lear Jet. A car, sent from Marine Corps Base Quantico, Virginia, waited for them on the tarmac.

"Welcome to D.C., gentlemen," the young Marine almost shouted as he pulled the rear door open. "Director Grimes and the Navy Secretary should be waiting for us by the time we get to Quantico."

"Navy Secretary?" Hansard questioned the driver.

"Yes, Sir," was the reply. He then pointed to three police cars with lights already flashing. "And that's our escort. The Director doesn't like to be kept waiting."

The NCIS agents looked at each other with blank stares. Monroe finally broke the silence with, "Whose idea was this anyway?"

~

The Navy Secretary had not argued with his old friend Jerome Grimes, not even for a second. The invitation to discuss the theories, held by Agents Hansard and Monroe, struck him as relevant. The fact was, Nelson Pharr held similar feelings about the matter, but had nothing or nowhere to start an investigation. His driver picked him up at the Pentagon and they drove through post-lunch traffic enroute to Quantico.

Ten minutes into the trip an impact struck Pharr's rear window edge, the most vulnerable spot on the half-inch glass. Wedging its way between the slotted metal channel and the glass, the 50 caliber projectile bent the metal trim and broke into three pieces. Two of those entered the vehicle itself.

The Navy Secretary felt a slight burning sensation under his chin before he noticed the chipped side window or even realized that he had been hit. There was more apparent damage to the seat than to him, but blood trickled down and began to pool in his lap.

"I've been hit by something," Nelson Pharr called out to his driver. "Pull it over a minute."

A second round struck the window glass squarely in the center and created a six inch web pattern along with its "thud" sound.

"Cancel that order, driver," Pharr barked as he grabbed the cut on his neck. "Get us the hell out of here."

The limo screamed forward and began to weave with the evasion tactics the driver had been taught. If there were any other follow-up shots, none of them found the car.

"Sir," the driver yelled over his shoulder. "Do you need a hospital?"

"Hell, I don't know. Might need a good size band-aid."

They had been enroute to Quantico but the driver began to recalculate in his head.

"Sentara is about a mile away," he declared "....hang on."

The extended Lincoln Town Car made a left turn from the right lane and increased speed toward the hospital. Pharr leaned back and pulled his hand down, trying to assess the damage.

"Don't kill somebody over this, Turner," he pleaded. "I think I've been pretty lucky so far."

The driver slowed down a bit, but still slid into the emergency room entrance at over sixty miles an hour.

~

Natalie Barrett was returned to her cell where a stack of requested library books awaited her. She picked them up carefully and turned the spines up to read the titles.

The first was by Julia Oliver, three other titles and then a book by Gregory Kelly topped the pile. The message to her was "OK."

Jackson Terrell was in agreement.

Barrett smiled and called for a guard to come.

"May I call my attorney?" she asked.

The guard nodded and went for assistance to move her again.

Though the call was monitored and recorded, she managed to get her instructions out through another code. She complained that time went by so slowly, "every hour felt like eighty-eight minutes."

Then laughing, Barrett told her lawyer that "clemency couldn't come soon enough" to suit her.

After the call, Attorney Hasbrough Fuller contacted a United States Senator with his orders. Attach a Presidential Pardon for prisoner number 37624-88 to a pending bill and make sure it was signed.

5

The tunnel lights beckoned as the Jaguar lunged toward the gas station exit. The six inch video screen in the dash showed that Highway 71 was clear of any on-coming traffic.

Jon held the wheel tightly as they came through the hologram wall and the front tires touched the road. He cut the steering wheel hard to the right and punched the accelerator. Twelve cylinders gasped for air as they responded to the request and the rear wheels spun a full rotation before grabbing the pavement. Jon smoothly rolled the steering wheel back and the front tires straightened up. They passed the mansion doing seventy-eight MPH.

"Temper fit?" Marsha smirked calmly.

"Naw," Jon answered but lifted slightly on the gas as he did. "I've just been wanting to try a fast exit...never can tell when you might need to."

His excuse wasn't so much a lie...as it was his reason. Whatever it was, Marsha could see through it.

"Right," she nodded slowly. "Well...it seemed to work."

"Yeah," he muttered as they got to the top of the hill. "It did, didn't it?"

IIis momentary distraction was now gone. The reality of the mission came back to him. It made him feel emotional and that was not comfortable.

He was taking her to the Dalton airfield where a plane from Charlotte's police department was waiting.

～

A solitary figure occupied the short bench. This bench was actually a bus stop outside Sentara Northern Medical Center. Salvatori Genevis sat there with a large paper bag in his lap. He had waited for almost an hour.

The long, black Lincoln swerved into the emergency driveway and Salvatori turned, glancing at it casually. He then pulled a cell phone from his pocket and stared at it. The phone had not yet rung.

Within a minute, the chimes for a text message sounded and the word, "Go" came on the screen.

Salvatori Genevis stood and began to walk toward the emergency entrance. Along the way he dropped his phone into a trash can.

~

Hansard and Monroe grabbed for anything solid in the car. Their Marine driver received a message and turned his head slightly to relay it to his passengers.

"Change of plans, gentlemen," he shouted firmly. Then slapping the brakes and spinning the steering wheel, their car did a mid-street U-turn as he calmly continued, "Just got new orders."

"How's that?" Special Agent Hansard asked.

"The SecNav has been shot or shot at," the driver told them. "We're to meet with Director Grimes at Sentara North."

"Somebody shot the Navy Secretary?" Monroe piped in.

"They hit his car, that's all I know."

"Where is this Sentara?"

"We're close..." the driver hit his lights and sirens, neither of which was apparent when deactivated, "Should be there in five minutes."

~

Salvatori Genevis lingered at the sliding glass doors to the emergency section. He noticed a large family group approaching with two distraught females among them. As the group worked their way inside, Salvatori melded in with them. After a quick look around, he found a seat across the large waiting area with full view of the reception desk.

Picking up a folded newspaper from the seat, Salvatori settled in and laid the paper in his lap. As the commotion from the upset family continued to occupy attention, he pulled a chrome plated .357 revolver from his bag and slid it under the newspaper.

~

Cheryl Duray rocked back in her chair and turned toward Ben. They worked together at the control center of Ben's private computer bank. One of her monitors had picked up a blur out on Highway 71.

"Did you see that?" she exclaimed.

"The green rocket ship that just went by outside?" Ben grinned. "Naw, I missed that," he added with a chuckle.

"That looked like Jon's Jag," Cheryl stood and walked across the second sub-basement. She put her hands on Ben's shoulders and leaned into his right ear. "Would you be that upset if I left?"

The young man was not about to fall into that trap. He quickly hit several key strokes on his system and pulled up a strange, insect looking device.

"Check this out," he pointed at the screen.

She leaned in even further, pressing herself against the back of Ben's neck. It was a tried and true incidental embrace that they both enjoyed. "What is that?" she purred and started to stand back up.

"Whoa..." Ben called out, "Not so fast. Take a good look."

"It's a bug," she declared indignantly. "Just a bug."

"A mechanical bug," Ben corrected her and smiled as she leaned back in... ever closer.

How small is it... really?" she lingered in place to ask.

"0.6 cm," he said flatly.

"I don't use metrics...you know that. Come on," she stood and half way slapped at his shoulder. "How big is it?"

"Just under one quarter of an inch."

"Cool," was all she could think to say at that moment. "What good is it?"

Ben spun his chair to look directly at her.

"That tiny thing has nearly one hundred moving parts. It flies, it can carry a payload, and it can land horizontal or vertical on most any surface, even inverted."

Cheryl was impressed but uninspired none-the-less.

"What good is it?"

Ben smiled broadly. "Have you ever wanted to be a fly on the wall?"

Cheryl looked at the picture on the screen again. "That thing?"

"It has a camera the size of a grain of salt, with audio," Ben explained with his chest pushed out. "It can attach the recording devices to a person or thing and leave the area undetected."

"You need to get some of those," she grinned.

"They're on order," he beamed, "Should be here in a couple of days."

~

The parking lot for the emergency room was packed. The Marine driver decided to let Hansard and Monroe out while he sought out a spot to park the car.

The agents walked up and past the full glass outer walls of the waiting area and Jake glanced in. As they approached the doors, he spoke under his breath to his partner.

"Let's keep going for now," he said without emotion.

Monroe knew well enough to simply trust Hansard's call, so with no hesitation, they both walked on by the doors.

At the corner, out of sight line from within the waiting room, Hansard stopped and turned back.

"Did you notice the guy sitting by himself?"

"No," Monroe admitted. "What do you have on him?"

"I caught a glimpse of a metallic reflection from under the edge of that newspaper in his lap," Hansard said while pulling off his jacket and laying it on the ground. Rolling up his sleeves and pulling his tie down, he changed his appearance if the man had noticed them.

"I'll take the spot near the desk," he told Monroe. "Does that suit you?"

They were on the same page without even a discussion of what to do.

"I'll sit near the glass and behind him," Monroe nodded and went in first.

As the limo from NCIS screeched to a halt in front of the doors, Hansard turned his back so that Grimes would not recognize him and then followed him inside.

Walking right to the admission desk, Grimes asked about Pharr. Across the room, Salvatori stood and leveled his arm and gun toward the Director.

Shots rang out from two sides of the waiting area before the assassin could fire his own weapon. Hansard fired three times and Monroe twice. In all, four 9mm rounds hit the "would be" killer. He froze in place before collapsing to the floor.

Jerome Grimes reached for his own sidearm and knelt down defensively. Monroe ran to the would be assassin as Hansard stood in front of Grimes and looked around for any accomplices.

"Director Grimes," Hansard called out, "Are you alright, Sir?"

Figuring it out as he climbed to his feet, the Director looked at Hansard quizzically. "They were after me?" he half asked in wonder.

"Looks that way, Sir," Monroe said from behind him.

"What the hell?" Grimes muttered and put away his Sig-Sauer, stainless, P-232. "What's going on?"

6

Murray Bilstock swooped in over his Caddo Mills ranch at over 250 mph. All appeared to be clear on the ground.

"Lucy Too to ground... LT to ground, are you there Slick?" he radioed for his cousin.

"Lucy this is ground," Slick responded. "I'm here. It's clear right now. Come on in."

"Slick, I'm gonna take a loop at five miles out just to be sure, you copy that?"

"Copy, roger and all that stuff. I'll see you topside in a few."

The deep blue Sikorski S-97 swung wide left and circled the area looking for anything out of place.

Murray found nothing, not even traffic on the highway. Satisfied, he did a 180-degree turn over the house and landed on the front pad.

Shreveport's bomb squad had been on scene at Phil Stone's lake house for just over an hour. The trip wire ran left from the dock ramp and into the brush.

"Looks like they ran out of time, Phil," the captain of the team informed the retired officer and his wife. "Can't really tell where they were headed with it, either."

"Could it be simply what it is?" Stone asked, "Just a warning?"

The other man looked down in thought and shook his head.

"I don't know about that," he said under his breath, "Looks to me like you have a serious enemy out there."

Having been through this before, Phil thought quietly, *or a serious friend they want to draw out.*

"Thanks guys," he said aloud. "What do I owe you for the house call?"

The uniformed captain grinned at him.

"Maybe we'll bill you."

~

Lori Seay knocked on Daniel's office door at their home in Pittsburgh.

"Danny," she called to him. "It's Bill White on the phone."

That's odd, Daniel thought, *he has my cell*, then looking at three clear lines on his office phone, *and he has these numbers.*

He went to the door and Lori handed him an extension of the house line. "Hello, Bill?" he answered with a skeptical tone.

"Daniel, I didn't know which line would be more secure. I need to tell, or maybe just ask you something."

"I can call you right back, Bill."

"Good," his former boss and editor of the Pittsburgh Post-Gazette responded as he hung up.

Lori followed him to his desk, where Daniel opened a drawer and took out a "secure line" cell phone that Ben had given him.

"What's going on now?" Lori asked.

"I don't know yet," he said dialing Bill White's number. When the man answered he looked down at the keys and hit, #21. The phone "beeped" slightly and then was normal. The communications were now scrambled.

"Bill?" he said. "We're good now. What's going on, sir?"

"Not sure what to make of this, Daniel, but there's a growing list of low level congressmen's aides turning up dead," he told him, " and a couple of unknown congress people as well, all in the last week."

"Any connection?" Daniel asked.

"Nothing except some work a cub reporter did for me. He collected a bunch of PR shots that included the dead folks and other political types."

"Okay," Daniel listened closely.

"Several had images of that "star" picture you were interested in a few months back, you remember that thing?"

"I sure do," the ex-reporter answered. "Can you send me those photos? I'll send a courier over to pick them up."

"That's a bit old fashioned, ain't it?"

"Yeah...but it might be called for. I don't think we need an electronic paper trail on this."

White smiled and opened a drawer on his own desk. He pulled a large manila envelope marked, "Personal – HR Records – Benefits" and told Daniel he "had just the package to use."

"You still in touch with 'him'?" White threw in at the end.

"Him?" Daniel repeated.

"Yeah...I thought, maybe so. You guys be careful," he then cautioned. "Looks like someone is doing some house cleaning."

~

Natalie Barrett's attorney was ushered into a room with no windows or apparent cameras. He sat at the small desk and waited, his hands folded in his lap.

When they brought her in, the attorney was taken aback. She was in shackles and chains at her feet.

"Is that necessary?" he stood and demanded from one of the officers.

"We got rules here," the uniformed man shot back firmly. "If you have an issue...talk to the warden."

"I plan to," the attorney shouted, "today!" as the three men left.

Barrett took her seat across the table and smiled.

"That's was kinda cute," she grinned at him.

"Are you alright?" the man asked sincerely. "This isn't what we expected in this move."

"I'm fine," she said calmly. "I actually feel more secure here. Can't say exactly why, but my paranoia was starting to get to me in the other place."

"You!" the attorney laughed for the first time. "Paranoid?"

"Just give me the report," she said and then said something odd. "I'm thinking of cutting my hair. What do you think?"

The attorney caught on quickly, realizing they could not trust that any recording devices might still be around.

"It looks better now," he told her. "Shorter on the back, isn't it?"

"Is it?"

"Yeah...I believe it is. The ones that were going a bit wild on you seem to be gone. Yeah...you count on that. It's looking better, for sure."

"Well, thank you," she said shaking her head to fluff her hair up. "Think I may need to fill back in around the sides?"

"That wouldn't hurt," he said. He was beginning to enjoy the role playing. "Could be done quickly too... maybe even as we speak."

"Good, good," she laughed. "It does grow fast. Not too much though, right?"

"Naw, I think a bit less than it was before. Does that sound about right to you?"

"I believe we're on the same page. Did they get the piano moved in my home?"

He had to think about that reference for a minute. Then it hit him, *piano...eighty-eight keys, eighty-eight! The last digits of Terrell Jackson's prisoner number, she's asking about his release!*

"That should happen next week," he told her nodding his head.

They spoke of other things for several minutes, just for cover.

7

Eight panels, all solid oak from what he could tell in the scant light. A thin coat of dust dulled the once proud finish. It appeared to be hung on hinges set into the wall, unlike its mate that stood angled against a heavy shelving unit nearby.

This must be it, he more muttered than spoke. Wrinkling his nose, the man wiped under it with the back of one hand, fending off a sneeze.

Dust was everywhere, the sticky pasty kind that could stick to anything. It had covered his shoes from the walk down to where he stood. What he had stirred up smelled like mold.

Yes, the man thought. *The damp was thick down here.*

He now stood at the end of a long, dark, rarely used passageway. The massive door he found was mentioned in the note that brought him here. In the faint light of the few lamps that still worked, he pondered what purpose had he been summoned here for.

Reaching out with his arms, he estimated this old door was five feet wide. He could raise his hand up to just past seven feet. This thing was a good foot above that in height. It had once hung, with its partner, on the entrance to the senate chambers. Replaced many years ago, they now collected dust in this hallway.

The note that had been left in his office requested he come to this sub-basement level of the Thomas Jefferson Building. Used for storage of old papers and other artifacts, the area was marked with row upon row of shelves and other items simply stacked where they would fit. Most long forgotten.

The last part of the message ordered him to slide the note itself into a slot beside the huge door. Searching with eyes and fingers, he finally found a crack in the plaster wall. Nothing else resembled a "slot" so he folded the small paper in half and pushed one end into the crack. Something within took it... and pulled it through.

Realizing he had stepped back impulsively, the man smiled at himself and reached out to knock on the large door. Before he could, the door cracked open with a groan and slowly swung from left to right exposing a dark room.

"Come in, please," an unseen voice offered. "There's a seat right in front of you."

Travis Gilbert paused. He looked behind himself and down the long hallway to the nearest light some forty feet away. Hesitation set in. It wasn't fear he felt, but more his common sense. It had long served him well and was working overtime at the moment.

"What is this?" he asked firmly. "Some joke?"

"To the contrary, Congressman Gilbert, this is quite serious."

Gilbert pulled his cell phone and hit "one." It lit up but did nothing else. Rolling his hand, he glanced down to see "no service" flashing on the small screen.

"'Serious' did not mean you were in any jeopardy, Congressman Gilbert. We simply take certain precautions when approaching an outsider."

"Outsider?" Gilbert now raised his voice. "I'm a member of the United States Congress." He strained unsuccessfully to see into the dark room, "I suggest you start making sense...and fast."

"Please..." the voice coaxed him, "won't you have a seat?"

"I'm fine where I am... and your time is running out...believe me," Gilbert did his best to sound threatening.

"How is your re-election coming along?" the voice asked.

Gilbert didn't answer though the question struck a chord in him. He leaned in and took a step forward still trying to see who was talking.

Through the shadows he could make out what appeared to be a long table with several people sitting, facing him. The dark made them little more than silhouettes.

"Who are you people?" the congressman pressed.

"A group that would very much like to help you stay in office," the voice answered automatically.

"I don't need the help of any secret group," Gilbert started to turn as he spoke.

"Don't you, now?" the voice challenged him. "You've been rather busy this last term. You haven't kept up with the rigors of re-election, have you?"

The congressman turned back to them but remained quiet.

"Third terms are always hard," the voice sounded sympathetic now. "It happens more than you know. We seek to keep those who do work hard at their job... in place long enough to have an impact. We ask very little if anything in return."

"Okay...there it is," Gilbert stepped towards the table in anger. "Who the hell are you?"

"We are the Celestial Enumerate..." the tone was solemn and very earnest. "It's not really as flowery as it may sound to you," the voice continued as a spotlight came on. Its light directed his attention to a star shaped medallion filled with numbers of all shapes and sizes.

"Someone once asked," the voice went on. "'Who can number the stars?'"

Gilbert more 'felt' the door close behind him than he heard it. He spun with a start and put his hand on the massive wooden object.

"Congressman," the voice went on calmly, "we have reached a particular point in this conversation...that cannot be undone. Of course, you understand that?"

Doing all he could to maintain composure, Gilbert stepped back to the chair he'd been offered earlier, pulled it out and sat down.

"That's much better," the voice assured him. It then paused to give Gilbert time to settle in more, to relax a bit. Then it continued.

"You asked who we are... I'm sure you suspect a conspiracy of rogue congressmen. We are more than that, considerably more. Our numbers include many like yourself, but we also have professionals from all fields. Men and women who see the need, no...the demand, that we keep things on a certain path."

"A path?" Gilbert interrupted. "What path?"

"The path that heads off mutual destruction."

"Oh, good Lord!" the congressman exclaimed. "I've been kidnapped by a bunch of Looney tunes."

The voice did not respond to his remark. There was quiet in the room for over a minute. Gilbert strained his eyes but still could not make out anyone or anything beyond the shadowy figures before him.

"The people of this world," the voice finally re-emerged, "outnumber us in this country by over twenty to one. Our gifts to them, payoffs, bribes, assistance...whatever you want to call it, have an increasingly smaller effect on their hatred of us."

"You're a one world order group?" Gilbert asked flatly.

"We are realists."

"Yet you refer to yourselves as 'Celestial Enumerates,' like you're special...some sort of chosen few."

"Enlightened, would be the term we'd prefer."

"And you believe you are making a difference?"

"We must."

"Then why all the skullduggery? Why not just be open about what you think?"

"Our numbers are vast, but not yet enough. We strive like you, to fund our existence and continue forward. We must keep our identities and our work sealed...protected as though in amber."

"So, this numbered star is your logo...is that it?"

"Our symbol is merely a sign to ourselves. It assures us we are with a like-minded believer."

Gilbert had added it up.

"So...you help me get re-elected, and then I help you down the road. Do I have it about right?"

"It could be that simple, yes."

"Or what...?" Gilbert asked flippantly. "You kill me?"

"That's extreme, don't you think?" the voice teased him.

The congressman stood, waving his arms.

"But I can just expose you," he challenged..."bring people down here."

A light in the room suddenly came on bright. It was a single, 100 watt bulb that hung down from the ceiling.

Gilbert's mouth fell open, his arms dropped to his sides. The room he stood in was merely eight feet deep and ten feet long. It was a closet, empty except for the chair.

The table, the figures, everything was an illusion. The voice spoke again, through a still hidden speaker.

"You, sir, can simply... lose your election." It said bluntly, "and you go away... with your tale of boogie-men in a closet."

Gilbert remained speechless, in near shock.

"Think about your response for a few days," the voice said. "We will contact you then."

The light in the closet went out and the door swung open. It was over.

8

Weston Duray took trips from Sault Ste. Marie to Kinross several times each week. He would always approach his home from the forest side and not the main highway.

Repetition can cause carelessness in some, but the old Pathfinder stayed on his toes. Before he entered the clearing, he noticed the barn door was not closed completely.

Westy scouted the perimeter of that clearing from fifty feet deep into the thick woods. The house seemed fine, just the barn was not as he had left it. He checked his Kahr 9mm and thought about his suit.

Jon had given him the black suit he'd worn to Mexico. It was in the truck, but the truck was over a half a mile back in the woods.

Walking upright from tree to tree, Westy moved ever closer to the rear of the barn. He could hear voices inside. A hatchway on the left side of the barn was used to load hay at a height of ten feet. Westy pocketed the weapon and climbed the exterior of the barn by grabbing the edges of one inch thick trim boards.

Slowly, he made it to the hatch and pulled on it hoping the hinges wouldn't squeal. They didn't.

On the floor of the barn he saw three men sitting at a wire wheel, playing cards. Two AR-15s and an AK-47 leaned against one center pole and he could see handguns in side holsters on two of the men.

Inching his way to the winch rope that lowered the hay bales down, Westy untied it and put his small handgun in his teeth. Just before swinging down to confront his unwelcome guests; he caught a reflection from near the opened barn door. A fourth rifle leaned against the heavy framework.

That's why it's open, his mind screamed and directed his eyes to the door once again. *There's another one here, somewhere.*

~

The house was as you would expect it, for the current patriarch of a six- generation, affluent family. Carlton Calvert enjoyed the mansion and lived there as though he were born to it. And he was.

"Good day, gentlemen," the uniformed butler greeted the guests at the front door. "Mr. Calvert is in his study."

The two men tipped their heads respectfully towards the butler. "Thank you, Williams," said the taller of the two. "We can find our way."

They walked side by side down the expansive hallway to the left of the grand foyer. Used to the extravagance at this point, neither man reacted to any of the opulent features they had seen many times before.

"Jasper," his voice sounded from the end of the hall, "Dil, you're earlier than I expected."

Carlton Calvert moved to meet them as he spoke. Gingerly, but still on his own, the seventy-six years of his life had been fairly kind to him.

"Sir," the taller man said as he accepted a handshake, "I fear we must talk about the wine."

Calvert's smile softened into a stare with little emotion whatever.

"I see," the host nodded and turned to allow them to pass. "My elevator is just over here." He pointed to a large wooden door, not unlike the others that lined the hallway. "You're familiar with it," he added.

The three rode silently to the basement and the wine cellar which lay at the far end. The house was built by his great-grandfather at a time when the family's fortune was worth even more than it was now.

|

The elevator door opened to a semi-dark, stone-walled corridor. "Sabastian would have thought he was stepping into a dungeon under the Tower of London," Carlton quipped as he had numerous times before. "This way, please." He led them to the wine cellar and its thick oak doors.

Sabastian Calvert, his third great-grandfather came to this country slightly before the turn of the century, the twentieth century. With few possessions other than his learned trade, he set forth to build his dream. He desired to print a newspaper.

After struggling to make his way in this new land, he finally published a weekly, folded pamphlet with local stories surrounding his own editorial thoughts. Within a year, he met another young man who came to him to advertise his soft drink product. Both business and personal relationships developed, as the two became good friends.

Revenue from this advertising pushed Calvert's dream into reality, and the Atlanta Sentinel was born.

The business began to grow and with capitol loaned to him by his wealthy friend, Calvert sought to buy other nearby newspapers. At first it was through benevolence, a desire to keep the news afloat. That soon morphed into a need to curtail competition. Calvert Publishing branched from its home in Atlanta, Georgia, to as far away as San Francisco. Still offering his opinions through the editorial page, Calvert soon learned his words could affect the thinking of others, even as these unknown people went to the voting poles.

The wine cellar doors closed behind the three men and Carlton Calvert became serious.

"Alright," he challenged them. "What is it?"

~

Weston Duray had refigured his plan. The unseen, extra man added a layer of problems to his attack. Staying low, he tied the rope to three bundles of hay, each weighing nearly eighty-five pounds and secured it all in place.

Slowly working his way further around the open loft level of his barn, he lay in a spot where he could see the men playing cards and the cracked open doors.

Was he outside? Maybe gone to the woods to take care of business, or was he just around the corner having a smoke?

Looking around carefully, he also considered the other possibility.

Maybe he's in here...off in a corner taking a nap.

What was clear was that Westy couldn't afford to move until all of the men were accounted for. He would have to wait.

~

"Are you aware of what is happening, Sir?" the tall visitor asked Carlton Calvert.

"In what regard?"

"She's apparently cleaning house...from inside that federal facility."

The old man frowned at his guests and stepped into the taller one's face.

"We had decided to let her run things," he said softly, "so now, you want to question what she does?"

"She moving too fast in my opinion," the tall man said bluntly. "We've got dead bodies being investigated all over the country and she's running a recruiting operation at the same time."

"The balance must be maintained," Calvert nearly smiled, "...you know that."

"But, Sir..." the man started to continue and then simply gave up.

Calvert stepped back and looked at both visitors before he spoke again.

"Is the balance in check?" he asked firmly. "We operate on a three-legged stool. Balance is not an option...is it in balance?"

""Revenues from the income side are holding," the shorter guest told him. "Influence is hurting but she's obviously working on that."

"Grant and Shanahan all but destroyed us there," the tall man muttered more loudly than he'd hoped.

Sheri Shanahan was an Atlanta attorney with big aspirations. Her plot had been to elevate then Speaker of the House Cyrus Grant to the White House by killing both the president and vice-president in an elaborate scheme. He in turn would then appoint her to the Supreme Court.

The plot failed and Jon Crane was the major cause.

"And you signed off on that entire operation," Calvert reminded him. "The impeachment mess could have been our downfall." He walked to a rack and pulled a bottle with a deep greenish-yellow colored glass.

The taller visitor had been in the wine cellar many times before but the subject of the wine itself never came up. He looked around at the vastness of the dark room.

"Just how many racks do you have down here, Sir?" he asked.

"Twenty-eight racks for 'reds', thirty racks for 'whites', three each for 'rose' and dessert wines, and five racks of sparkling wines," his host answered yet spoke into the bottle he held rather than to him.

"What's it all worth," the guest asked, "do you even keep up with that?"

"This room is worth over twelve million dollars, not counting the invaluable secrets it conceals."

Both guests stared at him in bewilderment. The old man had never spoken of that before.

"Without our secrets there would have been nothing left as collateral," Calvert smiled and stared at the obviously precious vessel. The bottle, a 1998 Petrus Pomerol, red wine, had small numbers on the bottom of the label, XXXVLIII20.58 -37XXVIXVII199. Calvert smiled even wider and turned the bottle lovingly in his hands before replacing it in the rack.

"It was almost over for us," he said as if whispering to the wine, "but Barrett gave Shanahan a free hand, and if it wasn't for that meddler..."

"We're lucky Grant had all his records with him in that cabin," the smaller man piped in, "We never considered anyone that high up getting caught."

"Speaking of the impeachment..." the old man changed the subject and turned back to his guests, "what is he doing?"

~

Weston Duray lay perfectly still in the loft of his hay barn. Keeping his eyes on the men playing cards and the door, he also noticed the location of the main rope's secondary tether line.

That tether was used to move the big rope into position from the floor off the barn. Westy had pulled on one to bring the rope to him, that one was tied to the end of the main rope. The secondary tether was attached to the big rope at the two-thirds mark and his pulling the others had left it hanging just behind the card playing trio.

With movements so slow, the air didn't notice, Westy checked his handgun. It was ready.

~

Carlton Calvert was asking his guests about any news on the former POTUS who Barrett had appeared to work for. Both answered the same, "Other than his people buying land in Costa Rica, not much."

"So," Calvert smiled again but only for a second. "He's planning his great escape, huh?"

"Everybody in politics is running scared," the other visitor finally spoke up. "Well...everybody we work with," he amended.

"Let him go...he's served his purpose," Calvert grimaced as he spoke and then became quiet. He walked to a large, leather, wing-back chair and took a seat.

"He's right," the tall man added. "Things are drastically different out there."

Calvert looked up at them, "Because of that fool, Beale?"

The publishing magnate referred to a powerful congressman from Connecticut, Ted Beale, who had worked with them, but mainly under Barrett's direction. Or so it was thought.

Beale's ego had led him to screw up and that got him killed, or to be exact... removed.

"Beale was just the tip of it," the tall man told him. Some reporter tied him to Leo Garnet getting wacked and now other newspapers are all over it."

"Cut the info stream," Calvert demanded. "Tell 'em to knock off all discussion of it till this dies down."

"Sir," the tall man said with a voice that nearly cracked with fear. "It's not like it used to be. We don't control all that anymore. Even our own papers are covering it."

"Fire the editors, damn it," Calvert stood defiantly. "I still run this operation."

"That won't do anything except make it worse, Sir. And then there's this 'Son' character."

"The meddler...Crane?" The old boss was surprised to hear that mentioned. "He's dead," he affirmed. Then a pause filled the air with silence until he added, "Isn't he?"

"He was seen, and it's been confirmed, at the beach house incident. On Nag's Head, where they killed that guy Ted Beale had set up. You know, the one who was killing the SEALs."

"There was more to that mess than just Beale, gentlemen," Calvert showed his awareness of the SEAL Team fiasco. "Besides, that guy in the black rubber suit was a helicopter pilot. That's Crane's former friend, the cowboy...not Crane."

"But Crane was there, Sir," the tall man insisted.

Calvert's look became one of concern. "You're sure of this?" he asked.

"As sure as we can be, Sir," the other man muttered. "Barrett's move to Wisconsin confirms she believes it, too. She's hiding from him."

"And cutting any ties that might lead to her," Calvert nodded almost affectionately. "Good move," he added.

"Do we rein her in, Sir?" the tall man asked pointedly.

Calvert sat back down in obvious consideration of what to say next.

9

Slick came up to meet his cousin as the Lucy Too touched down. Murray climbed down with his Glock in hand.

"It looked clear from the air," he announced, "Anything on the screens that you noticed?"

"Naw," Slick told him. "Not in a while."

"You're sure they didn't go in the house?"

"Look for yourself," the cousin shook his head. "I checked, but make yourself happy."

Murray stopped and turned to his insulted relative.

"Sorry, man," he said sincerely. "Let's go look at those tapes you have."

As they passed by the Lucy Too, Murray could hear his phone ringing from on the seat.

"I really need to quit leaving that thing lying around," he scolded himself.

"Hello," he answered abruptly.

"Murray, it's Phil Stone. Are you okay up there?"

"Don't tell me...."

"No, no...we're fine, "the retired captain assured his friend. "How about up there?"

"Slick has had some company we didn't ask for on film. I was just about to take a look. What happened there?"

"A trip wire was set up on my dock ramp," Phil explained, "Got lucky this time, though."

"Have you talked to Jon?" Murray asked him.

"No...thought I'd check with you first. Are you gonna call him?"

Murray Bilstock took a huge, deep breath. "Not just yet. I want to make sure Ben knows so he can be alert though."

"You don't think Jon should be told?"

"I got a feeling; if they're messing with us like this...he's got his own set of problems to deal with."

You're right," Phil agreed. "He doesn't need to be worrying over us every minute. Besides...Ben will likely know already."

"Probably," the cowboy nodded as he spoke, "I just want to be sure."

~

The door of the barn flew open as the fourth man burst in.

"Check this out," he yelled at the top of his lungs. He raised his arm holding high the black suit from Westy's truck.

"What the hell is that?" a card player asked without otherwise moving.

"There's a truck out there...in the woods," the new arrival said. "Hood was still warm when I found it."

At that point the card players stood and began looking around. One noticed the rope leading to the loft area. The large diameter rope had a smaller tether hanging from it.

"That wasn't up like that when we got here," the man shouted and pulled on the tether...hard.

The larger rope and its three bales slid from the perch on the loft and swung down and across the barn. The men from the card table tried to move but not fast enough. The bales spread out in a wide path and caught the men chest high at around fifty mph.

Westy stood as this was going on and leveled his 9mm at the man nearest the doors. Two shots spun the man and put him down. The others were not moving.

Duray climbed down, keeping an eye on them. Two had obvious broken necks and the third had been driven into a stall post, head first. His skull appeared to be caved in on one side.

Westy gathered the weapons and retrieved his suit from near the man he'd shot, then looked back at the others.

"Barns can be a dangerous place," he muttered, shook his head and then turned to go to the house where he called the local sheriff.

As The Atlanta Sentinel grew and became influential, Sabastian Calvert's stature also grew. He met the younger sister of his first big advertiser and a romance turned into a family union and dynasty. Camille Carlton pushed her new husband to even greater ambition, purchasing other papers. The power of Calvert's company soon equaled that of his brother-in-law's beverage operation.

Sabastian's work ethic and Camille's drive were passed down to their children. Franklin Calvert, the eldest son, continued the growth and included operating radio stations, the newest gimmick in communications. Calvert Publishing became Calvert Enterprises.

Carlton Calvert sat thinking about his visitors' concerns for several minutes. He was not used to the feeling he now had, that of not being in complete control.

"Why can't we fire the station managers who don't put out our message?" he announced suddenly. "This is still my company."

"The Grant-Shanahan thing brought too much scrutiny to the business, boss," the taller man reminded him. "We can't call the shots like that anymore...not right now for sure...and maybe not even for some time yet."

"So, Barrett is rebuilding her base?" Calvert asked them again.

"And... bringing too much attention with the purging," the tall man affirmed.

"Has she reached out to you in any way?"

"Well...no. Not yet."

"So, she's dealing with her mess on her own?" Calvert grinned. "I like that."

"What if it leads to us?"

"As long as you keep your finger out of the mix," the old man lectured, "you won't get any on you."

"I understand."

"One more thing," Calvert offered in his most serious, sinister tone. "If that 'Son' fella is still out there...find him and get him."

"Word is that Barrett has people on that already," said the smaller man.

Calvert's face froze. "So she does believe he's out there," he answered. "What steps is she taking?"

"Every known link to him is a target. It's happening now."

"That could get messy," the old man reacted with concern.

"Anything we should do, then?" the taller guest asked.

Calvert moved once again to his beloved wine racks. He laid his hands on two bottles as though protecting them.

"No," he finally answered, "stay back from it. I want no connection to us, not yet."

"If she screws it up...do we move in or wait?"

The old man turned to them solemnly. "Getting close to this 'Son' could be very dangerous," he warned. "Watch and learn, whatever comes of it."

~

The "beep" sound rushed Ben off his phone.

"Hey," the unmistakable cowboy voice started, "you guys okay over there?"

"Has something happened, Murray?" Ben pressed him. "I just got off the phone with Daniel."

"They after him, too?"

"What? Him?...Wait, he called to tell us about a bunch of politicians and aides getting wacked. He didn't say anything about himself."

"I want to hear about that, but right now, you need to let Daniel know some stuff is up and he needs to be watchful." Before Ben could answer, Murray abruptly went on, "Where's Jon?"

"He's at the little house...I think," Ben told him. "He took Marsha to the airport and went there to run. What's going on, Murray?"

~

The visitors left the mansion in silence. Neither spoke till their car was clear of the driveway.

"You're quiet all of a sudden," the taller man teased his friend. "What is it?"

"You heard what the old man said, right?"

"Yeah, he said watch and learn, but stay out of the way."

"Not just that," the smaller one paused as though he didn't really wish to continue.

"Spit it out," the other demanded in gest.

"That about getting too close to this 'Son' fella creeped me out."

The tall man laughed as he drove, "You? Creeped out!?"

"Didn't you ever read any Greek stories in school, man?"

"Sure, what of it?"

"The old man's warning was like that Icarus' dad gave him."

"Huh?" the driver didn't follow what he was hearing.

"Daedalus... Icarus's dad. He made the kid these wax wings, you know. But then he also gave him a warning. Our teacher made us remember it by calling it the 'Daddy Directive.'"

"You've lost me, man," his friend shook his head.

"It didn't work out well for Icarus."

"Make sense, will you?"

"Calvert just gave us the same warning, man."

The driver stared at his friend until he continued.

"The Daedalus Directive...Don't fly too close to the sun."

10

The meeting in Charlotte didn't take long.

"Lieutenant Hurst," the Chief of Police said bluntly, "we waited this long to allow some of your celebrity to wear off."

Marsha nodded her understanding of that but otherwise said nothing.

"Your departure and absence have been investigated and declared 'reasonable' and 'justified' by our review panel."

"Thank you, Sir," she whispered softly.

The Chief stared at Marsha, almost sternly.

"No need for modesty, Lieutenant. This unit, and the law enforcement community of these United States, is proud to have you in our ranks." As he finished with that, the man's chest puffed out and a round of "here, here," rose from the room.

"Your job is here, if you want it," the chief continued, "one change is," he paused for effect, "that you would be reassigned to the day shift as Watch Commander."

"Watch Commander?" Marsha repeated through her stunned expression. "What about Captain Hardy?"

"The city has... in its wisdom..."

His comment was briefly interrupted by laughter.

"As I was saying," the smiling chief continued, "I have been offered the luxury of having an Administrative Assistant Chief to help with my day to day functions. Captain Hardy has accepted that position...pending."

Yet another short round of laughter and then all eyes were on Marsha. She was not smiling.

"Sir, with all due respect to everyone here," she said while standing, "may I have a word in private?"

The room became quiet as a church. The Chief stoically paused and then offered a slight smile.

"Of course Lieutenant," he pointed towards a door at the rear and everyone in attendance stood at attention. "This way, please."

~

Phil Stone sat on the end of his dock ramp with the thin wire in his hand. He watched as Sara walked the last remaining investigators through the house and to their cars. He was still there when she returned.

"So," her voice was steady, "what do we do now?"

The retired police captain looked up at his wife and then rubbed his forehead with one hand. He pulled his cell phone from a pocket as Sara sat beside him in silence. Dialing a number he knew by heart, Phil looked at his wife while the phone rang.

"Hey, Phil," the voice answered at the other end. "How are you guys doing with that retirement?"

"We're fine, Matt," Stone replied. "I was wondering if I could ask a favor?"

"The answer is 'Yes', now what's the question?" his old friend and local newspaper editor, Matt Turlock said gleefully.

"Do you have room for me and Sara for a few days?"

Without hesitation, Turlock replied again, "How soon can you get here?"

~

Inside the small office an assistant closed the door and the Chief turned to Marsha.

"I was hoping to refer to you as 'Captain' by this point."

"Sir," she said as sincerely as she could muster, "was this a set up?"

"In what way, Lieutenant?" he asked.

"Watch Commander is a desk job. You'll be pulling me from any field duty...keeping me inside and...safe."

The chief shook his head and glanced down at the ground for an instant.

"Looks like it, doesn't it?" he said flippantly.

"So it is?" she was nearly spitting mad. "You admit it?"

"No," the boss responded in a calm, firm, and drawn-out tone. "I admit to nothing of the kind." He turned from her, looking out a window to conceal his smile as he attempted to sound angry, "I'm going to allow you this one shot at questioning my motives, but that's it. I simply said 'it looks like it,' now didn't I?"

Her expression went from anger to confusion.

"I don't understand," she whispered, but loud enough to hear.

"I need you in this job, if you'll take it. This would have happened months ago had you not been called away."

The Chief turned back and looked her in the eyes.

"Your assumption wasn't unfounded and what you've been through makes it harder to understand, I know. Traditionally, here in Charlotte, the job has been mainly an administrative 'desk' assignment. I've made provisions for you to operate more like the Chief of Detectives."

Marsha looked for and found a chair. She sat as he continued.

"You'll have three sergeants on the desk, as well as a Lieutenant. You are to concentrate on Tactical training and response. Any case you feel needs your attention...you deal with it. I'm giving you free reign but...I expect case closures."

"Sir, I'm sorry," she apologized and looked up at her boss. "I just thought maybe..."

"You thought Jon Crane called me?" he grinned, "Or maybe George Vincent or even the President himself."

Marsha's eyes reacted more to the mention of Jon's name than any other.

"Oh, I know your man is alive and well," he nodded. "But these plans were in the works, as I said... months ago. I can show you the paperwork if you still don't believe me."

She stood, sheepishly, and the Chief shook her hand.

"That won't be necessary, Sir," she told him.

"Can I call you 'Captain Hurst', now," he asked in jest.

"Thank you, sir," she responded sharply from attention.

"Now, let's get back in there and make this official."

11

A door cracked open to the large, quiet office and the voice coming through it stopped the occupant from his reading.

"What is it, Jesse?" the man at the huge desk asked.

"Sir," the aide stepped into the room with several papers in his hand, "the auto-sign machine picked up something this morning."

Leaning back, the man at the desk was clearly puzzled by the comment.

"What does that mean?" he pressed.

"S.B. 776215-29 was two pages over the expected count."

"Senate Bills often have last minute riders, Jesse. You know that."

"Yes, Sir...but this one is important." He laid the papers on the desk and stepped back. The cover page said, <u>Presidential Clemency Directive</u>.

After going through the other papers, the man looked to his aide.

"Who put this in here?" he asked, "and who is Jackson Terrell?"

"Interesting case, Sir," the aide explained. "He's a convicted killer up in Wisconsin. He's doing forty to life at Oxford."

"Is this a done deal? Is this man out?"

"He's not out yet, but yes, Sir... The machine just picked up the extra pages. The bill went through, it's law."

Flipping through the papers, the President asked, "Not out yet...when is that to happen?"

"Next Tuesday, Sir."

"Who did this?" was the next rapid question.

"Edgett, Sir," the aide answered, "That new Senator from Wisconsin."

"Get Senator Edgett on the phone, please," the President ordered. "I'd like a word with him."

~

Jon Crane sat at a table in the small kitchen of his first house. A once cold beer stood before him, collecting water that ran down the glass as he stared into space.

He had run eight laps through the woods, three more than his previous record, after returning from the Dalton airfield. How long he'd been at the table, he wasn't sure. His thoughts were of Marsha.

The meeting was probably over by now; he almost said aloud and glanced at his watch. It had been four and a half hours. His attention went from the watch to the growing puddle around his half-consumed beer.

Standing abruptly to seek a paper towel, he froze at the sound of his cell phone. Jon pulled the object from his pocket and looked at the caller ID. It was Ben.

"Yeah?" Jon answered tersely without meaning to.

"Okay, guess I won't ask how you're doing," Ben retorted.

"I'm sorry; I was cleaning up a mess. What going on?"

"Everything alright over there?"

Jon didn't care for such games. "Ben...has something happened? Get on with it, please."

"It's all good here," the younger man said. "But I have heard from Daniel and now Murray. Stuff is starting to get weird."

"Anybody hurt?" the voice was now clearly that of Silas.

"No... none of ours. Daniel says there's a rash of murders in the congressional ranks. Mostly low level staffers, but the big deal is that several of the victims are in pictures with that star thingy."

"The one you found downtown in Atlanta?"

"The same," Ben assured him.

"What's going on with Murray?"

"Somebody was snooping around at Caddo Mills, the ranch itself. But what's worse, there was an attempt on Phil Stone at his lake house."

"To kill him?" Silas barked.

"Looks like it. The cop in him, you know, instincts, saved his life."

"What...where are he and Sara now?"

"I'm not sure... but Murray said for you not to worry, they were handling it."

Jon rubbed his head and heard his phone beep. He looked at the call-waiting ID.

"Ben," he said, "I need to go. It's Marsha."

The elevator opened and Cheryl stepped out announcing dinner would be ready in ten minutes. Ben turned his chair towards her and noticed the action on a TV monitor, set for national news.

The banner of "Breaking News" was overlaid with another line of crawling text.

Navy Secretary hurt, gunman killed in shootout at Washington, D.C. area hospital, it read. The pictures on the screen clearly showed a face Ben had seen many times, in pictures if not in person. It was Jerome Grimes.

Scrambling for the remote, Ben turned the sound up and Cheryl approached the table with a look of concern.

"What's going on?" she asked and grabbed Ben's shoulder.

"I don't know yet," he injected and turned the volume up even more, "I'm trying to find out."

The story on the TV was fairly complete, given it was network news. Ben reached up and covered Cheryl's hand with his own.

"Have you heard from your folks today?" he asked.

~

The rain had ceased around noon time and, as Warren Dawes expected, the regular driver had called in saying he "felt much better." The normally patient man found himself pacing the floors of his Decatur, Georgia, home in anticipation of the job offer from this morning.

Once well known in those circles, Dawes had been out of that type of work for several years. Then came the call in 2014. It had gone well back then. So well, the thought of another challenge had his adrenalin pumping.

It will be close to a week before I see the details, he thought trying to gather himself. *Don't get worked up till you see the details.*

He needed an outlet for his building energy. With nothing else on his schedule, Warren went to the detached garage and made appearances of starting a project in his workshop. Neighbors often saw the man building or cleaning an odd piece of furniture in his shop. With the wind blowing slightly, it was not out of the ordinary for him to close the big garage door, cutting off their view.

Warren had a large rack of scrap lumber against one inside wall. This material was organized on heavy shelving with steel standards and rails. It looked like and it did, weigh a ton. Reaching in along the middle shelf, Dawes found and pushed a button, a button that was very neatly hidden.

An electric motor drove the impeller on a pneumatic system that sounded much like his shop vacuum. This instantly raised the shelving unit, a quarter-inch off the floor. With one hand, Dawes rolled the edge of the shelving unit away from the wall on tiny, almost invisible, rollers set behind the leg standards. The system had cost as much as his new pick-up truck and it took several months of night work to install. Both were now over twelve years old, but they still served his needs.

Under the bottom shelf, cut into the otherwise solid concrete pad, lay a steel door with a padlock. Its key hung on the backside of the shelving's standard.

Dawes unlocked the door and pulled it upright until it fell back on its hinges. The pit beneath the door was nine feet deep. Cut into the earth were rows of yet more shelves, these containing boxes rather than raw materials.

He let himself into the pit using a short section of extension ladder. Stepping down with caution, he then pulled a box from the center of the space and propped it into position with a piece of two-by-four lumber.

Cautious movements were all he could handle since the fall. That was now ten years ago.

With the lid raised, Dawes could see and select from several large caliber handguns, magazines for each, and boxes of ammunition. He took three weapons and spent that afternoon cleaning them. The exercise eased his mind.

12

Marsha explained the meeting and her new job offer into a mostly quiet phone. In his mind, Jon wanted to act surprised. The truth was, he wasn't.

"Are you there?" she frustratedly asked the silence.

"Hey," he managed, "congratulations. So, are you coming home to pack?"

"Actually, I have the things I left here. The department sealed up my apartment, so nobody got in there. I do want to come get some of my other stuff, but for right now, they need me involved with the transition and some orientation."

She was speaking so fast it took Jon a moment to realize what she said.

"You're staying there, then?"

"For a while," she answered meekly. It was the first time her voice had faltered. "Just till we get everybody settled. This doesn't involve just me."

Jon could feel Silas taking over within him and he changed gears suddenly.

"Be careful," he said. "And I mean extra careful. Things have started to happen."

What...what kind of things?"

"Somebody tried to hurt Phil," he said slowly, "and Murray's place had some visitors. That's all I know, but be aware, okay?"

"Are they alright?"

"Yes...yes, they're fine. It's a good thing in a way. Now we can all be on alert. Makes it harder for anyone to get to us, right?"

"You be careful, too," she cooed softly.

~

A button flashed on the huge phone set. The President leaned across from where he was standing to answer the intercom line.

"Yes?"

"Sir, I have Senator Edgett on line three."

"That was fast."

"I didn't call him, Sir. He called in."

"Thanks," the Chief Executive replied and quickly punched line three on his desk set. "Senator, I'm glad you called," he started.

"Sir, please let me speak," the rattled man said. "You need to know what I've done...and why."

"Go ahead, Senator."

Edgett was blunt about the rider he had attached without conferring with anyone and then went into some detail.

"I received the request in an unmarked envelope, somehow hand carried to my office. With it were pictures of my eldest daughter at school."

"At school," the president tried to picture the man's family, but could not. "What school?"

"She's at Wake Forest, sir, the Bowman School of Medicine. She's scheduled to graduate this fall."

"I'm assuming there was a threat included with the pictures."

"Subtle," Edgett told him, "but very clear, yes."

The President stood quietly for a moment before responding.

"Senator, I have an idea if you will give me some time. You're coming to me is very important," he didn't share with the man that he already knew about the clemency, "I need you to trust me and to stay quiet a bit longer."

"Sir?" the senator was puzzled and concerned.

"Just stay calm, tell no one else of this until you have heard from me, okay?"

"Sir, I'm so sorry about this..."

"I'm sorry this is happening to you, Senator. I want you to know, I'm sending plain clothes men to Wake Forest today. Don't tell your daughter anything. These men will not be intrusive into her business, simply protective. I can assure you of that. By the way, what is her first name?"

"Claire, sir."

"Claire is going to be just fine, Senator. I'll be in touch."

The president punched another button on the phone set, "Jesse, get me Farley at Langley...if he's not there, find him."

~

The alarm sounded and caught both Ben and Cheryl off-guard. He immediately touched a key on his computer lighting up a screen with a view outside the mansion. A small suction cup had attached itself to one of the front glass windows.

"What is this, now," Ben said out loud. He scrambled to roll back the recording from that camera. "Well, well," he smiled, "gotcha."

The recording clearly showed a sedan cruise by slowly and a shot from the backseat window. Instead of a bullet, the shot was the suction device.

"Microphone, I'll bet you," Ben proclaimed and half ran to the elevator. Cheryl started to follow but he asked her to stay and watch the monitor.

Doris Shaw, Ben's mom, had heard the 'thump' and was standing at the window looking at the object when Ben got there.

The glass suddenly turned black and actually bowed inward. The vibration from the blast projected through and knocked Doris to her rear on the rug.

"Mom!" Ben yelled and ran to his mother. She blinked a couple of times, as though stunned, but otherwise was okay. Ben looked up at the window and saw it was cracked on the outer layer and singed in a five foot diameter circle.

"It felt like the breath went out of me," Doris muttered while holding her chest.

"Are you alright?" Ben was trembling as he looked her over for any wounds.

"I think so," she answered, breathing better now. "What the hell was that?"

"Somebody didn't bother knocking at the door."

Ben stood and went to the far end of the room. From there he could see the damage to the exterior shrubbery and grounds. The Liberty Tree was leaning toward the road.

Cheryl's voice erupted over the house intercom.

"Ben, they're coming back. The car is back and there are two other cars with it."

"I see 'em," he said aloud, even though she couldn't hear him at that moment. Jogging to a desk, Ben picked up a phone. He could feel his fear turn to rage as he punched "9" for the intercom.

"Cheryl, stay put," Ben demanded, "we're alright up here. They can't get to us. Just stay put, okay?"

No less than ten men climbed from the three vehicles but didn't proceed very far. They looked very puzzled that the bomb had not allowed them access to the house. The leader appeared to be in disbelief.

Ben ran to the elevator.

Four of the armed men outside climbed the driveway on foot, still seeking a way into the big house.

The elevator slipped past the second sub-level and went on to the third. Ben rushed out before the door had completely opened and unlocked a cabinet he hardly ever used.

The men outside beat on the windows and doors with their weapons as Doris stood defiantly, staring at them through the thick glass.

Ben Shaw had his own secret. One he had not shared with anyone. From the cabinet he pulled a Kevlar suit he had ordered several weeks ago. It was not black like the others. This one was deep emerald green.

The leader of the attack team had begun to realize they did not have the ability to breach the outer walls of the mansion. He waved his men off and they began to walk back down to their cars.

In the third sub-basement, Ben pulled on the last piece of his own protective suit, the head covering cowl, and jumped into the armored pick-up truck. It rolled down the tunnel at over fifty miles per hour and screeched onto the pavement, rocking heavily to the driver's side before lumbering up the highway.

The four man-team had reached their cars but stopped at the sight of the intruding old truck. The others scrambled from their vehicles and all ten pointed weapons.

13

A young aide stuck her head into the senator's private office.

"Sir, there's a reporter from back home here," she announced.

An older, scruffily-dressed man nearly pushed his way into the office and pulled out a folding ID case. He laid it on the senator's desk in front of him.

"Sir, I'm Dilbach Hurtle from the Milwaukee Dispatch," he smiled and chirped rapidly. "As you can see on my ID," he pointed to the document, directing the senator to look at it, "I'm fairly new to Milwaukee but the folks back home would love to know how you're doing?"

Senator Edgett glanced at the ID, which wasn't that at all. Written out across the two sections was, "The president sent me. I need those pictures of your daughter that were sent to you. We're going to find these people."

As color came to the senator's face, his visitor spoke again.

"Don't be embarrassed, sir. The folks seem to love you. That ain't a bad thing."

Edgett looked up into the man's eyes. His guest nodded ever so slightly. "May I sit...please?" he asked.

"Yes," the senator stammered but became stronger with each passing second. "Please, have a seat. It's good to see you."

The reporter pulled a small digital device from his coat and held it for the senator to see.

"You mind if I record?" he asked. "You're probably already on recording devices anyway, right?" he winked at his host.

The senator understood the warning and replied verbally and with a hand gesture. "By all means," he smiled, "go ahead."

"I'm sure you have a standard press release already prepared."

Edgett thought a second and realized the opportunity that question offered. He pulled open a desk drawer and retrieved an envelope. Inside it were the pictures that had been sent to him.

"Yes," he handed the papers across to his guest. "This is the prepared standard package we make for home folks."

"Great," the man peeked into the covering without pulling the contents out. He flipped through and nodded again. "This is good, I recognize the format so if I can fill in with just a few simple questions, and I'll get out of your hair."

~

When his phone rang, Jon flipped it open without checking the caller ID. The rattled voice of his ex-neighbor and old friend, Doris Shaw brought him to his feet.

"Jon," she spoke rapidly, "some men have attacked the house. Ben has gone out after them."

"What?"

"He's in the pick-up, Jon. I can see it coming up the road."

Jon closed the phone without another word and ran to the Jaguar. The garage door slid open and the twelve cylinder beast roared toward the mansion. Silas was at the wheel.

~

Cheryl looked at the flashing red light while keeping her attention on the drama outside. She finally reached over and answered the special phone line.

"Hello?"

The caller was taken aback by the female voice. "I'm looking for Jon Crane...or Ben."

"They're not here," she said as the pick-up got closer to the three other vehicles on her monitors.

"Is this Cheryl?" Grimes realized. "Cheryl Duray?"

"Yes, sir," she answered meekly, "who is this?"

"I'm Director Grimes, of the NCIS in Washington, Cheryl. We've had a situation here I need Jon Crane to know about."

"Sir, we got one here right, now. I'll have to have Ben call you back."

"I may be on the line with the president," Grimes told her. "But have him call me ASAP."

~

The ten attackers began firing at once. Bullets struck and bounced from the truck's body and windshield. Ben lowered the protective steel plates over the wheel wells and pushed down on the accelerator.

He aimed the truck directly at the front cars and several shooters jumped out of the way. He struck the car a glancing blow, which shoved it backwards into the ditch alongside the roadway.

The car's bumper hung on the truck's as Ben tried to back away from it. A man, dressed in a dark suit, ran up to his driver's window and fired into the glass. One ricochet struck him in the neck and he fell backwards.

Ben reached for his handgun and the door handle. His power bent the handle and he let it go, initially shocked by his added strength.

Two other men rushed up and grabbed their friend and loaded him in another car. Then all piled into the remaining two vehicles and fled up the highway with Ben's truck still stuck to the last car's bumper.

He carefully opened the truck's door and climbed down. Flexing his hands, he looked at them and reached down to the car's steel bumper.

He raised it with little effort, well enough to dislodge it from his truck. Walking back to his driver's door, he heard the distinct whine of the Jaguar turning down onto Highway 71.

~

The fake reporter did ask several, "stock" questions and pretended to be making notes. The interview lasted about ten more minutes and then the guest stood and thanked Senator Edgett for his time.

"Hope my editor likes this enough to run it," he smiled and shook the senator's hand. "Either way," he added, squeezing his hand even firmer, "it's going to be alright."

The senator walked his guest to the door and thanked him for coming.

"Very nice to meet you," he told him. "I'm glad you're doing this."

"My pleasure, sir," the man smiled and walked away.

Edgett walked back to his desk and tried to be natural. His emotions were churning inside him, yet he needed to stay calm. And that he did.

14

Jon stepped from the sleek, dark green machine and looked at Ben in wonder.

"What is all this?" he asked.

"There were three cars," Ben started, "ten men, by my count. One of them is hurt... bad." He turned and pointed to the blood by the truck door and the trail of it away.

Jon walked closer to Ben and touched the suit. He looked it over sternly and then stepped back. Ben expected the absolute worst.

"Why green?" Jon asked him calmly.

At first, Ben didn't know how to answer. That wasn't the comment he thought would be coming. Jon noticed the head covering that Ben had pulled off, dangling from his right hand.

"A soft helmet, too, huh?" he reached for it. "I'll bet it's hot."

"Kinda," Ben heard himself answer.

Jon tossed it back to him and asked again, "Why green?"

His head clearing somewhat, Ben walked to the Jaguar. He leaned against it and began to explain.

"That night, coming back from Atlanta, when those guys were after me," he spoke slowly at first and then evened out. "I never felt afraid, not really...not in this car."

Jon noticed that the suit color blended in almost perfectly with the paint of the Jaguar. Saying nothing further about the color, Jon moved in closer. His eyes squinted as he stared Ben down. Then stepping into the young man's face, he leaned in tight.

"Okay..." Jon whispered in his ear. "But why did you take a chance like this... alone?"

Ben turned, stiff necked, to answer. His voice was unequivocal.

"They nearly hurt my mother, Jon." He seemed to stand even taller and added, "and my girlfriend is in there, too." He pointed at the mansion and paused but for just a second. "What did you expect me to do?"

There was no smile on Jon's face, but there was a look of complete understanding and even acceptance. He nodded several times and looked up at the house. The damage from the blast was evident, even from the road. At the top of the driveway, a single figure stood with a rifle in her hands. It was Doris Shaw.

Looking back at Ben he simply nodded once more.

~

Weston Duray completed the reports for the local authorities. Reluctantly, they called the situation into the FBI.

"You got four dead men here, Westy," the sheriff pushed his hat up on his brow. "Who are these guys, anyway?"

"I've got an idea," Westy muttered in his direction, "but it still doesn't tell me just who they are."

"What?"

"I know, Bob. It doesn't make sense right now but I'm afraid it will real soon."

"Where's Rita?" the sheriff asked.

"She's up in the Soo with family. We've been staying up there mostly since we got back from Georgia."

"Georgia?" the sheriff took his hat completely off his head. "That feller, we've been hearing about, a part of this?"

"He's probably the real target."

A deputy walked up and interrupted them.

"Bob," he said to his boss. "The FBI says they'll have people here in an hour."

"Thanks," the sheriff told him dismissively and the deputy bowed and walked away.

"You need any back-up, Westy?"

"I appreciate it, Bob, but I just don't know. I got this feeling I'm being used to get to my friend, ya know?"

"It's happened before," the sheriff started to back away, and leave Duray alone for a while. "Let me know what I can do, okay?"

~

Lori Seay walked out onto the rear porch and had to yell over the sound of saws and drills to be heard. "Danny," she nearly screamed, "phone!"

Daniel Seay turned from a discussion with a contractor.

"What?" he asked, but then could see his wife was waving a cell phone. He excused himself and went in her direction. "Who is it?"

"Bill White," Lori told him and reached out to hand him the phone.

With his face twisted in curiosity, he took the phone and mouthed at his wife silently, "Again?"

His friend and former boss sounded excited but hearing clearly was a problem.

"Hang on a second, Bill," Daniel tried to be heard, "Let me find a quiet spot around here."

Out the front door and walking toward the road, the noise died down. "Okay, sorry about that," Daniel finally could hear his own voice, "what's up?"

"There were some people here today, looking for you. Where the hell are you anyways?"

"We're checking on the rebuilding at the beach house. We're in North Carolina."

"Well, that's good," White said. "I believe they think you're in Pittsburgh."

"Whoa," Daniel realized Bill was seriously concerned. "Who were these people?"

"That's just it, Daniel. I don't know and they wouldn't say. They just wanted you and they looked serious."

"It's been months since I left the paper. They don't have very good information, do they?"

"Not current stuff, it would appear. With all this other mess going on, I just wanted you to know, okay?"

"Thanks, boss," Daniel said affectionately. "I'll figure out what we need to do. I'm afraid coming home ain't the thing right now."

"Is your friend home in Georgia?"

"We've always thought alike, Bill."

"I'll let you go," the editor told him. "Just be aware and stay safe."

Daniel punched "end call" and looked at Lori.

"Did you hear that?"

"Enough of it," she answered. "Are we ever going to live a normal life again?"

Daniel didn't respond. He pulled up Harold Foster's number on his phone and hit "dial."

15

Security was beefed up at Sentara Northern Medical Center, but oddly enough, it was all internal security and area cops.

Jerome Grimes was escorted down a long hallway to a private room where two uniformed officers stood guard. Sitting in a straight-backed leather chair was the Navy Secretary.

"Nelson," Grimes asked, "are you alright?"

His friend and boss tilted his head back, showing a tiny bandage below his chin.

"Three stitches and a God-danged shot for this," he pointed in disgust. "I've been hurt worse shaving, for Christ sake."

"How long have you been here?"

The Navy Secretary looked at his watch. "Two and a half hours now," he responded.

"Have you called the President?"

"No," Pharr said bluntly. "I'm not calling him over three stitches and I'm not even sure I was the target of this thing."

"I know what it looks like, Nelson," Grimes tried to explain, but his superior cut him off.

"I've got tons of questions, Jerry," he was getting red in the face. "How did they know any of this?"

Grimes stood without answers.

"How did they know we were meeting or the route I would take? Hell, how did they know they could get around inside my damned car and that I'd be taken to this facility for treatment?"

Grimes shook his head but he was in full agreement.

"You were the target, Jerry," Pharr stated firmly. "I was just the bait...but how in the hell... did they know all this?"

"I'll get on this investigation right away, sir."

"Hell, man," Pharr said in a calmer voice. "I know you will. I'm just pissed that somebody, with a bunch of apparent clout, is trying to kill my friend."

Jerome Grimes nodded that time. He was figuring it out in his head but the whole thing felt too weird. *Were they trying to use him to lure Jon Crane out?*

"Boss, do you want me to call the president? An attack on you is significant...no matter what we think is going on around it."

"I'll call him," Pharr said as though it was all one word. "I just wanted to talk with you first. Is my driver still out there?"

"Yes, Sir."

"And the agents from Florida are here...thank goodness."

"I did hear about that," Pharr smiled. "Make sure my driver is comfortable out there and bring your agents in here. We'll get on with our meeting."

Sergeant Gil Gartner of the Dalton, Georgia, police stood with Jon and Ben on the highway in front of the mansion. Ben's suit lay folded on the seat of the old pick-up. The three men looked at the disabled sedan Ben had pushed into the ditch.

"It's definitely a rental," Gil reported after calling in the vehicle's VIN. "Owner is Tanner's Car Rental; they operate out of downtown Atlanta and the airport. Airport would be my guess."

Gil's people were going through all the hard surfaces, on and in the car, looking for fingerprints.

"This technology we've got," he told them, "we can get a digital picture of the print and have an ID in minutes."

The FBI's IAFIS, the Integrated Automated Fingerprint Identification System, has a database of over 120 million domestic citizen's prints as well as nearly 200,000 internationally known terrorists. Access for matching can take as little as ten minutes or up to a full twenty-four hours.

A technician in a white coat walked up to Gil and informed him they had found three distinctly different sets of prints overlaying some that were obviously older.

"We hope to know something in a few minutes," he added.

Yet another technician had gathered some of the blood from the wounded man for possible DNA record-matching.

"You folks want some coffee?" Doris called down from the main door of the house.

Gil smiled and hollered back to her, "Thanks, Mrs. Shaw but we're still working at the moment."

Jon walked across the road in slow, deliberate paces. His thoughts were piling on top of each other and none stood out as more important than the rest.

Murray's place is breached, but there's no harm, Phil's place is booby-trapped and now this, he listed over and over. *Then there's all the stuff Daniel called about...Daniel?*

He turned and called to Ben, "Have you heard from Daniel again?"

The younger man shook his head, "No, Jon. I haven't."

~

After several hours of work, Murray Bilstock and his cousin "Slick" had set up more hidden cameras around the ranch house and hangar.

"How are we on food in the underground?" Murray asked.

"I probably should run to town and get a few things. If anything does happen and we're holed up...there's stuff we'd need."

"We'll go together," Murray was stern in his pronouncement. "No more getting separated until we know what we're dealing with, okay?"

"Yeah," Slick nodded. "I'll bring the truck up to the house."

Murray stood looking skyward without a word. Slick stopped and stared back at him.

"What?" he asked. "Do you see something?"

"I know Ben is monitoring the radar around here, but I may call him and have that circle widened out."

"He checks a fifty-mile radius, now."

"Yeah...well," Murray pulled his hat off and rubbed his forehead, "Those drone planes run pretty fast. I'd like to know if they're coming."

"I thought you and the president were big buddies? You're not worried about the government, are you?"

"The government, and those who use it, can be different as all get out," Murray muttered. "I don't know, I just got a feeling this ain't good."

~

Her eyes stayed glued to the monitors, yet Cheryl Duray sat with a phone to her ear.

"Mom," she said, "I need to know if you guys are alright."

"I'm fine, Baby, and your Dad called this morning. I had expected him home yesterday but he said some things came up that he had to deal with."

"Some things?"

"He didn't say what. You know how he is."

"He's okay?"

"Yes, yes...he's coming back up here tonight."

Cheryl and her Mother both knew his secrecy wasn't to be believed. They also knew that discussing it wouldn't change or help anything.

"Things are happening, Mom," Cheryl said seriously. "Ask Dad to call when you talk to him. He needs to talk to Jon, Murray, or Ben."

"Are you still in that mansion?" Rita asked.

"Yes, Mother. I'm safe."

Rita Duray stood with her eyes closed and a hand over her heart as she listened. Her voice was strong, but that was a cover. It was good that this conversation was over the phone, though. Could Cheryl see her mother, it would upset her.

16

A wrecker had pulled the mystery car from the ditch and was on its way to the compound. It passed George Vincent at the top of the hill. Either it or George's beige sedan caught the sharp beam of the setting sun, reflecting it off the front glass of the mansion.

"Nothing broken up there?" Jon asked. The sun's glare had drawn his attention to the house.

"I haven't checked from outside," Ben admitted. "But inside is fine. Do you want me to use the pick-up to pull the tree back into position?"

Jon stared at his beloved elm tree. It leaned nearly forty-five degrees away from the house, but still clung to its spot.

"Leave it," Jon said softly, "for now."

George had parked and was walking up before Ben could respond.

"Doris called," George started excitedly. "I know she's fine...how are you guys?"

"Shaken but not stirred," Ben laughed and quickly noticed he was alone in his humor. "We're good," he added with a much more subdued tone. "The house is amazing."

"I was on the phone with a friend when Doris called," George said as though it were important. Jon and Gil looked silently to him, waiting for the rest of his remark. "This friend's son is the congressman from the sixth district."

"Gilbert?" Gil injected. "Travis and I grew up together."

George paused then looked directly at Jon.

"My friend's son has been approached by a group. He doesn't know who they are, but they seem quite powerful and, well...scary, as he put it."

"You don't scare Travis," Gil threw in. "Not easily anyway."

Jon let Gil's comment fade before he spoke up.

"What did this group want him to do?" he asked.

"They offered help with the next election should he join in with them."

The next question was obvious, so no one actually asked it.

"They didn't say exactly what they wanted him to do," George continued. "He recalls something about 'a path' they were on and 'amber sealed secrets' or something to that nature."

"Why did the father call you?" Jon asked bluntly.

"To get your ear, of course. He knows I'm close to you," George stated as fact. "They need your help."

"Does this group have a name?" Jon asked him.

"Travis said the voice called them the Celestial Enumerates."

It was Ben who put it together first.

"The stars and numbers," he thought out loud and then turned to Jon almost shouting, "Numbers in the Star!"

Weston Duray got to Sault Ste. Marie, Michigan, just after dark. He called Rita from outside their friend's home.

"You okay in there?" he all but whispered.

"Yes," she answered and immediately went into full animation. "Where are you? What IS going on?"

"I'm right outside. I'll come in and explain."

He told his wife the story of the unwanted guests at their farm and without a breath between, asked her, "Have you talked to Cheryl?"

"Cheryl is fine," she said grabbing him in a bear hug. "Something is happening though... and it's big." She pushed back still holding his arms with her hands. "She says you need to call Jon right away. If you can't reach him... then Murray or Ben."

~

At 8,000 feet, Harold had been given clearance to land. The small Dade County Regional was not known for heavy traffic this time of year.

As he banked the G-5 towards the runway, Harold could see a line of cars coming across the Virginia Dare Bridge. He called Daniel.

"You guys there?" he asked.

"Sitting here, waiting for you," Daniel told him.

"Were you expecting a big send off?"

"No...what do you mean?"

"There's a convoy of vehicles coming over the bridge. They just turned toward the airport, Daniel."

"Get out of here then," Daniel yelled into the phone. "Don't take any chances on our account."

"You're kidding, right?" Harold snapped. "Run and I mean run, to the end of the runway. I'll drop the door long enough for you to climb aboard."

"What about our bags?"

"Screw the bags, Daniel...move."

The screaming jet dragged her tail slightly as she touched down and Harold locked the brakes to slow her. He could see Daniel and Lori running to position and he cut the front wheel hard, spinning the G-5 around.

The Seays avoided the engine and ran to the opening side door. They climbed aboard the still rolling aircraft as the line of vehicles approached the runway. They blew horns and flashed headlights, but Daniel helped the hydraulics close the door as Harold punched down on the throttle and released the brakes. The plane leapt and accelerated.

Through his port side window, Harold saw several men exit the cars and point weapons in their direction.

While listening in silence, Nelson Pharr picked at his new stitches. After a couple of hours the tiny wound had begun to bleed again.

"Sir," Jake Hansard noticed it first. "We need to get a nurse in here."

"What?" the Navy Secretary challenged but pulled his finger away from the aggravation under his chin. Blood on his finger tip explained it all.

"Damn," he muttered.

The break in the discussion was welcomed by all in the room. The two agents had expressed their concerns about a larger plot. As news trickled in of other incidents, they all began to see a larger picture.

Secretary Pharr watched the nurse leave and close the door behind her. He was the first to speak after that.

"Okay," he started and then immediately paused. "First of all, I think you two are on to something," he pointed to Hansard and Monroe. "Second...if Barrett is behind all this, she's cleaning house."

The stories on the press wires of the political deaths were coming in throughout their meeting.

"What do you want us to do?" Grimes asked as though he already knew.

"Whatever you do, don't let her know we suspect," Pharr proclaimed.

"Understood," Grimes nodded.

"Are you in touch with that 'friend' of yours?"

"Friend, sir?" the NCIS Director tried to play dumb.

Pharr offered a dirty look but continued, "Find out if he and his group...yes, I said his group," the secretary snarled his lip sarcastically. "I don't live in that bubble I pretend to."

Grimes smiled and again nodded.

"Find out if they've been affected by any of this," Pharr barked. "Offer any help you can give if they have."

"Yes, sir."

The top man in the room then looked to the two agents.

"You two are good agents. You're likely targets of this thing as well, you know that?"

"Kinda figured that out, yes, Sir," Hansard responded.

"I want you involved, but stay safe. Where is Dunbar?" he looked back at Grimes.

"I'll get in touch with her right away," he assured the boss.

"She uncovered this whole thing...keep her protected and in the loop."

"You're not looking out a window this time, are you, sir," Grimes teased his friend.

"Hell, no," the secretary smiled. "These bastards have come after me and my friends. I'm in this, too."

17

The low tone of a buzzer sounded just before a panel opened into the Oval Office. Actually a door, the panel hid behind moldings that matched the other panels in the room. A uniformed man entered and spoke out confidently.

"Sir," he said, "the forensics department has completed its analysis of those photos."

The president spun his large chair towards the man.

"What did they determine?" he asked firmly.

"They were all taken by the same camera, a Canon XT 8MP SLR with a 70-300mm lens."

"English, if you please?" the president barked.

"It's a fairly high-end camera with a long lens, sir. The important thing is that by reverse angling, they determined the pictures were taken from eighty to a hundred yards away. That would put the photographer in a parking lot in each case."

"How do you see someone from that far away?" the chief executive asked. "I mean...to tell who you are taking a picture of?"

"There had to be a spotter, Sir. Someone closer," the man explained. "Someone who could identify her but was too close to point a camera and get caught doing so."

"Like a sniper's spotter."

"Exactly," the man smiled and replied.

The president rocked backward and thought for a few seconds, then stared directly at the man before him.

"This is really your line of work, Conrad," he gestured at the uniformed man. "But doesn't this tell us there's a team involved and that they had to be in communications...somehow?"

"I can offer you a job when you retire from this one, Sir," the man grinned as he spoke.

"I'm sure," the president answered. "Nevertheless, can we trace the communications?"

"Satellite imagery would have needed to be recorded for that area, Sir. I don't think we have that."

The president's eyebrows appeared to become thicker and heavier as they slumped down from his brow. He turned to a drawer on his desk and found a piece of paper with a name and a number.

"Send copies of what you have to this number, attention Mr. B. Shaw," he told the man, handing him the note. "Tell him what you know but be sure it's handled as Top Secret. This must be kept quiet... that girl's life is at stake."

"Aye, Sir," the man turned with the note to leave.

"I want that paper back when you're done," the president called out. "That's not a number I intend to lose."

Rita Duray had not turned loose of her husband for almost a full hour. "We've gotten involved with some...high profile people," she managed to get out.

Westy stirred in his position on the sofa but kept her close.

"Can I admit something to you...without you coming undone?"

She looked at him with unabashed apprehension, but said nothing.

"I kinda enjoy this," he said. "I like these people. I like what they do and how they operate. And I'm glad we're a part of it."

Rita hugged him tightly. "I know that," she sighed.

~

Later that evening, as information and word of incidents piled high, Jon closed his phone and rubbed his tired ear. He had heard from Grimes, Phil Stone, and Marsha again. Weston Duray had finally called to report his adventure. Jon rocked his head back trying to organize all he had heard into something he could work against. The attacks, added to the information Daniel had called about and George's call from his friend, all presented a huge-scale conspiracy or random coincidences. He tried to allow for the latter, but his common sense told him otherwise.

Through closed eyes and little sound, he could still sense Ben walking up to him. Jon sat up straight, noticing the photos in Ben's hand.

"What's this now?" Jon asked him and reached out.

"A new senator in Wisconsin is being blackmailed," Ben started.

"Where did we hear of this?" Jon asked, studying the pictures of a young, blond woman. A story like that would normally overwhelm the news.

"The President's people," Ben answered, "just now."

Jon said nothing, but his stare into Ben's eyes relayed his next question.

"The concern is that it will cause the release of a career killer from Oxford Prison in Wisconsin," the youth continued.

"Isn't that where Barrett is?"

"Yeah," Ben answered and then followed with, "has a smell to it, huh?"

"Even under normal circumstances, yeah," Jon smirked. "Who is this in these pictures?"

"The senator's daughter. She's a med student at Wake Forest."

"So... she's the target if he doesn't play along?"

"The senator did what they asked, but then contacted the president about it himself."

"Brave man," Jon muttered, "and smart, too." He looked back at one of the photographs. "Who is it that's to be released?"

"Jackson Terrell," Ben told him, "the serial killer."

Jon silently wished he could isolate this into a separate case, but it fit too well into the growing plot. Another quick glance at one of the pictures triggered a thought like a shot out of the blue. First he stared at the photo closer, then holding it out to Ben, he asked, "Who does she look like to you?"

"I don't know," the boy stumbled to respond. "Where are you going with this?"

"You've met Dunbar, haven't you?"

"Colleen Dunbar, Agent Dunbar?" Ben thought aloud, "No, not in person. But I've seen pictures of her."

"Look at this girl," Jon almost grinned as he still held the photo to him. "Do you see it? There's a resemblance there."

Ben stared at the picture of the blond woman.

"Close enough," he said and nodded his head in agreement. "If she'll do it, it would be something we can work with."

"She'll do it," Jon assured him. "It's in her nature."

~

Having "buzzed" the Dalton airport, Harold thought he saw vehicles he didn't recognize sitting around. He made a command decision on his own.

"We're going to land at Calhoun," he announced through the intercom. "There might be company waiting for us in Dalton."

The pilot had prepared for such a need, using funds from his "budget," he'd had a special hangar constructed at a small private strip in the community. The runway, just off I-75, was lengthened but still obscured from view. World War II aircraft sat on display along the expressway, giving the strip the appearance of a neglected museum rather than an active airfield.

"Hang on back there," he warned on approach. "This could be bumpy."

The G-5 rolled directly into the hangar before any of them climbed down. Daniel was impressed when he walked outside to take a look at the structure.

"Harold, I always knew you were a sharp cookie," he grinned. "But this takes the cake."

The building blended into its surroundings as though it had always been there. It looked like an old hay barn with what appeared to be holes in the fading facade. One of the larger, fake voids went through the painted "See Rock City" sign on the mansard roof.

"Only used it once before," Harold smiled and then pointed back inside. "The car is in here, too. We'd best get going," he told them, "we're still thirty minutes from the mansion."

~

"Will," the voice said. "This is J.C. Chastain over in Gadsden."

"Yeah, JC," the owner of the wild animal park responded. He rubbed his forehead and pulled the phone tighter to his ear. "You need to speak with Cody?"

"Not really...no."

The tone of his old friend's voice suddenly sank into the busy man.

"Something wrong, JC?"

"Cody is alright out there, isn't he?"

"Get to it, Chastain," Will's patience was closing in, "You know what we've been through so don't play games. Out with it."

"I ran into Cody's dad at the grocery this morning. They'd had some visitors yesterday."

"What kind of visitors?"

"Said they was from the government, but Arnold didn't think so. They had black suits and all, just something about 'em put him off."

Will could see the story coming clearer now, "They wanted Cody, right?"

"Exactly."

"What did Mr. Arnold tell these men?" Will asked.

"He told them that Cody was back over at the VA in Atlanta."

"Why didn't he call me himself?" Will asked out loud without really thinking.

"Arnold thought those people might have his phone bugged or whatever. That's why he told me about it."

"Tell Mr. Arnold he did good," Will smiled. "Tell him his son is fine and that we'll watch out and take care of him."

"He knows that, Will. You be careful now."

18

Albany, Georgia, had seen better times. The once proud business and social center of southwest Georgia had become like many other urban areas in the country. Drought from years ago, a political climate that had been ignored for too long, and a bottomed-out economy left the old guard leaders in shock and denial.

They could drive down the once pristine US Highway 19, known as Slappey Drive in town, and somehow pretend not to notice. All that lay to the east side of that road was in near ruins. While to the west, a struggle to maintain dignity caused racial divide and unrest.

Dilward Putney could remember the heyday of Albany. He'd been there when the pecan business was king. His family has owned a grove of more than 450 acres for over 200 years. Fifteen years ago, when he took over the family business, David's Pecans, the wealth that accompanied his position was three times that which remained today.

Cost and the availability of labor had driven the price of his products too high. Add to that the failing economy and reduced incomes; pecans were no longer a staple in households. They had become a rarely used extravagance.

Dilward was easily spotted as he walked through the processing plant. His tall, lanky frame had been a huge asset in high school, where he excelled in both football and basketball, but those days were over fifty years ago. Now, it simply made him quickly noticeable as he came through on his inspections.

"The old man looks worried today," a worker whispered across the wide sorting table. "I think his color is leaving him."

The other man looked up and laughed under his breath.

"Yeah," he responded. "Staying up all night counting that money must be hard on an old man."

Putney didn't hear the exchange. If he had their days at the factory would have ended right then. Lucky for them, they were too far away. The owner had walked into his 100 yard long shop no more than forty feet, far from earshot of the men working at the table. The large building, that once held over three hundred "sorters," now housed a mere fifty experienced workers. Two machines now did the basic sorting for size. These people picked out nuts that were not to standard, due to color or some other abnormality. Demand for his product was down nearly half of what it had been. The production line showed that.

Dilward Putney stopped and looked over the activity with a disapproving glare, then turned to the sound of a speaker calling his name.

"Mr. Putney... phone call on line three," it bellowed, "Mr. Putney, line three please."

~

Jon had been cordial yet distant in the three days since Harold, Daniel and Lori had arrived. So much to consider and much more he wanted to hear, made him seem reclusive. He was trying to organize what he did know while Ben set up a secure conference video call, where he could listen and see everyone with their input. Ben and Daniel had been through this with Jon before and they understood.

"I see another big 'round table' discussion," Daniel said to Ben.

"Oh, yeah," the young man responded with animation. "All hands on deck, as they say."

Jon's concerns were for everything he could think of that might be a target. That included the mansion.

When Harold had called to say they were enroute by car, Jon told him to use the upper driveway. He feared the house was under surveillance and didn't wish to give the gas station entrance away. That did not mean Harold's party would be sacrificial lambs by any means.

A few weeks earlier, just after everyone had left, Jon and Ben had set up more holographic projectors along the driveway's sloping climb to the house. When turned on, they projected the image of an empty drive. A vehicle turning into that driveway from the road would simply disappear to anyone watching. The system worked perfectly and the arrival had been without incident.

Ben looked up from a secure text message on one computer screen.

"I need to tell Jon about this," he said to Daniel.

"What is it? Can you tell me?"

"That CIA agent who was hurt at your beach house," Ben explained. "Langhorn was his name."

"Was?" Daniel eyes became wider. "You mean the guy who everyone thought was the helicopter mechanic? Was?" he repeated.

"Yeah...he's been killed in an ambush."

"Dil, is that you?" a man's voice said when Putney picked up his phone.

"Yeah," the tall man answered.

"Hold on a second while I do this," the caller informed him.

The line filled with sounds of screeching wires and metal banging together. On the other end, the caller had pushed a button and was asking, "Can you hear me?" When there was no response, he tried more buttons but still received no answer.

Just before Putney gave up, the line cracked and a voice was heard.

"There," the caller sounded relieved, "can you hear me?"

"I hear you but you sound like you're in a tunnel. What the hell is going on?"

"Dilward, this is that new scrambling system I bought for the phones. So we can talk without being tapped."

More impressed than he intended to let on, the tall man simply answered with, "Okay, what's so important?"

"I got a message from Barrett. She ain't happy and she thinks we may be undermining her efforts."

"You heard from her?" Putney challenged angrily. "There's no contact, remember?"

"It wasn't direct," the other man quickly explained. "She sent word. Most of her tries to hit people associated with this 'Son' fella were absolute failures. Four of her men are dead to only one of theirs."

"I don't like this. Any contact with her can tie us all together."

"Look, Dil. She sent word through services. I got a bunch of flowers with a note to call a number. That led to another phone number directing me to a wire service location. A telegram from Spain had been relayed through Argentina."

"Enough," Putney stopped him. "So what is it she thinks we're doing?"

"She said her 'hired gun' was being released yesterday and for us not to interfere with him."

"What does that mean?"

"Apparently, she did something to get Jackson Terrell out of Oxford."

"Interesting," the tall man said. "You're sure nobody can follow what we're saying on this line?"

"Quite sure."

"Who is Terrell going after, do you know?"

"She didn't say. She just warned us to stay out of it."

"So why are you calling me?" Putney asked.

"What do you want to do?"

Dilward Putney grinned and looked around. He was alone.

"We watch and maybe learn something," he laughed.

19

Ben found Jon in the main living room, sitting and staring at the blackened window.

"Jon," Ben called out as he entered the room. "That CIA man from the beach house... Langston. He's been killed in Washington, D.C."

With his face nearly pale, Jon stood up as though hit by a bolt of lightning. He had not thought about those who were involved in that incident, the SEAL Team murders, and the termination of Clifford Wyckoff at Nag's Head. *That's the target list*, he realized. The puzzle pieces were falling into shape. His mind immediately went to the NCIS agents who had helped, and especially Cody Arnold.

"Notify those agents from Jacksonville," he ordered as he pulled a card from his wallet. The card read, Tigers of Tomorrow.

"They know about the SEAL case, don't they?" Ben figured.

"Call those agents, now please. Make them aware of what's going on. I need to make this call myself."

"I've got something else and I might as well go over it with you now," Ben held his ground and stared back at Jon sternly.

Jon looked down and noticed papers in Ben's hand, papers that had not been offered to him yet. His eyes came up to meet Ben's without a sound spoken. His glare meant "get on with it."

"After you supposedly died," the boy started, "the informant network got quiet... actually really quiet. Then in the last couple of months it began to pick up again."

"The network," Jon said as though a ghost from his past had suddenly reappeared. He had all but forgotten the wide spread group of volunteers who sent in suggestions for investigation, activities of local congressmen that were beyond the scope of the law. Jon's eyes turned down for a moment as it came back to him. "Something important come up?" he asked.

"There's three, really," Ben reached out with the notes. "There was a bunch more but I sifted through and culled out all but these."

Jon took the notes and led a short walk to a small table. There he laid the papers out, scanning them as he spoke.

"So these are cases...the kind of cases we started out handling?"

"Yes," Ben answered.

"Any connection to this 'star picture' bunch, in any of them?" he looked over at Ben.

"No...not that's apparent. And I dug deep as I could from here."

Jon picked up one Ben had marked in red.

"This is a priority to you?" he asked as he looked it over.

"Yeah...that congressman from Virginia is bad business. There's a dead man that has a tie to him. The man would follow the congressman to 'town hall' type meetings and harass him about a crime his son committed."

"I saw that on TV," Jon remembered. "I didn't hear about the death, though."

"That wasn't reported too much. Many in the media like this congressman."

"You feel like he did it, huh."

"Enough to bring it to you..." Ben said, "yeah."

"These others?"

"One is in Kansas and one is in Minnesota...similar stuff, though."

Jon folded the papers and stuffed them in his shirt.

"We've gotten ourselves off track, haven't we, Ben?"

"I wouldn't say that," the young man told him. "But that's really what we set out to do...isn't it?"

"Go call those agents, will ya," Jon reminded him. "I need to talk to Alabama."

~

He had studied the package several times and was going through the details again when the special line rang. It was a different number this time, but the caller was the same as before.

"This is Dawes," he answered sharply and sat up straighter, though it was a completely unconscious act.

"You have your answer?" the voice from the other end asked.

"Let me clear a couple things up...first," Warren Dawes told him.

"You do know who this target is, right?" the voice sounded a touch sarcastic.

"I've heard of him, sure. But why me...for this hit?"

"You're not far from him... for one," the voice responded. "Proximity is a good thing in this case. You can go about your normal business while you prepare."

Dawes had been in the business a long time. He knew that answer, while valid, wasn't the real reason. He didn't speak in return. He patiently waited for the voice to go on.

"Your style is why you've been chosen, Mr. Dawes. You're old school. This job will require calm and above all patience."

"He will be hard to get close to," Warren added almost as a question.

"Again," the voice assured him, "that's why you've been selected."

"What's the timeline on this?"

"Things are happening now...other things at all levels. There's not a particular hurry...we just don't want him to become involved. You know, and screw things up."

Dawes acceptance was in the form of a request. "I'll need some seed money ahead of my fee," he said.

"Ten enough?"

"Better make it fifteen for this job. Same account as before."

"Done," the voice told him. "We'll expect to hear results in...how long?"

"When they've happened," Dawes countered. "You want this right, not quick and messy. If I'm wrong about that, use someone else."

"You can expect your deposit by in the morning, Mr. Dawes," the voice said and the line went dead.

Warren Dawes leaned back in the straight back chair. A bead of sweat rolled into one eye. He looked down at the information about the hit.

Damn, he thought and wiped his brow. *Get a grip, man. You can handle this guy.*

~

"Agent Dunbar," the strong voice on the phone was instantly recognized by the young woman. "I hear you're back in the office, full time."

"Yes, sir Director Grimes, sir," she replied with an unseen smile.

"And the hand?" he blurted out, "They tell me your finger is doing good."

Holding her phone with that hand, Colleen Dunbar flexed the digit in question and nodded as she replied, "I'm very fortunate, sir...thank you."

Agent Colleen Dunbar had her pinky cut off by the SEAL Team killer. Doctors had saved the digit and she was now a celebrity in the agency.

"Let me get right to it, Agent Dunbar," the director stayed in character with his aggressive style of speaking. "There's a case... same one really, that you were involved with before. I need to know if you're interested in some more field work to do with it?"

"Your package just arrived a few minutes ago, sir," she told him. With her free hand she spread the photos, still studying them. "This senator's daughter...she's the target in this blackmail?"

"Exactly."

"I see a striking resemblance...don't you?" she offered.

Grimes grinned and softly muttered to himself, *she's in.*

"Silas noticed it," he shared with her. "He called a while ago... I agree completely."

"Silas is in on this?" her own nervous voice surprised her.

"This is part of a much larger situation...if we're right about it."

Dunbar turned her head and took in a breath, picturing the mysterious man she'd only met twice. In one of those he'd saved her life.

Her mind filled itself with one thought... *yes...yes*, it repeated over and over. But spoken words would not form for her. She stood in silence.

Grimes listened quietly, waiting for her reply. After a half minute of silence, he spoke again, "Conference call... MTAC, 1430 hours today. If you want in...be there."

Agent Colleen Dunbar could not resist. Holding a picture of the senator's daughter, she clearly understood what her job would be. It would be dangerous but that didn't matter. She was proud to be considered to be a part of it. "Thank you, sir," she said smartly. "See you then."

20

Jasper Jamison stood at the window of his expansive office, just east of Franklin, North Carolina. His view of mountains and a medium sized lake would make working difficult to concentrate on, but he'd managed to do well for over twenty-seven years.

La' J Furniture was now a fifteen-million-dollar-a-year business.

Jasper's father had started making picnic tables for home improvement stores. But after a cross country trip involving stays at many motels, he decided those places needed furniture with a more "upscale" appearance. The slightly downsized and lightly constructed furniture was priced right and his timing was perfect.

Hotels and motels had begun massive swaps, of both names and interior design. La'J bid with remodeling contractors, and the business grew nearly overnight.

"Mr. J," the speaker on his oversized mahogany desk bellowed out, "I have a call for you on line five, sir."

Jamison slowly turned from his view and stepped to the phone. He pushed a button, thanked the receptionist, and then answered the line.

"Have you heard from him?" a voice asked. "It's been two days, hasn't it?"

"He's not working for us, remember?"

"He knows the score. He knows to stay in touch."

"He'll call," Jamison assured the caller. "Two days is hardly time to organize your life... after where he's been. Besides," he went on, "he knows who arranged his release, regardless of what she thinks. He'll call."

The office door opened and Jamison's son stuck his head in.

"You got a minute?" the younger man asked.

Jamison covered the mouth piece of the phone and grimaced at his son. "Busy here at the moment," he said calmly, yet tersely.

The younger Jamison nodded and backed out, closing the door.

"I had an interruption there," Jasper told his caller. "If you said something just now, repeat it for me please."

What followed was a pointed silence to which Jasper did not react, other than to turn and look out his window while he waited. He clearly heard the caller take in a huge, deep breath before continuing.

"She sent word to Fuller through Davis. It ain't going so great," the tall man's voice began to crack slightly.

Henry Davis was a type of contractor, an independent go-between. He handled messages for Barrett and the lawyer Hasbrough Fuller.

"She's getting desperate," Jamison half muttered into the phone.

"She's not alone. The old man wants to hear who Terrell's target is and when this is in play," he ordered in an unpleasant tone. "This is your job, get it done."

"Who's creeped out now?" Jamison challenged his caller. For that he got a dial tone in his ear.

~

George Vincent had news. His entrance into the kitchen was abrupt and out of character for him.

"Gil just called me," he announced as though to a crowd. Only Jon sat at the table staring into a cup of cold coffee. He responded without looking up.

"Anything good?"

"DNA on that blood from the street is finally back. They had to go through Interpol to get an ID."

"Interpol?" Jon seemed surprised.

"The blood belongs to Klaus Scheffler, a German national with ties to Keane-Collopy...an Irish Drug Gang."

"What?"

"He was an enforcer for the Irish mob until he got too old to ride," George nearly laughed as he relayed the message. "It seems Keane-Collopy is a biker gang. Scheffler is, or was... depending on how bad he was hurt, fifty-eight years old."

"Is he registered here?" Jon asked.

"No...nothing. No Visa, Work Permit, nothing. No telling if he came in through Canada or the south."

"So that whole crew were his boys," Jon surmised, "Irish or Germans."

"More than likely... yes."

"Okay...no sense wasting much time on that then, is there?"

"No," George agreed. "The other cars have been found, one in Acworth and one in downtown Atlanta."

"Hospitals and clinics?"

"Naw," George shook his head. "They're 'in the wind' as they say."

Jon looked at his watch.

"The call is in ten minutes," he mostly mumbled under his breath. "Are we ready?"

"Ben has it under control."

The mention of Ben brought Jon to his feet. He stepped toward George Vincent in what could pass as anger.

"You know he has a suit?"

"Gil said something about it, yes."

"A green suit," Jon now sounded disappointed. "Are you and Doris going to say anything to him?"

"He knows his place, Jon. There's no need for that."

"The suits have a purpose," Silas' voice rang through now, "and that purpose isn't what he does."

"He did good in that situation...and you damn well know it."

Jon squinted and his eyes glowed as he lost his fight to stay quiet.

"I keep thinking about Jakes," he whispered.

"Ben is not Lamar Jakes," George argued. "Jakes was a good kid, but he was impulsive. Like a young Murray."

That comment brought a smile to Jon's face but only for a second.

"I need him doing what he does."

"And he will, Jon. Like I told you ...he knows his place."

With a nod Jon asked, "Is it about time?"

"Time we get down there it will be."

~

Even the splendor of his view couldn't help. It took four unconscious laps around his desk to get over the call and the interruption. When Jasper Jamison finally stopped pacing, he hit the intercom button on his desk phone.

"Sharon," he asked pleasantly. "Is my son out there?"

"He left the building, sir. I can page him for you."

"Please do," Jamison told her. "And have him knock before he barges into my office from now on."

"Yes, Sir."

21

Her knock was answered immediately by the Charlotte Chief of Police. Through his smile he appeared apologetic if not embarrassed by the opulence of the office. Large and surprisingly plush, it did not fit the current occupant, a man Marsha had known for many years.

"A bit much, I know," the Chief told her, "it's the way I inherited it. But it is the most secure spot and phone line I know of."

"Thank you, sir," Marsha Hurst tried to tell her boss. "I really don't mean to be this much trouble."

"You take your call in here Captain, and take whatever time is required," he said pulling the door closed behind him. His respect for Marsha Hurst was already obvious. The call he'd received that morning from the Director of the NCIS, did not impair that respect one bit.

"We'd appreciate your assistance in arranging a secured phone conferencing line this afternoon," Grimes had told him.

Marsha stood alone in the big office, and stared at the closed door, wondering for a moment what to do now. Then a four foot video screen, on the back wall lit up. A test pattern flashed and then became a scene she'd seen before.

"Good afternoon, Captain Hurst," a technician in uniform greeted her. "The others should all be signed on in a minute. Please stand by."

"Can you hear me?" she asked into the open air.

"I hear you fine, ma'am. We'll be right with you." And the audio went silent.

The screen began to resize into smaller sections. She recognized the underground at Caddo Mills in one box and watched as Murray was logged on. Then in an upper corner the second floor sub-basement, Ben's workshop, came into view. Ben sat at the bench and Cheryl stood right behind him. Daniel, Lori, George, and Doris walked into the frame, but not Jon.

Another box showed an area she wasn't familiar with, but she knew Phil Stone and his wife, Sara. The man she remembered as Matt Turlock was also there. Then the last box appeared and Cheryl's mom and dad sat in what looked like a secure room somewhere she didn't recognize.

Finally, the center box lit-up with the control room at MTAC in the background. Director Grimes, Tim Spiegel, two other men, and a young blonde woman were there.

~

A cloudy afternoon had held down the visitors to the park. Co-owners Will and Suzanne had discussed the phone call he had received and made their decision.

"Kiska, will you watch the front for a while?" Will asked an assistant, "We need to go talk with Cody."

With her nod a sufficient answer, the two walked toward the enclosure of Boris, one of the park's lions. They found Cody sitting at the outer fence, grimacing as he flexed his injured left arm. Boris became instantly more alert as Will and Suzanne came near.

Cody Arnold forced a smile when he saw them. It was more to cover the expression of pain his face showed from the exercise.

"Slow day, huh? "he offered.

Will wasn't much for wasting time or words.

"There's a big conference call, probably going on right now. We're not in on it, obviously...but the NCIS Director wanted us to be aware of what's happening."

Cody's smile went away and he stood. Boris stood with him, cocking his large head to one side.

"What is going on?" the retired SEAL asked.

"There's been trouble...damn near all over it seems. Those folks... the ones who investigated the case. Well... now they're being attacked."

"By who," Cody was almost demanding. "Wyckoff is dead."

"They don't know, but they aren't the type to sit around and just wait."

"Nobody has come here...have they?"

Will took a short look at the ground, then stared the youth directly in the eyes.

"Not here, no. But they'd been around your old place in town."

"Dad?" Cody leaned in toward his friend.

"He's fine...I assure you... he is okay. They were looking for you, and he told them you were at the VA in Atlanta. They bought it."

Rubbing his lower face with his good hand, Cody asked, "What do I do?"

"You wait here...with us," Will told him forcefully. "Right now, that's the best for everyone."

"I don't need you, Suzanne and," Cody swung his arm and looked across the vast animal park, "all this to be in danger because of me."

"Trust me, Cody," Will begged him.

"It's going to be fine," Suzanne grabbed his right arm and smiled at the SEAL. "You've got to trust us, okay?"

~

The noise had become more than he'd bargained for. Even with the phone held tightly to his ear and his free hand cupped over the other, he could no longer hear.

"Look," he yelled into his end, "I'll get it...here. I don't need anything traced back to you guys."

He thought he heard something being said but the operation of the twin loading machines had overtaken the human ability to hear.

The receiving platform was always a good location for privacy, except when a flatbed of new material arrived. The cranes worked well together. As soon as one load of hardwood reached the racks another would be lifted and swung into position. But their grinding chain hoists and gears could seem to be in competition for pure, intolerable screeching.

His hiding spot was compromised, for now.

"Listen if you can hear me," he tried again. "I've got this. I'll call later."

Closing his phone, he noticed the flashing light on its cover. He was being summoned. He straightened his tie and jacket.

The old man liked neat appearances, he reminded himself.

22

Jerome Grimes started the meeting with introductions.

"Most of you know each other," he looked straight into the camera, his expression quite serious and formal. "There are a few folks here with me I would like to introduce quickly."

Pointing to Colleen Dunbar he said tersely, "Agent Dunbar from our home office."

Marsha Hurst lifted her head and stared almost approvingly.

Grimes, completely unaware of her reaction continued, arm gestures and all, "And from our Jacksonville office, Agents Hansard and Monroe." The camera briefly centered on each man. "I believe you all know Tim Spiegel from New Orleans," he added with a nod in his direction.

An uneasy quiet took control for a couple of minutes as everyone obviously checked each other's view. Grimes used the time to step to a small podium and look at his notes.

"You're all aware of at least several incidents that have caught our attention in the past few days," he said while looking down. "Not the least of which is the death of a CIA agent who had been at the scene in North Carolina."

Murray spoke up. "The guy who got shot at the beach house?" he interrupted with raised eyebrows. "That man died?"

"Not from that," Grimes informed everyone. "He was killed outside a safe house in Louisville, Kentucky. But please, let me continue."

The NCIS Director listed off all the deaths of congressional aides and the few actual congressmen also killed. He told of the recruiting efforts brought to light by a couple of other brave congressman and recapped the attacks on the members of the meeting.

"We also have a congressman's daughter being stalked in Winston-Salem, North Carolina. Thus far, we've convinced the family to play along."

Grimes took time to briefly check each screen on his huge board. He then went on.

"Our best judgment is that there are at least three separate sets of activities on-going, all caused by the same people...or person."

Grimes' eye caught Phil Stone nodding in an animated fashion, "I see you are in agreement, Captain Stone?"

"I may have something to add, Mr. Director," Phil smiled as he answered. "But please, continue...you may cover it yourself."

Looking back down at his notes, the director went on.

"This syndicate...cartel, cabal," he raised both hands, palms up in another gesture, "whatever you wish to call it...is cleaning out weak or ineffective members, recruiting and adding new ones, and doing both on a rather large scale."

Searching the crowd for any input, he found only rapt attention from everyone.

"The third thing they are doing, in a somewhat clumsy manner, appears to be an attempt to draw out who they believe is responsible for many of their troubles. The man we know as 'Silas'."

"I think we're in agreement, Director," Phil spoke up. "To be clear, the attempt on me was not as serious as it was made to look."

"Go on, please," Grimes asked him.

"I heard about what happened with Westy, and I can't speak to that. But, the attack on me was a threat and not much more. Ben tells me the hit on the mansion was visual and heavy handed, yet when they were confronted, they left...with the numbers clearly on their side."

"They didn't want to mess with Ben," Murray cracked and there were a few short laughs that joined him.

Grimes stared down at his papers and concluded, "We feel the attack on the house in Dalton was not a serious effort. More, simply an attention getter that went bad."

Weston Duray squirmed in his seat and then stood.

"The guys in my barn," he shrugged his shoulders and shook his head, "it's hard to say. They were armed, but kinda casual about the deal. I really don't know what would have happened, had I walked into them."

"That's just it," Grimes pointed out. "You wouldn't have."

Westy cocked his head to one side in a non-spoken agreement and then sat down.

"Did we identify those men?" Grimes asked.

"A crew from New Jersey," Westy answered, "Muscle for a small time loan-shark around the boardwalk area."

"Not too professional for a job like...well, taking you on," Grimes said bluntly.

"That is right," Murray's voice chimed in. "Weston Duray would be no easy task. I agree...those guys were intended to fail."

Duray frowned but remained quiet.

Grimes looked down and to his right. "Have Jersey's office cross-check those men with the dead congressional aide from Asbury Park."

The technician sitting there made a note.

Ben Shaw turned away from the monitor to look at Jon. The boy's face was flush with color and his eyes squinted nearly shut. Jon's eyes shifted toward him while his head slowly shook. He deliberately mouthed three words but did not speak aloud. *Work with me*, his lips formed and then tightened. The fierce stares continued, from both sides.

~

Studying his newest assignment, Warren Dawes sat in the garage with his secret compartment open. He had notes from other jobs, filed by difficulty. He had only successes, failure wasn't acceptable to him.

It would be a few days until the money got to him, but he still could make plans. The house was an obstacle, but he'd dealt with large houses before. *Getting in was the key and there was always a way in,* he reminded himself.

At least it was not far away. Closeness would work in his favor. The get-away would be clean while authorities searched for a traveler.

~

With a respectful knock, the younger Jamison opened the door to his father's office.

"Hey," he offered meekly, "sorry about before."

Jasper looked up from his desk, eyes locked in a cold glare.

"You have to regard my privacy," he scolded. "Always."

"Hey...again, I'm sorry. I do have something I need to talk with you about, though."

"Money, I'm guessing," the old man smirked.

"Dad, I'll pay it back, if you like. I just got caught up trying to impress these guys I was with."

"Guys?"

"Okay...it wasn't guys," the younger man admitted as he crept closer to the big desk.

"How much this time?"

"Twenty will get me by," came the answer.

"Twenty? You lost twenty thousand dollars?"

"It was a bad night...won't happen again, I promise."

"Well...you make do with fifteen and if they come after you over the other five they can break your leg or something." The elder Jamison was bluffing about the latter part of his statement. Truth was, no one would come after his son. Not in their right mind anyway.

"I'll sell my car if I have to, sir," the younger man offered. "Fifteen will help and I thank you."

As he turned to leave, Jasper stood and called to his only son.

"Jamie," he said. "I hope you've learned from this."

"Oh...yes, sir," the younger man told him, "learned a bunch."

~

Ben had eased from his chair. Director Grimes was still talking on the monitor and Cheryl frowned at Ben with a silent stare. Her look was asking him, *what are you doing?*

Ben took her arm and gently pulled her into the chair. Cheryl could operate the board if need be and Ben pointed to it profusely before walking away, nodding back at her.

Leaned over below the camera level, the young man walked out of view to where Jon sat crouched in a corner. He was rubbing the side of his head but still listening and watching what went on.

"What does he mean they weren't serious?" he asked in a whisper. "That guy shot at me point blank."

Jon looked at him with one finger in front of his lips, his "hush" sign.

Red faced, Ben's head shook involuntarily as he started to repeat himself. He was cut off before he could speak.

"Hold it down," Jon warned, more with lip movement than sound.

Resisting the urge to blow up, Ben leaned down even closer.

"The heavy glass on the truck saved me," he said softly as he could. "That's about all."

Jon grabbed Ben's arm and pulled him down to sit beside him.

"The ballistics came back on the round fragments they found," he told Ben. "It was... a .38 caliber soft point."

"I knew that," Ben reminded Jon he had looked down the barrel, "it was a .38 alright, I stared right at the thing."

"Officially, we're saying what it was."

The youth's face wrinkled as he spoke, "I don't understand."

"Grimes wants to mislead these people. Put out bad info to see how they react."

"These people?" Ben was even more confused, "Us?"

"As secure as this communication system of his is...there could be leaks."

"Who?" Ben asked still in full whisper mode, "someone in his department?"

"He didn't have time to explain...totally."

"Okay, but this seems trivial. Why change that detail?"

"You weren't expected to come out. But when you did, they tried to kidnap you."

Leaning away, Ben asked, "Why would they do something that stupid?"

"They wouldn't, but their boss could be thrown off by this information."

"Grimes didn't even mention the attempt on his own life," he whispered strongly. "And don't tell me that wasn't a serious try."

"Ben, I agree with you. Grimes is treating that as an isolated event."

"More misdirection?"

"I don't know," Jon's mutter showed signs of his own frustration, "he didn't mention doing that." Looking back at the monitor as he spoke, he continued, "He might actually believe that one."

Ben too, turned to stare at the monitor... and stayed quiet.

"There's a bunch more going on than we're aware of, right now." Jon said handing Ben a small piece of paper.

"See if you can decipher this," Jon told him. "It was found in the car you forced off the road."

The note read 4555522.

"What is it," Ben asked.

"That's your job," Jon smiled. "Worry about that... not all this other stuff, okay?"

Ben sighed softly, closing his hand around the note.

"All of this is part of the same deal," he whispered, "Plain as day."

Jon turned a disciplinary stare at Ben and held it for several seconds.

"Work with me, here," he mouthed in total silence. Still the message came through to Ben who nodded that he understood, though he really didn't.

23

Congressman Travis Gilbert stepped into the tiny fast food shop in Avondale Estates, Georgia. He had driven the long way around from his home in Roswell, Georgia, using the southern loop of the city's perimeter highway, I-285. With no visible followers, he'd parked in a mini-mall lot across from the restaurant and walked from there.

The smell of fresh coffee hit him square as the voices of the staff shouted their welcoming greetings. Gilbert slowly let the door close behind him and stood tall, searching the area. An arm rose up and caught his eye from a booth near the back wall, it was Travis' father.

"You okay?" the older man asked with his hand outstretched.

Travis took his father's handshake and smiled, offering what confidence he could muster.

"I am," he professed and sat down. "You having breakfast... or just coffee?"

"Your waffle will be here in a minute," the older man said and took a sip from his steaming cup. "I saw you park across the street and ordered it."

The young congressman grinned and nodded approval but otherwise said no more.

"I've been in touch with George," his father told him.

"Yeah?"

"They want you to work with these guys until they can find out who they are."

Nodding again, Travis looked up and smiled at the waitress who placed a smoking hot waffle in front of him and then his father. He spread the butter slowly, then spoke while still looking down.

"I don't like you being involved in this," he said under his breath. "I appreciate their help, but..." He looked up to admit, "I really don't know what to do."

"That's why we have friends," his father told him as he pulled a small cell phone from a pocket. "George sent this... for you. It's a 'burner' phone," he explained with some question in his voice.

"I understand, Dad," the congressman reached over and took it. The phone quickly disappeared as he put it away.

"There's more about it," his father started again. He waited for that thought to sink in before finishing his statement, "it has some kind of encryption deal on it."

The congressman raised his own cup. His face wrinkled a bit.

"Who are these friends of yours?" he asked.

"The kind we need right now."

With the note in his hand, Ben returned to his chair. Cheryl slid quietly from her seat and knelt down beside him.

"What's that?" she asked, pointing to his closed fist.

"I'm supposed to figure out what this is," he responded softly and handed the paper to her. Cheryl looked at it for less than ten seconds.

"It's a phone number," she declared.

Without moving, Ben dismissed her guess. "Not enough numbers," he said.

"It's shorthand, silly.... Look, if you're writing something down, like a phone number, you abbreviate." She pointed to the first number, a "4."

"That's not an area code around here, is it?"

"What?"

"Is there an area code around here that starts with "4?"
Ben looked at her as a light went off in his head.
"Yeah, in Atlanta, there's "404."
"Ok," she smiled at him, "so it's '404975522," something."
"So...what's the last number?"
"Something easy to remember," she told him, "like, '1,' maybe."
"Huh," Ben mumbled and twisted his head to her. "Kind of a long shot, don't you think?"
"You are going to check it out though....aren't you?"
Ben's eyes locked on her's for several seconds, and then he wrote Cheryl's idea down under the other number.
"Worth a shot," he told her. "We'll see when this thing is over."
With a confident grin, Cheryl grabbed and squeezed Ben's hand.

~

The hollowness in the pit of his gut would not go away. Carlton Calvert had spent his life in a cocoon of confidence, never really having to be concerned about anything. But he was now.

This queasiness, coupled with a loss of concentration, had the man out of sorts. He was in unfamiliar territory and for a man of his years the experience was disagreeable. Obviously not known as a nervous type, the pacing he realized he was doing set him off even more.

"Damn it," poured out from him louder than he'd hoped and his assistant was quickly at the door.

"Mr. Calvert, sir...are you alright?"

The old man gathered himself and turned toward the helper.

"I'm fine," he tried unconvincingly, "tripped on the edge of this damned rug. My fault...really."

The door closed and Calvert was again alone. He glared at the phone. *That was the culprit, not some silly rug. That damned phone, and its silence.*

He had done something new, something he had not done by himself before. There had been ample time... yet no report of how it went.

Calvert had ordered such things many times before, just not directly. Through all the attempts to gain control of the political scene, all the murders and conspiracies and yes, the failures, he had remained apart from it all.

It had taken years to organize. That was after the years before; spent in deep thought figuring out the three legs to the stool that would be his Kingdom.

It was coming undone and he could feel it.

The revenue stream was choked off. First the simple drug business with the bikers and other distributors. What happened in Texas sent a chill through that community; the drug business nearly fell apart. Then the outright shot at a complete overthrow of the government. He had doubts, but their plan seemed sound.

That mess was all her fault, he grumbled inside. *That lawyer from in town got greedy and screwed it all up. I'm glad that damned tiger got her.*

His mind suddenly jumped all the way to the white slavery ring and its supporting operation. *That was on Barrett,* he reminded himself and then the SEAL Team mess. *That Sheik didn't even know about the amber.*

We shouldn't have even been in that, he nearly said aloud. *That was personal stuff. Her and that puppet boss of hers,* he thought about Barrett.

The troubles were all her own doing and now she was trying to clean things up. Should she succeed, that could mean even more problems for Calvert. The kind he couldn't tolerate.

If she establishes herself at the top again, he thought, *she could push me aside.*

Barrett was not likely to succeed. She had not performed well up to now, though there was more to it and he understood that. All the failings had one common factor. One man...one solitary individual...an obstruction to his vision that would not leave him alone.

Carlton Calvert had devised his own plan and initiated it himself. Only one trusted go-between was aware of the arrangement. A first for Calvert and it would remain his secret. He had taken matters into his own hands...arranging for a murder squad from Europe to stop this man, this "Son" person. They had arrived several days ago.

They should have reported in by now, he obsessed as he paced the floor. Experience shook him with what he needed to do. Though the words did not actually form within him, not even as a thought, instinctively he knew. It may be time to call his go-between, Henry Davis.

24

The conference call continued for most of an hour. Grimes relayed what was known about the Senator's daughter. George Vincent told the tale of his friend's son, the congressman who was being threatened and Murray touched on the visitors to his Caddo Mills ranch.

"You almost make it sound like it was no big deal," Tim Spiegel challenged him. "Why is everyone being so noble and tough?" his voice soared in octaves and volume as he went on, "this is a huge mess we're in. These are bad folks who ultimately want us dead. You all understand that, right?"

An unexpected answer came quickly, "I feel like I've been left out."

The voice was Marsha's. She was trying to break the tension while making her point. No threat to her had been made, that she was aware of.

"All this going on and I haven't even gotten a phone call," she added.

Then an unseen voice chimed in, "You still need to be careful," it warned. "They may not know where you are yet."

Everyone searched the screens. It was clearly Jon's voice, but he wasn't visible.

"We've had a report that someone was looking for our young SEAL friend," he continued, "just in the wrong location. We all need to be mindful of these threats. They are very real."

"What about the other SEALs who survived that case?" Phil asked.

"Outside of your group and those who were at the beach house, there are no reports of anything," answered Director Grimes. "That tells us something about our adversary."

"Yeah...They know who we are," Ben explained, "and they researched what happened at Nag's Head...and those who were there or involved."

Tim Spiegel stepped forward, as though to take the stage. His face showed no emotion.

"What of that woman?" he asked, "the one in prison that you were checking into. Is she behind all this or what?"

Ben answered him, "Barrett," he started. "We haven't found any communication or anything from her to the outside, other than conversations she's had with her attorney. But we know...she's involved, we just can't prove it."

"Well, look into the attorney." Tim's voice elevated.

"To the extent that we can...," Jon's voice came through in a deadpan, cryptic tone, "we are."

Tim understood, as did everyone on the call. Legal methods were slow, but that was all they could admit to on this call. Jon and Ben did not restrict themselves to the law when seeking facts. It simply wasn't going to be discussed here.

"You're right, Tim," Jon started. "This all adds up, it all fits together, and we need to deal with it." His voice went quiet for several seconds and while they could not see him, everyone seemed to know he wasn't finished.

"I have some requests if you will all allow me," he started to continue.

Colleen Dunbar leaned into Jerome Grimes and whispered, "Where is he? That's Silas, isn't it?"

"Yes ma'am," Jon had heard her. "I'm here."

Grimes leaned toward Dunbar, whispering, "I have an assignment for you when this is finished. Silas and I discussed it earlier."

Daniel and Matt Turlock got out notebooks and pens, others shifted where they stood or sat to the point the noise was audible to everyone. Jon spoke again, though he was still unseen. "Westy, can you get away to check on someone for me?"

Duray perked up and immediately answered he could indeed.

"I'll send the details, but there's a guy in Minnesota I need info on, quickly."

"To do with this?" Duray asked.

"Honestly...I don't think so. But it is important." He directed his stare at Murray now. "Murray, can you do the same on a man in Kansas?"

"Sure, what's going on?" the cowboy responded.

"I have a stop to make myself. There's three potential 'interests' we need to follow-up on. I hope you understand."

Grimes was the only one to answer.

"Hell... I understand," he said gruffly. "You're talking about that stuff on my call? For Gosh sakes, am I supposed to be dumb?"

"That wouldn't be helpful at all, Mr. Director. Just some latitude if you will."

George saw a need to change the subject.

"I've sent Travis Gilbert a secure phone," he blurted out.

"Travis Gilbert?" Phil asked, "That congressman from around your area?"

"Yeah, he's the one who was approached by the syndicate recruiters. He was threatened about his re-election chances unless he helped them."

"Well there you go," Phil countered. "We got our insider."

"Potential...insider," George corrected him.

"That's good, George," Jon spoke up. "All this is good. If you can chip away at them as well, do so. But I want to find out who's at the top."

"To kill a snake you've got to cut off its head, right?" Murray threw in. "That's something I learned in Louisiana."

"Speaking of Louisiana," Jon jumped back in. "Phil, I hear you and Sara are staying with Matt, is that right?"

"As long as is necessary," Matt Turlock answered for him.

"Hello again, Matt... and thank you," Jon smiled. "I need something else, if I can ask of you. I need you and Daniel to scour every story and tip across the country. Look for anything you even think has relevance to this."

Daniel and Matt responded at the same time.

"Phil...could you and Marsha monitor all police info, leads or anything, kinda like Matt and Daniel are doing with the press?"

Both nodded affirmatively on screen.

Jerome Grimes sought to regain control of his meeting.

"Okay, this thing is an expensive toy," he announced jokingly, "Captain Hurst, I have a message for you. You have someone, in country, seeking your whereabouts."

Marsha perked up, as did Jon.

"It's Nava Golan," Grimes told everyone. "The NSA picked her up entering Georgia a couple days ago. She's enroute to North Carolina as we speak. Do you require assistance?"

Nava Golan was Israeli Mossad. She had been here before to help with a perceived Al Qaida threat that was actually a domestic coup attempt.

Badly injured while here then, Marsha had nursed her back to health.

"No," Marsha nearly yelled out. "Nava isn't a threat to me or anyone. She has a reason for being secretive, I'll find out soon enough."

There was no disagreement from Jon so Grimes moved on.

"Are we about done here?" he jested.

"For now," Jon answered, still out of view.

A stolen van left the interstate somewhere south of Locust Grove, Georgia. Its driver fought off his anxiousness, though he could see in the rear view mirror a loss of color in his own face.

Three others rode in the back as he drove. One was seriously hurt.

They had split from their local hired guns on the Southside of Atlanta. It was there they had taken the van from a daycare parking lot.

The driver had not heard anything 'good' from the back in over an hour. The beginning of the last exchange had caused him to exit the expressway.

A voice asked in German, "How is Klaus?"

"Worse than yesterday, I fear," was the reply. "He has lost much blood."

Hearing that, the driver made his decision.

"The wound doesn't look that bad," the first voice responded. "Let's find a doctor somewhere."

"We can't go to a doctor...or a hospital, fool. We have no papers."

The first man frowned but then quickly had to grab the side of the van as it stopped suddenly. The second man braced himself while speaking, "We really need to check in ...find out what we should do."

"Klaus had the phone number on that piece of paper," the first man said, his expression even more troubled.

"I still can't find it," the other stuttered. "It is not on him anywhere."

The driver pulled open the rear doors and stepped closer, a bit too close. Blood had soaked the thin carpet flooring. It ran down through metal channels and dripped out, marking the rear bumper. Several drops hit the driver's shoe.

The hardened criminal reacted as if in horror. Color returned to his face in a sudden flush. His friends watched as he frantically rubbed the shoe on the back of his pants leg, smearing the stain.

The two conscious men in the truck remained quiet. The third lay still, looking more a shell than a man. The driver glanced at the injured man's face and reacted by turning his eyes to the ground.

"How is he?" he asked without looking up.

"I'm not sure he's even breathing anymore," answered one.

Rubbing his eyes with open palms, the driver finally looked back up at the others. It was up to him to take charge and now was the time.

"Still no sign of the note?" he asked sternly.

"No."

"Then we have no choice," his voice nearly moaning as he spoke. "We must get out of this country...now."

"We have no money!" the first man interjected.

"We'll do what we have to," said the driver.

"How? What do we do?"

"The ship leaves at 6:30am. We must be there."

"Back to Savannah? How far is that?" one asked him.

"GPS says we're within four hours of the town, maybe another hour to the docks."

"What of Klaus?" asked the other man.

Then, after a deep, labored breath, the driver issued his first order as leader.

"Strip him down," he said firmly. "There's a lake not far from here."

The others glanced at each other asking almost simultaneously, "Can't we do anything for him?"

"You want to get caught?" the driver lashed out. "Get him ready. He's probably dead already....We'll burn the clothes later."

Slamming the doors, the new leader scooped a hand full of dirt and rubbed it on his still bloodied shoe.

"Verdammen," he exclaimed at the result.

25

The main lights came up quickly in the M.T.A.C. Center as the series of linked calls were disconnected. Everyone, including Grimes, caught themselves blinking with the adjustment.

"Any questions here?" the director asked those in the room. The two Florida agents stayed quiet but their expressions were quizzical. Grimes walked them to the door.

"You realize you're part of the group that needs to be careful, right?"

Hansard stood very stiff and asked, "Just what is our stake in this? What do you want us to do?"

"I wanted you to see this, to understand as much as possible, what's going on and who is involved. As you've seen, that includes you two."

"So...we go home?" Monroe piped in.

"I want you both to go down to Alabama and brief Childs and Everson on this. They are in this neck deep, too. They're watching Cody Arnold from a distance. We all know the kid SEAL could be in real danger."

"He's in that animal park we heard about, right?" Hansard asked.

"Don't go there," Grimes said, almost as a direct order. "Meet the agents in Gadsden. Set up a perimeter watch for the area."

He shook their hands and the two left.

"Those men saved my life earlier," he said turning to Tim and Colleen. "Good agents."

"Back to New Orleans for me then, Sir?" Tim asked.

"Actually... I'd like you to go to Dalton, Georgia. Silas requested you as a backup there while he's on the road."

With a smile, Agent Tim Spiegel nodded and left the room. Grimes looked at a bank of chairs under a control panel. He pointed to them and asked Agent Dunbar to join him.

"You already know you favor that girl at Wake Forest," he started bluntly. "What we'd like to try is dangerous...you can say 'no' without fear of reprisal."

"I'm not going to say 'no,' Director." Colleen was firm but he noticed her rubbing her reattached finger as she spoke. "How do we precede, Sir?" she asked.

"Does that finger still bother you?"

She smiled and separated her hands. "I think I bother it," she grinned. "I count myself very fortunate in that whole deal. I thank you for your concern."

Grimes smiled a half grin himself.

~

In the second sub-level workshop of his Dalton mansion, Jon stood from the dark corner and walked to Ben at the desk.

"I'll need my old bag ready by later today, and my regular khakis and jacket...understood?"

"Where are you going?" Ben asked.

"Please just have them ready as well as two uniforms and all weapons that go with them." He didn't appear to be in a mood to discuss the request. Ben nodded once and Jon went to the elevator.

"What the heck was all that?" Cheryl asked.

"This is getting serious," he told her. "That's about all."

~

Senator Wallace Edgett sat at his desk in the Hart Building, doing all he could to concentrate on the papers in front of him. Thoughts of his daughter, Claire, under constant surveillance by both the government and whoever was threatening him came to one conclusion. *This won't end well,* ran through his mind over and over again.

He did not know when the next request from the unknown threat would come. This was not a way he wanted to live or conduct business.

A knock on his door was quickly followed by an aide stepping into his office.

"This just came by special courier," the man said and laid a large envelope on the desk. "It's been screened," he added.

With a fast nod toward his aide, the senator grabbed the envelope and ripped it open. Among several folded pieces of blank paper was a note, stamped with the Presidential seal. It read simply, "Lincoln House restaurant – 4:15 PM today."

~

Jackson Terrell walked out of Oxford Prison with his clothes, a bus ticket to Madison and one check for $250.00 from the State of Wisconsin. As he stepped onto the bus, a man bumped into him.

"441 North Lake," the stranger said in a low voice. He handed Terrell a small key that was stamped with the numbers 4823.

Terrell stared hard at the man who looked back at him, unfazed by the criminal's glare. That reaction sent a cold chill down Terrell's back. He realized the level of who he was dealing with.

Taking a seat on the bus, he rubbed the key and wondered where this would all lead. His concern lapsed as he reminded himself, *it beats sitting in that hole.*

26

The Mercury was loaded and ready to go. Ben slowly approached, head somewhat down and thought of a way to break the ice he had created.

"It's getting harder to find parts for that car," he said.

Jon turned to him and smiled.

"How long since they did away with this model, now?" he asked.

"They did away with the entire line. Mercurys are history."

"That's a shame," Jon said. "Something gets to be a good thing, and we get rid of it." He closed the trunk and stared at the huge vehicle. "Sign of the times, I guess," he continued. "The times... and the direction this country is headed."

Ben waited a second before asking, "Can you tell me where you're going?"

"I'll be in Winston-Salem, North Carolina, in three days. Set up full surveillance. Satellite, phone taps... everything you do, for that campus and wait to hear from me, okay?"

"Until then?"

"Listen out for a call from Colonel Swanson in Kentucky. I've asked her to see what she can find out about Langhorn getting killed up there."

"Will do," Ben answered sharply. "Anything else?"

"You'll hear from me in three days, Ben."

With a sheepish grin, the younger man stepped back, "You're sounding like the old days with all this mystery."

"You think?" Jon replied and fired up the V-8 and the tunnel control panel on the dash.

~

Parking behind the Verizon Center, Senator Edgett walked two blocks to the Lincoln House restaurant on 10th. It was quiet inside; the time of day had much to do with that. No hostess was in sight, but a man wearing an old baseball cap turned from the cashier as though he'd just finished paying. He walked close to Edgett on his way to the door and whispered, "Third table on the right side."

After unconsciously turning to look at the man in the ball cap, Edgett moved forward. A well-dressed man sat at the third table on the right, he was alone. The senator stepped beside the table and the man motioned for him to sit.

"Senator, thank you for coming," the well-dressed man said. "The President sent me."

"What is this about?" Edgett asked trying to play dumb.

"My name is Jerome Grimes," was the response. "My team and I... we're going to help you and your daughter."

~

"Captain Hurst," the young officer announced through her door. "You have a visitor downstairs. She asked for you by name."

Marsha stood immediately. "Did she give you her name?"

"Katy Mills," he answered, "from Texas, she says."

The captain tried to stifle her smile as she instructed the officer, "Bring her right up." The fake name was a play on the town where they had been while Nava healed, Caddo Mills, Texas. "Oh," she added, "and please, hold all my calls while she's here."

After two local transfers, Jackson Terrell stepped from a bus in Madison, Wisconsin. Looking around to get his bearing, he found he was on North Lake Street, the four hundred block.

The only building that matched up with the street number he'd been given was a Post Office.

"That's it," he looked down at his key. "It's a P.O. Box."

Once inside the building Terrell walked past the line of patrons to a wall of small metal boxes. His key fit neatly into the lock on number 4823 and the box door opened. One white envelope lay inside.

~

Phil Stone's cell phone rang suddenly. It was Ben Shaw.

"Phil, I need your help and ideas," the young man sounded excited.

"What's going on?" the retired cop replied.

"Local police found a body in a small lake south of Atlanta. We've got a leg up on the feds because George's people were watching the police blotter."

"Okay?" Phil said quizzically.

"There was a picture of the face...it's Klaus whatever, that German guy that was here."

"You're sure from just a photo?"

"Phil, I looked him right in the eye from two feet away...yes, I know it's him."

"Who have you let know?"

"Nobody is available...Jon's on a mission of some sort, Marsha's phone isn't taking calls and Director Grimes isn't answering either."

Alright," Phil began thinking like a cop and he enjoyed that. "You say it was found south of Atlanta?"

"Yes, sir."

"That tells me they're headed for Savannah or Jacksonville."

"Why is that?"

"They're in the country illegally. They had to have come in by ship. They're trying to get out the same way."

"Okay...I'm with you."

"Check all shipping logs at both ports for a ship that came in from Europe in the last...say week or so."

"Can do."

"And tag that with one scheduled to go back... around now."

Ben took a few minutes and came back on the line.

"Phil, the 'Ava Gentile;' a medium sized freighter from Glasgow arrived in Savannah last Tuesday, early morning."

"That's the day you got hit at the house right?"

"Yeah."

"Check private charter flights from near Savannah to Dalton or better yet, Atlanta on that date."

Ben worked the computer and Phil spoke up again. "They'll be three or four passengers listed, Ben."

"But Phil, there were ten to twelve men there at the house."

"The rest were hired local, I'll bet my life on it. The team came in here to run the operation and they hired guys on the way up."

Ben typed away and within minutes had an answer.

"A King Air 200 043, landed at Charlie Brown airport in south Atlanta that day from...damn." Ben paused, "It came in from Hunter Army Airfield in Savannah."

"Not surprising," Phil said bluntly, "we're dealing with high level bad guys. Ben, how many passengers were on the manifest?"

"Four."

"See if the Ava Gentile has sailed."

Switching to another screen, Ben typed in the information and waited, but only for a few seconds.

"She left early this morning...like 4:30 AM," he told Phil. "Wait though... it's not going back to Glasgow. It's going to New Zealand and then China by way of the Panama Canal."

"That's still where they are, Ben. Those are your boys... or what's left of 'em." After a thought came to him, Phil added, "When do they get to Panama?"

"Tomorrow. Around 4:00 PM."

"Doesn't Jon know some people down there?"

Ben smiled..."He does. He does indeed."

27

Marsha stood just inside her office door. *There must be a reason for Nava's secrecy,* she realized. And with everything else that was happening, who knew what was at the center of it all.

A shadow danced along the glass wall, preceding the knock on her door. She grabbed the knob and pulled the door open.

Nava Golan stood there, looking somewhat pale and concerned.

"Come in," Marsha reached for her friend's arm, "please."

Closing the door, Marsha pointed to a couch along the far wall and gave her friend time to speak first.

"Are you all okay, here," Nava spoke softly as she sat down.

The question caught Marsha off-guard. Shaking her head, she sat beside the woman she had nursed back from serious injuries just over a year ago. "We don't know," she admitted. "Why...what do you know?"

"Yinon has been hurt. Bad enough he has been replaced in Mossad."

Marsha squinted and unconsciously fired off several questions, "When did this happen? Why haven't we heard? Does Grimes know?"

Nava reached for Marsha's hand, to calm her down. "All is hush, hush," she whispered. "Reiss is under house arrest, I barely got out."

"You make it sound like a coup."

"Marsha, Reiss found a note in Yinon's briefcase. We don't know where it came from, but it mentioned Silas' name, yours and Grimes'. It also lists the cowboy's name."

"Murray?" Marsha asked.

"Bilstock is what was written down."

"I still don't understand."

"The new leader of Mossad is a man named Romach. Teo Romach. He has sent a team here to attack you all."

"Why the hell would Mossad come after us?"

"The new government is tired of war. The P.M. has been speaking out about giving up more land. Yinon was against this. He said he had information about weapons of mass destruction being hidden in Syria."

Captain Hurst stood up and walked to her desk. Did the note say anything about a Sheik and a SEAL Team mission... around a year ago?"

"There was one name we didn't know," Nava told her. "Beale. This has to do with a man named Beale and something called Amber."

"A woman?"

"No," Nava explained. "It said Beale was the closest link to finding the Amber. It is a thing of some type."

~

Director Grimes gave the senator time to compose himself. He pulled out photos of Agent Dunbar as she normally looked and some with her hair styled like the senator's daughter.

Edgett's color settled back down and he tapped one of the pictures with his finger. "You're going to swap this woman for my daughter?" he asked suspiciously. "How will that help?"

Sitting even straighter than he had been, Grimes spoke with stern resolution. "We're going to take these guys down. Get them to reveal who they work for and put an end to this...completely."

The senator put a hand to his forehead, rubbing his face in frustration. He then leaned nearly across the small table, directly into the director's face.

"That's a great plan," he said, "for a movie script." He then sat back and added under his breath, "This is my daughter's life, man."

"You came forward on your own," Grimes responded, unfazed by the man's concern. "We already know you have what it takes to work with us on this. It is more than a fictionalized game, Senator. We know what we're doing and this will work."

"How are you going to get these men to talk...if you even catch them?"

"Officially, I can't tell you that. But I can assure you...they will talk and I will get what I need."

Edgett partially slumped into the seat, his eyes nearly closing.

"Grimes?" he muttered aloud. "You're head of NCIS, aren't you?"

"That's correct."

"You just worked with that vigilante assassin on the SEAL murders, didn't you?"

Without flinching, Grimes answered, "I'll neither confirm nor deny that, Sir."

Senator Wallace Edgett sat in silence. His eyes darting inside their sockets until he finally put his hands on the table and stood.

"When will you start this?" he asked.

Pointing to one of Agent Dunbar's photos, Grimes told him, "She and I will get to the campus day after tomorrow. We'll do the first take-down the next day."

"What do you need from me?"

"Keep your daughter calm... and the day we begin, you will need to contact the bad guys and tell them the deal is off."

The senator stiffened his back and rolled his neck. He tapped on the table top, saying only, "Make this work."

Director Grimes nodded several times. "Roger that, Sir," he affirmed.

~

Jackson Terrell pulled the fat envelope from the post office box and walked back to the street. He looked left and right, noticing an alley down on the right side from where he stood.

Holding the envelope down, Terrell stepped into the alley and laid the package down flat. His trust was as "long as his little finger," he used to brag to friends. With a handkerchief held over his nose, he cut one corner from the envelope with a pocket-knife. Then standing up, nose and mouth covered and head turned slightly away, he pressed on the object with his foot.

Once, twice even three times he patted the envelope watching the corner for any sign of dust or powder. There was none.

Pulling the handkerchief down, he closed the knife and reached down slowly, sniffing the air as he picked-up the envelope. Reasonably sure it was safe, he ripped the end open completely and looked inside.

"Damn,' he said out loud at the sight of all the green. In all, there was $10,000.00 wrapped in a note.

It read, "Stay low and out of trouble till we call you. Another key will be sent to that same mail box in one week. That key, to a different box, will have a cell phone. When you get it, keep it close at all times."

Terrell didn't like being told to "sit tight," but ten grand made that easier to deal with.

Sticking the money in his pocket, he looked up and noticed a billboard. It advertised "Smokey Joe's Supper Club." "Best Steaks in Town" the sign read. Terrell waved down a taxi. *I could eat two steaks*, he told himself smiling.

He told the driver to take him to the address on the billboard.

28

Jon arrived on the north side of Roanoke, Virginia, at 2:20 AM. Driving through the night brought back memories, yet still allowed him to think clearly and uninterrupted.

He knew Murray would be in Atchison, Kansas, by now. Lucy Too was faster by far, but he wanted the time this drive had given him.

Westy should be arriving in Mankato later this morning, he thought with a smile. If either should find anything valid about their man, he would go to verify it. *It's nice to have him on board*, he admitted to himself. *Westy is a good man.*

As the Mercury neared Troutville, Virginia, a sign advertising a Comfort Inn caught his eye.

"Some rest would be good," he said aloud and then realized he had not yet picked a travel name to register under. Pulling off the expressway, Jon opened the trunk and flipped through IDs and business cards. He selected "Terrance Wassmon," a pharmaceutical rep from North Carolina.

Might as well go with what you're familiar with, he reasoned.

Once in a room, "Terry Wassmon" set an alarm for 6:30 AM and lay down. He was out in less than a minute.

Ben got to his workshop around 9:30 that morning, a late start for him. Working till the wee-hours on the set-up for the Winston-Salem campus had taken a toll.

Jon's private cell phone, which he'd left off so as not to be bothered, had vibrated to the edge of the table top. From it flashed a light indicating a missed call. In fact, there were two missed calls.

Ben picked it up. Seeing who the calls were from, he immediately hit "call-back."

Murray answered within three rings, "Well... there you are."

"Murray, this isn't Jon," Ben informed him. "It's me."

The cowboy took a second to absorb the voice he knew... but hadn't expected to hear.

"Didn't take his phone, huh?"

"Nope," Ben confirmed. "I'll hear from him in two days, as it stands right now."

There was a slight hesitation and an audible groan followed by Murray saying, "Well, I've got a situation over here that can't wait two days."

Ben sat down and grabbed a pen and pad, "What's the deal?"

"This guy I came over here to check on, the congressman, well he's still kicking, but from what I hear, maybe not for long."

"He's been shot or something?" Ben asked.

"No...but his brother-in-law was killed yesterday in a weird traffic accident and the locals all say our boy is freaked out by it."

"How weird?"

"An SUV came up on the sidewalk. Knocked him through a plate glass window hard enough to break about every bone he had."

"Somebody lost control?"

"The story is, they had real good control, smacking this guy without hitting anything else. Then driving back onto the road... they were gone."

Ben made notes and tried to think what he should ask. "When was this?" he offered.

"About an hour before I got here, yesterday. It took a while to figure out who the victim was and his connection to our guy."

"You saw the scene, then?"

"It was a mess, alright. The folks I talked to said it was not an accident either."

Ben inhaled deeply, his frustration welled up.

Why does this stuff happen every time Jon goes undercover...from me? He thought as he wrote.

Then his next question came to mind, "Do you know where the congressman is?"

"Nope, that's why I'm calling you. I need you to pin him down for me. You do have cell phone info on him, right?"

"The latest I have is from three months ago," Ben advised as he pulled up satellite feeds.

"Well, ping the thing...quick."

"Okay," Ben told him. Quicker than either man thought possible, information came back and pointed to the location of the cell phone.

"That phone is in a private cabin on the Missouri River, near ...well, it's south of a town called Elwood."

"Is that cabin in his name?" Murray wondered out loud.

"Give me a second...." Ben was typing as fast as he could go. "No...no it is not. Our records don't show he has a cabin."

Murray thought for a minute. "The brother-in-law was a guy named Leland Pierce. Is it by chance his?"

"No...," Ben answered slowly, "but why does that name ring a bell with me?" Continuing to almost mumble, he added, "Leland Pierce...hang on a second."

Murray waited while Ben searched his records. The time was not wasted though; he made up his own mind while he waited.

"Murray," Ben sounded excited. "That name, Leland Pierce is on the first list."

"What list are you talking about, man?"

"The list Jon found in that biker hangout, the drug cartel contacts."

"You're kiddin' me."

"No...I wish I were," Ben continued. "Damn...here he is on the Chicago Mayor's list, too."

"Holy crap," Murray felt his color leave him. "I thought all that stuff was done with!"

"Whoever these people are, they killed the brother-in-law. They are really cleaning house."

"We can't just let them guys kill our congressman fella, too. He could have a ton of information."

"What are you going to do?" Ben shouted into the phone. "We should wait... till Jon can be in on this."

"No time, Ben. If you could find this guy...so can they," Murray explained, "and just as fast."

"I don't know if Jon would...."

"Ben," Murray cut him off, "Jon ain't here now, but the bad guys are... And so am I."

~

The two-story Victorian building had been residential for over a hundred years. It now housed a flower shop on its main floor and the private offices of a U.S. Congressman on the second. Ben's research showed the building was owned by Walter Frazier, a local businessman. Frazier operated a plumbing supply house and a coffee shop down the block from the corner of Roanoke Boulevard and Tennessee Street, the site of his flower shop.

"He's not here today," was all the information Jon could get on Frazier from the plumbing company. A call to the flower shop was more fruitful.

"Mr. Frazier is away on vacation, can I help you?" the female voice told him.

"No, thank you," Jon replied quickly and hung up.

Vacation meant Florida. Frazier spent much of his time there... except when his friend and tenant, Congressman Herschel Briar was in town.

Jon put on a facsimile of a local fire department uniform and gathered the badges Ben had printed up for him. The drive across Roanoke to the small town of Salem took less than an hour, even in morning traffic.

Parking a block and a half away, he walked the long way around the block, approaching the corner building from the east. He saw that the young lady behind the counter was with a customer. Jon sat down a briefcase and began looking around at windows, the door hinges, floor vents, and other areas. His activity got the attention of the clerk.

"Can I help you, Sir," she asked looking past her customer.

"Annual fire inspection," Jon stated officially. "Are you the manager?"

The young lady excused herself from the customer and walked over to Jon. "The manager is off today...do you have to do this now?"

Jon gave a puzzled look that spurred her to continue.

"My client is arranging a funeral...I can't drop her right now."

The opportunity was too good. Jon quickly smiled and asked her, "How about I take care of the upstairs while you work with her, if I find anything wrong we can go over it later."

The flustered employee froze as she considered the idea and then stepped to the counter, holding up one finger to the client and grabbing a set of keys from the backside. "I suppose that'll be alright," she said handing Jon the keys. He was quite prepared to get in without them, but this was perfect.

Locking himself in, he took his time going through the private office.

29

The conversation had been simple the rest of that evening and the next morning at Marsha's place. Though Nava was a hardened agent, Marsha could tell her friend had been through hell. So she allowed space and time for her to compose herself. The talk finally became serious over coffee.

"My government knows you are here," Marsha told her.

The Israeli agent sat speechless, not sure what to say next.

"It's okay," Marsha tried to reassure her, "Director Grimes told me about two hours before you got to the office."

Nava stared down and put her cup on the table. "Yinon would have gone straight to Grimes," she started, "they are friends, but I do not think he knows me."

"He does," Marsha smiled. "None the less, you're here now. Can you give me details?"

"It's your man, they call 'The Son,' I need to speak to. He has the ear of your president."

That leaned Marsha back against her chair. She kept eye contact with her guest, though she felt her eyes drawing tight.

"You need to speak to the President?" she asked softly.

Nava looked down again, her head twisting to one side as she organized her words. "Yinon had been investigating a report from one of the action teams."

That term was new to Marsha, but she didn't need to ask.

"They had been following a lead about some holy man who held knowledge of a powerful nature."

"How powerful?"

"I don't know what it actually is," Nava admitted, "I don't know if Yinon does, but it is very vital... and very secret."

"Why the need to talk directly to our president?"

"It is believed the information is hidden here...in your country."

Marsha had added things up in her mind, but didn't want to appear foolish. "Why would information important to your country be kept here?" she asked.

"Israel remains torn between those who want peace, at any price, and those who see that as a threat to us all. The group within Mossad...the ones who took over when Yinon was injured, are very tight with one of your political parties. The one currently out of favor."

"You're saying this information could be important to people here?"

"The group I mentioned, here in Israel, is funded by outsiders."

"Americans?"

"There is no proof," Nava told her.

Marsha had one other question, she feared she already knew the answer but asked anyway.

"Where was this holy man from?"

Nava looked straight at Marsha and answered, "Yemen."

The young Georgia Congressman sat in his office looking mostly into blank space. Activity was brisk throughout the Rayburn Building, yet Travis Gilbert was alone in his cocoon of thought. Both hands rested on the desk top, one lay over the new phone his father had given him. The thought of it broke his concentration and he turned his gaze, looking down at the object.

This job had been his dream, he thought quietly, *now it was cloak and dagger BS and his family was in danger.*

He hardly remembered the flight back to Washington, the drive to his small apartment last night and the trip here.

"How can I do a job like this?" he muttered softly.

Gilbert moved his hand from the phone and, as if by magic, it rang. He saw the caller ID but did not recognize the number. There was no name shown. He felt his jaw tighten as his hand scooped the phone up.

"Hello?" he managed to get out.

"Travis, this is George Vincent," the voice said. "I'm a district attorney here in Dalton, Georgia and a friend of...."

"I know who you are, sir," Gilbert stepped in. "My father speaks highly of you."

"We've actually met several times," George added. "But you were quite a bit younger then."

"I'm in a pile of crap, right now Mr. Vincent. What do I do?"

"First...it's 'George,' please." He paused to hope that would sink in and take some of the tension off the conversation.

"You are a brave man," George restarted with. "To come forward like you did, as quickly as you did, there's no question about you or your loyalty."

There was no comment from Gilbert's end of the phone.

"That's more important than you realize right now," George went on. "The people working with me have high level security abilities and are equal in their loyalty. You can have faith in them."

"Faith and trust are simple when there's little choice, Mr...I mean, George."

"You sound as though you still take all this lightly," George challenged him.

"I don't mean any offense, but that set up under the building was impressive. This 'Celestial...whatever' has clout and power. They were there and then, nothing. I sent two teams into that building looking for signs of that room I was in...nothing."

"Travis, that room didn't exist."

"I was there...I saw it."

"You were in an illusion. The room you thought you were in... was only three feet deep."

"How do you know this?" Gilbert's voice rose for the first time.

"There's some conjecture, I'll admit. But I know others who have investigated that space. What you experienced felt real to you, we know that. But you need to understand that it wasn't. That's important in moving forward."

"You're talking in riddles, now."

"I didn't mean to get this deep into it right off the bat," George tried to explain. "You will next be contacted by the Director of The NCIS. It will be very undercover. Work with him, please."

"I thought you worked with that assassin everyone talks about."

George took a breath and let that comment hang.

"Do not get ahead of yourself, Travis."

"So...you do work with him?"

"I didn't say that. Director Grimes will be contacting you. You are a small part of a huge issue. I know that sounds belittling and I don't mean for it to. Just have patience and work with us."

The next thing Gilbert heard was a dial tone.

30

Twenty minutes was all Jon allowed himself in the upstairs office of Congressman Briar. There were pictures, lots of pictures...mostly of the congressman and his friend Walter Frazier, but nothing remotely connected to the numeral star graphic. No incriminating evidence of any type and worst of all, no leads.

The congressman's son had been charged with murder some years back, and a local man made it his life's work to harass the representative at every venue he could. That man's disappearance is what alerted Ben.

There just wasn't anything, not here anyway.

Jon completed his "inspection" and handed the young clerk her keys back. He then walked a more direct route to the Mercury and thought it was time to check in with Grimes about the Wake Forest case.

Taking a "burner" phone from the trunk, Jon dialed Grimes' private number.

"Busy here," the director answered a bit sarcastically, "yourself?"

Slightly taken aback, Jon cleared his throat before he responded.

"If we work together long enough, I may learn how to take you," he jousted back, then asked, "Just wondering if we're a go for Winston-Salem?"

"I believe you met the parties there as planned, yes. How are you doing? If you can tell me."

"Not so hot. Can't find anything over here in Roanoke, not to verify what we suspect, anyway."

"To do with this?" Grimes shot out.

"No...this is another matter."

Grimes quickly changed gears in his head.

"Roanoke, huh? I know of an old guy in Roanoke," he offered. "Retired NSA spook. They say he keeps an ear to the ground over that way."

"Seriously?" Jon asked.

"Oh, yeah, he's the real deal. I don't have a name, just a call-sign he went by. He's known as The Eagle."

Jon didn't respond in any way. The proposal was outlandish, yet from a man he trusted, and he couldn't imagine a way to say what was going through his mind. Grimes did so for him.

"Sounds over the top, huh?" the director said meekly. "I can get a hold of a guy who'll give him a message."

"You know, Sir," Silas' tone kicked in. "Over the top, you ask? With all due respect... it really does. I don't have time for games, and I don't know you as a game-playing sort. I'm a bit confused by all this."

"Jon, I wouldn't pull your leg."

That statement was as strong and firm as anything Grimes had ever said to him. The director wasted no time. He followed with, "I won't send word to him, if you don't want me to. But he is for real."

Hearing the hesitation still in Jon, the NCIS added one more push. "There are some out there..." he said, "Old school patriots, who are still active."

After thinking for a few seconds, Jon said simply, "Have them use this number. I'll keep it active for a day or two. Oh...and tell Dunbar I'll see her at the Dance Studio, on campus in Winston-Salem, 2 PM, the day after tomorrow."

"I'll reach out right now," Grimes told him. "I know a guy near Atlanta, a writer who can get in touch with 'The Eagle' pretty quick."

Grimes could hear Jon grunt audibly and picture the man nodding. He finished with, "I'll be sure Dunbar has all her equipment. And she'll be there on time, too."

"Okay, then," Jon answered, and the line went dead.

Topographically, the area around and south of Elwood, Kansas, was as bad you could get for hiding a helicopter. Murray found a farm with an empty field and though the idea was problematic in many ways, he struck a deal with the owner.

In the assumed role of a Texas cattleman looking for farm land in the area, he was allowed to leave Lucy Too in an open area and have use of a tractor for ground transportation. The price was $1000.00 and a promised ride in the copter.

Carrying his bag, the cowboy drove several hundred yards before he stopped and put on his protective suit.

Already answered enough questions, he told himself. *Don't need any about the black outfit.*

The cabin, more a low-cost frame home, was close to the bank of the river. It had a nice porch on both front and rear and Murray could see a path leading to a small dock. *If there's a boat, It's just a Jon-boat*, he surmised though he could not see to the water. To be sure he had the right location, he called Ben.

"Ping me and then the phone in the cabin again, will ya?" he asked. "I should be right on top of it."

Ben made the tests and confirmed his location.

"Thanks, now all I have to do is find a spot out of sight, to keep an eye on things."

"They might attack from the water," Ben threw out.

"Yeah...I know," Murray said while low-crawling through some short grassy weeds. "I'm trying to get closer to the river."

"I've pulled up a satellite image of the area around you," Ben advised him. "There's no traffic right now on any road or on the river. You got some time to get situated."

~

Marsha's knowledge of the SEAL murders case was limited, but she knew it had to do with the botched rescue attempt in Yemen.

"Tell me what you can about the Yemen connection to all this." She asked Nava Golan.

"A deep cover agent came to Yinon years ago. It was when they were investigating the chemical weapons Assad had used in Syria."

"We didn't even look into that until years later," Marsha remembered.

"The United States did not...but others did. Your news networks, for the most part, had their minds made up that the weapons did not exist. They had a lot of sway then. They knew they controlled public opinion."

Marsha nodded acceptance to that and Nava sipped at her coffee before continuing.

"No one ever could nail it down," she said using American lingo. "The trail was cold until one label was found near Aleppo. It appeared to be from Iraq."

"A label?"

"From a container, yes. Our agent reported this to Yinon and he assigned a team to look into it. This was before we came here to help you, in fact, it was why we came here."

"Israel thought the chemical weapons were here?"

"Some, maybe...but that didn't turn out to be."

"Where are they?" Marsha pressed. "That would be a game changer if they were found."

"We still don't know," Nava admitted. "But the information from Yemen, we really wanted to know what that was about."

Marsha tread very carefully, what she knew and what she had only heard discussed could be mixed together in her mind.

"Was your team tracking a Sheik in Yemen...the one that got killed about a year and a half ago?"

"One team was involved with that, yes. They reported a huge fight that was not expected."

"Who all was involved?"

Nava shook her head.

"You never had any details at all?" Marsha asked her.

"Everyone backed off," the Mossad agent told her. "The subject is still very sensitive and to many countries."

Marsha sat her cup down and leaned back. She tried to be sympathetic but knew she looked skeptical, at best.

"I don't understand the connection to the missing WMD's," she almost whispered. "What makes you guys think that could be it?"

"Only one cryptic word... it was overheard on a transmission between Syrian and Iraqi ambassadors four years ago."

"Were they actually talking about the weapons?" Marsha seemed suddenly concerned much more than before.

Nava looked at her friend sternly before answering.

"What one thing would mean so much to a political faction in both our countries?" she sounded almost lecturing. "The denial of which has grown into more importance than the thing itself? It caused them to attack Yinon...to stop him from looking." She paused to give Marsha time to understand the seriousness of her reasoning.

The slightest blink from Marsha gave Nava the signal to continue. "Now they are here, perhaps to stop your Jon... and his friends."

"I'll have to warn Jon," Marsha acknowledged. "But I need proof. He always requires proof. Are you sure it's the missing weapons?"

Without flinching or change of expression, Nava Golan spoke in strong words.

"Be it them or something else, they were assuring the Iraqis it was secure," she explained. "The secret, as the Syrian called it, was safely hidden in Amber."

"That's an odd reference."

"It definitely means something...big," Nava was adamant.

Marsha rose from the table taking her half empty cup to the counter. She poured the contents out and unconsciously refilled her cup without thinking about her guest.

"So, the secret is either Amber... or perhaps encased in amber somehow," she said, turning the carafe still in her hand. Nava smiled and lifted her cup in Marsha's direction.

"Oh, sorry," Marsha snapped out of her thoughtful trance, "Where are my manners?"

31

The Fillin' Station Coffeehouse had a disappointed customer that morning. Not due to their coffee or anything else they had done. Weston Duray sat in a booth near the window with a local paper in front of him.

Below the fold, but on the front page of the Free Press was a two column story about Congressman William Bowers. He was in the University of Minnesota Hospital in Minneapolis, the victim of a major stroke.

Bowers was accused of sheltering drug dealers, if not being a main distributor himself. Several investigations over the years had come up empty, but when four high school kids died from overdoses at a school dance Ben raised the congressman to third on the list.

Westy called Ben.

"Hey," Ben told him. "Sorry, it just hit the wires...happened early this morning."

"Yeah, well from what I'm hearing, in my short time here, there's no love lost for the guy."

"Is he going to recover?" Ben asked.

"What I'm hearing is no. Not beyond being a vegetable. I suppose I'm done here, huh?" there was disappointment in Westy's voice. Duray would have loved to deal with this guy on his own terms but that was not to be.

Ben thought about Murray and an idea came to him. "Say," he said while grabbing his notebook. "Can you catch a flight to....give me a second," Ben looked up the closest airport to Elwood, Kansas. "It looks like St. Joseph, Missouri."

"What's up there?"

"Murray has a problem. Call him, would you...see if you can help?"

The Michigan cowboy smiled. "I'll do that," he answered.

~

Colleen Dunbar and Charles Burr, her assistant, left Washington, D.C., that afternoon. They drove one of the agency's black Dodges as far as Annandale, Virginia.

She recalled something another agent had warned her about some months ago. "Those things are like wearing a badge around your neck," he had told her. The black Dodge was a three-piece suit at a swim party.

"Boss," Dunbar said through her phone, "I'm trading this car in on something else at the first rental shop I find."

Grimes didn't get it at first, but his instincts told him to, *just go along with it*, and he did.

The trip from Annandale would be in a new Ford Taurus, light blue in color. The couple now appeared to be just that, a couple on the highway, on vacation or a trip home. The "look" of "cop" was off of them.

Dunbar kept her new "bag" up front with her after the change of cars. Burr drove while she checked out her new bullet-proof suit.

"This thing is unbelievable," she said. Burr looked over and smiled but had no idea just what she meant.

"Feel this stuff," she handed an arm to his reach. "It's lite-weight, but they say it will stop a .357magnun."

"Let's hope you don't have to prove that."

"Really," Colleen grinned. "How far to Winston-Salem?"

Burr punched a button on his GPS unit. "It says about five hours."

"I wonder if he's there already," Dunbar muttered.

~

The lavish home of Herschel Briar was in a community known as Catawba near the foothills of Brush Mountain. Entry had been little problem for Jon, but he still found nothing incriminating. Mainly more pictures of the congressman and his obvious BFF, Walter Frazier.

Walking down the sloped drive to the Mercury, Jon's burner cell rang.

"Yeah?" he answered.

"Is this Silas?" the old voice asked.

"Who's asking?"

"The Eagle," the voice responded. It sounded rough yet firm. Like a piece of raw leather dragged across sandpaper.

Jon stopped in his tracks and looked at the caller ID. It read "out of area." He took a breath for patience and said, "Thank you for calling, Sir. I'm told you might have some information for me."

"First, let me say it's nice to speak with you. I've followed your exploits for some time."

"Is that so?" Jon challenged. "How's that?"

"Why...it's what I do, son." That was followed by a slight chuckle and, "No pun intended."

Letting all that go, Jon started in. "Herschel Briar, I have reason to believe he may have had someone killed. Do you know anything or where I might find something about that?"

"Briar's an idiot," the old man was blunt. "You're barking up the wrong ass-hole."

"Excuse me?"

"You need to look closer at Walt Frazier. He runs everything in that district...no questions dare be asked."

The voice paused for a few seconds and then added ominously, "He's what you're looking for."

Jon had reached the Mercury. He leaned against the hood, asking his next question as it came into his mind, "But it was Briar's son that raped and killed that girl, wasn't it?"

"Oh, sure...and Jacob Watson followed Briar around, giving him hell about it."

Jacob Watson was the citizen who attended civic meetings and heckled the congressman relentlessly.

"I'm listening," Jon told him.

"The boy and Watson are both dead. It's just Briar didn't do it. Hell he didn't even know it was going to happen."

"Wait a minute," Jon asked. "I knew the son had gone missing, but now you say Watson is missing as well?"

"You need to listen better, Silas. That's just what I said."

"Frazier killed his best friend's son?"

"In a heartbeat," the old man said. "Frazier makes good money from having Briar in office. He doesn't let much get in the way of that."

"I haven't heard any of this," Jon was puzzled. "When did this happen?"

"The boy... about two weeks ago...Watson two days ago."

"How do you know all this?"

"I told you...it's what I do. I ain't been in the intelligence business for all these years just to earn a pension." The voice started to take an unfriendly tone, but quickly calmed down. "I have contacts in every agency you can name," he added. "And most of them owe me favors."

Jon rubbed his forehead and took out a notebook.

"How do I prove this?" he asked the voice.

"I just told you...that's not good enough?"

Jon laughed out loud, "For what I do... no, Sir. That's not quite enough."

"Hell, I knew that...I was just checking you out," the old man laughed back. "The proof is where the bodies are, but be careful. The Salem authorities are all...and I do mean 'all,' in Frazier's pocket, neck deep."

"You know where the bodies are?"

"Of course."

"Could you share that with me, please?"

"There's a field outside Bent Mountain. That's southwest of town, about twelve miles out. There's two Dogwoods, oh... a half-mile off the road. The bodies are between them. Not too deep from what I'm told."

Jon scribbled his notes and asked the obvious, "Why haven't you acted on this?"

"I've got more important stuff I deal with, every day."

Shaking his head, Jon asked yet another question. "I don't see how Frazier is doing this on his own...who is helping him?"

"Very good, Silas," the old man seemed pleased. It not so much 'helped' him, as it is beholding to him."

"And you're going to tell me who that is...right?"

"Silas, some men of wealth sponsor little league teams or cub scout packs. Frazier sponsors Richmond's worst street gang, the Los Tiburones Rojos. They take care of his heavy work."

"Red...sharks?" Jon guessed with his translation.

"Very good... And they watch the burial site, so don't go out there on your own, son."

There was another short pause. "Damn," the old man laughed. "I did it again."

"That's alright," Jon assured him. "But... why? Is that part of this gang's territory?"

"Their territory is pretty much all of Richmond. The current cops leave them be and nobody wants to mess with them too much."

"Current?" Jon asked.

"Long story," The Eagle answered, "but things aren't as they used to be here."

Deciding not to push that issue Jon moved on.

"Are we talking kids...or what?" He asked.

"They use kids out front...but it's a regular drug cartel outlet. They distribute around here and in Blacksburg and far east as Lynchburg."

"It's strange... that I've never heard of them."

"Count yourself as lucky and again, that area off Hwy 602, near the dogwoods is part of their unchallenged territory. The area is watched, 24/7. Just be careful like I said."

Jon was familiar with the description of gang activity, particularly the way they used young people. The thoughts that came to him stirred a deep anger.

"Thank you Mr. Eagle," he offered respectfully.

"<u>The</u> Eagle," the voice corrected him. "Nice talking with you."

32

"Man, that would be great," Murray told Weston Duray over the phone. "Any help would be nice. Truthfully...I don't know what might happen here... if anything at all. It just feels hinky."

"Alright then," Duray smiled as he spoke. Being needed was a good thing and he was re-inspired. "There's just this... I can bring my suit on the plane, but not my weapons."

"I've got you covered on that. Lucy has whatever you think you need."

"Good," Duray told him. "My flight gets to St. Joe at 4 PM and I'll grab a rental car. I'll call you when I get near... Elwood? Is it?"

"Yeah...see ya then. Oh...and... thanks, man."

~

Jon called Ben, earlier than both had thought, but the situation had changed.

"I'll need everything you can find on this Walter Frazier. If it's so, I'll deal with him later."

Ben explained what happened in Minnesota and that Westy was on his way to help Murray in Kansas.

"Can you even believe all this is happening?" Jon said more rhetorically than anything. "They work together well...it'll be alright."

"What and where are you going now?" Ben asked.

"I'm gonna find a couple of dogwood trees and then head for North Carolina."

"Dogwood trees?"

"I'll explain later," Jon answered and then he was gone.

~

Nelson Pharr knocked, but just barely. The door to Director Grimes office swung open and the Secretary of the Navy strode in with his usual intensity.

"Nelson," Grimes said without looking up.

"There was a time you'd stand when I came in your office."

Jerome Grimes did glance up briefly at that remark. "Yeah, guess there may have been," he quipped. "Is that what you came here for?"

Pharr issued a cold stare but said nothing.

"What's on your mind...boss?" Grimes asked while looking back at his work.

Pharr pulled a chair up and sat down, "Thanks, I will have a seat," the joust continued. Once comfortable, the SECNAV got serious. "I understand there's a whole lot going on."

"You got that right," Grimes smirked. "We're kinda busy around here Nelson. Is there something in particular I can do for you?"

"I got an anonymous tip that you were using the MTAC facilities for your own clandestine activity."

Grime laid down his pen and looked at his friend. "I knew it," he said with a grimace that bore resemblance to a smile. "Any idea who or where it came from?"

"Nope, but we now know how we can leak stuff we need to get out there."

"How are you going to play this?" Grimes asked.

"Quietly. If I'm asked, I'm conducting a private investigation."

Grimes nodded and went back to his notebook.

"So...are you going to North Carolina?" Pharr inquired.

"No. That's under control."

"By control, you mean your assassin."

"It's under control, Nelson...okay?"

"You might consider dividing the assets you capture," the Secretary said smugly. "Play one off the other so to speak. Worked well for me in the field."

Grimes leaned back, stared at his superior, but did not say a word.

"Information is a valuable thing, Jerry. How you get it sometimes isn't as important as getting it."

Nelson Pharr stood, pushed his chair back and stepped toward the door. Jerome Grimes picked up his phone before Pharr got to the door.

"Reserve a jet for me," he said into it while looking at his boss. "Today...Winston-Salem, North Carolina."

~

Studying the house occupied most of Warren Dawes' free time. There wasn't much information on it because of whose it was and where it was situated. But he knew one thing for sure. To accomplish what he needed to do, he would have to get inside.

Security would be tight, he told himself over and over again. *Whatever means of access probably wouldn't work twice.* He'd need to get in and do his thing on the first try.

His normal day off from driving a school bus for the county was tomorrow. Dawes planned a trip to go drive past the house several times if not discovered.

I need to get the feel of the area, he said as another idea came to him. He would rent a large panel van. He had noticed some retired UPS vehicles at a lot on Chandler Road.

I may wait till my money gets here and do it that way, he smiled to himself.

~

An early dinner was called for in Salem. Jon drove the streets through the older downtown district, seeking a place to eat and listen.

A small shingle hung from a building in the 200 block of East Main Street. The large parking lot next door told him it was a popular place. As he parked and walked up to the door he was even more pleased, a tiny section of the restaurant was cordoned off to itself as an intimate bar.

He sat as close to the bar area as possible and nursed his beer and salad for almost thirty minutes. The clientele was mostly locals, or so it appeared. They came in small groups, a few just pairs. There was little discussion about the congressman or anything political. The small talk was mainly baseball.

Jon was enjoying the skinny steak that did have a nice flavor and the home fries that came with it. Then the main door opened and the entire place became quiet.

A tall Latino man, mid to late twenties, strode in. The most noticeable feature to him was his cowboy boots. They were bright red.

He walked straight to the bar, right where the bartender was. This man may have been the owner, or perhaps the manager, of the place. He glared at the newest guest in his bar without saying a word. The young Latino laid one hand on the bar top, palm up, and waited.

After a short staring contest, the bartender pulled an envelope from beneath the bar and put it in the Latino's hand. Stuffing the package into his shirt, the man in the red boots turned and saw Jon looking at him. He stopped and tried to stare the stranger down with a contemptuous gaze.

Jon laid his fork on the table and smiled at the young man. The Latino seemed to bow up at the lack of respect, but Jon kept his smile and let his right hand slide from the table to his pants leg holster.

The aggressor huffed under his breath and walked out the door, not looking back at the stranger who did not fear him. He joined two friends outside and the group went down the street.

Several of the customers in the diner and bar turned to look at Jon, but only briefly. It was clear he had broken protocol and it was time to go. Paying his check at the counter, he took one look back at the still quiet restaurant on his way out.

He'd killed an hour and a half, had a nice meal, but learned nothing. The man in the red boots had to be part of the gang he'd been warned about, but that was obvious. Keeping his right hand low along his leg, Jon walked to the car with no incident. As the sun peeked around the three story buildings on its way down he pulled away from the parking lot.

Once out of town, the Mercury headed southwest on Hwy 602. He measured twelve miles and there they were. Just past the area called Bent Mountain, the two dogwood trees sat well off the road.

33

Sunset on the Isthmus of Panama was something that never got old to Luke Diaz. He pulled his jeep to one side just over the Bridge of the Americas to watch. The harbor master at Pedro Miguel Locks called as he sat along the road.

"Yes, Henry," Diaz answered.

"The Ava Gentile is ahead of schedule," the man told him. "She must have picked up some good currents coming down."

"Okay," the CWO and friend of Jon and Murray's told him, "How does that effect getting a search party on board?"

"You need to wait until it gets into Miraflores. She's approaching the locks here, right now. I have a visual on her. I just don't have enough men to safely do what you ask."

"Thanks, Henry...I understand and appreciate that. Makes it less travel on me anyway," he quipped. "I'll get a team together at Balboa and be waiting for them."

"The ship is scheduled to get to Miraflores at 12:00 AM."

"Less travel and...less sleep!" Diaz laughed. "Oh well, these are supposed to be some bad eggs on that boat. Thanks again for your help."

In his years there, Luke Diaz had made friends with several ranking officers in the Panamanian Defense Forces.

"Time to take a couple of buddies to dinner," he said aloud and headed for Balboa.

~

Murray Bilstock had found a spot behind some tall grass. He could see the cabin-like structure clearly and some movement from within. As the sun began to slip away, lights came on, confirming a presence inside.

The person or persons would go to the windows and peek out but never opened a door. It was like they were hiding and if his guess was right, it was the congressman and he was. Then the thought struck him to check-in with Ben.

"Hey, "he started when Ben answered. " Heard from Jon?"

"Not yet," the boy told him.

"I'm sitting here, watching this little house. There's definitely somebody in there."

"What's the plan?"

"You know Westy's on his way, right?"

"Yes, Sir."

"I guess we give it some time, see if the place is hit."

"By the way," Ben injected, "I checked around Washington. Your boy isn't there. His office says he has been called away on personal business."

"This could be him here," Murray said. "We'll find out. I just don't want to get in the way of an attack. I'd love to see who is after this guy besides us."

"Be careful...oh hey, I've got another call coming in."

"Jon?"

"Nope...it's Luke Diaz in Panama."

"Hey!" Murray exclaimed. "Tell him I said 'Hi!'"

"Will do."

~

The setting sun can work in your favor if you know how to use it. Jon drove past the two dogwoods and pulled off the old road at the base of a ridge of mountains. With binoculars in hand, he climbed to about forty feet above the roadway and looked back at the trees.

The glaring sunlight bounced off and lit up three locations where look-outs were hiding. Two appeared to be glasses like he was using but one reflection was clearly a single, most likely a scope on a rifle. That would be his first assault.

Checking his location on a GPS unit, he texted Ben to scan the area for phone conversations. After first reporting no traffic, Ben quickly changed that.

Call me if you can, the text read.

"What do you have?" Jon asked in a whisper.

"In Spanish, looks like from about two hundred yards in front of you, one guy said he was going in for the night. Another answered that was okay."

Jon watched as a faint glimmer from what had to be a belt buckle bounced along from one of the locations he'd identified.

Cars lights came on and the vehicle left, going back towards town.

"Got him," Jon whispered again, "That one's gone. Any other voice traffic?"

"No, not yet."

"Can you tell me, was the person he spoke to on his left or further away from my position?"

"Oh yeah, he was definitely to the left at about the same range from you."

"Thanks," Jon told him and hung up.

The other caller, the obvious boss for this detail, was on the rifle. If he went carefully around behind the shooter, the other spotter would not see him.

Time to move, he thought as he slowly rose to a standing position.

34

Cheryl Duray stepped from the elevator and quietly walked to the table where Ben was working. She saw the note from Luke Diaz's call and picked it up.

"This is about those guys from Germany, isn't it?" she asked.

Ben nodded without thinking what would follow.

"Have you ever tried to call that phone number?" Cheryl opened with.

Stopped as if hit by a log, Ben turned to her with a sheepish grin.

"It's been really busy down here...no, I haven't?"

Digging through piles of other notes, Cheryl found the small piece of paper with 4555522 written on it. "Why not now?" she asked while holding it up. There was no good answer against it.

They tried, 404-555-5221, but that was not a working number.

"Another two, maybe?" she suggested.

Ben dialed it but that also came back as "not in service."

Cheryl scratched her head; still convinced it was a phone number while Ben was losing interest in that whole idea. Neither heard the elevator open again before Daniel Seay walked up.

"Try "zero" at the end," he said, looking at the note in Cheryl's hand.

Ben paused a second but then dialed the number as Daniel proposed.

The other end rang several times. A man's voice finally answered, "Where the hell have you been?"

~

Darkness settled across the field where Murray hid. The muted sound of a fishing motor floated through the thick, humid air. It was, in fact, two small motors.

The cowboy slowly turned toward the river and saw two flat bottom craft running into the bank of the Missouri. Six men climbed out, three from each vessel and they gathered into a small huddle around a huge bag.

A leader of the group distributed weapons and flashlights.

Murray reached for his silver plated Colt .45 and checked it. He also carried a Glock 23 and a XM8 assault rifle. Lying flat in the grass, he watched the team spread out and approach the small house.

Two were heading into Murray's area, the rest several yards away. Murray rolled onto his back and held the Glock with both hands. The two infiltrating men did not expect anyone to be waiting out there in the grass.

As they got within twenty feet of him, Murray opened fire. Three rounds and the men went down. Camouflaged in the dark by his black outfit, Murray rolled four times to get behind a small berm of sand and grass. He heard voices call out in Spanish to the men he'd taken down. Shots were fired in his direction, but none close to him. It was clear they didn't know what was happening.

As he peeked around, two of the assault team continued on to the house. Murray couldn't let them gain access to that, so he crouched into a firing position with the XM8 and opened up.

Every seventh round was a tracer, so Murray could see where his fire was landing. He couldn't tell if he'd hit any of them, but the advance appeared to cease. When he stopped shooting, the return fire began, more direct this time.

He rolled again, away from his position and behind the tall grass so as not to disturb it and give away his location.

It was then he heard a loud scream and two shots.

~

Weston Duray could see the bright flashes of gun fire before he was close enough to hear it. Parking the rental car, he pulled his protective suit on but had no weapons with him. Then running across the field, he stayed near the water until he was behind the first group of two shooters. They didn't hear him or see him coming. Westy got to within four feet before one of them sensed his presence and whirled around. It wasn't quick enough.

Duray grabbed the man by the throat and the rifle. When his neck broke, the rifle fell from the man's grip and Weston turned it on the other shocked attacker. Two shots and that was that.

Duray knew Murray had to be out there somewhere, and there wasn't much choice in what to do.

"Got two down over here, Texas!" he yelled out.

Murray rolled through the grass once more, smiling... and hollered, "That just leaves two more, by my count."

The sound of men running through the grass and sand got their attention as the survivors made it for the water. Turning the rifle in that direction, Weston fired into the dark. One was hit several times but the other got to the water and dove in. Allowing the current to take him, he was gone quickly.

~

Daniel pointed frantically to the computer and took the phone from Ben, "Klaus ist tot," he said in the heaviest accent he could muster.

The other end was silent for a few seconds. Ben typed away setting a trace on the phone's location. Then the voice spoke again.

"Who is this," it asked.

"Dieses ist Wilfred," Daniel tried again, "Klaus ist tot."

The voice didn't speak again. The phone line went to a dial tone.

"He's hung up," Daniel slammed the receiver down.

"It's okay...I've got him," Ben declared. "He's in Washington, D.C. on the 100 block of Seventh Avenue."

"That's the Hart Senate Building," Daniel exclaimed. "Our guy is a senator or works for one."

Cheryl looked at Daniel with a blank stare. "Where did you learn to speak German?"

With a smile and a blush, Daniel shook his head and shared, "I spent a year in Berlin when I was in the service."

Leaning back with his own broad grin, Ben lightly challenged him, "You never mentioned that before," he said.

"It never came up before," Daniel shrugged.

~

Jon/Silas moved cat-like through the Virginia countryside. In the ten minutes it took Silas to flank the shooter, darkness had become a major factor. Stopping to slide on his night vision goggles, he realized that any shots fired would alert the man or men watching on the far side of the trees. He didn't want that, and getting close enough to manhandle this shooter was a long-shot at best.

Jon searched the ground around him and found two good-sized rocks... almost baseball sized objects that he felt would work in this case.

Quietly, he crept through the brush, looking for his prey through the green colored lenses. Suddenly, there he was, lying on his stomach and staring through a scope at the piece of land between those dogwoods.

At less than ten feet from his target Jon stood straight up, one rock in each hand. The noise of him getting up caused the gunman to roll to his side and sit forward.

Jon unleashed the rock from his right hand. It missed slightly, but did catch the gunman in the right shoulder. The blow knocked his hand from the trigger housing as it broke the clavicle. Pain registered hard on the man's face so fast his breath left him and a scream would not form.

Silas flipped the other rock to his throwing hand and let it fly.

This time, accuracy and the power from the suit did the job completely. Silas' stone caught the shooter square in the forehead sending his head backward with a snap. The sound of the body hitting the ground, though muffled, did carry enough to be heard.

The next noise was a clicking sound coming from the man's body. Jon found a cell phone and knew he could not answer it to the caller's satisfaction.

He hit the answer button and rubbed the unit across the ground and a clump of grass. The static noise made it sound, to the other end, as though the phone had malfunctioned.

Silas heard a voice in Spanish call out what must have been the shooter's name. Again, he rubbed the phone through the grass and then stood. With the dead man's hat on his head and the rifle in one hand, Silas waved toward the area he knew the others were hiding in.

He quickly took a picture of the shooter with his own phone and checked again for a pulse. There was none. He then began to walk forward.

~

A young and thoroughly shaken man stepped out on the porch of the small house. Murray walked up to him and the man fell to his knees.

"Don't do that," Murray scolded him. "I'm not with those people."

The frightened man slowly climbed back to his feet as Murray asked him, "Are you alone here?"

"Yes," he answered. I'm the personal aide to Congressman Harvey Waters."

Murray was now confused and upset.

"He's not here? What's going on, we tracked his cell phone to this location."

"That's what he figured," the aide told him. "After Leland got run over like that, Harv became frantic. He sent me out here with his phone to draw attention from him."

Weston Duray approached the house dragging one of the bodies.

"What do we do with these guys?" he asked.

"Leave 'em," Murray slapped Westy's shoulder as a greeting, "we need to get this guy out of here and find out where Waters is." He pulled the young man by the arm and asked him, "What's your name?"

"Charlie," the aide answered, "Charlie Higgins."

"Well, Charlie Higgins," Murray informed him, "when we get back into town, you're gonna call the cops and tell them you had a shoot-out with some bad guys. Got it?"

"That's insane," the aide protested. "They'll never believe I did this."

"They're gonna have to," Murray told him with his head cocked to one side. "You see...we weren't here."

35

Seeking cover for his advance on the other position, Silas knelt down and looked behind him. He realized the darkness had become his friend.

Once distinct objects like trees, boulders, and brush were now mere shadows and silhouettes that blended into the low mountains lying further away. The sun cast itself skyward now, distinguishing only the highest points that stood against the glowing backdrop beyond them.

Jonathan Crane now stood and again moved forward, trying to stay between the men he sought, and the shadows behind him. The tactic worked well up to about thirty feet from them. It was there that they could see his form.

Continuing to move closer, Jon threw down the rifle and pulled his Glock, holding it down next to his leg. One of the men approaching him suddenly stopped and yelled something in Spanish. Not knowing the language well, Silas kept moving forward without answering.

The man raised a weapon and fired at Jon. The 9mm round struck mid-chest and bounced from the suit. Still moving forward, Jon slowly raised his Glock but did not fire.

The other man fired again, but neither he nor his partner moved from where they stood. The second round missed Jon completely.

This guy is really nervous, Jon thought and kept moving forward.

At a distance of less than twenty feet, the Spanish gunman opened up with three shots in rapid succession. Two struck and again bounced from the suit. Jon raised his Glock and fired into the ground in front of the others.

"Alto," he yelled at them, using one of the few words in Spanish he knew. He was now close enough to see these guys were just kids.

One started to run and Jon shot just ahead of him as a warning. In the next few seconds he had them in control.

Language was a big issue for both sides. The young men were terrorized by the man in the black suit, but couldn't answer his questions. Jon finally pointed to the spot between the dogwood trees. It was clear the others did not wish to go there.

"Move," he ordered them with a push and they walked to an area of freshly turned dirt. Jon kicked at the loose soil and then spoke again.

"Dig," he barked at them. They seemed to understand.

The clerk at the desk appeared confused when Colleen Dunbar asked for a third room to be held.

"Your office asked for two rooms," she said as though there was a limit.

"We'll be requiring one more, please. Is that possible here, or do we need to go elsewhere?"

The indignant desk staffer searched her room bookings and found another availability.

"Here we go," she now smiled. "I can move a few things around and put you all three on the same hall. Will that work?"

Dunbar smiled and nodded at the woman who began writing up the guest tickets.

"Hold that last one for a late arrival, please."

Charles Burr walked up with a rolling cart, "Everything good here?"

"Yeah, we're fine," Colleen told him.

"What's with the boss deciding to come himself?"

"Same deal," she told him as they walked down the corridor. "He just has an idea about the interrogation."

~

The phone rang in Carlton Calvert's office. He had to stop and think what it was. His normal desk phone wasn't lighting up and then he realized it was that cell phone. That special one he used for contact with Davis.

"Yeah," he answered gruffly.

"Something is wrong," the caller said, "bad wrong."

Calvert didn't care for the sound of that.

"Have you heard from him?" he asked.

"I heard from somebody, but it wasn't him."

Calvert tried to think of the possibilities. "Is there any news from Dalton," he asked.

"Nothing I've heard about. They should have been done by now and then I get this mysterious call on the number we set up."

Then a thought caught Calvert. "How long were you on the phone with this person?"

"Just a couple of seconds," Davis assured him.

"Long enough for them to trace you?"

"Naw...I'm sure of that. I figured out real quick it wasn't our guys and hung up."

Calvert was slow to respond. "I hope so," he said, "we don't need any more trouble."

"No...I agree. I hate this, but we have to assume the hit didn't go well. The authorities must be keeping it off the news wires somehow."

"I'll call the office to be sure, but I think you're right. Just stay low until we know what happened, okay?"

"Yes, Sir," Davis told him and then hung up.

Carlton Calvert sat down behind his desk. His gut told him there was a huge loose end that had to be dealt with. He'd known Davis for years, but this was business. After only two minutes he dialed another number from the cell phone. When the voice answered, Calvert identified himself as "Carl."

"I need a job in D.C." he told the man, "Quick and messy, like a robbery."

"$25, 000," the voice said bluntly, "who's the party?"

Digging by hand wasn't nearly as bad as it may sound. The loose dirt had not had time to settle and compact, and the two youths scooped it out in no time.

At the four-foot level, one screamed and jumped up from the hole they had created. He had unearthed an arm and it looked to Jon like he came a good two feet above the surface area when he jumped.

Pointing with the Glock, Jon insisted they sit and not move. He then cleared the soil from around the corpse's face and took a picture with his phone. There was no need to dig down to the other body, he would take The Eagle at his word on that one, especially now.

He did cut a piece from Jacob Watson's shirt and handed it to one of the young men sitting by the hole. Then, stepping back, Jon took several pictures of the hole itself and the surrounding area. Even in the dark, it was apparent where they were.

After motioning for them to rebury the body, enough to protect it from animals, he touched the piece of fabric from the dead man's shirt.

"Tell them, 'I know,'" he said firmly.

The look of total confusion made him lean into their faces and repeat, "I know...tell them, 'I know.'"

Finally, one of the youths answered, "si...si."

Jon waved for them to leave and he walked back to the Mercury. *It was getting late*, he thought, *and he still needed to get to Winston-Salem.*

Backtracking as he had come to the area, he stopped the car near the trees and took a mini-camera from the trunk. With a hair-thin antenna and a solar battery pack, the unit was still invisible to the naked eye. He settled in for the drive, figuring it would take just over two hours.

36

Murray had Weston leave the rental car with his new farmer friend.

"What was all the racket out there?" the farmer asked.

"Some men tried to attack our young friend here," Murray told him. "Is the fee still as we discussed?"

"Yeah...I suppose," the farmer mumbled. "That chopper ride can wait, though."

Murray did a double take before nodding his agreement, then added, "And all you know about the rental car is that it showed up here all of a sudden."

"You guys criminals or something?" the farmer's voice was now a bit shaky.

Murray lifted his hat and smiled at the man.

"Do I look like a criminal?" he asked. "And if I were, we wouldn't need to be talking like this...would we?"

The farmer blinked and his eyes stayed wide for a moment.

"You're right about that."

"We got an agreement then?" Murray concluded.

Sticking the money in his pocket, the farmer nodded and looked down. "Never seen you guys," he said softly. "That car just appeared out of nowhere this morning."

Murray stuck out his hand and shook the farmer's.

"Thank you, Sir," he said.

They loaded the Lucy Too, including the still shaken Charlie Higgins, and flew off in the direction of Kansas City.

Higgins had made his call to the police from the farm house and left his contact information in Washington for the authorities.

They took on more fuel at an airport north of Kansas City and went on to Winston-Salem, North Carolina. Touching down just off runway 33 at Smith Reynolds Airport placed them near the terminal. The apron area allowed service trucks to bring fuel and tie-downs.

Inside the terminal, Huggins felt he needed to call and make sure the Elwood Police had been to the scene of the shooting. He came back from the call looking almost pale.

"What's the matter?" Westy asked him.

"The house...by the river....it's been burned down," he told him. "And you won't believe what else."

~

Calling in markers from old friends in the media business late at night was difficult, but Daniel Seay was getting closer to the information he wanted. He sought a list, by whatever means, of who was working in the Hart Building at that hour when the call was made.

Most of the senators and staff had left for the day, but a few stragglers were still signed-in. The list was right at fourteen and Daniel was sorting them when his phone rang back. It was one of the friends he had called a few minutes before.

"Daniel," the security guard started sounding out of breath. "You were just asking about who was here tonight."

"Yeah, Smitty. What's going on?"

"We've had a mugging in the north parking lot. A senator's aide is dead. Looks like he tried to fight them off, and got knifed for his trouble."

"Do you know who it was?"

"Oh, yeah...one of my guys found him. It was Henry Davis, an aide for Senator Pilmont of Ohio."

"Smitty, this is a tough thing to ask you...but did he have an odd cell phone on him, you know... like a burner cell, not a Blackberry, or anything, just a simple burner phone?"

"I don't know about that. You want me to check with the coroner? I know him...we play cards on Thursday nights."

"Would you? That would be great, Smitty, thanks. You can reach me here."

~

CWO Luke Diaz waited at the gate to the Miraflores Locks. He had received word that Panamanian National Guard troops had boarded the Ava Gentile and a short gun battle had ensued.

"Is there any word on what happened?" Diaz asked his friend, a Colonel in the guard.

"They didn't even get to talk to them," he said. "The minute the troops set foot on deck, the shooting started."

"Any of your men hurt?"

"No...that's the weird thing. It looks like one of the three men shot his friends and then himself."

"Damn..." Diaz said. "Didn't want to talk to anybody, did they?"

"No...my men never really saw them alive. The crew pointed below deck, to where they were hiding, but the shots came before we got to them."

~

There was a short phone call from Jon in Virginia to Ben around midnight.

"Set camera number," and he read off the serial number for him, "to record continuously for the next several days. I don't think it'll take more than one, but keep it running, okay?"

Ben dialed it in and answered, "Got it," the younger man said and stared at the freshly plowed spot of ground. "You growing tomatoes now?" he all but laughed.

Jon grunted, "Looks like a little garden, doesn't it?" He thought a second and added, "Keep this view to yourself. When what I want you to film happens...it won't be pretty...Understood?"

"No tomatoes, huh?"

"No..." Jon said solemnly. "Look...I'm going silent while I drive. I'll check in again tomorrow."

As Jon hung up, Ben's phone rang again. He looked at the caller ID and shook his head.

"It's Luke Diaz," Ben said to Daniel and Cheryl. "What a night!"

37

The town of Salem, Virginia, in the western suburbs of Roanoke, had been, until recent years, a stronghold of law and order. The police force was respected not only locally, but nationwide. One of the finer law enforcement training facilities in the country was located there. The optimum word is, "was."

The ability to have what Salem had came through the process of information. When people have accurate and truthful information from which to make their decisions on issues truth and honesty prevails. As the heat grew, under the disgraced presidential administration some years ago, that information stream was compromised.

The Times-Register, an arm of the larger Roanoke paper, did not follow the lead of its parent. The publisher, though a go-along to get-along type, didn't apply the pressure his outside forces wanted to see.

The Atlanta Sentinel quietly bought out the owner/publisher of the larger paper and had the Times-Register closed down.

The vast arm of Calvert Publishing also bought a local television affiliate, to affect that aspect of the news as well. The idea was simple and proven by the large media networks to have an impact. If stories that were detrimental to their agenda didn't get into the news, people didn't know about them. Should some other news outlet or radio station mention those stories, they would be attacked on a personal level with no rebuttal to the story itself.

The system, silly as it may sound, worked. The constant chatter over who was trustworthy to report the news and who wasn't turned people off. Citizens became preoccupied and paid little attention to any of it.

In regard to the corrupt administration on a national level, the gambit did not work. But the confusion and discourse soon brought major changes to the Salem area. Political turnover led to changes in the police force and a spiral downward.

The Los Tiburones Rojos came to the Salem area soon after that turmoil. They came at the invite of Walter Frazier. A fishing trip to Bahia Kimo in the Sonora Province of Mexico introduced him to the Red Sharks, a Mexican division of The L.A. Crimson.

The gang offered drugs and prostitutes to the tourists who visited their island home off the coast of Mexico. The gang would force visitors to pay for the services they offered... or protection from an unnamed, ominous source... or both. Frazier paid the extortion fee with a smile and asked for a meeting with their boss.

It took a day to arrange, but they finally met.

"I offer you virgin land and people to run over," he told their leader. "But you must follow my lead and obey my decrees."

The leader listened, at first unsure whether he should kill this fool, or take his offer seriously.

Frazier's demeanor stayed upbeat. He would never know how that alone saved his life. Through the talks, he began to make sense to the gang leader.

He described the conditions in Salem and offered a large facility for use as a hangout.

"It used to be a police academy," he laughed. "There's a gun range and everything."

Frazier talked and the Red Sharks boss loosened up. That gang leader, Renaldo Guies, known for his red sharkskin boots, moved to Virginia with twenty young men later that year.

~

Jerome Grimes got into Winston-Salem just after 10:00 P.M. He went to his room and made one phone call, to Senator Wallace Edgett.

"I apologize for the hour, sir," he started, "but this is what I need you to do."

"I haven't slept much lately, so no apology is necessary. I'm ready when you are."

"At noon tomorrow, eastern time, contact your 'handler' and tell him the deal is over. Say you just can't do it anymore."

"So...you will have your agent in place of Claire before that?"

"Absolutely, Senator. My team is in Winston-Salem now. We're ready."

"Can I call my daughter tonight?"

"We'll have her call you after we do the switch... in the morning," Grimes said. "Look to hear around 11:00 A.M.

"God's speed, Director," Edgett said with a quiver in his voice.

"She'll be fine, Sir. You have my word."

~

The two young gang members got back to Salem within an hour of their encounter with the man in the black outfit.

Their leader was asleep and no one dared to bother him. They told those who were awake of the Diablo Negro, the Black Devil, and the message he sent with them.

"He knows of the bodies?" one asked them.

"Si," came the trembling reply. "He forced us to dig."

Renaldo Guies, that feared leader, was with his girlfriend. Disturbing him could be painful if not fatal, yet this seemed important. The senior man there called his leader's phone.

"What?" the angry voice answered.

"The bodies have been found, Reggie. I knew you would want to know right away."

The phone went silent but Renaldo stepped into the room with them in only minutes.

"Tell me about this," he ordered. "What and who has done this?"

Checked into his room on the north side of Winston-Salem, North Carolina, Jon sat on the edge of his bed and dialed Murray's number.

"You here?" the cowboy answered in lieu of 'Hello'.

"I am," Jon told him. "Everything good with you?"

"Yeah, I suppose...Westy's here with me. We had a bit of a snag in Kansas."

"A snag?"

"The congressman pulled a fast one. This guy is definitely one of the 'star picture' people. He left an aide with his cell phone figuring we'd track him with it. Long story short, it fooled us and a hit team."

"Hit team? Did you have a run-in?"

"Yeah, Westy got there just in time, like the cavalry ya' know? We had five down and one got away in the river."

"That's a tough river to swim in," Jon commented.

"Well, that ain't all. Apparently he got where he needed to go."

Jon sat in silence, waiting for what could come next.

"Before we left, the congressman's aide called the police. He told them about the house, the bodies and that the bad guys had attacked him...which is true. He just didn't mention me and Westy being there."

Still silence from Jon.

"Well, anyway..." Murray continued, "When we got the aide away from there, he called the police to see if they found everything."

"Okay," Jon finally spoke.

"He said the damnedest thing, Jon. The cops found the little house burned slap down and get this...no bodies, no blood, no signs of the fight at all."

Jon was quiet for longer this time. He was stunned by the revelation. This was something he had not seen or heard of since Argus.

When he finally spoke he uttered one word, "Colombians."

"They were Hispanic alright," Murray confirmed. "Why do you say Colombians?"

"We've dealt with them before, remember?"

Murray paused for a second as what Jon said sank in. "I'll say..." he finally admitted. "By the way...Luke Diaz called Ben. Those Germans that were part of the hit team on your house...well, they're dead, all of 'em."

"You're way ahead of me on that...what's going on?"

Murray explained in shorthand about the phone number trace and Luke's help tracking them through the Panama Canal.

"Didn't find out who they worked for, huh?" Jon exhaled hard.

"Maybe," Murray snapped. "Daniel is working on something that might pay off on that."

Not satisfied with the answer but too busy to worry about it right then, Jon let the subject go and went back to Murray's situation.

"Where is the congressman?" Jon asked.

"The young aide who worked for him didn't know, or claims not to."

"Is he with you, there?"

"Yeah, we got him in a room down the hall," Murray said proudly.

"Go check...I'll bet you he's gone."

38

After listening to the tale of his young gang members, Renaldo Guies spoke again.

"Carlos is dead?" he asked them.

Both shrugged and one said he assumed so.

"Who was this man?" the leader demanded.

Again, they told of the black outfit and little else.

Guies pointed to four others of his group, "Go get those bodies...now!"

"Where do we put them?" one asked almost frantically.

"Take them to the compound," Guies barked. "These two will dig new holes there," he gestured to the messengers as he spoke.

~

As the clock worked its way to noon that day, Daniel Seay got a return call from Washington, D.C

"Danny? This is Smitty."

"Yeah...did you find out anything?"

"The coroner said Davis had a cheap cell in his pocket, like you suspected. The number for it was 404-555-5220."

Shaking his head as he tried to write a note, Daniel couldn't believe how simple that was.

"Thank you, Smitty," he told the caller. But that was all he shared. He didn't want to tip his hand totally just yet.

"Danny, you're very welcome. Is there something I should know about this deal?"

"Possibly, my friend," Daniel hedged. "If I can verify it I will call you back."

"Good enough for me," Smitty told him and hung up.

Daniel laid the phone down and another rang beside it. He looked around, but he was alone for the moment. Ben and Cheryl had stepped up to the kitchen for something to eat. He answered the phone.

"Is Jon there?" the husky woman's voice asked.

"No, ma'am. This is Daniel Seay. Can I help?"

"I've heard of you," the voice told him. "Jon speaks very highly of you. This is Sharon Swanson calling from Kentucky."

"Oh, why certainly, Colonel is it?" Daniel tried to remember what he'd heard about her latest promotion.

"Yeah, I guess. I'm just a cop, but thank you for that. Look, I've been looking into the Langhorn case up here."

"The CIA Agent, yes."

"I need to talk with Jon, first chance he has."

"I take it you can't share with me?" Daniel stated the obvious.

"No offense," she said firmly. "I'd just rather give this directly to him, and as quickly as you can reach him...okay?"

"Indeed...he has your number?"

"Oh, yeah," she assured him. "Nice talking to you."

The elevator opened as Colonel Swanson hung up. It was George Vincent.

"Heard from Jon?" he asked.

"Nope," Daniel swung around in his chair, "but I just got confirmation that the murder in D.C. is connected to the guys that hit this house...and, I've heard from Colonel Swanson in Kentucky."

George's eyes got a bit wider. "This is starting to heat up, huh?"

"Has that feel to it," Daniel grinned.

Yet another phone rang.

"Your turn," Daniel pointed to George.

"Go ahead," the DA waved at him. "Put it on speaker if you like."

"It's Marsha," Daniel proclaimed as he picked up the phone.

Jackson Terrell awoke and tried to get his eyes to work. His night of fun in Madison, Wisconsin, had taken a toll on him. After his first attempt to lift his head, he lay still for another fifteen minutes.

Two bottles of Johnny Walker 'Black' were in his line of vision and as the blurring subsided he began to remember. One bottle sat completely empty, the other mostly and it was on its side. A smell of something having gone bad came over him and he forced his upper body to move. Finally sitting on the edge of the bed, Terrell noticed a food cart across the large hotel room. The smell came from the cart and a brown bag from Smokey Joe's Supper Club. Something on the cart and the left-over steak in the bag had not fared well sitting out as long as it had.

Three deep, labored breaths later, he stood and made it to the door. Two newspapers lay atop one another in the hall. The date on the newest one gave Terrell a start.

"Damn," he muttered aloud, realizing he'd lost a full day.

On his way back to the bed, he tried to deal with the smell. A piece of fish sat on the food cart as it had for over twenty-eight hours, at room temperature. He found a silver cover and placed it over the offending dish. That helped, but just a little. The brown bag was tossed into the small refrigerator and sealed in there. Staggering toward the large covered window his eye caught an ornate object on the wall with large numbers. The clock read 1:35.

Pulling back the window's heavy curtains instantly proved it wasn't night time. He grabbed at his cell phone, dropping it at first and then noticed he had missed three calls.

"Crap!" he yelled out this time and tossed the phone across the bed. Laying down next to it, he rubbed his aching head with both hands. That seemed to help.

As his senses came more and more into tune, he looked for the clock again. It now shouted 1:57. Jackson Terrell finally rose and pushed the food cart into the hall and then found his way to the bathroom. A long hot shower was called for. He'd return the calls later.

~

At 2 p.m. the team met on the west side of the campus at Wake Forest University. Jon thought he would arrive last. As the Mercury pulled in, he was surprised to see his friend Jerome Grimes drive up right behind him.

"Sir?" Jon greeted the NCIS Director quizzically as they walked toward the group. "I didn't expect to see you here."

"I've been given an idea, Silas," the director answered. "You'll appreciate it, I assure you."

The two met Colleen, Agent Burr, Murray, and Weston Duray at the place and time specified.

"Where's your new friend?" Jon asked Murray.

The cowboy offered a stony glare, knowing Jon meant the congressional aide. Weston Duray stared off in another direction.

Grimes delivered his own look of disapproval.

"What new friend?" he demanded.

Murray turned to the director, "It doesn't matter. Not right now anyway."

"If it pertains to this it does," Grimes shot back.

"It doesn't," Jon said with a taste of Silas' voice and attitude. The answer seemed to be sufficient. Jerome Grimes grimaced but moved on. The immediate plans were discussed.

"Ben Shaw has selected and set up a vantage point for Mr. Duray to use as a sniper position," Grimes told them. He held a map of the area which Ben had sent him and notes from his investigation.

Through study of the phone transmissions between the men watching the senator's daughter, he had located the building where their sniper would likely be placed. Weston would be two hundred yards across the campus. Murray would be Westy's spotter.

"Ben calculates the shooter will be on the second or third floor," Grimes advised. Then looking at Murray and Weston, he said, "You two will be here," and pointing to the building across the common area and added, "on the fourth floor."

"Higher ground," Murray mumbled out loud.

"Exactly," Grimes nodded at him. "But there's one change in plans I want you to be sure you carry out."

He then abruptly turned to Colleen without finishing and began her instructions.

"You have your outfit?" he asked her.

She stepped back and held her arms apart; displaying the dress Ben had sent. All eyes but two were on her at that moment. As Agent Dunbar confirmed what she had on to be the correct apparel, Murray looked to Jon in confusion.

Shrugging his shoulders, Jon put a finger to his lips and then went back to listening to Grimes.

The director, now pointing to a building located in the center of everything, said, "You'll come from here and walk straight toward Jon at the edge of the parking lot."

Dunbar pulled up a girlish bonnet around the sides and back of her head. The frilly cap was lined with Ben's special impervious material. She then pointed to a spot near the front of that building.

"I'm told the closest guard will approach near here," she said. "Is that correct?"

"According to Claire Edgett, that's right," Grimes told her, "He'll follow you to the parking lot to mark you as the target."

"If you get hit," Jon interjected, "go down right away. Don't invite an extra shot."

There was a moment of silence at that thought, but then Grimes picked back up, "By then, our shooter will have them zeroed in, right?" he looked at Murray and Westy.

Agent Burr became nervous suddenly. "But the follower," he blurted out, "won't he run up and coup de grâce?"

"He won't have a chance," Jon spoke again, "and neither will the sniper."

"That's what I want to talk about," Grimes added. "Jon, you will have thirty minutes alone with your captive to get information."

"Thirty minutes?" Jon reacted negatively. "Naw...I need more than that."

"Work with me here," Grimes cautioned. "My way will get what we both want and give the operation credibility."

Jon tilted his head to one side but stayed silent. He wanted to hear what this man had in mind. Instead of an explanation, Grimes folded his papers and directed his attention to the group as a whole.

"Be careful out there," he said sternly.

Colleen put on an overcoat and headed to her assigned spot. Most of the others nodded and began to move toward their positions.

Murray smiled at Grimes and whispered as he walked by, "Hill Street Blues fan, huh?"

Jon Crane did not move. He and Grimes just stared at the cowboy in confusion.

"Late night cable," Murray laughed. "TNT has everything, man."

39

Marsha spoke to Daniel and George about her visitor. They all knew it had been predicted by Grimes but it was still a bit of a surprise. Her tale of a Mossad death team in the country was an added shock.

Knowing George was there prompted Marsha toward the other matter that Nava had brought to her.

"George," Marsha called him out. "Didn't Travis Gilbert say something about 'Amber' being mentioned? You know, by that voice in the basement?"

"Yeah," the DA confirmed. "Does Nava know what that is?"

"No, but it was on a note they saw. This whole thing is tied together somehow."

"Amber," Daniel repeated as Ben and Cheryl stepped from the elevator. "It's used to preserve bugs and stuff, right?"

"Prehistoric bugs, yeah," Ben jumped in. "Actually, it comes from tree resin, old...tree resin."

"That comment struck me because of what George had told us," Marsha tried to get hold of the conversation. "But the news here is there is a team from Mossad looking for me and probably all of us."

Everyone became quiet until Daniel offered a quip.

"Looks like their politics is a bit more overt than ours," he said.

"You may think so," George corrected him. "I wouldn't bet on that."

"Mr. Grimes said in the meeting that he knew Nava was in the country," Marsha recalled. "Has he said anything about the others?"

"No," Ben spoke up. "I just talked with him this morning. He said nothing about it." Then looking at his watch, he told them. "In fact, I need to get set up. I'm part of their operation that starts in ten minutes. I need you guys to leave or quiet down, please."

~

It was early in room 958 at the Aston Waikiki Beachfront Hotel. Sunlight crawled into the room past every seam in the curtains. Noise from the beach drifted up as well, but by the time it got to that level it had combined into a mild humming sound. Together, the dancing light and the wave-like droning added to the restful state he was enjoying. But all that soon ended.

He became aware of a new sound, a jarring sound that prodded Walter Frazier from his trance. A low growl came from him as he reached for the offending object. His immediate anger lessened when he saw who was calling.

Guies wouldn't bother me unless it was serious, he thought through the hazy fog in his head. Still, he remembered, he had an image to maintain.

"What the hell is this about," he yelled into the phone. "It's too early for this crap... why are you bothering me?"

"The dump site is compromised," Reggie told him in excellent English.

Hardly able to comprehend what he'd been told, he rolled to one side and began the process of lifting his upper body. His senses concentrated more on the pain his own voice had caused him rather than what he'd heard.

"What?" Frazier muttered back as he sat up and tried to clear his head. "A dump site?"

"The trees, Mr. Walt. You know...the dump site."

Understanding shot electric currents through his brain, the gang's benefactor launched to his feet.

"Who's doing this?" he screamed and then realized he needed to calm down.

"I don't know, sir," Guies answered meekly. "Some guy attacked the watch team last night."

Frazier thought and paced his room.

"What have you done, so far?" he asked.

"I'm moving the packages."

He was still groggy but his mind questioned that idea.

"That may not be the thing to do," Frazier heard himself say. "They could be watching the area."

"It's already done," Guies told him. "Three hours ago."

The boss exhaled and sat back on the edge of his bed.

"I'll be home soon as I can," Frazier advised him. "Stay low till then."

~

Congressman Travis Gilbert heard a ringing sound he'd not heard before. Laying down his pen, he sat back from his desk and listened.

That cell phone, his memory finally told him and he walked to his coat hanging across the small office.

"Hello," he answered in a firm voice.

"Travis?" the man asked.

"This is Travis Gilbert, yes."

"George Vincent."

The congressman knew that was the only person who should call on this line, but this was all new to him.

"Yes, Mr. Vincent," he said.

"Travis...I want you to keep people you trust around you at all times for a few days."

"Just how do I do that? That's not my normal thing."

"I don't know, but just do it. There may be trouble and we don't know from where it might come. Just keep folks near you, got it?"

A frustrated congressman relented and agreed.

"I'll do what I can," he offered.

40

The Benson Center's side lot at Wake Forest was not busy. Agent Dunbar found a parking spot near the building and walked through the auditorium to the backside of Reynolda Hall. She placed her hand on the dark glasses she wore but left them on, even inside the building.

A lingering lunch crowd stood near the stairs. Colleen got by them with little recognition. She found the assigned room on the third floor and knocked.

"Yes?" a timid voice asked from within.

"Claire? It's Colleen."

The door opened and the young woman stepped back, her hands held close together in front of her.

"You wore a sweater this morning," Colleen noticed.

Claire looked down and nervously pawed at the blue knit garment.

"It was chilly this morning," she excused herself.

"Not a problem. I'll just need to borrow it for a while."

They walked to a window overlooking the plaza.

"Your normal route to the parking lot is on which side?"

"I usually go to the right of the quad."

"Does the man who follows you ever talk to you?"

"No, he stays back about ten yards, I guess. But he's always there."

"Okay, good."

Colleen suddenly touched her ear and spoke for the others in the team to hear through the communications devices.

"Right side through the quad area, blue sweater added."

Claire looked startled but Colleen touched her arm below the shoulder. "My team is in place," she said assuringly. "You stay in here till I come get you...Okay?"

"Yes, ma'am."

Dunbar stared back at her oddly for a moment, not sure how to take that remark. She didn't consider herself much older than this girl and the respectful, "ma'am" was not often thrown at her.

She recovered with a quick smile and put on the blue sweater. Once again touching her ear, she twisted her left arm up to see her wristwatch.

"Moving down to the exit now," she said. "Will evac through the right side doors in three minutes...check?"

Colleen received "checks" back from each location the team occupied. She smiled at Claire Edgett once more and nodded.

"I never wear a bonnet," Claire said as she noticed the old fashioned cap hanging from Dunbar's neck.

"You will today," the agent grinned and rubbed the material with her fingers. She suddenly stared at Claire with a very serious expression.

"You've done good," she told the girl, "real good."

~

Many miles away, an older model pick-up truck rolled past a large house. Its driver studied the house, its position on the property and looked for access points. He stopped several yards beyond the building to turn around. From that spot, Warren Dawes took pictures.

He then placed the camera on a tripod pointed out the passenger side window. As he drove back by, Dawes used a remote trigger to snap pictures along the way.

~

Jon called Ben Shaw.

"Any voice traffic yet?" he asked.

"Yeah, there's plenty, just not what we're looking for."

Ben continued to dial out those voices he knew were not involved in their case.

"It's helpful though," he advised Jon. "I can tune them out now, rather than listen over them later."

"When did you talk to Grimes?"

Ben knew that tone and he knew to be careful.

"He called about an hour ago," he answered.

"Okay, you understand what's going on then?"

"I think so," Ben told him. "You okay with this?"

"It's his party now. I just hope it works like he thinks."

"Do you see her yet?" Ben asked.

Through his binoculars Jon saw a woman approaching the side doors.

"Yeah," he told Ben. "But I don't see the spotter yet."

~

"Okay," Murray whispered. "She's coming out. Do you have a good line on that building?"

"Yeah, those maples are new, aren't they?

"What?"

"The trees along the sides," Duray repeated. "Those are young maples. They don't fit the area."

"Are they in your way?"

"Naw, the foliage isn't that thick. But they couldn't be more than four or five years old."

Murray shook his head and watched as Colleen Dunbar emerged from the large building. Weston checked and set up his MX109 25 mm rifle.

"Here we go," Murray said aloud.

Grimes and Agent Burr stood at separate windows in the bookstore.

"Keep an eye on the floor above the post office," Grimes said into the radio.

"Have you seen something?" both Murray and Burr asked at the same time.

"No, just got a feeling."

Charles Burr stared down the length of the common area, the Quad as the students called it. He could see a young woman in a flowered dress with a blue sweater walking along the opposite sidewalk. Turning his attention back to the building across from him, he listened intensely but in his mind Burr was praying for safety for his boss, Colleen Dunbar.

"Go across to that post office," Grimes ordered.

"Who?" Burr asked.

"You...now. Stay on the first floor till you hear more."

Charles Burr walked briskly from one side of the quad to the other. He fought off the urge to glance toward Dunbar who was still a good distance away. Behind Dunbar, a man stepped from the stairs of Reynolda Hall and walked in her direction.

"Contact," Grimes alerted them. "Everyone get ready."

41

The call skipped across an ocean and a continent. Though not clear as normal cell traffic, it was too clear for Virginia Congressman Herschel Briar.

"I'm coming home in the morning," Walter Frazier told him from Hawaii. You stay put, understand?"

"Why is this happening?" Briar couldn't believe his ears.

"That doesn't matter right now. I know about it and I'll handle it. Just stay put and don't say anything, no matter what you may hear."

Matt Turlock laid down his telephone and walked to the patio. His house guests were there, enjoying a warm Shreveport day.

"Phil," he said through the door. "There's a call for you."

Captain Phil Stone put down his glass and reached for his cell phone. It was dead.

"Damn," he exclaimed. "I let the battery go down."

"Well, there's a Chief Merlot on our line."

Stone rushed to the corded receiver and scooped it up.

"Danny," he started. "Sorry man, I let my cell die."

"Phil, we picked-up two guys at your house this morning."

"Inside?"

"Yeah," the Chief told him. "A traffic copter with infrared caught them in a fly over. We 've got them here and there's something you need to know."

"Who are they?" Phil asked.

"That's kinda it, Phil. They have no ID on them, but when we ran prints they came back as foreign nationals... Israelis."

"I'll be there in forty minutes," the retired Captain told his friend.

~

As she walked down the sidewalk, on the quad at Wake Forest University, Agent Colleen Dunbar heard a voice call out to her as "Edgett."

"What do you think you're doing, Edgett," the voice sounded closer with each word. "Your daddy has lost his senses, huh?"

Colleen kept moving, slowly. Her instincts were to reach for her weapon, but it was too early for that. As she reached the edge of the residence hall and post office building the voice behind her spoke again, not as loud this time. It sounded as though it were speaking to someone else.

"Take her," she heard it say.

~

Claire Edgett was trembling. Her third floor window offered a clear view of the quad and the young woman walking through it, pretending to be her.

She recognized the man who followed Agent Dunbar the instant he stepped into view. When her father told of the plan to end this, she cried. She wanted to cry now, she wanted to scream as well, but felt she could do neither through her shaking.

A noise startled her. It wasn't in her room or the hallway outside. *Someone is moving furniture*, her mind calculated, *But where?*

Then the sound of a window opening drew her to one she stood near. With her face pressed hard against the glass, she gazed to her left, to where the noises came from. What she saw scared her even more.

Claire dropped to a sitting position after seeing an object protrude from the opened window to her left.

The odd looking barrel with the strange vented square on the end was still unmistakable. It was a rifle.

~

Grimes noticed a window opening on the second floor above the post office as Ben suddenly shouted into his ear over the cell connection.

Grimes watched from across the quad while Ben, in Dalton, Georgia, watched through satellite and cell phone interceptions.

"They're going to shoot her!" Ben screamed, "They're going to shoot!"

Grimes, in turn, yelled into his microphone, "Second floor, first room on the right...go go go !"

Charles Burr raced for the stairs while across the quad, Murray locked in on the window with his range finding binoculars and gave Weston the coordinates. "Got him?" the cowboy asked.

"Got him." Westy confirmed.

Murray spoke now into his microphone, "Target engaged...ready."

Hearing this, Jon jumped from the Mercury. He wore a new, enhanced version of his street uniform. Making no attempt to hide his hurry, he ran toward Colleen at full speed.

Grimes watched the shooter, across the quad, close down the bolt of his rifle and calmly ordered through the com-system, "Fire...fire."

Weston Duray did as he was told. The entire quad resonated with the crack of the Barrett MX109. His round struck the thick granite window casing just under the shooter. Its .25mm thrust penetrated seven of the casing's ten inch thickness.

Shards of stone and glass flew in every direction. A dense dust cloud formed around the gunman obscuring any view except for that of the rifle falling from the man's hands. His spotter fell backwards but quickly scrambled to his feet and grabbed the shooter's collar. Glass lay all around them and each man suffered cuts around their face and hands.

"Let's go!" one yelled and both spun, running toward the door. It burst open before they got to it.

Charles Burr stood in that doorway with his Sig Sauer .40 cal held in a double hand grip.

"On the floor," Burr ordered. "Move any more than that... and I will kill you."

~

The roar from the Barrett rifle had echoed through the quad like a sonic boom. Campus police, housed in the residence hall next to where Westy and Murray had set up, were not spared the shock.

Three young officers jumped while in their chairs, falling over and then crawling to the windows. Their sergeant, an ex-military veteran, pulled the door open to see what had happened.

He saw the damage to the window across from him. With a hand on his holster, he ran toward the post office and yelled for his men to follow.

42

Jon appeared from the far corner of the post office building as Colleen's stalker climbed to his feet. Both he and Dunbar had dived to the ground when the shot rang out. Colleen lay on her side, wrestling with her long dress to get to her leg holster.

The aggressor stopped some ten feet from the downed woman and leveled a handgun at her. Silas' strong voice rang out.

"No," he barked and raised his Glock.

After a brief look in Silas' direction, the stalker again took aim at Dunbar.

Jon, now in full Silas mode, fired once hitting the sidewalk in front of the attacker. Pain from the concrete chips stung the man who raised his weapon at the approaching stranger and fired. The .44 caliber slug struck Jon's jacket and fell harmlessly to the ground. The impact stopped him for a second, but only that. Silas rubbed at the impact spot with his left hand and fired his Glock again.

Another shot sounded in Silas' ear as his round slammed into the aggressor's lower leg, fracturing his shin bone and spinning the man to the walkway. The other shot wasn't from the stalker. It was a warning shot from the campus police sergeant, in full run toward them.

Colleen, now on her feet, held out her ID in her left hand and screamed at the police, "Federal officers...stand down!"

As Silas secured the injured man and cuffed him, he saw Jerome Grimes walk past without speaking to either him or Dunbar. The NCIS Director went into the post office building and up the stairs.

~

George Vincent reached out and shook Ben's shoulder.

"What was that?"

The four long-distance witnesses had a bird's eye view through the satellite and fairly clear audio of the activities. Daniel and Cheryl sat speechless. Mesmerized by the scene they were watching. Ben and George took it all more in stride.

"I don't know," Ben responded without moving his stare from the monitor. "He didn't say what would happen past this point."

Out of their view, Grimes joined Charles Burr in the second floor room.

"Have you told them anything?" he asked Burr.

"No, sir," the young agent smiled, "Saved that for you."

Grimes pulled his badge and held it right in the two prone men's faces.

"My name is Jerome Grimes, gentlemen. You are under arrest and being held by the NCIS."

"NCIS?" one man asked in confusion.

"Yeah, yeah," Grimes knelt down over him. "I'll ask the questions."

~

Dunbar's assailant lay on the concrete walkway, his eyes unable to focus through the pain of his shattered leg.

Added strength from his jacket helped Jon lift the injured man. He pulled him toward the parking lot as Dunbar approached.

"I'll go with you," she offered.

"No," Silas' voice answered in strong terms. "Your job is to go back and secure the girl, remember?"

The rebuke startled Colleen. She stared at him, half stunned in embarrassment, and half struck with an emotion she didn't understand.

Silas turned away with his prey almost off the ground. Dunbar watched him for a minute before going back to the campus police.

She explained a senator's daughter had been extorted and used against her father. She told them what she could while stalling for time.

Silas stuffed the now unconscious man into the trunk of the Mercury and as the sirens began to grow closer he drove off campus, back to his motel on the north side of town. The real police would soon be on the scene.

~

The sound of breathing started up again in the second level basement area. Ben, Cheryl, and Daniel sat while George Vincent stood behind them.

"I can't believe that," Cheryl spoke first. "That was too cool!"

Ben looked at her in disbelief as Daniel noticed a light flashing on another system.

"What is that," he asked.

Ben slid his chair down the table. It was the alarm for the camera in Virginia. Remembering Jon's admonition, he warned the others he'd been asked to keep this private.

"Does that have anything...?" George started to ask.

"No, sir," Ben cut him off. "Nothing to do with any of this, I assure you. It's a totally different matter."

After the others were on the elevator, Ben viewed the video twice and then called Jon.

"It was worse than I expected," he told him.

"What's that?" Jon's mind was on the Edgett case and Ben's comment didn't make sense to him.

"The tape from the trees," Ben said again. "Worse than I thought it would be."

Pulling into the motel, Jon stopped and turned the engine off.

"What did you see?" he asked.

"They dug up bodies, Jon. They pulled bodies from that hole."

"Two, right?"

"Two?" Ben repeated sarcastically, "They pulled four out of there."

With the communication system now turned off, Grimes had Burr secure the two men in chairs. One, more aggressive in attitude than his partner, glared at the director.

"You're not getting a thing out of us," he spit angrily.

Grimes nodded and smiled at him.

"Don't have to," the director retorted.

The man sat quietly after that for several minutes as Grimes stood, looking at his cell phone. Curiosity finally getting to him, the man blurted out, "What the hell, man? What's going on here? You can't do this."

Grimes slowly moved his eyes from the phone to the man.

"I can and I am," he answered softly. "Just sit there while we wait."

"Wait for what?" the man raised his voice.

The director stepped closer to the mouthy prisoner and stared into his eyes.

"You've heard of the guy they call "The Son?"

Without an answer, the man squirmed in his seat.

"Well," Grimes smiled through a short pause. "I see that you have."
The director leaned in yet closer. "You see smart-ass, I have you two...he
has your pal."

Grimes then turned and walked away a few steps before looking
back at the man. "I'm under strict rules of how I can question you...he isn't.
When I get the call that your friend has rolled over on you two, then we go
to the FBI."

"Roll over?" the man pulled at his bindings as he spoke. "What roll
over? What difference does that make?"

"You're dumber than I thought," Grimes baited him. "He who
speaks first gets a deal. The others go down hard. What's been happening
here amounts to kidnapping of a Government official's daughter. That's the
chair in North Carolina."

"We deserve a chance," the other man spoke up.

"Shut up," the leader threatened him.

"Shut up, hell. I don't want no chair." The frightened man
continued. "What is it you want to know?"

The first man started to speak and Grimes silenced him with a
finger point. Addressing the other, the director answered him with a
question.

"Who do you work for?"

"They'll kill us both," the first man muttered.

"Your way and we're dead for sure," the other snapped back at
him. "Wilkins will talk...and fast. That 'Son' guy does things. He makes
people talk."

The room filled with the sound of a ringing phone. Jerome Grimes smiled and answered his.

"Yeah?" he said.

Jon was on the other end.

"I've got nothing," he told Grimes. "Thirty minutes just isn't enough time."

"I see," Grimes nodded. "That's good...real good work!"

"Good work?" Jon repeated him, "This guy won't wake up enough to talk. You want to let me in on this game or what?"

"Really?" Grimes smiled even broader. "What was that name again?"

Before the slightly confused Jon Crane could sort out what his friend was up to, he heard another voice from the room Grimes stood in.

"Fuller," a man screamed out. "Hasbrough Fuller."

There was a slight pause as that name rattled around Grimes' mind. He pulled the cell phone close to his mouth and whispered for only Jon to hear, "Fuller...that's Natalie Barrett's lawyer."

43

Natalie Barrett had been in prison for four years and ten months. It all began some fourteen months prior, but these things take time.

It had ended, as most things do in Washington, D.C., with a deal. Not necessarily a good deal or the right thing to do, but that was normal as well.

The House charges for the impeachment had been vague to start with: Breach of Oath of Office. It sounded serious and it was. It just didn't define anything.

Unanswerable questions began to pile up. Blatant lies, scandal, and cover-ups led to Executive Orders in an attempt to avoid culpability. Threats to disband the Supreme Court raised eyebrows at all levels. Once supportive media outlets now sought to get in front of the collapse. Slowly, they exposed an agenda which turned popular opinion against him.

While people on both sides held their own beliefs, it was clear to a combined majority that he had gone too far.

The press secretary quit under fear for his life and senior advisors could not curtail the POTUS' drive to use the power while it was his.

Talking heads on television ran amuck, suddenly on the side of truth and the Constitution. A full blown trial would have been devastating to our entire system. A deal was the only way out.

Truth about the Administration was damning. They had ignored the Constitution and the separation of powers, but that was nothing new. Attempts to override citizen's rights in favor of global policies went beyond anything imagined. Members of their own party, who had been supportive to a point, finally realized the danger the country was in.

Partisanship had kept their eyes closed for almost too long. When they awoke they swung hard against their leader and his minions.

Somebody had to take the fall. That part took the longest to negotiate.

"You will be rewarded nicely," they told her.

No one, even the man who considered himself her boss, knew who or what she really was. She was allowed to plan for the future, to set up and secure her reign over her organization, even while incarcerated.

The President resigned, his cabinet resigned and his Chief of Staff was allowed to plead "nolo contendere" and accepted a ten to fifteen year sentence for her role in the "plot."

That had been six years ago.

Congressional hearings took nearly a year, sentencing took seven weeks. After that there were still questions from reporters and the public but the ruling class pulled together and held silent.

In time, things appeared to settle down.

~

Police Headquarters in Shreveport arranged for retired Captain Stone to drive into a basement parking lot for security. A short ride in the elevator stopped on the third floor. The sign said simply, "Robbery Homicide."

A greeting party of old friends stood several feet down the hall. Led by Chief Jack Merlot, the group seemed shocked by his sudden presence.

"Phil," the Chief exclaimed and reached out with his hand, "you got here quick."

"Where are they?" Stone asked sharply. He then looked at the Chief and took his hand as an afterthought. "Sorry, Jack. I appreciate you calling me in. My attitude may not be the best right now, there's a bunch going on."

"Phil, I understand that," Merlot told him. "I'll let you in, if you promise to remember protocol. Let's go in here for a minute first."

He opened a door to the observation room with one-way glass. The men sat at opposite ends of the short table, neither looking at the other. They did not speak or even offer a gesture.

"That's been the demeanor since they got here," Merlot explained. "Nothing, not a word. We identified them through their prints."

"I don't recognize them, but that's not really a factor. Can I go in?"

Merlot gave a strict, unspoken stare to which Phil Stone finally nodded his agreement. The Chief walked him into the hall and opened the holding room. Stone walked in and closed the door behind him. Still in silence, he stood looking both men over and then pulled out a chair between them.

"Yinon didn't send you," he started with. "That much I know."

Neither man uttered a sound though one offered a brief, glaring look in Phil's direction. The retired cop sat placing his hands in his lap.

"You know Yinon, don't you? But you don't work for him," he stated as fact. Then leaning back, Phil placed his fists on the table. "Yinon is a friend of mine," he said in low tones. "He's why you were in my house, isn't he?"

The defiant men remained quiet. Phil sat there looking back and forth at them, but didn't add anything more to the conversation.

After about five minutes of that he stood abruptly, knocking the chair against the wall. A detective standing with the Chief started to move to the door. "No," Merlot stopped him. "He's alright. Just wait."

Phil continued to stare the men down. They chose not to look back, their eyes on the table top.

Captain Stone stepped to the door and pulled it open. "Contact DHS," he yelled as though an order. "These two are terrorists."

The men still didn't speak, but they did look at each other in concern.

With the door closed, Stone looked at his old friend, Merlot.

"That got their attention," he said.

"Believe it did," the Chief smiled.

Before local Winston-Salem police arrived on the scene, Colleen called for Burr to relieve her down on the quad.

"I need to get back to Claire," she told him. "She's waiting for me."

Her walk back to Reynolda Hall didn't take as long as she wanted it to. Dunbar knew her job but she was trying to sort out her attitude and these strange feelings that nearly got in the way.

Her training and operation of her former job required strict discipline and focus. Statistics allowed for no variance and neither would this new position as field agent. Yet being in close proximity with this man, this Jon Crane had caused her to almost lose that focus.

She reached the third floor without remembering the climb. Turning down the hall Dunbar encountered a man she did not know. Instinctively and rapidly the agent drew her weapon.

"Who are you and what are doing up here?" she demanded.

The man threw his hands up.

"Whoa," he said and stopped dead in his tracks. "You're Colleen Dunbar, aren't you?"

"How do you know who I am?"

"I'm Bilstock...Murray," he tried to get out. "I'm Murray."

Colleen slowly lowered her weapon.

"The cowboy with the copter," she acknowledged with a nod.

"Two," he corrected her. "But Lucy is still my first love."

"Are you alone?"

"Naw," he grinned. "You can't see it, but that red dot on your forehead is from my friend Westy...in the doorway behind me."

Murray stepped to one side and the agent could now see the barrel of a Glock pointed at her.

"Weston Duray," she guessed correctly. "You're Cheryl's dad."

"Now that we've got the introductions out of the way," Murray perked up. "How about dinner?"

"What?"

"Dinner...you know...food."

"I'm on the job. I can't just go to dinner." She looked at her watch and added; "besides...it's only 3:00 o'clock.

"I could eat," Murray quipped and turned to look at Weston. "Would you tell Grimes I'm taking Agent Dunbar to dinner?"

"Sure," he laughed and stepped into the hall.

Colleen shook her head and opened the door she had come to check on. The still frightened girl stood against the back wall. Colleen motioned for her and reached out.

"I've got a duty here," she said as Claire Edgett stepped out. "Guys, meet the senator's daughter, Claire."

Murray looked briefly at the girl. "You're a brave young lady," he told her, but quickly found his gaze back on the female agent.

Dunbar placed an arm around Claire and said, "It's over...we need to call your dad."

44

In the still busy second level sub-basement, Ben heard the phone Jon had left behind ringing again.

Seeing who it was on the caller ID gave him a start.

"Gosh Colonel," he answered, "I'm so sorry. He hasn't gotten back to you, I know."

"What the hell is the situation down there anyway," Sharon Swanson bellowed through the phone. "I need to let him know about this CIA deal. He ain't gonna like it and I can only keep the lid on this for so long."

"Ma'am, let me call him right now," Ben tried.

"Ma'am?" the Colonel was all but spitting. "Do I sound like your mama to you?"

"No Ma'am, I mean no Colonel," he stumbled. *Sound more like my grandma*, his mind reacted. "I'll have him call you right now."

Jon was leaving the motel, having loaded the injured man back into his trunk. He punched in the number Ben gave and hit send.

"Sorry, Sharon," he went for the soft approach hoping it would soothe her feelings. The Kentucky State police commander was all business.

"This CIA dude that got killed here in Louisville," she started. "He had two visitors while in rehab. Both of them CIA by the way they signed in."

"Okay," Jon was waiting for the revelation to come.

"One checks out...the other doesn't."

"Doesn't check out?"

"He's not an agent with anybody, much less CIA."

"Did Langhorn say anything to anybody about this guy?"

"No, but the word is they both worked together."

"Langhorn worked with this guy?"

"Keep up will ya?" she scolded. "The two visitors worked together."

Jon was totally lost at this point.

"How is that possible? Only one was an agent."

"The other was retired, so we thought. No record on him at all. He was a total spook."

"I never heard how Langhorn died," Jon looked for more information.

"Garrote," Swanson told him. "And here's where it gets weird. The thing broke. They left one small wooden handle at the scene."

"Great...so you got prints," Jon assumed.

"Oh yeah...we got prints. They only came back through Interpol."

"What does that mean?"

"The prints are from a Syrian national. A guy named Varkey Al Halbi."

Jon's mind reeled as his thoughts were tossed back to the SEAL Team incident in Yemen and the murders back home afterward.

"Sharon," he asked deliberately, "You're aware of that thing about the dead SEALS, right?"

"Way ahead of you, son. That's why I wanted to talk to you."

"This Al Halbi was connected to the dead Sheik ?"

"Closely..." she stated slowly, "he was a member of the brother's body guard squad."

"Was Langhorn working with him?" jumped from Jon before he could think.

"I don't think so," the Colonel told him. "The CIA guy was tortured before he was killed. We're keeping that little fact under wraps along with another one you need to know."

"Another one?"

"The coroner found blood and small bits of brain matter on Langhorn's body that wasn't his."

"The other visitor?" Jon guessed.

"We haven't found that body," she admitted, "but DNA comes back to Langhorn's old partner... when he was in Lebanon. The killer used him to get to Langhorn," she stated as fact. "That's my guess anyway."

"This thing keeps growing," Jon muttered low but Sharon Swanson heard him clearly. "I'm losing track of where I should start."

"Well for one thing, you'd best get your ass in gear on this part," she ordered boldly. "I can only keep international murders quiet for so long. The clock is ticking on this."

"Thanks, Sharon," Jon told her. "I'll get right on it."

Pulling over in a diner parking lot, Jon called back to Ben.

"Listen," he started rapidly. "The SEAL thing may not be over. Set your satellite to where Cody Arnold is and watch that. I'll find out from Grimes where the others are."

"Jon," Ben nearly shouted to be heard. "I've just heard from Captain Stone."

~

Jerome Grimes had separated the two captives immediately after the revelation of lawyer Fuller.

Suspect number one yelled and protested as he was dragged away by two campus police officers. They stuck him in another room down the hall.

The talkative one stayed with Grimes, who let him stew for a few minutes before going back at him.

"In for a penny," the director baited his prisoner, "might as well go for a pound, right?"

"I don't understand," the man muttered humbly, "Pound of what?"

Grimes grinned and pulled a chair for himself up next to the man. He sat down, leaned toward the guy's ear and out of the blue, he asked a direct question.

"When was the last time you heard from Natalie Barrett?"

"What?" the man seemed sincerely confused, "Who is that?"

Grimes paused and studied the man's face. It was part of his job to recognize a lie and a liar. He wasn't seeing any of that right now.

"How many jobs have you done for Fuller?"

"Two...other than this, I mean."

"Murders?"

"Naw...we just strong-armed a couple folks, that's all."

"So, you three are a team?"

"Me and Pete, yeah. Wilkins joined us on this gig."

"You mentioned that name earlier; he was the leader I take it."

"Fuller told Pete we would work with Wilkins. He said it would just be for a week or so. But then it went longer."

"You watched the girl every day?"

"No...no, no," the man shook his head profusely. "She was supposed to think we were. But really just every now and then, ya know?"

"Did you know you were going to try to kill her today?"

The man got quiet. He lowered his head and didn't want to look up.

"I asked you a question," Grimes pushed him.

"Yeah...Pete told me this morning." He paused again. His head appeared to shake as though unconsciously. Then he continued, "She stopped cooperating...so we had no choice."

"Quite a step up for you, huh?" Grimes taunted him.

"I never thought..." the man's voice slipped down to a nearly inaudible level. " I just never..." he then looked up at Grimes with, "stuff just happens sometimes."

"How did you get your orders from Fuller?" Grimes went in a different direction.

"Pete...Pete always talked to him. Phone usually. You know...one of those cheap cell things you get at a Walmart."

"A burner phone?"

"Yeah...that's what Pete called it. Said no way anyone could trace it."

"Who has that phone now?"

The man looked at the oversized bag in the corner. It was the one they had used to bring the rifle in with.

"It's in there," he said solemnly.

45

Agents Hansard and Monroe arrived in Gadsden, Alabama, and found Leland Childs and his partner Walt Everson at a fast food place just off the main road.

Intros were short and sweet, then Hansard asked, "How's it going?"

"Terrific," Everson quipped through a mouthful of French fries. "If you like baby-sitting."

"Does the kid even know we're here?"

"I doubt it," Childs answered. "He's hid out at the animal park. We put out word that he was in Atlanta at the VA hospital. It's been quiet."

The new arrivals ordered food and the meeting continued for another half hour. Then Walt Everson suddenly rose from his seat and walked to the large front window.

"You guys drove that black Charger parked out there, didn't you?"

Hansard and Monroe looked at each other, puzzled and Monroe answered him, "That's all the office in Atlanta had for us."

"Might as well have driven a sign truck," Everson added as he continued to look outside.

"What do you mean? Were we tailed?" Hansard asked as he got out of his seat.

"Maroon SUV, Georgia plates," Everson advised.

"Where?"

"Wait for it...." He held a finger in the air, watching his wrist watch more than the window. Then slowly pointing to the left added, "there."

A dark burgundy SUV drove by at normal speed. The tinted glass made it impossible to tell how many were inside

"That's the fourth time around since I first noticed," Everson told them.

"I'll be damned," Monroe offered to the conversation.

"Nothing like bringing your work with you, huh?" Leland Childs piped in.

"Sit down," Hansard almost ordered with his tone. "Play like all's normal," he went on. His expression had become deadly serious and he asked, "Which vehicle is yours?"

"That grey Taurus right outside the doors."

"Good," Hansard smiled. "This might be our fault, but I've got an idea."

~

Jon Crane climbed the stairs and had to convince one of the campus cops to let him into the room.

"We need to talk," he told Grimes as he came through the door.

The director threw a finger in front of his nose and then shook it at Jon. "Outside," he said tersely.

In the hallway, Grimes began telling Jon what all he now knew.

"This guy gave it all up," he grinned. "We've got a straight line connection to Barrett. I'll bet those Germans were on her team as well. We've got her!"

Without smiling, Jon blinked and kept a serious look on his face.

"What's wrong?" Grimes asked him.

"We've got to keep this quiet...for a while anyway. There's much more to this that we can't let go of by busting her."

Grimes expression changed and though he said nothing, his face asked for details.

"Langhorn was tortured, probably for info on where we all were. I'm guessing particularly the SEALs who are still alive. The prints found lead to a Syrian national that worked for the Sheik's brother." He took a breath and then added, "Phil Stone had a couple of uninvited guests at his house, Israelis."

The NCIS director rocked back and leaned against the wall. He rubbed his face with both hands and asked, "Your reputation is to go after the head of the snake, right?"

The stare he received back from Jon offered little more than squinted eyes and a head cocked to one side.

"God..."Grimes groaned. "You don't think it's her, do ya? You don't believe she's pulling the strings on all this?"

"I don't know," Jon threw his hands up. "That's the problem." He stood and continued to stare at the man against the wall. "My guts says to look further."

Grimes was obviously thinking through this new situation. His gut told him to trust Jon, but his evidence was overwhelming.

"I've even got their burner phone," he offered. "It called that number you gave me, several times."

"I don't doubt her involvement," Jon said solemnly, "just her place in the pecking order."

Grimes turned to the window and muttered, "Keeping a lid on this...I just don't know."

"Does the press know about it yet?" Jon asked him.

"No," he spoke automatically without emotion. "I don't know if we can keep it that way for long." He turned back to Jon, sternly stepping toward him and asking, "What do I tell those real cops down there? What kind of story could cover this?"

"Three dead... unidentified gunman?" Jon guessed out loud.

Grimes' expression froze. He backed up and returned to the window looking around.

"There's four campus cops headed by an army vet," he thought as he spoke. "I'll bet he'll work with us. Beyond that, I can't say."

"I'll call Daniel...with a U.S. Senator involved he and Matt can call around and make it a national story."

Grimes headed for the door, now suddenly in full operation mode.

"Okay, I'll deal with the cops," he announced adding, "Both groups," as he saw the local and state police now on the scene. "Which leg do you want?"

"What?" Jon didn't catch the reference.

"There's two live avenues we need to check on, Jon," the director chided him, "Israelis or Syrians?"

His first instincts were to Phil and a desire to protect him, but Jon realized Grimes had a direct link to Mossad through an old friend... he had the same type connection with Sharon Swanson in Kentucky.

"I'll deal with the Syrian connection," Jon announced. "If you'll try to call your friend Hinon and find out what's up with those Mossad agents over here."

"First things first," Grimes said while nodding his agreement. He turned to one of the young campus officers and demanded in no uncertain terms, "Go get your sergeant for me, quickly."

46

Dilward Putney had been waiting for this call, but now that it was ringing it only made him madder. The cell phone lay on his desk, the desk he'd inherited from his grandfather, David Putney.

It was he who had started the business in Albany, Georgia, many years ago when pecans were king and David's Pecans amassed its fortune. Business today was so-so. It had been that way longer than Dilward cared to remember. He now had time to study politics and decided he would rather be behind the scenes. That too was fun for a while.

He met Jasper Jamison through a mutual friend and acquaintance in the publishing business. Before long, he and Jamison were confidants of Carlton Calvert. They were the king makers but even more they were a final layer of insulation between Calvert and exposure.

Putney now felt that also crumbling around him. He was helpless to stop it. Though he'd never admit it out loud, that's how he saw it. The feeling angered him and shortened his patience.

He picked up the small, screaming phone and took it into his private bathroom just off the office before accepting the call.

"Yeah," he answered in a way that was not his norm.

"Is that you?" the caller asked.

"It's me, Jasper...go ahead."

"Names? So you're using names now?"

"I thought you had some fancy do- hicky that scrambled everything."

"I'm not in my office," Jamison complained, "I'm on the road, damn it. Watch what you say."

An exasperated Putney slammed his fist into the sidewall.

"Will you tell me what's going on?" he spit out.

"Henry Davis is dead," Jamison whispered.

"Who?" Putney feigned convincingly.

"Davis...you know that go-between for Fuller. Calvert mentioned him a time or two."

"Why is he dead? What the hell is going on?"

"I don't know that," Jamison said a bit louder and with much more frustration. "Did Calvert say anything about him in the last few weeks?"

"No," the tall man told him. "No mention at all, why?"

"The word here is that Davis wasn't working for Fuller anymore. That he had gone rogue...we just don't know with who."

Putney opened the door from the bathroom, walking and thinking at the same time. His personal dealings with Davis needed to be kept secret, especially his order to have the man taken out.

"You think it was with Calvert?" he asked approaching his grandfather's desk.

"That's why I called you...I don't know."

Dilward Putney sat slowly behind oversized, oak desk and rested his head in his hand. Calvert wasn't the best diversion, but it had to be that for the time being. The truth would not be understood right now.

"What is that old crow up to?" he asked, continuing the distraction.

"Don't go running off with that idea, Dil. I just wanted to ask what you knew."

"But it makes sense...he could have been checking up on us, for God's sake."

"Well I didn't kill Davis and I don't think you did...so what sense does that make?"

"You haven't mentioned our other friend," Putney changed the subject to a contractor who was late checking in. "That's who I was hoping you were calling about."

"He's in the country," Jasper shared, "has been for a while. Outside of that, your guess is as good as mine."

~

"Sit up straight and try to smile a bit," the young man repeated what he'd heard. The quote was delivered with as much accuracy of tone as the man could muster. His interrogator at the Saint Simon's Island, Georgia, police department was not impressed.

"That's it..?" the detective pressed with his thick southern accent. "That's what he said?"

The witness looked up with a faint grin. "Yeah...I was standing right behind him taking an order."

"What did that mean...do you have an idea about the conversation they were having?"

"It was pretty tense, I can tell you that much. She was upset...and I've seen them in the place many times... so I know she was acting differently."

The young man was describing a local personality. Suzanne Glesser was a free-lance writer on Saint Simon's Island, off Georgia's coast. She wrote human interest pieces for both the local paper and the Brunswick News, the larger paper on the mainland. Her specialty was movie reviews, celebrity sightings, and other fluffy stuff the papers used as filler copy. The readers loved her.

Her boss at the island paper, Gerard Styles, knew Suzanne well. Some say too well. Styles paid his writer by the number of submissions, whether he used them or not. Though the editor was married, he and the younger Ms. Glesser were often seen together at dinner. The meetings were business, should anyone ask, and while no other "evidence" of an affair was known, the local gentry had begun to look down their collective noses.

"A lover's quarrel, maybe?" the detective asked suggestively.

"Naw... I don't believe it was," came the response. "It was deeper than anything like that."

"Deeper?" the detective became sarcastic. "A waiter at Tramici is telling me he understands the human psyche?"

Tilting his head toward the man standing over him, the witness looked up, paused, and calmly answered, "Perhaps... yes."

"So you're a psychiatrist now?"

"Actually," the witness smiled, "when I finish my doctorate this semester, the State of Georgia will say I am a psychologist. It's a bit different."

The detective looked across the room to his partner who nodded her head affirmatively. The waiter was telling the truth.

The male officer leaned forward over the table. "Did she say anything about David Eastling?" he blurted out.

The reactions from both the others in the small room came quick and emphatically.

"What?" the waiter gasped as the female officer stepped forward, waving her fingers across her throat.

"Are you talking about the ADA they found dead last week?" the waiter pushed on his chair nearly standing as he spoke.

The detective stood back and remained silent. Their case in the death of an assistant district attorney was going nowhere. His luxury yacht had been found tied to a private slip along the mouth of the Black Bank River. Eastling's body was found in the cabin.

"Why would she do that?" the waiter asked, looking between the two officers for an answer.

"She wouldn't," the woman officer spoke up. "Did Eastling dine at your restaurant as well?" When the witness remained quiet she followed with, "We still don't have the answers to that situation...we just check everything."

The young man didn't appear satisfied with the response but said nothing else about it. "Yeah, sure...he used to," was his reply.

"Did you ever see them together?" she asked.

With a strained look of puzzlement, the waiter paused and responded, "No. Not together."

The female officer kept control of the proceedings. Closing the file she held in her hand, she thanked the young man telling him he was excused. Little was gained from the interview that they could use. The hoped for motive of a "love triangle" had not been forwarded by his comments. A connection to the other open homicide case was not made.

As the door closed behind the witness, she turned to her fellow officer nearly glaring at him.

"It's way too early to bring that up," she scoffed.

"We'll have to sooner or later... All this ties together somehow, I can smell it."

"I agree, but timing is critical," she paused. "Lives could be at stake here."

"You mean 'more lives,' don't you?" he countered.

"We don't know yet what we've got here. We keep that to ourselves for now...understood?"

Her subordinate partner nodded and then shook his head.

A fact that was unknown to most was that Suzanne also wrote under a pen name, Felicia Goodman. Through that name, she was a regionally known investigative reporter whose work was syndicated through several news organizations.

The police on the island knew that she had been looking into the mysterious death of the assistant to the DA. They also speculated that could be why she and her editor were now dead as well.

47

Captain Marsha Hurst sat at her desk in Charlotte. Her hands flipped through paperwork that her mind wasn't interested in. It was more focused on resisting the urge to call and check on the plane. George Vincent suggested it when she talked with him and she agreed.

Harold Foster was on his way to pick up Nava and take her to Dalton.

"You staying here will endanger us both," she told her Israeli friend. Nava had asked her what she would do.

"I'm fine right here," Marsha told her. "They can't get to me while I'm on the job. Everybody here knows...they're on alert, so to speak."

A short knock at the door was followed by her boss sticking his head in.

"The plane just left for Georgia," he said with a slight smile.

"Thank you, Sir," she answered and before she could add anything he was gone.

That helped, but one urge for knowledge was quickly replaced with another. She really wanted to talk to Jon.

Daniel Seay had, from time to time, been going through the list of casualties. Congressional people, their staff, and others across the country, who might in some way be connected to this case. Many were flagged because pictures of their offices showed the ominous star formed by numbers on their wall.

Though the stack was vast and sat nearby, recent events had taken priority over his search. He was typing out a press release on the Senator Edgett story when the intercom came alive.

It was Lori and she sounded like it was important.

"Ed is on the phone up here, Danny," she said. "He needs to talk to you."

Ed White, Daniel's former boss and mentor at the Pittsburgh Post-Gazette, also had a copy of the list and had been going through the names.

"Daniel," he started, "there's a name on here that rang a bell. I didn't remember at first but then it hit me."

Daniel listened respectfully, offering only a single, "Okay," as Ed went on.

"You remember our program to 'safe keep' information through others?"

"Sure."

"Well, Jerry Styles, an editor down in Brunswick, Georgia, sent two or three emails a few weeks ago about a story one of his reporters was working on."

"Did you look at them?"

"Not till just now," White sounded a bit indignant. "It was about a corruption case. No names or real details, just the initials, DP."

Ben began looking through a list of current or past congressmen and staff in Georgia for those initials. While still searching, he did comment to his former boss.

"Something happened to Mr. Styles, I'm assuming."

"Both he and the reporter are dead."

Ben froze then adjusted the phone to his ear, "Both of them?"

"Yeah, just in the last week. I called down there and the paper is in turmoil. The reporter wrote nationally too, she's actually a pretty big deal."

"Why hasn't the story gone national?" Daniel asked.

"That's a great question! It's almost like the old days... when powerful publishers could squash a story they didn't like."

"Do you know how they were killed?"

"Pretty grizzly," White told him. "She was stabbed in the neck, down through to her lung. He was strangled with a thin wire of some kind."

~

NCIS Agents Hansard and Monroe finished their meal and left the hamburger joint, walking casually to the black Charger. Monroe added to the charade with his own theatrics. He took off his jacket and slowly hung it in the back.

A dark red SUV turned the corner and stopped when seeing the agents at their car.

"They're here," Monroe smiled and slid into his seat.

"Good," Hansard responded without looking. He got into the driver's seat and started up the vehicle.

"This will mess with them," he said as the Charger pulled out and turned toward the SUV, driving past them in the opposite direction.

After waiting a minute, the larger vehicle u-turned in the street and continued to follow. By then, Childs and Everson were at their Ford and from a good hundred yards back joined the parade.

~

Colleen Dunbar followed Claire Edgett onto a plane bound for Los Angeles. They boarded separately and under assumed names as did Senator Edgett from Washington, D.C., and his wife from Madison, Wisconsin.

The planes landed within an hour of each other and all were met by Agent-in-Charge Terrance Barker. A secured safe house, for the family, had been established in Oceanside, California. They would remain there through the duration of this situation.

As the Edgett family headed to the car Barker brought for them, Colleen hugged the girl and wished her well.

"Why aren't you coming with us?" Claire asked.

"I have business back home," she smiled and shook both the girl's hands with her own. "We still have to catch all the people involved in this."

The Senator reached out to her, "Tell your boss how grateful I am...please," he told her.

"I will. You all did great."

"I know there was someone else who helped with this, I never heard who it was," Edgett added.

"He's a personal friend of mine, sir," Barker jumped in. "He's very happy he could help, I assure you."

Colleen smiled and nodded at Terry, then left to catch her plane back to D.C.

~

Outside the city limits of Gadsden, Alabama, Agent Hansard turned right on highway 11 and picked up speed slightly. Monroe kept an eye peeled to the rear. The dark red or maroon SUV continued behind them.

The two lane road was nearly as straight as any he'd ever seen, but Hansard found a stretch that had severe dips and rises. These variances were enough that the SUV would disappear from sight momentarily. As they entered an area with several of these dips, Hansard increased his speed to almost eighty-five miles per hour and Monroe contacted Childs and Everson on the cell phone.

"We're taking off," he informed them. "We'll execute in about thirty seconds"

At the bottom of a steep decline, Hansard suddenly stepped hard on the brakes and as the Charger slowed, he cut the steering wheel positioning the car across the road, diagonally. Both men jumped out and took places on the far side of their car, with guns drawn.

The SUV came into view at high speed and slammed on its brakes with a fishtail stop. Still some thirty yards from the Charger, the SUV attempted to run, backwards up the slope. They were quickly cut off by Childs and Everson who slid their Ford sideways and climbed from their cars aiming at the aggressors.

Walt Everson popped the trunk on the Ford and extracted a Ruger mini 14 tactical rifle. The .223 caliber was a cousin of the AR-15 but only held a twenty shot magazine. Everson grabbed three of them with the weapon.

A short standoff in dead quiet was followed by an eruption of gunfire. Initially, those in the SUV shot at both cars blocking them. Then just as suddenly, the SUV smoked its tire in reverse and then lunged forward toward the Charger.

When it became clear that they had no intention of stopping, Everson unloaded a magazine into the back glass of the fleeing vehicle.

From the range he had to work with, it was difficult to miss. When the horn blew with a solid tone, Everson knew he had swept the interior clean.

The huge, lumbering vehicle continued forward but now wavering from side to side.

Monroe called to Hansard to join him on the left side of the road and he yelled out, "Left front...left front," as the SUV barreled down on them.

Sixteen total shots from their Glocks hit the left front wheel, bursting the tire and causing the rim to dig into the asphalt.

The whining hulk of metal dropped into the ditch and rolled through the kudzu vines. It stopped on its top momentarily and then rolled again, finishing upright in dust and smoke. There was no sign of life as the thing ignited and went into flames.

~

Before Colleen would arrive back in Washington, D.C., news reports of the kidnapping attempt on a United States Senator's daughter were spreading through the country.

With the cooperation of the North Carolina authorities, Grimes had the three assailants under heavy guard in a hospital in Charlotte.

"I'll check on them myself...daily," Captain Marsha Hurst told Grimes by phone.

The news, as Daniel and Matt Turlock had described it, didn't take long to reach Wisconsin's maximum security prison. According to the reports, all three kidnappers had been killed in the assault and, the identities of these men were unknown at the present time.

That last part was little solace to Natalie Barrett. After pacing her prison cell for nearly an hour, she unconsciously threw a book across the space. It's slamming into the aluminum sink and toilet sounded a tone that carried through the cell block.

A guard appeared within seconds, peering in without speaking. Barrett forgot her years of experience in keeping cool. Circumstances were closing in on her and the control seeking portion of that devious brain was in full command.

She demanded a private phone call to her lawyer.

Another phone rang in the Oval office.

"Sir, they are safe," a voice advised the President.

"Confirmed?"

"Yes, sir," the man informed him. "There's one other thing."

"Go ahead."

"NCIS is keeping the details and the connection to Barrett under wraps for right now."

"Okay," the President acknowledged. "If Grimes is going in that direction we need to back them up, is that clear?"

"Yes, Sir!"

The President changed course and went into a question. "We still have Terrell under surveillance?"

"He hasn't left that hotel room, sir."

"Pick him up, quietly."

"Roger that, Sir!"

48

The office was hot when he arrived. His earlier than expected return had not been communicated to his regular staff. Walter Frazier realized he didn't even know where the thermostat was, but what he wanted was his unlisted cell phone. The one he used to speak with Renaldo Guies.

He took it from the lower desk drawer and unlocked the glass doors to the balcony. It was seventy-six degrees out there but that was some twenty lower than inside.

"What have you done about the problem?" he asked when Guies answered.

"They are moved."

"To where?" Frazier demanded.

"The compound, sir. They're in the compound," Guies stated. "I want to burn them."

"No...no," Frazier grumbled. "That would draw attention, we can't risk it." Frazier suddenly understood what that meant. "Where are they, exactly? You haven't reburied them yet?"

"They are in bags, in the van at the compound."

"Bury them, damn it...tonight!"

"The hole is ready," Guies told him. "I just wanted to check with you about burning."

"Have you learned who the man was that found them?"

"Nothing on him," Guies admitted. "No idea at all."

Frazier thought about the job he had authorized several months ago.

Could he know? He asked himself. *That was so far from here, there's no connection. It can't be him.*

"I'll call you back later," Frazier told Guies and hung up.

~

Lucy Too approached Louisville International Airport with Murray and Jon Crane aboard. They had left Jerome Grimes in Winston-Salem with Agent Charles Burr and the cover story of the kidnapping attempt.

Jon spent most of the flight time engrossed in notes Ben had sent about Editor Ed White's concerns.

"You're a cheerful passenger," Murray prodded him. "I thought everything went pretty damn good back there. Why so quiet?"

"What?' Jon looked up, not having really heard what his friend said.

"Never mind," the cowboy shook it off. "Tell me about this female agent, Colleen. You've been holding back on me, son."

Jon stared at him. "Is that what you're thinking about, really?"

"Hey! She's attracted to me, what can I tell you? I just want to know more about her."

"Murray..." Jon mumbled. "Get your head in the game, will ya?"

"Well, what's got you so wrapped up in work over there?"

"There have been three murders off the coast in Georgia," he explained. "From what I'm looking at, it's possible they could be connected to the case we're going to."

"The Langhorn killing?"

"There's a weird similarity that needs looking at."

"This thing is like peeling an onion, huh?" Murray swung the copter to the left as he spoke.

"When we get to Louisville..." Jon tried.

"We're there, buddy," Murray cut him short. "I'm holding for a spot to set down."

"While I'm meeting with Colonel Swanson, I'd need you to contact Brunswick police and see if they have cause of death on the ADA they found in his boat."

"This dead guy got a name?"

"David Eastling."

"Sounds like a DA," Murray said. "By whose authority am I doing this?"

"Use Grimes' name if you have to," Jon told him. "Just see what they'll tell you."

Lucy Too began to drop toward the tarmac.

"Sit tight...we're cleared to go in," the cowboy told him.

~

Agent Leland Childs called in and asked that someone check on the animal park while they waited for the flames to subside. Local authorities arrived, including a contingent of Alabama State Patrol.

"How many are in there?" one officer asked as he tucked in his shirt. The smoldering hulk of the SUV still groaned of expanding metal. The bright orange glow kept everyone back.

Jake Hansard, the senior agent on the scene answered the uniformed officer. "At least three, we think."

Leaning toward his shoulder microphone, the State Patrolman yelled, "Give me two more meat trucks and have anothern' on stand-by."

He then looked back at Hansard and added, "That thing holds a bunch a gas, don't it?"

Hansard nodded and the officer turned to walk to his car. He was heard to say, "This could take forever," as he got to the cruiser's door.

~

Cheryl had been watching the satellite monitor from over the former police academy in Roanoke, Virginia.

"Are you sure something is going to happen there?" she asked Ben.

"That van drove in there, didn't it?"

"Yes," she answered with dripping sarcasm.

"This is what we do," Ben shot back. "We watch and wait...a lot."

Daniel Seay looked over at them and smiled.

"I need to go upstairs for a few minutes," Cheryl abruptly informed Ben. It wasn't in the form of a request and he knew that.

"Sure," Ben grinned. "Just make sure the recording is on."

As the elevator closed, Daniel spoke without looking away from his monitor.

"You handled that nicely," he teased.

"Huh?"

"Nothing," Daniel went on. "Some guys take years of marriage to learn that move."

Ben's eyebrows rolled down on his forehead as he sought a dignified come back. A light on his control panel quickly changed the subject.

"They're on the ground in Louisville," he said as though to no one in particular and then focused on another screen showing the upper driveway. "And Tim's back with Ms. Golan."

~

The phone in the Oval Office rang again. It had only been an hour.

"What?" the President answered. "Do you have him?"

"No, sir..." a timid voice responded. "Terrell wasn't there."

"He got away?" the President stood in shock. "How did that happen?"

"The room had a vagrant in it, Sir," the voice sounded completely despondent. "We don't know how he pulled the switch, but he set us up with a street person in that room."

There was silence on both ends of the line until the caller swallowed hard and added, "The best we can tell, Sir... Terrell's been gone two days, at least."

49

A tiny conference room near the luggage claim served as their meeting place. Jon and his friend, Colonel Sharon Swanson went over notes and pictures from the Langhorn crime scene. The raw images were brutal.

"This was a fight," Jon said, throwing one picture across the table.

"We call it a crime of passion," Swanson corrected him.

Jon's eyes rose to meet hers. He understood anger and rage, but to do this under passion didn't register with him.

"Where was the piece of wood found?" he asked.

"The handle section was wrapped in Langhorn's coat material. It must have broken off and fell under him." She demonstrated by wrapping her hand around the flap on her own coat. "As he rolled, it was tangled in the jacket."

"Do you know how this Syrian came into the country?" Jon asked.

"No," she shook her head. "No trace at all."

Jon stared down at the photos and thought about what he was going to say next. Then it just came out.

"There was a double murder on Saint Simons Island in Georgia," he heard himself say, "just a few days before this happened."

The Colonel held her stare, waiting for the payoff to what he had said.

"The man was killed with a wire around his neck there, too."

Sharon Swanson's eyes got wide as she tilted her head back somewhat.

"I've got Murray trying to get details on a third killing that could be connected to the others."

"I take it there are no leads down there either," she guessed.

"Not yet."

The door suddenly swung open as Murray came in.

"Sorry guys, but I knew you'd want to hear this," he blurted out.

Jon pointed to a seat at the table. "Go on," he told the cowboy.

"The cops on the island and in town are all hush-hush over this. I did get a guy in the ME's office to read me the report on the ADA's death."

He looked at Jon and the Colonel as both leaned in slightly.

"The initial finding was decapitation by unknown object," he told them. "But that was later revised."

"They found other evidence?" Jon asked.

"They found bits of metal in the neck wound like old piano wire."

"Garrote?" Swanson asked before Jon could get it out.

"Exactly," Murray smiled like he'd won the lottery. "This killer is the same guy."

"It looks possible," Jon admitted. "I need to go down there and see what I can figure out."

"What if he's after you next?" Swanson asked. "He could be going to Dalton."

There was an extended pause before Jon spoke again.

"I've got some good people at that house. They can take care of themselves...till I get there."

Murray looked around and then stood trying to see out a window. He was checking to see how his refueling was going.

"I suppose we're going to Brunswick?" he guessed out loud.

"Saint Simons, actually," Jon answered. "I know a guy from college who lives there."

"You're going to visit an old pal?" Murray sounded confused.

"The island is not that big. A stranger snooping around would draw attention and real quick."

"So, you're using this friend as cover?" Sharon spoke up.

"I'll check with him first, of course," Jon stood, his indignation showing. "I wouldn't do anything to endanger him or his wife."

Calvin Earl was a business major Jon had known at school years ago. Earl also loved the beach music. Jon attempted to explain what he remembered about his old friend.

"He's kind of a small time writer and producer in his own right." Jon explained.

"Oh, yeah?" Murray grinned, "Beach music. Like the Tams and all that?"

"Something like that. He was more into it than I ever was. His friends and the locals call him, 'The Duke'."

"The Duke? Is that his name?"

"Naw," Jon smiled. "His name is Calvin Earl."

Murray grinned from ear to ear.

"The Duke of Earl, huh? I like it," beamed the cowboy.

He was with Rahem in south Yemen a year ago when they found the Sheik's body and those of the others. He witnessed the pain and anger felt by his friend and boss. The Sheik was Rahem's brother.

Varkey Al Halbi was also in Syria when the American came to see Rahem. That man was given a task Al Halbi would have gladly done himself. But that was not to be.

Just months ago, more Americans came to Rahem ali Kupla's compound. They asked impertinent questions of Rahem and as he watched, his friend, boss and benefactor grabbed for a weapon and was gunned down.

That had been the deepest cut of all. In that instant, Al Halbi lost not only a friend but a means of livelihood. One he had worked hard for and that could not be replaced easily.

Trust was important. It took years to gain trust these days. The role of a household bodyguard was sacred. It was best to die when the house master did for such a role could not be obtained again.

Another American came to Syria, only weeks ago. This one sought out Varkey Al Halbi with a proposition for him. The job in America remained unfinished and there was one who was the cause. This man with the strange name, "The SON" he was called, appeared in black dress... to interfere with what must be done.

Al Halbi asked but one question, "How do I find this man in black?"

"There is another who was there. One who knows who this man is and can point you to him," the stranger explained. "This man was injured and is in hiding. You will reach him through a friend of his, this man." And Al Halbi was given the name of Langhorn's old partner.

"This one will take you to Langhorn," the man said.

Al Halbi was given money and a contact number. He was boarded on a merchant ship that crossed the sea and slid down the coast of America near a city called Brunswick on its way to the port in Savannah.

The small craft that sailed within meters of that ship appeared as sent from God himself to Al Halbi. He donned his wet suit and with his information and money safely tucked inside, he dove into the sea.

The single man on the smaller craft never saw him coming.

50

The view from the hallway window was quite breathtaking. Jackson Terrell had not run far. He was suspicious about being followed, so he opted to stay within visual range of his old room. His concerns were valid.

Fifteen floors above the city, he could see the activity. He'd heard the sirens when they first discovered he was not across the street as they believed.

The sound of people in the stairwell of the building he was in sent him back to his new room.

They'll think I'm long gone, he told himself behind the locked door. "I'll find out who snitched," he heard his voice say. Then silently assured himself, *they'll pay...they will pay.*

Georgia's newly carved out congressional district snaked along the coastline taking in both port cities of Brunswick and Savannah and their heavily unionized labor force. The deal wasn't clearly understood, but state leaders seeking solidarity to pursue and approve of the impeachment proceedings six years ago agreed to this new district.

Headquartered in Brunswick, the staff operated basically on its own. The congresswoman, Agnes Pugh, stayed in Washington until needed for each re-election cycle. At which time she would show up, attend a few union rallies, and go back to her apartment in D.C.

Agnes preferred the Washington social life over her past in Brunswick.

District business was handled by the Chief of Staff, Darcy Brown, and his decisions were not questioned. "Aces," as he was known on the streets, was well connected and had been heavy into gang culture and drugs for most of his younger life. Turning his talents to organization of impoverished communities, "Aces the white boy," had been influential in Agnes' run for office. He kept his connections secret. No one knew just how high they went.

"Darcy," a young aide stormed into an office on the third floor. "Someone has been calling police departments here and on the island asking about David Eastling."

"Do they know who it was?" Brown scowled through his words.

"He wouldn't say. Just some "interested party" is all he'd give them."

"Have they done the cremation on him yet?"

"The family objects. They want the body for burial."

Brown paced his office for a few minutes and then turned abruptly to the aide.

"Accidents happen," he blurted. "Burn it and tell the family mistakes were made. I'd like to burn that damned boat too, but that would draw attention we don't need."

"We've gone all through it, Darcy. There's no note or anything that points back here on that boat. How the killer got to the reporter and her boss I just don't understand."

"Well," Brown pointed at him threateningly, "we need to find out before somebody else does."

~

Tim Spiegel had taken the Jaguar to the airport. With Nava and Harold with him, he pulled up the front driveway to the main garage doors.

"This is it," he smiled at Nava who still seemed distant and quite concerned. *Especially for a trained Mossad agent*, Tim thought quietly.

Stepping from the car, she noticed the tree first. It still leaned away from the blast marks that were also still visible on the front of the house. A heavy-gauge wire held the elm in place and dirt had been brought in to cover exposed roots, but other than that, all remained as the bomb had left it.

"Jon won't let them fix it," Tim said in seeing her stare, "until this is finished."

"What is finished?" she asked.

Her words struck Tim and Harold. The men glanced to each other before Harold answered her.

"We're starting to wonder that ourselves," he said.

They were met at the door by Doris Shaw and Lori Seay. Each in turn hugged the new guest and told how much they had heard about her. Nava looked around the vast interior and her expression showed her disbelief.

"Marsha told me," she muttered, "but I had no idea."

"There's a room set aside for you upstairs," Doris told her. "Do you need anything?"

Nava looked at her with nearly a blank stare. "I'd like to rest for a while," she said with little emotion.

Lori stepped back and let Doris show their new guest up to her room. She looked over to Tim Spiegel who shrugged his shoulders.

"She didn't have much to say on the drive over here, either," he offered.

Harold Foster reached for Tim's arm asking him, "You going to put the car away, or do you want me to?"

Spiegel looked back at Lori Seay but she had nothing to add to the question they clearly shared.

"I'll get it," Tim told Harold, "thanks."

~

When her call was finally connected, Natalie Barrett startled Hasbrough Fuller with her frankness over the phone.

"What the hell is going on, Fuller," she demanded, "I get nothing and then I hear about this on the friggin' news?"

Fuller took in a breath to compose himself.

"Ms. Barrett," he tried to sound calm and cool, "we must remember these communications are fairly open to scrutiny. The retrial motion you're concerned about is before the judge and I should hear something soon."

He could hear her breathing... hard. She was trying to regain some decorum herself.

"Has our representative called in?" she asked under much more control.

"I expect to hear any time...there's no news on him and I'm sure he's out and about."

"Our other business," she went on, "any word on them?"

He didn't want to tell her that most of the other "teams" had been scared off by the results the first ones had suffered, but he had to.

"There's some delay on those transactions over concerns of recent events," he said carefully. He could hear her fist hitting the concrete wall beside the phone she was using, but she said nothing in retort.

"I'm planning a trip up there so we can speak in private," he said dispassionately. "There are a few details about your case I wish to discuss with you."

After a slight pause she answered, "Be quick about it, but before you leave, clean up Carolina."

Fuller paused at the bluntness of the order. "Yes, ma'am," he said.

51

It was confirmed that three bodies were in the burned SUV. Near darkness covered the Alabama roadside as the coroner's vans left for town.

"Anything on them... or in that thing indicating who they were?" Hansard asked hurriedly.

"Crispy critters," the technician replied through the side window. "The truck is pretty well gone, too. We'll have to peel the clothes back at the lab, but you can have the truck. We're done with it for now."

The three NCIS agents went over the burned-out hulk for an hour. All they came up with was a VIN number and small corner of a document that was in the center console.

"Rental agreement?" Childs guessed.

Leonard Monroe looked over the frame of the seat back. "That would be my guess," he added to the discussion. "No sign of anything personal in here at all. Had to be a rental and I'll bet that VIN will match with something from the airport in Atlanta."

Nodding in full agreement, Hansard pulled his phone and called in. Walt Everson leaned against their car in silence as Agent Childs approached him.

"Something bothering you, Walt?"

Everson looked at the SUV and then back to his partner.

"Those dark stains in there," he said. "Right where the bodies were. That's just weird."

"Grease fires," Childs said without having to think about it. "Once those bodies got going, the fat in them burned hotter than most of the rest in there." He stared back toward the SUV himself. "I've seen it before in Afghanistan, it leaves a mark like that."

~

From the exterior, the Charlotte Police Headquarters building was half alive with lights. Most of the offices were closed or should be, but many still offered glowing shades or even dancing silhouettes on the blinds.

Captain Marsha Hurst sat at her desk pondering a call she wanted to make. She finally punched a pre-dialed number and Jon answered from the Lucy Too.

"I was just getting ready to call you," he said shifting his body toward the window for as much privacy as he could get. "You okay?"

"I've heard some of what's going on," she told him. "You're the one I'm worried about."

"It has been busy," he tried to laugh it all off but she could make out the concern in his voice.

"Say 'Hi' to Murray," she quickly changed the subject, "I can tell where you are."

"Yeah, we're not far from you actually," he told her, "On our way down to Saint Simons. I need to check something out there."

"Oh...okay," she said and then her voice changed completely. "Hold on a second, will you. I'm in my office and there's someone at the door."

Jon could hear her answer the knock and let the housekeeper in.

"I'm in the way here at this hour," she joked at Jon. "I'll let her do her job though."

Marsha went to the corner of her new, larger office space and sat on the sofa to continue the talk. The cleaner went about her duties.

"I've heard from George," Marsha advised him. "Nava is in Dalton."

"Good," he nearly shouted. The noise of the machine he was in seemed jealous of the conversation. "It sounds like she's been through a bunch. I've got Grimes trying to get through to find out what's going on over there. Some Israelis were found in Phil's house earlier today."

"My gosh," Marsha exclaimed, "are he and Sara alright?"

"Yeah, they're fine. It was pretty much amateur hour, really."

The housekeeper moved across the room and reached up to open the venetian blind on the big window. Marsha watched for a second and then looked back down as she spoke.

"Nava seems distracted. I could barely get through to ....."

Marsha's words and thoughts were instantly cut off. A loud shattering of glass to her left, quickly followed by more to her right made no sense at first. Marsha's eyes darted toward the window.

The metal blinds heaved inward as though they were exploding and the housekeeper appeared to spew from them, folded in two. Three rounds from an unseen weapon had blasted through the window.

The lifeless body flew several feet before landing in a shower of glass from the other wall and sliding against the door.

Marsha's phone fell from her grasp as she stood. Then instinct and training took over unconsciously. She slapped the light switch throwing the room into darkness and dropped to her knees. There would be no more shadows for the shooter, not just now.

Jon's coloring faded as he called for Marsha with no response. He turned to the already concerned Murray and muttered, "We need to go to Charlotte, now."

The Lucy Too leaned hard to her left and the cowboy got on his radio, seeking clearance to change his course. He could hear Jon still yelling into the phone.

~

News from Winston-Salem reached Franklin, North Carolina, quickly. Though limited in information, Jasper Jamison understood the potential hazard the story represented.

Putney had called him from Albany, Georgia.

"What did Calvert say?" he asked without thinking.

"Dil, I haven't talked to him and don't expect to. He's too smart to expose himself while this is going on."

"I didn't hear mention of Fuller. Did you?"

"I can't talk to you right now," Jamison scolded his friend. "You're not thinking straight." The use of names on the public phone lines was becoming a problem. Jamison hung up, loudly.

What would Fuller do if discovered? Jamison thought. *Take his poison pill like a good solider or try to run?*

He stood from behind his desk and was startled by his assistant coming in to check on him. It was late. He didn't realize she was still there.

"Sir, I heard a loud noise," she explained. "Are you alright?"

Through the door Jasper could see his son waiting to come in. He didn't have time or patience for him right now.

"I'm fine, Sharon," he answered dismissively. "Sorry to keep you so late. You can go, and ask Jamie to give me about an hour. I can't talk right now I have something urgent I have to deal with."

With the door closed again, Jasper let out a huge deep breath and threw a hand up to steady himself against the window frame. He looked at that hand as though it belonged to someone else.

"I'm getting too old for this shit," he heard himself mumble.

52

A slight U-turn put Lucy Too within ten minutes of Charlotte's police headquarters. Murray called for and received emergency clearance to land on the rooftop heliport.

The two minutes since the incident seemed like an hour, Jon had calmed down after hearing the voice talking to Marsha through her dropped cell phone. He continued to listen until she finally remembered what she had been doing.

"Jon?" she asked in a controlled panic. "You still there?"

"We're just a few minutes out, literally. We're coming in."

"I'm fine," Marsha told him through the noise of a gathering crowd in the office. "Someone shot and killed a housekeeper...through my window."

The building was in sight and CPD already had three choppers in the air with lights searching everywhere.

"What floor are you on?" Jon asked her.

"What?"

"What floor is your new office on?"

"The second."

"Does it face Davison Street?"

"Yes, why?"

"Is that new parking tower completed across the street?"

Marsha knew what Jon was thinking.

"They've already got it surrounded but, no...it isn't finished yet."

Jon looked at Murray, "Can you put me on that parking deck?"

"If it'll hold," he answered. "I guess I could just kiss the surface..."

"Do that," Jon concurred. "Just let me out there."

~

Jackson Terrell stayed in his room across the street from the hotel getting all the attention. He had the news on, he'd heard about Winston-Salem only because the story involved a U.S. Senator from Wisconsin, and he was still hiding in Wisconsin. The connection between his release and this senator was never explained to him. All he knew was the "heat was on" and travel to Georgia would now be more difficult.

After checking the hall one more time, he settled down.

Might as well get some rest, he thought. As he watched yet another report on the Senator's daughter, a thought came to him.

Maybe this stuff across the street, he began to wonder, *has nothing to do with me. It could be just a coincidence.*

Either way, it wasn't worth the risk of going out there.

~

He'd just turned out the lights in the garage and locked everything up. Walking to the truck to make sure it, too, was securely locked, Warren Dawes heard the ringing.

"Damn," he spit out. Pain rippled through his injured hip as he hurried to the extent it would allow. The ringing continued as he went through the kitchen and to his bedroom where the phone was down in a dresser drawer.

"What?" he answered rudely and meant every bit of it.

"This is Jamie," the caller's voice announced.

"Young man, I know that," Dawes added. "Who the hell else is gonna call me on this?"

"Are you about ready?" Jamie asked without sounding put off in the least. "Things are beginning to happen and I need you to move on this."

"If you're in a hurry, call somebody else," Dawes barked. "What I do takes planning and that takes time. If you need it sooner, you called the wrong guy."

"We never discussed a time table," Jamie tried to calm the discussion down. "I just wondered how close you are."

"A week...maybe two," the old man told him. "Getting in that house will be a handful."

The caller took a long, hard breath and finally said he understood.

"Please..." he added. " Just let me know when you're ready."

"Working on it," Dawes told him. "I'm workin' on it."

~

Murray informed the other copters of his intentions and they backed away, giving the Lucy Too full access to the area.

"Hang on for me," he told Jon but looked over to see him pulling his bullet proof jacket on. Murray reached over to the back over Jon's helmet and pulled loose a cable. Then pushing Jon's head forward so he could reach the switch, the cowboy turned a knob from "I" to "W".

"Can you still hear me," he asked Jon.

"Yeah. What did you do?"

"Took you off intercom and put your helmet on Bluetooth. You can talk to me from down there...should you need something."

Jon nodded and grabbed the door handle. When Murray signaled, he pushed the door open and stepped down about a foot to the concrete surface. Once he was clear, Murray pulled up steeply and circled away.

With a scope mounted flashlight on his Glock, Jon searched for a ramp or stairs. The parking deck was four stories tall. He figured the shooter was probably on level two or three.

~

Marsha stood at her shattered office window looking across the street. Through the haze of darkness and the harsh street lamps she could see a small flickering light. It trailed along one edge of the under-construction parking deck. Appearing and disappearing as Jon worked his way down the yet unfinished stairs.

She tried to call him, but Murray answered.

"He didn't take his phone with him," the cowboy told her. She could hear the sounds from inside Lucy Too, and when she glanced up she could see the blue chopper circling the area.

"Just tell him I said to be careful," she asked.

"Are you okay?" Murray threw back. "That window shot was close, huh?"

"Too close, I'm afraid. The bastard killed an innocent."

"He'll find him...you know he'll find him."

"He's on level two now," Marsha gauged by the dancing light. "From the angle of the shots, I think that's where the shooter was."

~

Jon's search uncovered little at first glance. A portable generator sat next to a stack of signs for Halliburton Construction. Heavy steel door frames lay beside a concrete block tower that would be fitted with a small elevator. Other construction tools and equipment were either on pallets or in job boxes, huge metal containers scattered about on each floor.

Steel re-enforcement rods, called rebar, lay in piles and some were strewn about on the fresh poured concrete floor. A thin layer of dust coated everything, even footprints. But one set stood out.

The difference was subtle yet enough that Jon had followed it down a set of stairs to the second level. The tracks led to the floor area and then stopped. Near a pile of rebar the prints stood together and there was a circular spot in the dust in front of them.

He knelt down to open a case, Silas thought, *his gun case. Look at the top of the metal bars.*

With his light, Jon could see that something had indeed been placed atop the pile. The dust covering had been disturbed and in several places looked clean, as though rubbed.

Stay alert, Silas warned from within as Jon nodded.

53

Chief Merlot of the Shreveport Police opened a door to the room Phil Stone waited in. The retired captain spoke before he could.

"Did you get anything out of them?"

Merlot stopped as though he needed to re-gather his thoughts.

"Very little, Phil. They came in with a group of seven, through Mexico."

"Mexico?"

"That's what they tell us, six guys and one female. They've been in our country for five days."

"Did they say where the other five are?" Phil had taken to his feet as he asked.

"The only thing else they gave up was a contact phone number."

"Can I see it?"

"After we've processed it... maybe."

"I know a young man who can tell us both who has that phone," Phil pressured him.

"I understand that, Phil. But these guys are in my custody and we have to do this by the book."

"The book's gonna get people killed," the retired captain muttered aloud.

"What did you say?" Merlot stepped toward him angrily.

"You heard me and don't look so insulted. I wore that badge for too many years. I've worked with this other guy for a little over a year now. He gets it done, and only the bad guys die."

The Chief sighed and shook his head. "Do you need a ride home, Phil?" he asked respectfully.

~

The footprints in the dust of the parking deck were now obscured by a netting material that lay on the far side of the rebar. The nylon wrap, used to carry the awkward metal bars, did not hold the light dust so the prints did not show. The material had been rolled out in the direction of a sidewall.

The sidewalls, lining the exterior of each floor, were also poured concrete, but only to a height of three feet. More like a pediment wall, they were to keep vehicles from going too far.

One such wall was adjacent to Marsha's window. Jon slowly stepped in that direction looking for the prints to reappear but the concrete was clean. Nearly broom-swept clean.

The downdraft from the police helicopters, Silas told him. *It blew the dust from the tops of those short walls and the floors nearby.*

No tracks in evidence, *but still this had to be the spot*, he thought. Jon studied every inch of the ledge atop the pediment and the junction of wall to floor. At one support column, he found a scuff on the wall near the floor. Close inspection with the light detailed what he'd found.

A shoe rub, he told himself. *This is the place.*

Seeking further confirmation, he examined the column and found a damp spot, slight as it was, and a greasy spot above it.

This is where he leaned against the concrete to steady his aim, he heard himself proclaim, and Jon could feel Silas agreeing with him.

A sweaty arm there, he touched the column, *and his head just above that.*

There was no casing, no powder burn on any surface. The weapon protruded out away from the building. *Where would he go so fast?*

Jon looked behind and around the big tool boxes marked "Knaak". Then the thought hit him, *he wouldn't hide on this floor. He'd go up.*

Moving to the ramp instead of the stairs, Jon walked slowly, his eyes scanning everything. He wanted this guy. Suddenly there they were, the footprints led up the ramp way.

Another scuff showed on the new concrete. This time it was along the wall. Fabric from a coat of some kind, *or maybe a shirt*, Silas suggested.

The third floor was wide open. There were three metal boxes for tools sitting on one wall. Two were flat top, and one had an angled top. All were locked...or appeared to be.

Wheel marks in the dust indicated that the angled top box, the largest one, had moved ever so slightly. A padlock hung from a hinge as it should, but expensive tools, two fourteen-inch, portable Husqvarna concrete saws sat against the wall behind the box.

A man could fit where those saws had been, Jon figured. He looked closely at the padlock and it had been rigged to appear closed. The hasp was not locked at all.

Taking several steps away from the box, Jon looked around and calculated he was near the northeast corner of the structure.

Keying his radio, he softly told Murray, "Call the cops at street level. Tell them I heard something on level two, the far southwest end of that level. Tell 'em to hurry."

He could hear the activity below as he walked back to the metal box. Jon leaned against it and spoke. He didn't shout, there was only one person he needed to hear what he had to say.

"You have twenty seconds, and that starts now...to come out. Hands empty and reaching skyward. Otherwise I pepper this thing." Jon had his Glock .40 cal in hand but decided to exaggerate a little.

"This .50 caliber Desert Eagle," he exclaimed loudly, "can eat up that sixteen-gauge metal."

There was a creaking sound from within the box, and then the lid lifted.

~

On the bluff across from the Dalton, Georgia, mansion, a solitary figure crouched down in an odd cut-out on the side of the hill. It was as if it had blasted away, but it fit the purpose and his form.

Varkey Al Halbi found this carved out spot to be an excellent observation post during the dark hours. He'd spent the prior evening there and was still tired from that, but he'd gained little, if any, knowledge.

The burn marks on the front glass gave him cause for concern.

What kind of place is this? he thought. His binoculars showed an impact but no fracture in the window.

Lights came on at dusk and stayed on until morning. There were people inside, but they kept to the back of the house. He had checked the surroundings the day before and there was no access to the rear of the building.

It sprang out from the mountain, he recalled thinking.

With a brown tarp pulled over him, Al Halbi watched and studied. He would spend a little while longer doing this, then retreat back to his motel for the night.

54

Jon stepped back a few feet from the metal box and touched the button activating his hydraulic arm. Slowly, a man's head rose following a skinny arm that raised the box lid from within.

"Stand on up," Jon ordered, his Glock held down to his side. "Let me see that other hand."

The man wore a work uniform and a patch for Halliburton Construction. With both hands in the air, the man appeared somewhat confused. "You are no policeman," he managed in broken English.

"Nope," it was Silas who answered him. "It's much worse than that for you. Get out from there!"

After a brief look down, the man put his hands on the edge of the tool box and climbed from it.

"Who you are, then?" he asked once more.

"I'm a dear friend of the person you just tried to kill."

Assuming a position on his knees, the man acted like he understood Silas' answer.

"So, are him?" he stuttered.

Jon stepped to the box and looked inside. The shooter had obviously planned both his entry to the site and his escape. There was food and drink, a bottle for bodily waste, and even an air tank should it become too stuffy.

A case lay there as well, and he didn't have to guess what was inside. Turning back to his captive, he asked, ".308 or 7.62?"

"Busha-master," the man said with some difficulty, .308, yes."

"You sound eastern European...am I close?"

"I tell you nothing," the man tried to sound defiant. "You kill me anyways."

"It could come to that," Silas answered. "But you will talk to me first."

Looking up at Jon with fear clearly in his eyes, the man said nothing else right then.

"You think you know of me," Silas taunted. "Then you know I do not lie. I will have you talk."

The assailant's head lowered. "I am Alexander," he said. "I am of Chechnya, raised in Finland."

"Finland?" Silas smiled. "We may have a mutual friend."

"I doubt this," the man sneered but still in total fear.

"Who do you work for?" the next question came sharply and bluntly. "Time is short," Silas added, "so don't waste what we have."

"We are jihad," the man proclaimed.

"Yeah...yeah," Silas dismissed that. "Who do you work for ...here?"

"I have no name," the man said in a tone too afraid to lie. "I get letter at post office... I call number on letter. They send instructions, money, and supplies and I do job."

"You have a phone?" Silas demanded.

"No, I not carry phone."

Silas moved toward the man who twitched and reached for a pocket on his coat.

"You wanting to die right now?" Silas asked him and grabbed his hand.

"In my pocket," the man trembled. "My notes...everything I know... in little book."

"Take it out," Silas ordered and as the man handed it to him a swarm of officers stormed up the ramp with guns and lights in hand.

Slipping the notebook into his own jacket, Silas looked at the officer in charge.

"My name is Silas... I work with your Captain Hurst."

"We know who you are, sir," a plain-clothes officer responded. "Is this the only one?"

"This is Alexander," Silas told the detective. "He's your shooter. The gun is in that box."

~

The scene on Highway 11 in Northwest Alabama had the feel of a shopping center carnival. Bright lights, a whining generator, and the sound of metal rubbing against metal were at migraine levels.

Two wreckers, parked at ninety-degree angles, worked together extracting the SUV from the vine-coated ditch. Then the rubbing metal noise subsided as a winch finally secured the burned out hulk on a flatbed trailer.

Agent Childs leaned into Agent Hansard's ear. "How about they leave the lights on for a bit?" he asked the senior man in charge.

"What do you have in mind?" Hansard turned the question on him.

Childs pointed to the tire marks where the SUV left the road.

"That thing rolled over from there," he drew a line in the air with his finger to the burned out spot in the vegetation, "to there."

Hansard nodded and walked to the generator truck asking the operators to stay a while longer. "We're not through searching," he told the driver.

Childs and Everson had their coats off and began at the tire marks. They worked their way down into the dense, matted foliage. Monroe saw them from the Charger and smiled. He climbed from the car and joined in the search, starting several feet in front of the others.

Digging through kudzu wasn't easy. "I've got a metal detector at home," Monroe chirped. "This is like looking through piles of..." he stopped a moment trying to come up with a word, "it's just hard," he finally said.

Agent Hansard walked up to them.

"Just got a call from Gadsden ME's office," he said solemnly. "No ID on any of them. The DNA doesn't hit anything on file, but that's not surprising."

"They say you can't take it with you," Everson joked. "These guys did."

"Well, all is not lost," Hansard continued. "The VIN number was a rental from the airport in Birmingham," he smiled at Everson who had guessed Atlanta. "The name on the paperwork is Al Habni. A Syrian national here on a student VISA."

"Student VISA? That's bogus as hell," Childs straightened up as he spoke. "Did they pull the paperwork on that VISA?"

"Issued two weeks ago," Hansard told him. "Obviously you're right, this guy is no student. But the paperwork is clean."

Leonard Monroe had an arm almost shoulder deep into the green mass. He grunted and then froze for a second. Looking to the others he yelled out, "Hold on..." He grunted yet again and pushed his body in deeper.

Childs rushed toward Monroe, fearing the worst.

"Are you snake bit?" Childs called out, "What's wrong, man?"

Agent Monroe cut his eyes in their direction and his face beamed as bright as the search lights. With a sudden jerk, he pulled his arm from the tangle of kudzu vines and held high a prize.

"Maybe they didn't take it all with them," he proclaimed loudly and showed the cell phone he had found. "This has to be from that red truck."

"Careful with it," Hansard grinned at his partner. "There might be prints on that thing, Leonard."

55

When Jon and Marsha got hold of each other, the stares lasted longer than the hug, but it too, was substantial.

"Okay, break!" Murray called out after what seemed an eternity to him. He walked past them slapping Jon on the back.

Silas took a back seat as Jon held the police captain by both arms.

"I need to talk to Ben, right away," he said before he released Marsha from the grip. She nodded and stepped back.

Murray was now at the window. He looked across and then back at Marsha.

"You were lucky..." he said sternly. "Again..."

"I still don't believe they would do something this brazen," she said, moving toward him. She grabbed the cowboy's hand. "Thanks for being there with Jon," she added.

"I know this a weird time to ask," Murray blurted out. "But what can you tell me about Dunbar? Have you met her?"

The name went through Marsha like a knife.

"No," she spoke in a sharp tone surprising even herself. "I haven't met her." She tried to reign herself in but felt her eyes flash as she added, "Jon has."

Murray's eye's squinted though he tried not to react. He could tell something was amiss but he also knew he didn't want to pursue it. Quickly looking at Jon, he sought to change the subject.

"He's got a notebook from the shooter," Murray confessed. "He knows he has to give it up, but not till Ben takes a shot at it."

They looked over at Jon, his phone in one hand the notebook in the other. He turned pages and snapped pictures, sending them directly to

Ben. They heard him say something about a number on the first page, but couldn't be sure. Jon turned toward Murray and spoke louder.

"Did the pages all come through?" he asked into his phone.

Ben told Jon he had heard from Captain Stone in Shreveport.

"I'll call him in a few minutes," Jon told Ben. "Is everything okay there?"

"Far as we know...it's all quiet."

It all took less than a minute. Jon closed the notebook and thanked Ben... then hung up. He walked over to Marsha, holding out the small brown cover book.

"Captain Hurst," Jon said quite officially, "I have a piece of evidence I found at the scene. It may be vital to your investigation."

Marsha took it from him and smiled with a wink. "I'll see that it gets to the lab," she answered him. "Can you two stay for dinner?"

"Seeing that we're already here," Murray spoke up.

"I need to be on Saint Simon's by morning," Jon told her. "But we've got a few hours."

As they left the building heading for dinner, Jon looked at Marsha and asked her in a loud voice, "Do you know somewhere that cowboy can spend the night?"

~

Tim Spiegel felt all along the need for caution was high, but the news of the attack on Marsha sent that to a new level. After a complete inspection of all empty rooms, including the attic space, he stepped off the elevator on the second sub-level and walked up to Ben asking, "Didn't you guys say a hole had been blasted in the bank across the road?"

"Yeah," Ben grinned at the thought. "That was cool...it really was."

"Well I didn't notice it just now," Tim reported. "I went to the attic, checking around, and I looked out two of the gun ports up there."

"It's right beside the little tree over there," Daniel added to the discussion.

"I know that's what you told me," Tim went on, "but the area appeared smooth. It's dark and all, yeah, but a hole like that should show up."

Daniel stood up; he was there when Gil Gartner cut loose with the T-Rex rifle. He remembered the hole the .557 super round left in the hilltop.

"Come on," he waved at Tim. "I'll show you where it is."

The two men went back through the house and up the stairs to the attic. Daniel looked out and immediately said, "There it is."

Tim climbed up and looked. He, too, now saw the hole contrasted by the faint moonlight from the rest of the hill's surface.

Looking back at Daniel, Tim said sternly, "Nobody goes outside until I figure out who's out there."

"What?" Daniel stared back at him.

"That hole was filled in by something not twenty minutes ago. We've got company, and I don't like it."

~

It was late, but the old man could not sleep. Sitting in his wine cellar, Carlton Calvert held the mysterious bottle in his lap.

Such a simple thing, he thought quietly, *but such importance to so many people. If this got out, it would change the world.*

He had tried a special cell number for a contact he had in the Washington area, but it didn't answer.

The news all around him felt like a vise and without knowledge he was suffocating. He dialed a more direct number for his person. It answered after six rings.

"Mid-East Operations... Magill," The man said.

"Are they here?" Calvert muttered as he asked.

The man on the other end hung up immediately and in a minute's time, Calvert's phone rang from the special cell.

"Are you out of your mind?" the caller screamed at him.

"Nearly," Calvert confessed. "This is way too much drama to kill one damned man."

"It's deeper than that, you old fool. And if you come apart you'll screw up everything."

"Where are they?" Calvert demanded this time.

"They are here, but they must draw this guy out first." Magill's voice all but cracked as he went on, "There's a rumor of another here, also from Syria. What do you know of that?"

"Another?" Calvert was shocked, "Nothing unless she arranged it."

"Too much rides on this," Magill warned. "Do I need to come get the prize?"

"It's safe here," the old man sounded insulted. "Who would ever suspect?" he snapped and then added, "and if they found it, they wouldn't know what they had."

The man on the other end was quiet for nearly a minute. Then he said calmly and steadily, "They are here and working on the problem, you...on the other hand, don't want to become a problem. Am I clear?"

56

With the sun still beyond the horizon, Lucy Too headed south toward Savannah, Georgia.

"So," Murray broke up the beginning trip silence, "You two get caught up?"

The inference got him no more than a glare from Jon.

"Okay then..." the cowboy tried to follow.

"Don't go there, Murray," Jon snapped, "Not funny and not your business."

The pilot stiffened his back and thought a minute before responding to that. But then could not hold himself back any longer.

"Ain't you the cock of the walk, then?" he bristled.

Jon looked up from his notes and offered a quizzical stare.

"What are you talking about?"

"Something-something going on with you and Dunbar?" Murray just spit out.

"You've lost your mind, man!" Jon's expression and complexion flashed. "Where the hell do you get anything like that?"

Murray was happy to hear the denial, but now his troubles were even deeper.

"You...well... You wouldn't tell me anything about her and then when I asked Marsha, she blew up over the mention of her name."

"She what?" Jon stiffened his back.

"Marsha seems to think something ain't right there," Murray told him.

"What exactly did she say?"

"She didn't say anything, Jon. I just knew to back off the subject. It kinda hit a nerve, ya know?"

Jon shook his head harshly and Murray could hear him mutter under his breath, "I don't need this."

The cowboy wanted to divert the whole conversation but this subject had to be closed out.

"Well," he offered naively. "Now you know. You can just tell her she's wrong."

Jon could not believe what he was hearing.

"Sure thing, Romeo," he managed through clenched teeth. "What do you suggest I say?"

The remainder of the trip seemed to take forever, though the sun was barely up when they reached Savannah. With Saint Simon's Island just ahead, Jon spoke again.

"The Earls are going to meet us on a small curved road to the east of the secondary strip at McKinnon airport."

Murray offered no reply but Jon was quite sure he'd heard him.

"They'll be in a Buick sedan," Jon added without looking at his friend. "Cream color."

The pilot finally responded. "Roger that," he said very officially.

The evening's excitement settled into more of the same that morning. Cheryl had talked with her folks. Westy was back in Sault Ste. Marie with Rita and they planned a trip to check on the ranch again, this time with extra hands along just to be sure.

The younger Duray sat down at what was now "her" station and checked the monitors. After less than three minutes, she picked up the intercom and called for Ben.

"It happened," she said excitedly. "They did it last night."

She referred to the former police compound in Roanoke, Virginia. A hole had been dug a day before. Last night the satellite caught it being filled.

"Four," she said. "They dumped them from the bags into the hole. They just dumped them."

"Could you see what they did with the bags?" Ben excitedly asked while on his way down.

"They threw them behind a building on the property," Cheryl answered, "in like a trash pile."

Ben went straight to Tim Spiegel.

"I need to get Harold to take me to Roanoke," he announced.

"No...no," Spiegel objected. "It's too dangerous to even go outside right now."

"We can leave out the back door. No one will know," Ben tried to assure him.

"Something happens to you and Jon will have my head."

"Those bags most likely have DNA inside them," Ben pressed in. "We can't get to the bodies without them knowing, but the idiots gave us what we need in their trash pile. We just have to get to it before it's hauled away."

The boy made perfect sense and Spiegel knew it.

"I'll go," he said.

"Tim, sir," Ben sounded as respectful as he could muster. "You're needed here."

~

Jon was on the phone with Jerome Grimes when Lucy Too touched down at St. Simon's Island. The call had just come through.

Jon waved at his old friend and put up one finger, asking for a minute. "Director, I need to go," he said into the phone, "what do you have?"

"I've got three dead Syrian assassins in Alabama," he started tersely. "There's more if you give me time to explain."

"I'm sorry, sir," Jon apologized, "What happened?"

"What happened isn't important right now...what is important, is how they got here."

"By boat?" Jon guessed.

"Huh?" Grimes was stumped by that. "No...they flew in with a CIA escort. Some flack named Magill. We got a leak in the chain somewhere."

"Why Alabama?"

"Appears they were going for Cody Arnold," Grimes said like there was nothing to it. "Best guess is they were really after you...just wanted to use him to draw you out."

"Sir, there's a whole lot more going on and I have people waiting for me. I've got a lead here on another Syrian...he did come by boat, I believe. I just need to prove it."

"I've heard about the Charlotte thing," Grimes told him. "Glad she's okay."

"Thank you...I'll call you as soon as I can talk. We've got to figure this out. They are literally everywhere."

"Be careful," Grimes signed off. "Talk to you later."

57

Murray had walked over and introduced himself to the Earls. They were having a great time getting acquainted.

"You're from Texas, right?" Patricia Earl asked him. "How did you and Jon meet?"

As he got off the phone and walked closer, Jon heard Murray's answer.

"We met through my father," the cowboy told them.

The comment stunned Jon but he said nothing.

"Oh, a social thing?" Patricia followed.

"No...they had a business transaction some time back."

"I see," Calvin smiled, "must have been a good one, huh?"

Murray twisted his head toward Jon for a second, then looked back at their hosts. "It worked out best for all concerned," he told them.

"Who's hungry," Pat asked them. "We can all go to Dressner's. This early, we shouldn't have any trouble getting in."

"Can we talk there?" Jon asked.

Calvin looked at him with a blankish stare.

"I think so," he grinned. "It's pretty tame."

The discussion between Spiegel and Ben brought the Virginia situation to Daniel's attention. Roanoke had not started as part of the larger case, but what the retired reporter heard intrigued him.

The Salem community, as a whole, had undergone a transformation. The gang's influence and seeming control did not happen in a vacuum.

A comment Daniel overheard about Calvert Publishing struck a chord and now his instincts pushed him to look deeper.

A call to Ed White was in order.

"Yeah," his old friend and mentor answered. He quickly found his records in a file cabinet under "open" investigations. "The Calvert thing happened really damned fast," White began.

"The Calvert thing?" Daniel didn't understand.

"The paper in Salem was the first to go," the editor explained. "But then it spread to the main paper. Then the investigation just ceased."

"What investigation, boss?"

White took his file to his desk and sat down, "Give me a second here," he muttered loudly. "I remember this, but not all the details."

Daniel did a computer search on the Calvert organization as he waited.

"Goodness," he said out loud. "I knew they were big, but I really lost track of what all they were in to."

"Yeah...you were up here," White told him. "The New York rag ran everything up our way. Calvert's bunch dealt with the south and west. I think he was into TV and radio, too."

"Oh, yeah," Ben read off the monitor, "The company bought up stations and formats changed overnight."

"Okay...okay, here it is," the old editor had found what he sought. "A reporter was looking into a connection to some local power broker in Roanoke."

"A connection to Calvert?" Daniel asked.

"Indirectly, but yes."

"Who is the reporter?"

"Gail Monahan," White read from his notes. "That's the thing about this case...she disappeared completely."

"Well they had to look for her," Daniel threw in. "What ever happened?"

"Nothing," Ed sounded disgusted at this point. "The changes went through shortly after and the papers lost 'interest' in her case."

Daniel could hear paper being turned rapidly through the phone.

"They just quit saying anything about her...nothing! It's like suddenly, she never existed."

"Hang on a second, will you, Ed?" Daniel pulled his phone from his ear and stood. "Ben," he called out.

The young wizard and Tim Spiegel were still talking about the mission to Virginia.

"Whatever you decide," he cautioned, "Be extra careful. Those bodies could be more significant than you realize."

~

When the phone rang, Marsha expected it to be Jon. It was not.

"Captain Hurst?" the gruff female voice asked.

"Yes," Marsha answered thinking she recognized the tone.

"Sharon Swanson...of Kentucky."

"Colonel! Why yes, ma'am," Marsha nearly stuttered, "how are you?"

"My question is to you, young lady," came her response. "When I saw the report on the wire I was concerned. Then your name came across. Are you alright? Has Jon been there?"

"Oh yes, I'm fine and Jon found the guy hiding in a tool box. A big tool box," she added laughing at herself.

"Understood," Swanson was still being very official. "The report didn't mention Jon...they never do. But it did say something about a man with ties to Finland."

"He does, so he claims. He's a Chechen national actually."

"Well, you may have heard, we have a guest here at the Ashland Facility. Jon and Murray helped lead us to him a while back. The name is Renio Petteri."

"The guy from Minnesota?" Marsha guessed. "The one involved in Cheryl's kidnapping case?"

"The same," Swanson confirmed. "He's still here in my state, will be for some time. Anyway, I went to see him to ask if he knew anything about your situation."

"Thank you," the new captain said graciously. "Did you find out anything?"

"At first he didn't seem interested in talkin' or sharing much. Then I reminded him of a friend I knew who could come up and ask him. I told him that friend asked about how his elbows were coming along?"

"What?"

"Anyway," Sharon remembered that Jon didn't talk about those things. Tilting her head back, the Colonel continued, "he opened up like a school girl's diary. Your boy 'Alexander' used to work for the Chicago group run by that mayor. Petteri doesn't know his real name, but he and a few others are now freelancing. Hits, muggings, whatever will earn them a buck."

"So he was tied to the kidnapping bunch?"

"Loosely, yeah... A part of that organization. Which...by the way, is pretty well done for, from what I'm hearing around here."

58

The sun began to light up St. Simon's Island. After the eggs and French toast, a third pot of coffee opened up the conversation. Jon asked about the trouble Murray had with getting anything from the local cops.

"That's fairly new," Calvin explained. "Many of them are quitting when they find another job. This district's political change has caused a lack of trust. It's gotten worse in the last year."

"Well," Murray jumped in, "that Medical Examiner was nice enough."

"You must have talked to Jacobs," Calvin guessed through a sip of coffee.

The cowboy nodded and Patricia Earl spoke up, "He's one of the few left with any nerve," she said flatly. "Everything is all hush–hush now."

"Where were these folks actually killed?" Jon asked.

"It looks like Eastling was killed on his boat. Suzanne and Styles were found in Styles' office," Calvin explained.

"Can we get into the office?"

"No, not in daylight...They keep it locked down and guarded."

"How about the boat?"

The old college friend grinned and glanced at his wife before speaking. "I can get you on the boat," he bragged.

"Cal?" Pat Earl elbowed him. "Are you sure that's safe?"

"No," he mumbled to his wife, "but it'll be fun."

~

A knock on his door interrupted the first pleasant morning the young congressman had that week.

"Yes?" he called out sitting a bit straighter in his chair.

The door opened and a man mostly pushed past his assistant, entering the office saying, "He'll see me."

Travis Gilbert stood angrily, "I don't know who you are, sir. How did you get in this building?"

The stranger flashed a card that only Gilbert could see. It was a representation of the Star of Numbers pictures.

"We come and go pretty much as we please around here," the man bragged.

Gilbert looked at the card and raised his hand toward the assistant.

"It's alright, Charles," he said, "I'll talk with him a minute."

The door closed and the man helped himself to a seat in front of the desk.

"What do you think you're doing?" Gilbert challenged.

"We need you to do something."

"A call wouldn't be enough?"

"Naw," the man smirked at him. "We felt you needed a visit to see we were serious."

The congressman sat down and glared at his guest.

"We want you to call a friend of yours up here for an important talk."

"Who?" Gilbert asked.

"George Vincent of Georgia."

"What do you want with Mr. Vincent?"

"We'll worry about that, not you."

The congressman picked up his desk phone. A move that brought the guest to his feet with an arm extended and a finger pointed.

"You don't want to do that," he said, "I assure you. We have people outside your father's home right now."

Though putting the phone down, Gilbert remained defiant.

"What do you want with Mr. Vincent?" he repeated himself slowly and with sincere determination.

The stranger at first appeared confused but quickly sat back down.

"Vincent has a friend that has been getting in our way too much," the man explained. "With George as our guest, this friend of his will surely come looking for him."

"You're gonna kidnap George Vincent?" Gilbert was smiling sarcastically. The unwanted guest didn't know quite how to respond, and he did not.

"I tell you what, my friend," Gilbert said confidently. "I'll play along if you're sure you want to try this. But you're signing your own death warrant, I can tell you that."

The man leaned back in the chair. "We'll take that chance," he said.

~

The lawyer Fuller's trek through Oxford Prison's security checkpoints seemed to go faster than usual this morning. Perhaps it was because he felt no hurry to get where he was going.

His client sat impatiently waiting in the private conference room, visible through heavy glass but supposedly sound proof. A loud creaking sound from the door announced his arrival. Barrett glared at him before any words were exchanged. At the door's closing, Fuller tried a greeting. "Good morning," he said and sat across the small table from his client.

"Why is all this happening?" she belched out as one word. "This is crazy. You can't kill one man?"

"Would you watch what you say, please?" Fuller attempted to stay calm. "I'm sure you're speaking rhetorically when you talk like that."

"Aw, screw you, ya wimp," she lashed at him. "They can't use anything they get from in here if they are listening."

"The few misfires are unfortunate," the lawyer tried to calm the discussion. "But we have other avenues that are still being worked."

"You and your damned flowery words," she spit. Literally, she spit on the table as she spoke.

"I talked to Magill this morning," Fuller told her. "His guests are enroute to their assignment."

"Which guests? The ones he brought with him or the Israelis?"

"I'm talking about those he brought in. The others are underground and I can't reach them."

"You can't reach them," she shook her head. "What is the old man doing? Is the prize still safe?"

"Yes...yes, it's safe. But as he says, what could they do with it if they had it?"

"It could be figured out, you fool."

"I suppose," Fuller admitted. "But in the time that took, we could have everything moved."

"It took nine months to get it all there the first time. I don't want anything to happen to those bottles. If it does, we're done; the whole idea of what we've worked for is done."

"Why the drama," he shot back. "You're just letting everything out of the bag this morning. This isn't like you. Get it together...I'm warning you."

Barrett leaned back and stared at her guest. "You're excused, counselor," she mocked him. "Get out of here."

59

The drive through St. Simon's Island led to Sea Island Road where they turned toward the ocean and the still climbing sun. Calvin Earl, the driver, lowered his visor while everyone else in the car looked to the sides avoiding the glare.

Low growth vegetation and tall grass lined the roadway. There was nothing big enough to block the view that went for miles.

Just before the bridge over the Black Bank River, Calvin turned right onto a dirt road along the riverbank. The ride became dusty and much rougher, but he plowed on.

"You were studying pharmacy back in school weren't you?" he asked Jon.

"Yeah," Jon smiled, "that's a pretty good memory, there." A harsh bump caused him to grab the seat back, but he grinned and went on, "I don't do much with it these days."

"He can when he gets mad," Murray popped off while still looking out a side window.

The others silently let that moment pass and then Calvin spoke up again, "Is that where you made your money? The drug business?"

"No...actually it was in computer technology."

"Huh," Calvin shrugged as he slowed down through the dusty bumps in the scratched out road. "I never learned how to do Facebook. I mean, I can do what I need to for my business, ya know? But I just never got that into it."

"Whatever happened to Facebook anyway?" Jon asked him. "I never did that either."

"From what I hear...when folks found out what they were doing with the information...you know, in collusion with the government of that time, well...everybody started loading up their 'profiles' with bogus stuff."

"Aw," Jon managed to throw in, "Pretty smart."

"That was the end of that," Calvin concluded. "Okay...we're just about there."

~

Spiegel made one demand before going along with Ben's plan for Roanoke. He wanted time to scout the area across the road, the carved out spot that seemed to disappear on him the night before.

He took Jon's old Jeep through the tunnel and looped around the backside of the mountain. Turning down Highway 71, he passed the mansion and took the right turn onto the ridge across from it.

Most of the tracks had been obscured but there were enough signs left to know someone had definitely been there.

"We've had company, alright," Tim said into his radio. "Looks like one man." He walked away from the edge for several yards and found more confirmation of his fears.

"This is where he quit wiping his tracks," he told them and followed the footprints to another ramp area. Tire tracks were in clear view.

"What are you going to do?" Ben asked.

Spiegel looked down at the marks his own boots were leaving. He smiled and turned back to the Jeep.

"Nothing," he said confidently. "I'll just let him know I've been here too. He can't get to us; by now he knows that."

"You coming in?" Ben pressed.

"Yeah."

~

Lori Seay was in the upper hallway as Doris Shaw left the guest room.

"How is she doing?" Lori asked softly.

Doris pulled the door closed and with a puzzled expression, waited until she was away from the door to answer, "I don't know."

Together they walked to the stairs where Doris told the reporter's wife, "Nava was clearly on a cell phone when I went in just now. She hung up right away and seemed nervous about it."

Lori tread deliberately down the next couple of steps, staring down at them while forming her next question.

"How well do you know her?"

"This is the first time I've met her," Doris reminded her, "just like most of us here. She was with Marsha and Jon at Murray's place during the government mess. Daniel was there! What did he say about her?"

"Not a whole lot; back then," Lori recalled. "She was hurt and unconscious just about the entire time. Marsha stayed with her and the other Israelis."

"I'll keep an eye on her," Doris proclaimed as they reached the main floor. Lori grabbed her friend's arm, nearly spinning her in her tracks.

"Do you have a gun?" she whispered.

"A gun?"

"Wouldn't hurt," Lori reached out and grabbed both of Doris' hands. "I don't have a good feeling about all this," she continued in low tones. "I'm sorry, but I don't."

Realizing she agreed with Lori, Doris nodded, then looked straight at her.

"I know where George keeps his," she answered reluctantly. Then before Lori could ask, she added, "And, yes...I do know how to use it."

~

They left the Buick along the side of the dirt road and walked toward a craft tied to a tree along the river. Calvin Earl pointed at the thirty-one foot Camper & Nicholson floating slightly bow away from the shoreline.

"Eastling has a dock further up, near the mouth of the river," Calvin explained, "but the cops pulled it back in here thinking they'd hide it from curiosity seekers."

Jon and Murray pulled the rope drawing the sailboats' stern closer to the bank and then jumped aboard. Calvin followed while Pat stayed on the bank, keeping watch down the river.

"The body was right here," Earl pointed at the blood stains. "He pretty much 'bled out' as they say."

Jon dropped to look at the small steps leading into the cabin area. He rubbed the nosing with his hand and then pointed to a slight reddish smudge at the bottom of the steps.

"He dragged the man up here to kill him," Jon said, explaining what he saw. "There's a rub spot on the steps, each one. And then the killer went back into the cabin for something." He pointed again to the smudge.

"What is that?" Calvin asked.

"A bloody footprint," Jon declared, "Left by a very smooth object."

Though the comment made little sense to anyone else at that moment, no one challenged it.

The small craft's interior cabin was tight and efficient. Space was at a premium. Everything had a place and many of those were obscure. Pictures on the wall were doors to storage. Even the trim along the staircase could move, exposing a place to keep rope, a sexton or whatever would fit.

Jon stood in the middle and slowly scanned the area with his eyes while Murray checked every obvious nook and cranny.

You're here, Jon thought quietly, *and you know someone has boarded your boat. Do you have a gun hidden?* His eyes sought a spot large enough. *Or*, his thoughts changed rapidly, *do you think of hiding something?*

Murray rose up, smiling ear to ear. From under one drawer, beside the built-in sofa, he'd found something. It was actually taped to the bottom side of the drawer. A small note bearing what appeared to be a phone number. Murray showed his find to Jon who quickly recognized the area code.

"That's a D.C. number," he said. He wanted to say he recognized it but held that to himself. "What else is here?" he did add.

The cowboy shrugged and continued looking. Jon went back to his silent, visual search.

Calvin Earl stepped out onto the stern deck and shrugged his shoulders at his wife. She nodded back in understanding.

Jon's attention suddenly went to a small mounting on the wall near the entrance from above deck. The brass instrument cluster was three pieces on a single backboard. Thermometer, clock and humidity gauge, all side by side on the shiny plate. He pressed his face close to it without touching. While the unit, as a whole, showed no sign of having been moved, the clock portion was askew slightly. That had left a minor rub on the back plate.

Jon twisted the clock gently and it moved to the right. Swinging up, the clock exposed a tiny hollow cut-out in the wall. With his fingers, Jon reached into the dark void. He twisted his wrist and pulled out a three inch by five inch notebook-style day planner.

He sat on the sofa without saying a word, flipping through the pages.

"What have you got?" Murray asked.

"Not much here," Jon told him as Calvin returned to the boat's cabin, "Looks like this was used for limited items only."

Past the alphabetical listing area, Jon found the calendar section. It too, was mostly blank.

Then he found what they were searching for.

"Here's a listing for the day of the killings," he announced, "says he was meeting the reporter and her boss to discuss a story."

"Where?" Calvin asked.

"The initials 'r' and 'd' and the numeral '20' is all that's with it."

Earl smiled at them, "Hell, that's easy," he said. "River dock, eight o'clock PM. He met them right here."

"You said their bodies were found back at the editor's offices." Jon recalled.

"Yeah, Glesser and Styles were. But that doesn't mean they didn't come here first," Calvin was rolling now. "That's how they got caught up in this. That's how they got killed!"

Jon left the cabin area, saying, "You told us the dock is back near the mouth of this river."

"Yeah," Calvin confirmed.

"Is the dock on this side or across?"

"That side is way too narrow," Earl told him, "His dock was on this bank."

Carefully negotiating the catwalk to the bow, Jon lay down and took out a tiny flashlight. He leaned to the right side of the bow asking, "He would have docked to port, right?"

"Yeah," Calvin called to him from the rear.

Jon searched the bow with his tiny beam of light. A heavy scratch, almost through the outer hull, appeared above the water line.

"He hit it hard coming in," he reported, "What injuries to his body were there...other than the obvious decapitation."

"I heard he had two broken ribs and his right arm was broken in three places."

Jon stood and nodded his pleasure with the response. "That could be the answer," he said returning to the stern.

Murray emerged from the cabin. He had been looking at a rubber wet suit, folded neatly near the bed in the rear portion of the cabin.

"Was Eastling a diver?" he asked from nowhere.

Earl turned to him, confused at first by the subject change, but then looked down into the cabin area. "Not that I'm aware of, no," he said.

Murray went back and retrieved the suit.

"Can we find DNA inside this thing?" he asked.

Jon smiled and reached for the arm and its attached glove.

"Maybe even better than that," he said. Carefully cutting the index finger from the glove, he turned the rubber inside-out. "I need some powder," he said, "like talc or even flour."

There was none to be found on the boat but when Pat asked what they were looking for, she dug into her purse and pulled out a tiny compact.

"It's loose powder and a brush," she offered sheepishly.

Jon dabbed the brush into the powder, then held it above the rubber fingertip. Taps on the tiny brush handle dropped the powder onto the surface. The print began to appear.

"Nice," Jon muttered, nodding his head. He then took a picture with his cell phone and sent it directly to Ben's phone.

"Thanks, Patty," Jon added.

"Let hear it for Avon," she grinned back at him.

60

The Floyd County District Attorney reacted smoothly answering his personal cell phone, but George Vincent's demeanor quickly changed.

"I need to go to the office," he announced.

Ben was monitoring Tim's excursion on two screens. He looked to his mom's fiancé' and said, "Tim doesn't want anyone to leave right now. It's too dangerous."

"I've had a call from Carl Gilbert," George explained with urgency distorting his face. "I have to call him back, on my secure line."

Ben looked back at the monitors. Agent Tim Spiegel was nearing the top of the hill. Everything was quiet.

"Do you know the number assigned to that secure line?" he asked George.

After considering the question for a few seconds, the DA had to respond, "Never thought about it. I just call out on the damn thing."

"Does Gil know where it is?"

"Yeah, I'm sure he does."

"I'll call him and ask him to turn it on. I'll clone it for you from here."

"You'll what?"

"You'll be able to use it from right here...same security, same phone...just from here."

Without totally understanding the process, George had no doubt that Ben could do what he'd said. "I need to call him as soon as possible," he affirmed.

~

Jackson Terrell had studied maps of the area. He arrived in town by bus and rented a mountain style motorbike. He approached the house from the far side, high above the roof's ridge. The view of the house, the road and the area was excellent from there.

One of the first things he noticed was the man across the road.

~

Three days in a row, Phil Stone came to the jail. He would sit outside the cell block and speak to the guards loud enough for the prisoners to hear his voice.

"Anything new out 'em today," he would start with.

The guards all thanked him but said they had lunch.

Nodding, the retired captain would take a seat and begin unwrapping his brown bag.

"Got an extra roast beef in here today," he said. "You guys hungry?"

The guards answered they were fine, but everyone knew he was trying to tease the Israelis in the cells.

With his iced tea jar on one side of the chair, an open bag of Fritos on the other and his sandwich in his lap, Phil didn't even attempt to stand when Chief Merlot opened the door.

"Phil," the man said seriously. "I have something for you."

~

Cheryl watched the monitors until Tim came back in. Ben had received the fingerprint from Jon and was running that against the files he had.

Local crime and government lists came up empty, but then the Interpol registry stopped with a ninety-eight percent match.

"Jon," Ben said when his call was answered. "Why didn't you tell me right away? I'd have run Interpol first."

"So, it's our guy?" Jon replied.

"Varkey Al Halbi," Ben confirmed, "The Syrian."

"Okay," Jon was on to another level and his voice showed the change. "This is our boy and we know he was in Lexington, that's where he killed Langhorn."

"I'm with you," Ben pretended.

"How did he know to go there? He was after him because he thought Langhorn knew about the entire operation." Jon was speaking very fast now. "He has a contact at CIA!"

"We figured that from the start, didn't we?" Ben asked before thinking.

Jon shot back, "One high enough to know what's going on."

It made sense but was still a wild accusation in Ben's mind.

"I'll check into it," he told Jon anyway

Jon thanked him and folded his phone. After a quick glance at Murray, he winked and then looked over to Calvin.

"I know you said it would be tough," he implored him. "But I really need to get into that office... where the others were found."

Calvin Earl started walking to his Buick. He hung his head in feigned frustration.

"You always were a pain in the ass," he laughed.

~

Chief Merlot took Phil into a private office.

"This must be something big," Phil said in jest.

His old friend turned to him, nearly pale.

"That phone number these Israelis had on them," he said as his tone filled with concern. "I don't know what we're in for with this."

"What?" Phil pushed.

"The number goes to CIA Headquarters in Virginia."

As the surprise sank in, Phil stood in silence for a few seconds. The scope of this attack on him had just changed dramatically.

"Look," he finally said. "I'm sorry to have gotten you guys mixed up in this. It does sound like it's big."

"That friend of yours?" the chief asked.

"Well," Phil explained. "It's not so much his fault as it is so many bad guys that think he's on to them. He scares the hell out of 'em."

"The CIA, too, Phil?"

Nodding and looking mostly at his feet, Phil answered, "Yeah...it would appear so."

61

Afternoon had drawn to a close in Roanoke. Darkness set in and Walter Frazier had not yet turned on a light. Questions piled up with no answers as to why this stranger in the black uniform was snooping around in his business. One of his young gang members was dead and his hiding spot was now compromised.

He had ordered steps to move and conceal the damning evidence but would that be enough? Frazier was used to being in charge and having all the answers. This was suddenly different. He was lost for the first time in his life. Making matters worse, he did not know what to do.

He'd already refused three calls from his friend, Congressman Herschel Briar. Sitting in a tiny office at the former police academy complex, Walter Frazier searched the internet, hoping to find a story that threw light on what was happening. As the sun fell behind some trees across the street from his building, he broke down and called a contact in Washington.

The voice answering was not pleased to hear from him. "This is not a good time, man," it said bluntly. "My boss is dead and I don't know why."

"Davis is dead?" Frazier was both shocked and stunned.

"Where have you been? Under some rock, some place?"

"When?"

"Just a few days ago, "the voice told him. " He was wacked, man. You need to stay off the grid until you're contacted. Not knowing anything is a good place to be right now."

A lump formed in Frazier's throat. He was about to say something about this strange man in black snooping around, but his experience saved him from it. After a quick look to the wall on his left, viewing the picture of the star formed by numbers, his mind warned him, *they'd kill me just to seal off the link.*

"I'll stay low," he told the man instead.

Frazier stood and walked to a rear window and looked up. The noise of a small jet roared overhead, catching his attention for the moment. He didn't know it...but that jet noise was Harold Foster's G5 on approach to Roanoke's Woodrum Field at the regional airport.

~

Hours passed and Jackson Terrell turned his collar up against the Georgia wind as he watched and made notes. From his vantage point overlooking the large house he could see the road and the hilltop across from the house. What activity there was came in small doses. This business required patience and he was good at it. Time spent in prison didn't hurt the ability either and it had paid off to some degree.

The movements across the road were both interesting and concerning to him. From his vantage point above the roofline of the house he had watched a man snoop around and then leave. That had been several hours ago, really. The only other activity he'd made note of was one car that drove by from the lower end. A green Jaguar went by and left the area, he wasn't sure where it had come from but assumed some other large homes lay beyond this one.

The cliff across the street was interesting and once things settled down it would make another good location to watch from. Information was what he sought, lots of it. If he was to be successful, he would need a plan that addressed all possibilities. Watching and learning were the best ways to do that.

Terrell started to stand as the sun was leaving the sky, but its glow lengthened the shadows of folks who he'd not noticed before.

Three, no four, were stationary and to the west, near the main highway. Another singular shadow extended from its maker along the southeastern edge of the roadway. This one was moving.

Terrell knelt back down, watching the lone figure approaching the cliff. The others didn't seem to be aware of him, or maybe he thought, *they are all together*.

From his build, this wasn't the man from earlier today. This one wasn't as tall nor as broad shouldered. When the solo shadow reached the edge of the cliff, he stopped dead, frozen in his tracks. He was looking at a dug out spot on the edge and something there appeared to upset him.

The other man had looked at that spot, too, he remembered. Terrell looked over to the other shadows. They were all motionless, but that didn't help how Terrell was feeling.

This job is getting crowded, he thought. *I don't like crowds.*

Two rental cars awaited Ben and Harold at the Roanoke airfield. The nearly matching, small SUVs were parked next to a service hangar.

"Couldn't make up your mind?" Harold asked facetiously.

Ben looked up from his task and out a side window.

"Good," Harold heard him say, "They're here."

As the plane's engines wound down, Harold turned off switches and unlocked his belts. He hollered back, over one shoulder, through the open cockpit door, "You about ready to tell me what you've been working on back there?"

"A diversion," Ben answered.

"Okay. So I suppose this involves me?"

Ben stood and turned toward the approaching pilot.

"I'm sorry," he started, "I didn't mean to assume you…"

"Don't apologize," Harold laughed and cut him off. "It beats sitting here, waiting. What do I get to do?"

Ben pulled his device out from between two seats. It had been all in one large duffle bag when they loaded the plane. The pilot noticed it, but had his own list of "to do" items and didn't say anything.

The young man had worked on his contraption through the flight.

"It's basically a noise maker," he told Harold, "A really loud one."

Ben explained the three foot long board with the speakers and four high intensity LED lights.

"You can turn it on here, but delay that by five minutes with this timer."

"So I can get out of there before it goes off," Harold guessed.

"Yeah," Ben said slowly. His mind hoping fiercely this would work.

They loaded the contraption into one of the vehicles and Harold excused himself, going back into the plane.

"Just need to get one thing," he said with no further explanation.

The Buick pulled up a block short of a three story building on Frederica Street. Several local police units were still parked near-by.

"First time I've seen them here past dark," Calvin Earl commented. "This isn't good."

"Which office is it?" Jon asked.

"You see those lights on the second floor, right there?" Calvin answered while pointing, "it's just above that one."

"Kinda small for a newspaper," Murray threw in.

"It's just Styles' office on the island," Pat told them. "The main paper is in Brunswick, this was his local bureau."

Jon had stepped from the car and walked back down the street, looking and figuring. Calvin started to follow him but Murray grabbed his arm, "Leave him to it," the cowboy suggested. "He'll ask questions when he sorts it all out."

"So... y'all still plan to go in there tonight?" Earl asked.

"Oh, yeah," Murray said confidently. "It's looking like it."

Now "in charge" of the monitors on the second floor workshop, Cheryl Duray nearly jumped when something actually showed up.

"Mr. Spiegel," she called over the intercom, "there's something you need to see."

When the elevator doors opened, Agent Tim Spiegel was running to the desk.

"He's back, huh?" he asked.

"Somebody was," Cheryl said. "He looked at that dug-out spot and stood up, looked around and left."

"I must have left a mark or something," Spiegel muttered, "Scared him off, probably."

"Wait, wait," Cheryl pointed to another screen that watched over another section of the hilltop. "Do you see that?"

He stared at the screen, which was mostly black anyway in the dark and saw what appeared to be figures moving slightly.

"Is that two or three?" he asked Cheryl.

"Could be more," she responded in a serious tone. "I thought I saw, maybe four."

The intercom came alive as Doris whispered from upstairs, "Somebody...pick-up down there."

Tim grabbed the handset, "Yes, ma'am, this is Spiegel."

"I don't know what she's up to, but Nava is in the bathroom and on her phone. She speaking in Hebrew or something," Doris sounded very disgusted and concerned, "whatever it is, I don't like it."

62

With the sound bar loaded in Harold's SUV, they both drove towards Salem and the former police academy compound. Ben pulled to the side of the road just before a right hand turn that lay ahead.

"Around that corner, it's five blocks straight in," Ben said over their radio.

Harold keyed his microphone. The old style two-way radio was out of fashion, but less likely to be monitored.

"Do I go up two more blocks or three?" he asked.

"By the map, it's two," Ben advised. "That should put you on Central Avenue. It's a dead-end past the complex so I'd turn around first."

"Thanks for that," Harold said. "I'll do that. Give me five minutes to get into position, okay?"

As Ben keyed his microphone to respond, Harold's vehicle came around him and headed down the street.

"See you back at the hangar," Ben told him.

Turning right on Bowman, Ben followed it to the dead-end. An activity field lay to his left and an old basketball court to the right.

Where's the trash dump? he thought in near panic. *The map showed it right here.*

He backed up and noticed a small cut-through going toward the main buildings. Turning left, with his headlights now off, Ben slowly proceeded through the dark. The sound of Harold's voice over the radio all but jerked him from his skin.

"In position," the voice said.

Ben considered answering with "wait," but he saw the pile of rubbish just ahead. It lay beside the main building along an unmarked alley.

"Good. Go for it," he replied and pulled alongside the trash.

"In five," Harold told him.

Jonathan Crane suddenly spun on his heel and briskly walked back to the Buick.

"Where can I get a coat and tie?" he asked.

"Now?" Calvin gestured with both hands.

"Yeah...right away."

Looking around at all the closed shops on the street, their host looked to his wife and offered, "At this hour, our house, I guess."

"Make it business appropriate," Jon directed while Murray stifled a grin, "Blue or Black, no gray."

With eyes bugged out in non-belief, Calvin Earl climbed into his car.

"Are you coming?" he asked as Jon stood where he'd been.

"No," was the blunt reply. "I'll be right around here. I want to keep an eye on things." Earl's head still shook as he started the car.

Watching the Buick drive away, Jon reached for Murray, tapping his arm.

"Would you go back to Lucy and get me some stuff from my bag?" he asked.

"You're not going to tell me what you're thinking are you?" Murray said while raising his arm for a taxi.

"I'll need the small black tote and a Gold Badge...any of them that look official. You know what? Just rent a black car and bring everything."

The cab stopped. Murray climbed in and Jon walked away, his eyes glued to the building in front of him.

~

Tim Spiegel placed a call to Washington, D.C. It rang in the Director's office of NCIS.

"Grimes," the voice answered gruffly.

"You're in the office kinda late boss," his agent said.

"Spiegel, is that you?"

"Boss, I need to know something, damned quick."

"Okay?"

"Have you talked with your Mossad friend, that guy that helped us some time back?"

"I can't reach him, Tim," Grimes admitted. "They say he's in the hospital but I can't get any confirmation. Reiss is 'unavailable' they tell me."

"Well, we've got Nava Golan here at Jon's."

"Are you sure that's wise?" the boss asked.

"Well not now I'm not. Seemed like the thing to do at the time."

"She and Reiss are very close," Grimes said. "And Harel is like her father. I'm afraid she's been sent here by someone, but I can't figure it out."

"Here's my situation," Spiegel told him. "They have two Israelis in custody in Shreveport that tell us there are five others who came with them, four men and a female. Nava is in here with us and we have four bogies across the road playing hide and seek."

"That's not too hard to figure out," Grimes mumbled into the phone.

"Yeah, I didn't think so...I just don't want to possibly hurt her before I talked with you."

"Go easy with her, if you can. The four bogies are probably hostile, but I still think she could be under duress."

Harold drove to the end of Central Avenue which did, in fact, dead-end. He turned around, pulled forward, and finally parked near a frame house on the right.

Lights left on in the main complex building to his left showed movement inside. He sat still for a minute, and then opened the driver's door. He had not thought of it before, but the dome light inside did not come on.

Ben pulled the fuse, he bet to himself. *How 'bout that!*

The rear door likewise, did not illuminate anything. Harold grabbed the device and lifted it from the vehicle.

A large, actually oversized Azalea plant stood by its lonesome in the frame house's yard. Harold placed his diversion unit just under the plant and set the timer. As it began to quietly tick, he grabbed his microphone and said, "Less than five...I'm gone."

Ben could hear the SUV driving away. Other than that, there was silence.

With two minutes to go before the noise, Ben pulled his car forward and turned onto the alleyway. Parking just beyond the trash pile, he waited.

The lights flashed first, seeming to penetrate the building and all around it. Then, before his mind could decide what the lights were, the sounds kicked in. Ear smashing, metal to metal grinding at such high decibels it was painful. Like a collision that wouldn't end or a plane crashing into a steel structure.

Ben jumped out and rushed to the trash heap. Two of the bags he sought stuck out from about middle of the pile. He grabbed those and pulled them free.

The smell was incredible, but he held his breath and labored on, digging with gloved hands through the junk and debris.

Another bag was uncovered and he dragged it out. Rolling this one up, Ben put the first three into another large bag he had brought for the purpose. It would hold down the smell, he hoped.

Returning to the trash, he dug deeper, finding the last one more by feel than sight. As he stood, his worst case scenario came to life. A man came out from a back door and froze when he saw Ben.

Throwing the last bag into the SUV, Ben jumped into the running vehicle and screamed away. The man had gone back inside, trying to be heard over the loud noise from across the street.

Three blocks through the alley, Ben looked to his right and saw nothing. His speed was curtailed by the narrow, rough, driveway he had to negotiate and then as he got where the main road was in sight, he saw the headlights coming up beside him.

The car was on the main road, Central Avenue, and traveling at a much greater speed. Ben reached the cross street and pulled the steering wheel hard to the left, flooring the accelerator at the same time.

His right side tires lifted but he managed to stay on the road. Within a block he noticed another SUV parked on the right side. It was Harold.

He stood outside his truck, his hands wrapped around a handgun. As the chase vehicle roared around the corner and came that way, Harold leveled his arms at the headlights.

Squeeze, he remembered, *don't pull.*

And squeeze he did. Two at first, then another shot, erupted from the gun. The rounds flashed against the metal of the on-coming car and the asphalt in front of it. A tire blew, loudly...and the sound of steel rim against the road screamed while Harold continued to squeeze the trigger.

Ben had stomped on his brakes and put his car in reverse. For the first time, he could smell the bag left outside the other one.

The chase vehicle lurched to its right, then its left and hit a pole, a heavy steel one that did not move. The car became a fiery mass, wrapped around the pole's base as Ben climbed from his SUV. He opened the back glass and stuffed the final bag in with the others.

The fire lit up the area in a hellish red glow that consumed metal and flesh alike. Responders would later find one red boot laying fifty yards from the burned out hulk.

Harold turned away from the wreck to look at Ben. He was closing the rear of his SUV, waving his arm at Harold and yelling, "Let's go!"

The two nearly matching SUVs took off, heading for the airport.

With their prize stowed away, they were in the air in twenty minutes.

Ben walked to the cockpit area and looked in.

"Where did you learn to shoot?" he pressed the pilot.

"Jon gave me that one last year, before we went to Mexico." He grinned, "Never got to use it down there."

Ben smiled back and searched for what else to say.

"Well, I guess that went smooth enough," he tried.

"Yeah," Harold looked over his shoulder. "Let's keep it between us, just how smooth... okay?"

Ben nodded. "Deal," he agreed.

63

A small gathering in the second floor workshop had decided on a course of action. Led by NCIS Agent Tim Spiegel, Cheryl Duray, George Vincent, Daniel Seay, and Doris Shaw discussed the situation about Nava.

"We don't know that she was talking to the men outside," Spiegel pointed out, "but then, we don't know she wasn't."

His eyebrows nearly met as George asked "What is she doing now?"

"Lori is watching her door," Daniel answered. "She has an intercom button with her. If there's any change she'll let us know."

After a brief pause, the agent took over once again.

"Cheryl picked up several moving targets out there," he explained. "Jon and Ben told me about a path around the back side of this mountain. It leads to a trail up over the roof ridge. If I can get there, I can watch what they are up to."

"You're our resident bad-ass at the moment," George pointed out. "With you gone, how do we defend this place?"

Doris smiled at her dear friend.

"This house will defend itself and us," she said confidently. "I know where the switches are. We can lock this place down and put an electrical charge on the entire perimeter."

Cheryl nodded in agreement while Daniel walked across the room to a munitions locker.

"There's enough firepower in here to last a month," he added.

The room became quiet again. Then a voice called out, "So we're good then?" It was Agent Spiegel. "I'll take the Jeep," he went on. "I assume it's a series of left turns around the mountain, right?"

"Right," George told him and walked toward the elevator with him.

"I've talked with Travis Gilbert," George whispered. "Ben set up a secure call for me."

The former SEAL was in full game-face, pulling on one of Jon's jackets.

"And," he stopped and stared right at George.

"I need to meet with him, ASAP."

"Doesn't he know what all we have going on?" Tim asked.

"I didn't ask him about that," George answered sharply. "He's thinking they are still trying to kidnap me...and so am I."

"Or worse," Spiegel stepped into the elevator saying. He fiddled with the jacket and asked, "How does this thing work?"

"The little button on the waist band," George pointed.

"Oh, yeah. Thanks."

Tim pushed the elevator control and nothing happened. He looked up to see George holding the door with his hand.

"First things first, okay?" Spiegel assured him. " You know I can't let you go right now. Let's deal with this mess outside."

George knew he was right. With a slight nod he removed his hand from the elevator door and watched it close.

"You... be careful," he offered sternly.

Harold rolled the G5 into a space at Reagan National that had been arranged by Jerome Grimes. Ben called the NCIS director about the body bags as soon as they had left the ground in Virginia.

The EMT vehicle, escorted by Colleen Dunbar and Charles Burr, took the large bag and they sped away toward Quantico.

"Jon knows about this?" Dunbar asked Ben.

"Ugh...not yet. It's been really busy," he admitted.

"You guys left quite a mess back there, ya know?"

"How bad?"

"Three dead, according to local reports. We know they are searching every laboratory facility in the area so they know what you were after."

"If there is anything to this... would you please call me first?"

She nodded and smiled. "I understand," she told him. "I'd want to tell Jon myself, too."

The lights of the ambulance were getting smaller.

"We better go before they get far ahead of us," she said, pointing at the flashing van.

A fuel truck was already reloading the G5 tanks and a swarm of men were checking her out.

"That's on Grimes' tab," Dunbar hollered as they drove away.

The plan had been to leave much earlier, but the show below him was fascinating. Jackson Terrell watched as one man backtracked from the area while four others slowly crept forward.

He'd long since put his notebook down.

This is way beyond notes, he thought and adjusted his position. *I've never done a "first come – first served" hit before.*

The single figure was now out of sight. Terrell grabbed a small tree trunk to pull himself to a better position, but the man was gone.

Was he part of their group? Terrell wondered, *a point man or something?*

The others had moved still closer, but were down a slope and not in view either. Pushing now against the small tree, he slid back regaining his original spot.

Then a noise behind Terrell caused him to jump.

~

Murray returned first, in a black Dodge Challenger. He had the bag with him.

"You look like one of Grimes people in that thing," Jon said flatly.

"You said black," Murray snapped at him. "I got you black."

The Earls drove up while Jon went through his bag. He took out a gold badge that hung on a piece of leather.

"Come here," he called to Murray. He stuck the leather strip into the cowboy's belt with the badge showing. "You're...agent Bowers, okay?"

"Jack Bauers?" Murray smiled.

"No relation..."

He thanked Calvin and Pat for the suit and stepped behind a nearby building. When he reemerged, he was transformed into a stuffed shirt Federal Agent.

"Put these in your pocket," he handed Murray several thumb drives and other recording devices. "You ready?" he asked.

"What are we doing?" the cowboy demanded.

"Just follow my lead," Jon said as they got into the black car and drove down the block and pulled up right in front of the office building.

Murray followed as Jon, now more in Silas mode, walked into the building like he owned it.

A plain clothes officer jumped from a chair and confronted them.

"Where do think you're going? He said.

Silas turned his head and leaned into the detectives face. Nose to nose, he replied to the man.

"Hancock, DHS," Silas spit out and moved in even closer. "Who are you?"

"I'm Lieutenant Sullivan, just hold it right there."

Silas turned his head slightly and took out a cell phone. Holding it in clear view he spoke in soft, even tones.

"Where is your Captain?"

The Lieutenant blinked and answered, "At home, I suppose."

"Your Chief as well, I assume?" Silas pushed.

"Well, yeah... what is this about?" the Lieutenant began to appear concerned.

"I told you...I'm Hancock from DHS," Silas repeated his claim. "That's Homeland Security, if you don't know."

"I know what DHS is, sir."

"Good...well, my lab tech, Bowers, here and myself are investigating the late Gerald Styles for passing information to the enemy."

"What?" the man's face wrinkled.

Silas held up his phone.

"I can have your Chief and Captain here in thirty minutes with one phone call," he threatened. "Need I do that?"

The Lieutenant thought about the ramifications of that.

"Third floor," he said as though it was an order. "Don't move anything."

Silas grunted at him and he and Murray stepped on the elevator.

64

Agent and former Navy SEAL Tim Spiegel parked the jeep a couple hundred yards below the tree line. He'd come up with lights out and stayed a quiet as he could.

With a Navy-issued light in one hand that was not on, he walked up toward the overlook spot. It didn't take long for his experience and training to warn him. He was not alone on the mountain.

The footprints were hardly noticeable. Had it not been for the bent and broken pine branches, he wouldn't have looked for them.

They were obviously street shoes, flat soles that slipped along the dirt surface. From the size, they were a man's.

Tim left the main trail and proceeded up alongside it. Moving in total quiet, he was near the ridge before he saw the figure lying under a small pine.

Spiegel had a gun, but he didn't want to alert the others that he was there. Not knowing, but assuming the man ahead of him was armed, made the task a challenge.

He found a baseball-sized rock and tossed it across the trail into the sparsely wooded landscape. The sudden disturbance got the man's attention.

The figure rolled to his side and pulled his own handgun.

That answers that, Spiegel thought. He sat perfectly still while the man stared into the dark where the sound had come from.

~

Inside the office of Gerald Styles in St. Simon's it was clear what had happened there. Rugs were gone but blood stains still marked the parquet flooring.

"Looks like the same guys who worked the boat scene did this one, huh?" Murray quipped.

After a quick look around, Jon nodded agreement.

The cowboy immediately pulled the drawers and looked underneath, this time without any luck.

The office appeared searched, but not ransacked. Computers were gone, but a desk pad lay as it had been. The current month page was torn away, the one with doodles and scratched-through notes. Silas tore the next page off as well and folded it neatly.

"Ben can read the slightest imprints from the page underneath," he said in a near whisper. "Looks like they took his desk phone."

"There's a couple of back-up drives here," the cowboy announced. "They were under these empty notebooks in a drawer."

"They're probably empty, but copy them to a thumb drive and put 'em back," Silas asked him. "I wonder if Ben can access the back-up memory on these FAX and printer machines."

"Do you know how to copy that data?"

Taking out his phone, Silas smiled, "I will in a minute."

The call found Ben at 40,000 feet on his return to Dalton. He started not to answer but that wouldn't do at all.

"Hey," he said and then covered the mouthpiece with his hand, "how's it going?"

"I need to know how to copy the memory off a FAX and a..." Jon became quiet and then continued, "Why do I hear the G5 in the background?"

"What's that?" Ben tried weakly.

"The plane, Ben. Why are you in the plane?"

"Something came up and I had to check it out," he tried. "I'll explain in detail later. We're good and we're on the way home."

Ben was able to help him copy the memories to thumb drives.

"People don't realize those things store everything for up to three weeks," he told Jon. "Those haven't operated in a while, so the storage goes back even further."

"I look forward to your explanation," Silas said by way of a thank-you. "And tell Harold I'll want to speak with him, too."

Ben hung up as Murray called Jon to a small indenture he'd found on a separate desktop. It looked like it had marked through a piece of paper into the soft surface of the wood.

"What do think this means?" he asked and pointed to a tiny hand written pyramid. It was made with the initials, "C" over "P" and "J".

Doesn't look like the writing matches any other notes around here," Jon pointed out. "Kinda...female, maybe?"

"Yeah, "Murray agreed. " I see it too."

The cowboy pulled the center drawer from the desk.

"You tried that already, didn't you?" Jon reminded him.

"I just thought of something Charlene used to do... to hide her diary from Daddy," he said grinning.

"Did it work?"

"From him...yeah," he grinned more, "but not from everybody."

With the drawer completely removed, Murray stuck his head into the knee hole of the desk and looked up.

"Bingo," he said in a self-satisfied grunt. Taped under the bottom of the desk top, hidden by the drawer was a small notebook.

Pulling it out, he began to sift through the pages.

"Kinda like that one you found on the boat," he said. "Not much here. It seems to start about two months ago."

Jon walked closer as Murray turned a few pages. "This date on the calendar," he touched it with his finger, "That's the day she and her boss got killed, right?"

"That's the date they all got killed, I'm thinking. I still need a connection to the Eastling thing. I see why he got nailed, bad luck...but what drew the killer to these two?"

In tiny scratching in the margin of the calendar, Murray found something else. "What would "BRD22w/S" mean to you?"

Jon stared at the scribble. His eyes clenched as he remembered seeing this type of thing before, in Missouri.

"Give me that," he said and held the notebook closer. Remembering what Calvin said about the other scribble, he said, "22 is 10:00 PM. You know, short for 2200."

"Okay," the cowboy wanted to play and tried to think himself. " 'w/' means 'with', right?"

Smiling now, Jon agreed. "With Styles...10:00 PM with Styles!"

His glee was short lived and he quickly stared at Murray, still confused. "But she and her boss had dinner together that night, didn't they?" he asked, "and much earlier than that."

"BRD," Murray repeated several times until Jon's eyes lit up.

"Black River Dock!" he said out loud. "She was supposed to meet Eastling at his dock...with Styles! That's how they got caught up in this."

"But why kill them way back here?" Murray quizzed him.

"Something about this all ties together," Jon surmised, "we just don't have the lynch-pin yet."

"They either had something on them... or said something that made him want to search this office. He needed them to bring him here."

"What's missing in this?" Jon tried to think.

"That phone number I found on the boat?" the cowboy asked him.

"That was still hidden, though," Jon recalled. "I'm not saying it isn't important. It's a D.C. number. I'll have Grimes check it out."

~

On the evening they would die, Suzanne Glesser and Gerald Styles had dinner at Tramici, a steak and seafood restaurant on the St. Simon's Island.

Glesser was trying to convince her editor and friend that she had a link between three regional businessmen and a jailed former member of a now disgraced administration.

"Eastling has the phone they call to get messages to her," Suzanne leaned across the table, emphatically making her point.

"Sit up straight and try to smile a bit," her boss warned her. "You'll draw attention we don't need."

"Will you come with me?" she pleaded. "I need you for support."

"What's the big deal?"

"He wants to meet us at his boat dock, out near the mouth of the Black River inlet."

"Tonight?"

"He's coming in around 10:00 PM," she told him.

"He's got a phone number," Styles repeated her words. "That's it?"

"A number that has records and ties to Dilward Putney, Jasper Jamison...and Carlton Calvert."

"Calvert?" Styles leaned back. "You're not serious...you've got a link to him and Barrett?"

The reporter nodded that she did.

65

Jackson Terrell knew he was no longer alone on the hillside. He couldn't see the threat, but he felt it. The noise he'd reacted to came from an area illuminated by what light there was. That space was not occupied; he could see the individual trees.

Immediately his instincts had him move away from his spot and behind a large boulder to the left. Any sound he made was of no circumstance since the threat already knew where he was. He looked at his gun. If the other person had a gun, *wouldn't he have used it by now?*

Terrell slowly stood behind the rock.

"Who's there?" he called out in a normal voice.

Agent Spiegel lay under a shadow. He knew he was not visible to the man calling to him.

"I'm just hiking here, man," Spiegel said. He spoke intentionally to his right, letting the sound travel through the darkness before the other man heard it.

"Show yourself," Terrell responded, "now."

"You've got a gun," Spiegel feigned concern. "I saw it. What are doing with a gun?"

That exchange gave the killer confidence that he held the upper hand. Stepping from behind the rock and moving toward the shadows and the dark he spoke out, "Show yourself I said... I'm not foolin' around."

The NCIS Agent checked the weapon in his rear waist band and powered the arm on the jacket.

"I'm coming out," he said.

Warren Dawes had his "toys" lined up before him. He'd managed to make them small enough to be carried together, in one bag or perhaps a small box. He had not decided which, just yet.

The receivers would help them work in mass, from varying locations, as one large unit. The main concern he still had was entry.

"I must get inside," he murmured over and over. Sneaking in was all but impossible, that much he had determined. It would need to be straight on, allowed if not invited in.

The master control would unleash a force strong enough to take down any mansion.

A thousand feet, he figured and set the control for that range.

Pushing back from his table, Dawes rubbed his sore leg. He had sat too long in one spot. The doctors told him about that.

The man stood, admired his line-up of killing devices one more time, and began storing them away for the night.

Those in the workshop on the second sub-level monitored Spiegel's progress through audio and what visual the darkness allowed.

Cheryl tried to call Ben. He had left his phone on the seat to walk up front and tell the good news to Harold, the news that they had been busted by Jon.

"Oh boy," the pilot laughed. "It could be Southwest Airlines for me."

"It ain't funny," Ben shot back though he caught himself with a small chuckle. "I'll handle it...but he'll probably say something to you, too."

As he turned he could see his phone flashing in the seat.

"I've got to go get that call," he said excusing himself and ran to grab the phone.

"Hey," he answered. "What's going on?"

A second car left the compound some thirty seconds behind the first. By the time they reached the main road Ben and Harold were gone and the car with their leader was a burning heap at the base of a utility pole.

They quickly turned back, returning to the compound.

Frazier was beside himself at the news. His number two man lay at the coroner's with his head caved in from a rock, and now his number one was gone. He needed a new leader and the pickings were slim.

With the boys of the gang gathered around him in the gym area, Frazier asked one question.

"English?" he called out...twice.

Several of the young men looked at each other and one finally stepped forward.

"I speak the English, Mr. Walt," he said.

"What started the chase?"

"Enrico saw someone messing with the trash pile."

"The trash pile?" Frazier was confused. "Why the big deal over that?"

"I'm not sure, Mr. Walt, but it happened as the noise went off."

Frazier tried to make sense of it all.

"Did they take something?" he asked.

"Si...Enrico say he took a bag."

"A trash bag?"

"No...no...a big, black bag."

"What is your name?" Frazier asked him.

"Orlando Miguel Benitez," he answered.

Frazier waved him to come closer and put his arm around him. Turning Benitez to the group, Frazier spoke loudly.

"Bennie here is your new leader. Understood?"

Heads nodded but little was said.

"Good," Frazier declared. He looked at Benitez and instructed him, "When the cops get here...that other car was going out for pizza. Capiche?"

"I think so, Mr. Walt."

"Excellent," Frazier tried to hide his worry with a smile. "I'm going home...I was never here."

On his way back to Roanoke, Walt Frazier pondered the black bag.

Why a black bag from our trash heap?

The answer hit him like a migraine headache.

"No...no...no," he told himself out loud then followed with thoughts alone. *How could anyone know about that?*

66

Tim Spiegel stood and walked one small step at a time into the clearing. As the faint moonlight cast definition on his image, Terrell also moved forward.

"Hands up," he ordered with his gun gesturing upward.

Spiegel raised both hands, more in front of him than up, but it seemed to satisfy the gunman.

"Are you with those other men?" Terrell asked.

"Who? What other men?" Tim pretended. "I told you. I'm a hiker. I just live a couple miles from here."

Terrell was now close enough that Spiegel could see the gun and the look on his face. It was a look of disbelief.

"You're the guy that was over there earlier today," Terrell surmised. "That's who you are."

"No man," Spiegel tried once more. "I'm just a hiker. Can't I go home now?"

Terrell stepped closer, now within feet. He looked at his gun and remembered the men across the road.

No need making a bunch of noise over this guy, he thought and stuck the gun in his shoulder holster.

"We're way passed going home, friend," he snarled and drew a long bladed knife from behind his back.

Only three feet away, Spiegel took a defensive stance.

"Don't do that," he said firmly.

Jackson Terrell's eyes winced. He felt the change of tone in the man's voice. It was no longer meek or weak. His words came as more of an order or even a warning. But Terrell's actions were beyond the stopping point. His knife welding arm thrust forward toward the man's mid-section.

~

Varkey Al Halbi sensed someone had been to his spot in the cliff across from the mansion. There was no discernible mark left by Spiegel, yet the Syrian knew, or sensed, it was somehow different.

He had withdrawn back down to his car where he sat thinking for several minutes. In his two prior nights watching the house, he'd noticed the trees standing behind it.

There must be ground back there, he thought, *no trees could be that tall. Not here anyway.*

He had slowly driven around, searching for a path up the back. He found the driveway and followed it as high as the car would go.

Fresh tire tracks led him to the Jeep. The hood was still a bit warm. The trained Syrian fighter put his gun in his hand and followed the path up, staying to one side, the sky peeking through tree limbs, his only guide.

Then he heard the voices.

~

From his home in the Hurt Park district of Roanoke, Virginia, Walter Frazier hurried to his bedroom and opened a drawer full of cell phones. He dug through till he found one marked, "H.P." and quickly dialed it. The phone took multiple rings and nearly a minute to be answered.

"Damn Walt, it's dinner time, man. What is it?"

"Hill, how many men can you count on in Salem?"

Hill Pence was a Lieutenant on the Salem police force. The entirety of which were under Frazier's control, but he needed loyalty for this job.

"Count on?" Pence thought as he spoke. "What's going on?"

Frazier explained the details and his fear of the man in black his gang had told of. Though he'd never seen him, this figure was now his worst enemy.

"I've got eight to ten that'll fight anybody I tell 'em to," Hill spouted proudly.

"That's not enough," Frazier was blunt and his stare cut through the other man.

Pence thought, then raised his estimate to fourteen.

"Get them to the compound in the morning," Frazier ordered. "Plain clothes, personal weapons only... no department traceable stuff."

"Some of them are scheduled for duty, Walt."

"That's why I'm calling you now. Work something out, Pence. Fix the roster, do what you have to. I'm under siege over there."

Pence had never heard Frazier like this. He stood quietly, phone pressed to his ear, letting this conversation sink in.

"Are you there?" Frazier almost yelled.

"Yeah...yeah, Walt," the man said. "I'll take care of it."

~

The blade's tip nearly touched the jacket when Spiegel's first move stopped it cold. With his left arm, he had caught Terrell's forearm in a blocking thrust. The knife was pushed back, but Terrell maintained control of it. Tim stepped forward, his right leg finding ground between Terrell's feet as he landed his own left forearm strike against the aggressor's chest.

A loud "pop" coincided with Terrell's eyes bulging outward. The knife was released from his hand and he fell backwards at a rapid rate.

Tim's right hand was already in motion, reaching for the wrist holding the weapon. He grabbed it, hard. There were more cracking noises as the body continued backward, its feet now off the ground.

Blood oozed and then spurted from Terrell's mouth as he twisted in Spiegel's grasp and hit the ground.

Tim stood, still holding the man's wrist, in a mildly confused state. He had not factored in the mechanical arm. The blow to Terrell's chest broke his sternum in two, the upper section pierced his lung on the right side, and the lower section scraped and tore into his heart.

Tim dropped the arm and looked at him. Jackson Terrell was dead before he'd hit the ground.

Spiegel straightened up and felt a blow strike him hard in the back, then the familiar sound of a gunshot filled the air.

~

Cheryl spoke so fast that Ben had to ask her to slow down.

"Tim is still out there?" he tried to clarify.

"Yes...yes," Cheryl was all but in tears. "Someone just shot him."

Ben started toward the cockpit of the G5.

"He's wearing that jacket I gave him, right?"

"I think," she said. "I don't know...it knocked him down, the images are really dark up there and it's hard to tell what's going on."

"Hold a second," Ben said to Cheryl and then spoke with Harold.

"Are we close to home?" he asked the pilot.

"On approach to the airfield now."

"Can you 'buzz' the house?"

"Do what?" Harold didn't think he'd heard correctly.

"Can you do a tight fly-over of the house?"

The engines roared back to full and Harold turned slightly.

"This is going to be VFR so hang on."

Without a charted course, Visual Flight Rules applied.

67

Spiegel fell face first across Terrell's legs and rolled to his right side. Though dazed by the impact he knew he was still in some form of combat, even though his main adversary lay dead beneath him.

Varkey Al Halbi moved forward confidently. Believing he had administered a kill shot, he walked straight toward the man, putting his gun away. The Syrian killer fiddled with his garrote, new handle and all, preparing for his signature mutilation.

Limbs high in the trees began to wave side to side and front to back. There was only a muffled roar at first. Then the overwhelming blast of a low flying jet rocked the mountain top. Trees now swayed down to their roots from both the air and noise vibration. It was mesmerizing.

Al Halbi stopped and stared skyward. All he saw was a stream of fast lights ripping past the stars overhead. Small limbs and pine needles rained down making the killer blink as he brought his chin to his chest. Once his eyes registered back on his victim, Al Halbi realized the scene had changed.

Tim now lay on his back, his head up and his Glock in hand. The weapon was pointed directly at the Syrian.

"Drop it," Spiegel ordered. "I don't really care if you understand or not. Drop that thing now...or you're dead."

With all they could recover or copy from the office, Jon and Murray came back down. The detective sat on a bench in the lobby.

"Bowers," Jon barked at Murray. "Give Lieutenant Sullivan one of your cards so he can reach us later."

The cowboy grimaced then played along. He patted his chest pocket and announced, "I'm all out, boss. Didn't get my newest order yet."

Jon stopped in his tracks, as though there was another solution to the situation, but instead looked at Sullivan saying, "Screw it." He then walked toward the man and asked him, "You don't want to see or hear from me ever again, do you, detective?"

Sullivan stood. He glared back at Jon, angrily at first, while his mind sought a snappy comeback. When nothing came to him, he decided he was better off being done with these two.

"You know," he snarled at Jon, "I really don't."

"Well, 'Good Night' to you, too," Jon smiled and they left.

Murray drove down the street and around the corner where the Earls waited. Jon climbed out and went straight to Calvin.

"I'll send you a letter for four complimentary suits at one of my stores. I think they're in Savannah and Jacksonville," he said seriously.

"You don't have to do that," Earls told him.

"I can't thank you two enough, "Jon took his friend's hand. " You've gone to a bunch of trouble for me on short notice. I won't forget it."

"You are so welcome," Pat smiled and then looked at Murray to include him. The cowboy tipped his 'imaginary' hat and smiled back.

They climbed back in the black car and Jon pointed to Calvin.

"That letter is still coming," he stated with no room for argument. "And pick out some shirts and ties to go with it. This one is a little itchy."

As they drove away, Calvin Earl pretended to take off a shoe to throw at them. "He never changes," he said to his wife, "probably never will."

~

Cheryl yelled into the phone, "Was that you guys?"

"I think so," Ben responded. "Could you hear us?"

"Man!" she said. "The whole place shook."

"What's going on now?"

"Daniel and George are headed out to help Mr. Spiegel."

"Who's watching Nava?" Ben asked.

"Mrs. Seay," she got a look from Daniel over that, "I mean, Lori, is up there now."

"We're circling to land, I think. We should be there within thirty to forty minutes."

"Okay," Cheryl's voice was cracking just a bit.

"Hey," Ben said softly, for only her to hear. "You did good. Really good!"

~

Tim Spiegel had Al Halbi pick up Terrell and carry him. When they got to the Jeep, Tim knew he had an issue with Al Halbi being awake and not tied up.

He didn't have a set of cuffs on him, nor was there rope in Jon's Jeep.

After the Syrian dumped the body in the back, Tim said, "Thanks," and then pushed the button, turning off the hydraulic arm. He followed Al Halbi to the side door and suddenly called to him, "hey."

When the Syrian turned, Tim nailed him with a right cross. The man bounced off the side of the jeep and to the ground.

Turning the arm back on, Tim loaded him into the Jeep and checked to be sure the killer was out.

~

Daniel and George each took weapons and a jacket from Ben's closet, loaded themselves into Ben's old Ford 500 sedan, and roared out through the tunnel.

"You've done this before?" Daniel asked as George left the accelerator on the floor.

"Just watch the screen," he pointed to the unit on the dash that showed the road out front. "If you see anything...scream."

"Count on it," Daniel laughed and they made a hard left onto Highway 71, going the way Spiegel had, to get to him quickly.

Not far up the dirt road on the mountain, they saw headlights coming down.

"It's the Jeep," Daniel hollered.

They stopped nose to nose and Daniel jumped out to check on Spiegel.

"I'm good," the agent said, "let's get back inside before this one wakes up."

"The other guy is dead?" Daniel asked.

Tim looked up at him and took in a deep breath.

"This jacket thing," he pulled on the front flap, "saved my life twice tonight." Then he looked toward the back of the Jeep. "But that arm enhancer, I had no idea it was that strong and...well," he breathed in twice more in rapid succession, "hell yeah... that one, back there... is dead."

Daniel quickly returned to the Ford. George put the car in reverse and asked, "Is he alright?"

"He's got two in the car with him...one's dead."

The Ford stopped after sliding on some loose gravel. George threw the car into "park" and looked at Daniel.

"He moved a body from a crime scene?"

68

Captain Marsha Hurst arrived at the Mecklenburg County Jail later than other days. The drive to the facility was delayed by a traffic jam. Her round of checkups on the three secret prisoners from Winston-Salem took longer that afternoon. All was well at the hospital ward, where the wounded man stayed silent. The injury to his leg was now stable and expected to heal, though he'd lost a great deal of blood.

Doctors kept him heavily sedated, so it wasn't clear what he was aware of, if anything. Marsha read through the medical reports, as well as those of the guards and made her own notes.

The men at Charlotte Jail Central were kept in solitary. One spent most of his days issuing outlandish threats.

An undercover officer, housed in a cell near this man, made hourly reports to guards of what the hit man had to say. His primary concern seemed to be making everyone know he had said nothing, and that he would kill his former partner at his first opportunity.

The third man was kept on a separate cell block. Marsha's walk to that area went through the main officer's entrance. One exterior window, some nine feet off the floor showed a red glow in the darkening sky.

Reminded by the darkness that she'd skipped dinner, a "PayDay" bar from the lobby vending machine went into her purse for later.

After processing into the next holding area, Marsha walked by the cell where another volunteer undercover officer sat doing surveillance on this prisoner. The officer knew who Marsha was. His eyes and head became oddly animated as she walked past. But he said nothing.

The prisoner was only two cells down so she kept moving and stopped only when in front of that cubicle. The man sat on his bunk, tightly gripping the metal edges of the bed railing. His eyes stared at the floor.

He had chosen to stay quiet after his initial outbursts to Grimes. He had given partial names of his partners, Pete and Wilkins, but not his own.

A noise to her right caught Marsha's attention for a second and she looked in that direction. A guard had come to take the undercover cop to an interview room. She knew then he had information for her.

The pleased smile that came to her was short lived. As she turned back to the cell her color left her and her body shook. The prisoner had stood and silently moved to within inches of her, standing just inside the bars that separated them.

His face was gaunt, pale and the eyes were dark as though sleep had evaded him. He grabbed the bars and leaned even closer.

"Who are you?" he muttered at first. When Marsha did not answer, he tried again, but ten times louder. "Who the hell are you?" his scream echoed through the cell block.

"He sent you, didn't he?" the man continued but in more subdued tones. He turned loose of the bars and walked away. "Do it," he challenged her. "Just do it and be done."

"Do what?" Marsha asked him calmly.

The man sprung his body back to the bars, arm high above his head.

"Kill me," he screamed again. "That's why you're here, right?"

"Who has you so frightened, sir?" she asked. "Fuller?"

He again turned loose of the bars and leaned away slightly.

"You should be afraid, too. Everyone should be afraid."

Marsha tried several more times to get anything sensible from him, but it was all more of the same. As she got to the gate, a guard pointed to the interview room and she nodded. The iron gate clanked heavily behind her as it was pulled tight.

~

Murray looked over at Jon as he drove the rental car back to the airfield. In full "Silas mode," Jon was deep into his notes already.

"I've set a flight plan to stop back by Charlotte first," the cowboy told him. "I figured you'd want to go there before Dalton."

Jon looked up as though the thought was new to him.

"Absolutely," he said twisting his head and nodding at the same time, "thanks."

"So, we know we're after this Syrian guy, but we don't know who he works for?"

Jon sat up straight with Murray's question.

"Ultimately, no," Jon said somewhat quizzically. "But initially, he's working for the same group Barrett is."

"Well now, that's new," the cowboy grinned in surprise. "I thought she was the boss."

"People thought her boss was the 'boss' for a while, too."

"You're gonna need to slow it down or back it up, okay?"

"This is bigger than it appears, Murray. I know it looks like she is after me...and using everything at her command to get me."

"You noticed that, huh?"

"I'm not that important," Jon said seriously. Enough so that Murray didn't try to joke about it.

"Then what is going on?" the cowboy asked instead.

"They're protecting something...something huge. Not just to them, but to everything."

Shaking his head, Murray mumbled to himself, "I shouldn't have even asked."

"They think...at least that's what I'm working on, that I can somehow have an effect on this thing."

"So, they are after you, then?"

Jon folded his notes, seeing that they were nearing the Lucy Too. Stoically he looked at his loyal friend.

"The threat that I represent to them, yes," he said. "That threat is you, Marsha, Ben...all of you, right up to and including Grimes and his people."

Murray understood now. It made sense.

"Why stop there, Jon?" he added, "The President, hell... the whole dang country, maybe."

Murray's words hit Jon solidly.

The whole country, he thought silently. *It could be at that level.*

~

The interview room was small. Twelve by fourteen, she thought, with the ubiquitous, one-way glass wall.

The undercover officer stood in a corner, his back to her.

"What are you into with this guy?" he asked without turning around. He'd heard the door and knew it could only be her.

"What do mean?" Marsha asked in return.

He turned to her now, his face almost flushed.

"Look, Captain...I've worked vice and narcotics for twelve years. Undercover for the last three and I've seen fear, believe me."

He walked to the table and leaned over the chair with his hands pressed down on the metal top.

"This guy beats all I've seen. He is consumed by his fear. He shits himself at night when he dreams."

Marsha pulled the chair out on her side. Very officially, and with all dignity authority can provide, she sat down and then looked up at the bearded man before her.

"Officer," she started, "While I fully appreciate your analysis, I'm assuming there's something you have to tell me." She stretched out her hand to the chair he'd ignored. "Please," she went on, "sit or stand, just get to it."

The man raised a hand to his temples and rubbed them. It took him a few seconds but he finally sat.

"Do you have an identity on him yet?" he asked still slightly agitated.

"Whatever there was has been wiped," she told him. "He's another ghost like the mobs use."

The officer rocked back in the steel chair and shrugged his shoulders. "This guy is a stone cold killer," he said in a near whisper. "But he's broken by something. Something he thinks is not stoppable."

Marsha stared at the officer's eyes until he finally looked back.

"What is it," she asked, "that you've seen or heard... that has you riled up?"

Her words seem to be a comfort to him. He became quiet for several minutes and then took three very deep breaths before speaking.

"Ma'am," he started much calmer now, "he talks crazy stuff all day. There's not much of a pattern to it, mainly fear and...well beyond that."

Marsha listened. Her tendency would be to again rein the officer in, get him to focus. But this man wasn't some new rookie. He was a hardened officer and what he had seen affected him. She allowed him to tell it his way.

"At night," the officer started again, "he sleeps for the first few minutes...once he does fall asleep. Then there's some repeating dream his mind won't let go of." With his right hand, the man drew circles in the air above the table. "He's sorry about something and wants to go back. He keeps saying 'Albany'."

"Albany?" Marsha took out her notebook and wrote it down, "Albany, where? There are more than a few of them in this country."

"He never says more than that, just a mumble about something to do with 'putt,' not like 'put it here,' but more like putt. You know putt-putt?"

"Do you have any theory of what it could mean," she asked respectfully.

"No ma'am. Like I said, it's kind of a loop in his head. He wants to go back to Albany and this 'putt', whatever has something to do with it."

"Anything else, officer?"

"No ma'am."

"Thank you, Officer..."

"Conrad, ma'am. Clinton Conrad."

"You're a good officer," she said standing. "proud to work with you."

69

As George and Tim Spiegel stood outside the Jeep, arguing, Daniel noticed the Syrian stir a bit in the front seat.

"Guys," he tried, but they were too into the discussion of law and a dead body.

"We need to search him," Tim insisted. "We can take him back before Gil and men come out."

"That's not the point of the law, damn it," George let out all his pent up frustration over how he'd learned to sidestep the law. As he spoke he realized that was what he was doing.

George saw Daniel pointing to the Syrian and understood there could be a problem. He picked up a hand sized rock and leaned through the driver's window on the Jeep.

A clunking sound, the rock to his head, rendered the dark haired man, once again, unconscious.

"You were explaining the law, I believe," Tim teased George.

"Let's get inside before I arrest your ass, okay?" he grimaced.

Jerome Grimes called Colleen Dunbar from his office.

"Sir?" she answered.

"I know it's late," he blustered. "But I've just gotten a report on some DNA found in Virginia."

"Virginia, sir?"

"It's a strange connection to start with, but the tie-in possibilities are too many to count."

"I'm not following you, sir."

"The lab hit on three out of four bags brought to us with positive IDs. Two are clearly local cases there, but the third one is huge. It allows us into this if we can justify getting the evidence."

"Who brought this in?"

"Some members of Jon's team flew them in a few hours ago."

Sitting up in her bed, Dunbar asked the obvious question.

"What can I do, sir?"

"I need you and Burr to go with me to Georgia."

"Georgia? I thought you said Virginia?"

"We can't go there yet," Grimes attempted to explain, "but pack enough for several days. Virginia will be next...before we come home."

"When do we leave, sir?"

"Wheels up at 0700," he said and then grinned.

Grimes closed his phone, still smiling. It wasn't about the case, his mind was just having fun.

"Wheels up," he thought and this time, laughed out loud. *I've always wanted to say that.*

~

They left the body on the third sub-level. Daniel found a cool spot in a dark corner and they dragged it there. The Syrian was another matter.

They considered tying him to the bumper of the pick-up truck. George didn't like that. "Too easy to get undone," he said and the others agreed.

Then they noticed Daniel stepping off the distance between support columns for the parking bays.

"Fifteen feet," he announced. "That should work."

His skeptical helpers followed his lead and helped Daniel place the Syrian between two of the columns. With his arm stretched above his head, the man reached a total span of nine feet.

"Tie his feet to that pole," Daniel suggested, "and I'll tie his hands to this one. He can't move to untie himself."

George and Tim looked at the space and thought for a moment. They quickly joined in; Tim added his expertise in knot tying.

As they finished and stood over their captive, the alarm bell sounded for the tunnel entrance. Everyone stepped away from the door and watched as Ben and Harold drove up in the Jaguar.

Seeing the man tied between the poles, Ben smiled and offered, "Holy Crap!"

"That's not the half of it," Daniel told him and pointed to the dark corner.

Ben slowly approached the body as though it might spring to life. Once he got close enough to see the face, he turned back to the others.

"Damn guys!" he said. "That's Jackson Terrell!"

"I thought it might be," Tim muttered.

"Somebody needs to call the president," Ben said with emphasis.

"Call?" George ran to the elevator. "I have to call Travis Gilbert. He's expecting me in town in the morning."

"What are you going to do?" Spiegel asked chasing after him.

"I don't know...I really don't. This mess could change everything. I mean, what if all these guys work together?"

"Speaking of," Tim reminded the group. "What happened with the four Israelis and what's Nava doing?"

~

Marsha arrived back at headquarters and noticed the rotor blades extending over the rooftop from the helipad.

Jon and Murray awaited her in her office. They had much to talk about and much to share.

"We're going home in the morning," Jon told her. "I'd like you to come, too."

"I've got work here," the new captain excused herself.

"I really want to have a big talk and share session again, this time in person and with most everybody there."

"Everybody?" Marsha asked.

"Well, Phil can't be there but he's about the only one, and I can put him on speaker. Grimes called a bit ago," he went on. "He's got some new stuff, says he'll give details when he gets to Dalton, but he's coming and bringing Dunbar and her assistant with him."

She tried not to show any reaction, but could feel her face changing color. Turning away, Marsha flipped through a day planner on her desk and said, "Well, I suppose I could go for a couple of days."

The cowboy looked away and smiled, but he said nothing.

70

The sun crept into the bedroom that next morning and found Jon sitting with his notebook. He stared across Marsha's sleeping form, toward the window, deep in thought.

He had been up for an hour, maybe more. Dedicating each detail he'd found to memory hoping they would connect on their own. The story was shaping up but still had many holes in it.

Marsha's addition of the terrified killer's mumbling about "Albany" and "putt" was intriguing, though it did not yet add up.

The man's identity remained a mystery. He'd been "washed" as they say in mob talk. His life reissued in a way that destroyed the past. There was a picture of him and that gave Jon an idea.

There's an Albany in many states but Georgia has to be considered a high probability. He made a note to call Grimes and have a copy sent to him.

Perhaps he knew an agent in the Albany area who could take the photo around. It could work, he convinced himself.

The form before him moved slightly. He really didn't want to disturb her. He enjoyed just being there... watching her sleep. The covers suddenly flew back and she smiled at him.

"You're up early," she said sounding almost surprised.

"I was just about to wake you," he reached for her. "It's about time to go."

With Marsha in the shower, he called Grimes on his private cell.

"You up?" he asked.

"On the way to the airport," the director told him.

"Care to share anything, yet?" Jon asked.

"When we're together later today. I promise this is worth it, I just don't want you flying off on your own before we meet."

"You don't trust me, Director?"

"Au...contraire, my friend," he nearly laughed through the fake accent. "I trust you explicitly. That's why I'll wait."

Jon griped a bit more and finally moved on to why he'd called. He explained the man in custody in Charlotte. Grimes knew him quite well and the possible connection to Albany.

"Send me the picture now. There's an FBI field office down there. I'll have it sent to him."

Within an hour, the photo sat in front of newly assigned Agent Andrew "Andy" Thomas of the Albany, Georgia, FBI.

He stuck the picture in a folder and headed out to ask around.

~

Vehicles gathered and filled the back parking lot of the complex. Salem officers, all in plain clothes, walked to the main auditorium without speaking or even the pretense of noticing each other. It was not a happy get together.

Walter Frazier was at the front, no microphone, or bullhorn; he expected them to pay attention. His disheveled appearance was concerning enough to emphasize the importance of the early meeting. Everyone took a spot, standing, and listening closely.

"What I need you to do is important and you may not like it," he started. "To insure the success of this operation, I have taken a couple of steps to enhance your loyalty."

With that, a mild murmur began to swell in the room and the men looked to each other and whispered.

Frazier let this go on a minute or two and then all but screamed at them.

"Do you want to talk to yourself or hear me?" he bellowed. "I suggest you hear me out."

The whispers quieted and, the room was again still.

"I have asked different things of you over the past few years. These things have all put dollars in your pockets and drugs and booze at your disposal."

The quiet was again uneasy but held.

"It's time to earn the big prize," Frazier told them. "Something is going to happen and I require your back-up."

He let that thought settle, or unsettle those he addressed and then went on, "I did not say 'need,' you may have noticed. I said 'require'. And require it is. You have no choice in this, be clear about that."

A short wave of unrest flowed through the room but quickly calmed.

"If your complete support is compromised in anyway... by any one of you, I will destroy you all. Is that clear?"

"What do you mean?" one angry voice asked from the crowd.

"I have taken steps to release information on each and every one of you here. Details of your work with me, what you have done, and have been accomplice to...from the beginning. Any problem through this admitted hardship, and it all goes to the media."

Through the din of noise that followed, a voice was heard to say, "kill him now."

Frazier laughed an odd, broken laugh.

"That would only hasten the release of what I set up," he threatened.

Finally another stepped forward to ask, "We have done some rough stuff since you've taken over. What's so bad that's coming now? That you have to threaten us...to stay with you?"

"Someone is out to kill me," Frazier told them, "Someone who I don't know or understand. But I am going to draw this fool out...tonight."

"What do we do?"

"You set up a protective perimeter around this place and defend it and me with your very lives."

"What are you going to do?"

Frazier looked down, almost as though ashamed of his own thoughts.

"What I must...to bring him here," he told them.

Lucy Too could have landed on the hilltop across from the mansion. Murray had done so many times before. But in lieu of the "visitors" reported, they set down at the Dalton airport and waited for Grimes and his party to arrive.

Harold and George brought cars, George had an urgent matter to discuss with Jon.

"Where are you supposed to meet?" Jon asked him.

"At Carl's office in town."

"Can you put it off till this afternoon?"

George thought..."I can try."

"Do that," Jon looked straight into his eyes. "I have an idea."

The DA wandered off to make a call and get away from the noise. The NCIS jet roared in and landed with squealing tires.

The only necessary introduction was Colleen and Agent Burr to Marsha. Grimes handled it deftly, mainly because he was oblivious.

Murray stood off to one side, waiting for her to notice him. It finally happened when she turned his way and smiled.

"Nice to see you again," the cowboy's words were smooth as silk.

Dunbar nodded and continued her smile, but Murray did catch her glancing at Jon.

After waiting for George, who returned nodding affirmatively at Jon, they rode to the mansion.

"We're coming in topside," Jon alerted them by phone. He didn't want to give away the tunnel entrance with all this attention.

"Driveway cameras are on...now!" Ben told them as Cheryl threw a switch on the control panel.

"Just follow me," Jon radioed to the car behind his. The "cameras" were holographic images that covered their approach up the driveway.

"Got ya' covered," Tim said in return. And he wasn't kidding. He and Ben sat at gun turrets in the attic, Daniel and Doris stood behind the garage doors with weapons at the ready while Lori stood guard at Nava's door.

Cheryl monitored everything from the second sub-level.

71

Jasper Jamison took the call reluctantly. Direct contact from his counterpart in South Georgia was dangerous and becoming more frequent. From his large leather desk chair, the furniture maker picked up his phone in disgust. "Yes, Dil," he said.

"That tone isn't called for," Putney snapped at him, "Not with me."

"Look," Jamison snapped back. "I'm getting pretty much the same as you...nothing."

"Her man Terrell is off the grid," the pecan man listed. "The Israelis are nowhere to be found... and what about the tie to Gilbert? Have they used that yet?"

"It got bogged down... but is supposed to happen today."

"Him or a lure?"

"Are we on a secure line?" Jamison asked.

"Absolutely."

"What was to be a lure is now scheduled to be a firm reason for him to come out."

Putney had to think about what that meant. It was a bold step.

"They're gonna kill the lure?" he asked rhetorically.

"I think it's time," Jamison told him. "The old man agrees."

"Remember what you said about Daedalus and that decree?" Putney reminded him. Jamison laughed under his breath.

"I can't get it out of my mind. But do we just sit and wait?"

A large sigh was followed by silence...then the voice from South Georgia answered, "I suppose not."

The butler called out for Carlton Calvert.

"Sir, there's a phone call, says he needs to talk with you."

The old man walked to his study and picked up the phone, "Carlton Calvert...what is this about?"

"Sir, this is Fulton County EPA calling. We've had a series of calls about radon gas permeating in your area. Do you have sensors in your home, sir?"

He thought and unconsciously shook his head.

"I don't really know; is there a danger?"

"Not immediately, no sir. But we would like to come out next week and put a few of our super sensitive sensors around your home for a day or two. Would that be alright, sir?"

"Super sensitive? Really...is that what you call them?"

"Sorry, sir. No offense intended. They have a name about long as my arm and it uses most of the alphabet, you know?"

"When are you planning to come out?" Calvert asked.

"Tuesday or Wednesday be alright?"

"I don't see why not. Just not too early in the morning, okay?"

"Thank you, sir."

Jon wanted to meet with everyone so he could listen, but there were a few things to do first. The thumb drives had to get to the workshop level and Jon needed to look at the new guest in his house. The Syrian was now awake but not talking.

Jon nodded at him, mumbling under his breath, "We'll see about that." He knelt down and went through the man's coat pockets. "I'm sure you searched him, right?" he asked Tim.

"Nothing on him except that Smith and Wesson and his garrote," Spiegel advised. "He had a car, keys were in it."

"How about Terrell? How'd he get here?" Jon interrupted.

"Haven't found a car yet," Tim looked slightly embarrassed, "didn't take time to look very far."

"No keys on him?"

"Naw. Sorry about..." Tim glanced over at the body. "You know, I wore that suit in Mexico but never really used the power gizmo."

"The jackets react a bit different," Jon said standing up. "You launch that arm and its full tilt." He looked down on the body and added, "Don't worry about it...he was a killer sent here to do more."

Grimes didn't know what to make of the situation. "The complications, legally, are monumental over this," he said as they walked away.

George Vincent was in full agreement, but added, "There wasn't much choice at the time, believe me."

It was decided that the main floor living room would be best for the meeting. A rarely used security door was lowered, blocking the stairs and upper level from access and sound.

"First time I've seen that door down," Ben commented.

"Same here," Jon admitted. "We don't know what our guest is up to, so...anyway I'm glad we have it. Here we can be comfortable. The workshop wouldn't be so for this many folks."

Ben set up a visual link for Phil Stone and Matt Turlock. Lori Seay had an ear piece as she sat outside Nava's door.

"Does she know I'm here?" Marsha asked.

"She hasn't come out since yesterday," George told her. "I hate to think what she could be up to."

"That's one thing I can shed light on," Grimes said while standing from one of the large leather chairs. "The Israelis have had a tough time in the last number of years. Our former and now disgraced administration nearly bankrupted them through non-support. The Social–Democrat Labor party pushed hard that it was too expensive to keep the level of defense they had under Netanyahu. The country underwent many hardships and people didn't like it."

"But our current administration is back on their side, isn't it?" the question filled the room from afar. It was Phil Stone asking from Louisiana.

"That's true, Captain Stone...but the reality is funding for them is still not back where it had been. The conservatives lost the last two elections and many now want to seek parity with Hezbollah. Nava's family was among those."

"But wait a minute now," Marsha protested. "Nava came here to help us not that long ago."

"She came because of her expertise. She is against the use of nuclear weapons and was here to identify them, if they were from Iraq."

"So, you're saying she wasn't loyal to Yinon Harel?"

"I'm told she was very loyal...to Reiss, and he to her. That's what I found out through contacts, just this week."

"Coercion?" Jon asked.

"Reiss is being held captive by the ruling party," Grimes said while nodding to Jon. "Nava is here at their insistence...to help eliminate...you."

"Okay," Jon said coldly. "Now...what is the really big news you've been holding back?"

Grimes gave him a look and noticed Marsha seemed shocked as well. He took a folded paper from his inside coat pocket.

"Let me read this, so I get it right," he said. "Four body bags were brought to us last evening by Ben and Mr. Foster, here. The contents of three of them were primarily human remains...actually, residue from human remains and three had some level of cross contamination."

"What about the fourth?" Ben asked.

"That one was dry, as they explained it."

The group looked around, most not sure what the subject was about.

"We filmed a gang moving and reburying four bodies up in Virginia," Ben volunteered. "With Jon and Murray tied up, Harold and I went to retrieve the body bags before they could be taken or destroyed."

"And," Grimes picked back up. "They brought them to us, so...the cross contaminated bags were still heavy on one set of DNA in each bag."

"What does that mean?" Doris asked.

"It means the residue of one person was strong in each of those three bags. Strong enough for identifications."

Ben clapped his hands and leaned back, nearly dropping the laptop. He looked over to Harold who was smiling and then to Jon...who was not. "Two of the identities are local Virginia cases and I believe Jon, you expected as much."

"Jacob Watson and Harold Briar," Jon guessed.

"Exactly," Grimes confirmed. "This third one...we want in... on a federal level... if we can justify the evidence."

"Who is it, Director?" Ben asked.

"West Virginia Congressman Charles Stanfield. He's been missing for over eight months, since he was to meet Ted Beale at Rock Creek Park."

"Small world," Jon said dryly.

72

Darcy Brown had a call that morning. One that upset the Chief of Staff to the new district's U.S. Representative greatly. He searched for and dialed a cell phone that he had been given for such use.

The call went to Langley, Virginia.

"A Lieutenant Sullivan from Saint Simon's Island reported visitors to the sealed office of Gerald Styles," he told the answerer.

"What kind of visitors?" the man asked in return.

"You're not aware of it?" Brown was now completely rattled.

"Who was there, Brown?" the voice now demanded.

"They told the officer they were Homeland Security...Damn!" he more sighed than spoke. "I was afraid of this. That's not who they were at all, was it?"

"Don't worry about it," the voice told him, "Stay calm." Which was easier said than done for the man in Virginia. This was the third inquiry call he'd had in two days about things that were never supposed to happen.

"Just sit tight," he told Brown. "We've got everything under control, there's absolutely nothing for you to concern yourself with."

Darcy Brown heard the phone click before he could follow up. He sat at his desk in a near stupor for over an hour. Then something told him to get out.

Later that afternoon, the congressional office in Brunswick was hit in a random break-in. Computers and other equipment were stolen; three staffers were killed, and there were no witnesses.

Darcy Brown sat in his car across the street as police cars and emergency vehicles surrounded the building. He took out the cell phone which he'd carried with him, wiped it with a handkerchief and threw it out the window. A passing truck hit it with a large tire.

Brown reached with a shaking hand to crank his car and drove away.

~

Director Grimes was explaining to everyone why the DNA evidence on Congressman Stanfield was unusable.

"Those bags were grabbed on a hunch and not by law enforcement with a legal warrant," he told them, "which would have been impossible to justify anyway."

No one argued. George finally said in a low voice, "Fruit from the tainted tree."

"I'm afraid so," Grimes added. "The law had no business being there, beside the fact that we weren't."

Ben cupped his ear and turned away for a second. The move caught everyone's attention.

"Something wrong?" Grimes asked.

"It's Cheryl," Ben repeated what he'd just heard from her. "Those thumb drives we were downloading into the system. One page just hit a pre-programed stop. It printed out a picture from some office."

He continued to listen as Cheryl explained more.

"The picture shows that Star of Numbers hanging on a wall behind some people."

"Where did this picture come from?" Jon stepped in.

Ben listened for another minute.

"From a memory stored on one of the FAX machines in Gerald Styles' office."

Jon got up and pointed to Grimes.

"We need to take a break for a bit," he said.

"Yeah, I'll go with you," the director said. He waited as the steel door lifted so they could get to the elevator.

"Two at a time," Jon warned as he saw the entire crowd deciding to follow.

~

Agent Thomas was new to the office. The "third man" of a two man team they teased him, so he would often be left to answer the phone or run the left-over cases. A photo had been on his desk that morning. A picture of a young man with a note from the Director of the NCIS attached to it.

The new agent studied the picture, checked what other duties were listed on the roster and stood from behind the small desk.

"Road trip," he said with a grin. This would be his ticket for a day trip out of the stuffy confines of the building.

FBI Agent Andy Thomas carried the photo with him everywhere. He drove out to the far East side of Albany, Georgia, on Oglethorpe Boulevard. Stopping at fast food shops and restaurants along the way, he would show the photo and ask people if they recognized the face.

Toward noon Thomas then headed north on Slappey Drive and finally west out Dawson Road. He'd worn a dog-ear on the picture from holding it in front of folks.

Driving back that afternoon, he saw that a healthy crowd had gathered at the Moon Harvester Bar. He decided to drop in and show the picture around in there.

Within twenty minutes, a guy at the bar leaned in, stared at the image, and declared, "That's Henry Collins...where the hell did he disappear to?"

Agent Thomas quickly took the man to one side, identified himself and made it clear the man's words needed to be truthful and not a hindrance to a lawful inquiry.

"Whoa, dude!" the man said. "I wasn't lying or nothin. That's a guy I used to work with out at the pecan plant. We was on security together, night shift.'"

A few additional questions convinced Thomas this guy was legitimate and actually did know this man as Henry Collins.

After checking with other patrons in the bar, Agent Thomas returned to the office. The pecan plant was several miles south, out Newton Road, and it was fifteen minutes to closing time.

Agent Thomas called David's Pecans asking for the personnel office. A woman answered and Thomas asked about an ex-employee named Henry Collins.

The response struck him as odd. It took less than two minutes.

"Nobody by that name ever worked here," the woman told him.

"Would you check again, please?" he asked.

"No need," she told him flatly. "I told you, there weren't no one here by that name, now or ever."

Hanging up, the young agent leaned back in his squeaky chair, and stared at the picture of the man in question. After reading the note that came with it yet again, he called his boss in Washington, D.C.

"Have you verified this ID other than with the one witness?" Thomas was asked.

"In a way... yes. Completely."

"How do you mean?" the supervisor asked him.

"Director Grimes' note said the unidentified man was tied to "Albany" and the word, "putt," right?"

"That's correct."

"David's Pecans is owned and operated by Dilward Putney."

The supervisor paused for a moment and then thanked Agent Thomas.

"That's good work," he told him. "I'll be sure Grimes is informed right away."

~

Marsha, Doris and Colleen had stayed in the living room with Charles Burr. As the last pair going to the workshop entered the elevator, Marsha announced she was going up to talk with Nava.

"I'd like to go with you," Colleen stood and told her.

"That's not necessary," Captain Hurst cut her off somewhat rudely.

"Please..." she said again, "I can possibly help."

Without agreeing, Marsha withheld further discussion and the two climbed the staircase to the hall. Lori stood outside the closed bedroom door.

"Anything out of her?" Marsha asked.

"No...who's this?"

As though she couldn't find the words, Marsha turned to Colleen but said nothing. The NCIS Agent reached out to Lori with her hand.

"Colleen Dunbar, NCIS," she said.

"Oh yes," Lori smiled. "I've heard of you, hello."

Niceties were cut short as Marsha opened the door and walked in. With Dunbar on her heels, she found Nava Golan sitting near a front window, staring out.

When Marsha called to her, the Israeli turned, recognizing her voice.

"You should not be here," Nava said without thinking.

73

Cheryl had the photo and other documents from the memory cards pulled up on monitors. Ben got to her and placed his hands on her shoulders. "Nice catch," he whispered into her ear.

"Was this from the FAX machine or a printer?" Jon asked. "Can you tell?"

"That code on the top indicates it was a telefax," Ben told him.

"From who?"

"The number is a blank. You don't have to input your real number to send a FAX."

"So we don't know who sent this to her?"

"Fraid not," Ben admitted.

"But she was onto the Celestial Enumerates, wasn't she?" George said.

Jon walked away from the screens. He turned back and looked at Murray. "Do you remember that scuff mark I found on the boat?" he asked him.

"Up on the bow? I heard you talking about it, yeah," the cowboy confirmed, "but I didn't see it myself."

Jon went from screen to screen, checking the papers that had been either faxed or printed in Gerald Styles office. He said nothing further.

"What are you thinking?" Murray pressed gently.

"I don't know," the voice was clearly Silas. "I just don't know."

Grimes walked over to Jon and said in a soft voice, "I was going to save this until I had more time to look into it...but those phone numbers you and I have been collecting all go to the same building."

"The ones these people have had on them?" Jon pointed at the Syrian as he asked.

"Yeah, including one found in Alabama. Those bodies came back as Syrians, too."

"Let me guess? The numbers go to Washington."

Close enough," Grimes complimented him. "Langley, Virginia, actually."

Jon looked straight at Grimes in wonder.

"CIA?" he asked. "I thought you worked with those people?"

"Again with that?" Grimes didn't appreciate Jon's tone. "Come on...it's a big agency. I do know many good people there. They've given me a name we're checking into. That's why I'm moving slowly on this."

"Makes sense really," Jon thought and looked back at the captive tied between the poles. "They're the only ones who could have allies like this."

~

In the upper bedroom, Nava now stared at her friend Marsha as though she didn't belong.

"Why?" Marsha knelt beside her, "Why shouldn't I be here? What's going on?"

"Nothing," the Israeli agent uttered softly and looked away once again.

"Have you heard from Yinon?" Marsha tried.

Nava shook her head but remained silent. Colleen moved forward and placed a hand on the Israeli's shoulder.

"Ma'am, Ms. Golan? My name is Colleen Dunbar. You don't know me ...but I work with Director Grimes and I know...you know him."

Slowly, Nava twisted her head to Colleen's direction. She stared at her and then Marsha.

"Has Grimes talked with Yinon," she asked as a trick question.

"Nobody has been able to reach Agent Harel," Colleen jumped in, "But our director has been in touch with our agents in Israel."

Nava stood and got nose to nose with Dunbar.

"What do you mean?" the Israeli sounded almost threatening.

"He has men watching him and Amzi Reiss." Dunbar glanced at Marsha before adding, "They are protected."

"This is possible?" Nava said while turning to look at Marsha.

"Yes," Colleen stressed. "We know you were being extorted and that threat to you has been eliminated."

"I need to talk to Reiss," Nava said defiantly.

Marsha stared, her mouth half open. Dunbar spoke again.

"Soon," she said. "Just not until we know what is supposed to happen here."

Stepping back from her, Nava clearly showed signs of disbelief.

"That makes no sense. None at all," she sat back down and turned away.

"We can't contact him...or Yinon at the hospital, until we have neutralized the situation here," Dunbar explained. "You must trust us."

With Nava again staring silently out the window, Marsha grabbed Colleen's arm and pulled her toward the door.

"Give her a few minutes," she said tersely and then closed the door once they were in the hallway. "When did Grimes talk to anyone over there and set up this protection?" she demanded of Dunbar.

Walking toward the stairs, Colleen lowered her head and half muttered back to her, "As soon as I ask him to...I hope."

~

The last day and a half had been slow in Northwest Alabama. Agents Childs and Everson drove over to the animal park to check on Cody Arnold.

"He's up and walking more," Wil told them at the admission building. "His legs weren't really hurt...the walking motion pulled on his chest muscles and bounced his arm around, that's all."

"Could we talk to him," Childs asked respectfully. "He needs to know we took down a carload of guys looking to do him harm."

Wil waved his hand for them to follow him. "Is this deal ever going to be at an end?" he asked with serious concern. "I've got a business to run here. We attract kids...or we try to. This type of thing isn't helpful."

"Yeah," Everson spoke up, "everything comes to an end at some point. These guys won't keep on taking hits like they did the other night. They know we're serious and that will sink in eventually."

"Eventually can be a long time. And I don't want to have to ask Cody to leave here...actually...I won't do that. It's just something we need to have go away, you know?"

"Yes, sir...I do very well," Childs answered. "This started as a big ole cabal...we're wearing it down, big time."

They had reached the area near the cage belonging to Boris the Lion. He was already aware of their presence. Cody stepped around the corner as Boris let out a small but substantial roar.

"Agents," Cody smiled and stuck out his good right arm, "How are you guys?"

"Good to see you up and about," Childs grinned. He then feigned a ducking motion. "You don't plan to take another swing at me do you?"

Cody looked down and nodded. "Hope you can forget about that one of these days," he half moaned.

"I'm just kidding you, son," Childs went on. "We're glad you're doing better."

Cody walked back to Boris' cage and the big cat moved to him from his side of the wire and rubbed against it, affectionately. Cody's hand pressed against the chain link, palm open, and Boris nudged his head on it.

"My buddy here keeps me motivated," he told them.

"My wife is the only other person I've ever seen," Wil whispered to Everson, "who could get that close to Boris and not upset him."

Childs told Cody about the trio they had stopped.

"We don't know if there's any more out there," he said to the SEAL straight faced. "But the greeting that bunch received will send a message."

"If they're getting this close," Cody said and looked right at Wil, "maybe I should not be here."

"Can I make any decisions around here?" Wil laughed, then quickly changed his tone to deadly serious, "It ain't time for that...not yet."

"We'll be in town," Childs shook Cody's hand, "You just be alert, okay?"

"Tell 'em, Boris," Cody said loudly.

The lion raised his head and let loose with another roar.

"Try sneaking by him," Cody challenged.

74

Colleen and Marsha were met on the stairs by Ben.

"She's just now on the phone again," he told them.

They started back up the stairs when Colleen grabbed Marsha's arm.

"I need to get to Director Grimes, fast," she said.

"Yes...you do," Marsha agreed with sharp words. She and Ben continued up and Colleen rushed down.

She found her boss just inside the kitchen on his phone. He held up one finger asking her to wait a second.

"Okay," he told the caller, "thanks to the agency and that young man down there."

Grimes looked at Dunbar smiling and shoving his phone into a pocket. "We've got a name on one of our guys in Charlotte," he told her.

"Don't put that away just yet, sir," she pointed to his hand with the phone.

Grimes head lifted and his expression dropped to neutral.

"What now?" he asked.

Dunbar explained what she'd told Nava and her reasons. The director stared at her... bewildered.

"You're writing checks we can't cash...you know that, right?"

"Something is wrong over there," she pleaded. "That I do know."

"What is she up to?"

"I believe she is acting under duress. She may have philosophical differences with our side, but she isn't a willing participant in this."

"So you're sure she's involved?" he asked as he opened his phone.

"No doubt, sir," Dunbar stated firmly.

When his phone was answered, Grimes said, "I need a show put on in Tel Aviv, and don't let Magill know about it."

He listened for a minute and then nodded affirmatively at Colleen.

"Yes, I'll hold," he said into the phone and then placed his hand over the mouthpiece.

"You'd best be right about this," he told her with a straight face.

Agent Dunbar nodded.

~

Jasper Jamison picked up his cell and walked to a sofa while it rang. He'd had enough of this. He wasn't supposed to be involved this directly and the constant calls were making him more than nervous.

"What now?" he answered.

"Something crawled up your ass, Jasper?" the voice said.

Jamison realized who it was and sat up. "Just about, yeah," he complained. "Tell me something good, will you?"

"Not this time," the voice sounded serious. "I just had a hit request I want to check on with you guys."

"From who, her?"

"Absolutely."

"Who is it now?"

"Fuller," the voice told him.

"Hasbrough? You're kidding me."

"Oh no. She's serious and wants it done quick."

"I take it you haven't called the old man."

"You got that right," the voice joked. "That's your level, not mine."

"Let me look into this," Jamison told him. "Hold off till you hear from me, okay?"

"Hey, I didn't want to do this one anyway, just keep her from tagging me over it, alright?"

Jamison found something to smile about. "It's kinda nice having you by the short hairs for a change."

"Just don't get too comfortable."

~

Still seated at the window, Nava held the now silent phone in her opened hand.

"Was that them?" Marsha asked, "the men outside?"

"Does that girl tell the truth?" the Israeli asked in return.

Marsha looked at Ben for a moment. He was obviously in the dark about the discussion and it showed on his face.

"That was the first I heard of it, myself," Marsha told her. "Grimes doesn't tell us everything. But ask yourself this…would Harel stand by and let something happen to his friend, Grimes?"

Nava tilted her eyes up but said nothing. She opened the phone and hit redial.

"What are you doing?" Marsha moved toward her but could only watch as Nava hit the number "2" on the keypad. She then dropped the phone and handed Marsha a small piece of paper. It was in Hebrew.

She looked at it, held it out at Ben who shook his head, and then stepped even closer to the other woman.

"You know I don't read your language," she said in frustration.

"They asked me, in code," she told her. "By the number of the questions listed. They asked if you were all here now."

~

Mid-afternoon approached Roanoke, Virginia. Walter Frazier left the compound in the charge of Orlando Benitez.

"You must trust and understand what I do is for the best," he told the youth. "Just hold your ground and protect the packages I send you."

"When will they get here?" Benitez had asked.

"Overnight."

Frazier's next meeting was with the police officers he'd recruited. They waited at his plumbing supply office.

~

Jon sat next to Cheryl, studying the pages of notes from the thumb drives and the memory cards of the machines from Saint Simons Island.

The details were vague but pointed to ever increasing corruption in the new congressional district on Georgia's coast. That corruption centered around and grew from the takeover of the local news outlets.

Suzanne Glesser, writing as her nationally known pen-name, Felicia Goodman, was preparing to expose connections between drug trafficking along the coast and the office of Congresswoman Pugh in Brunswick. The Saint Simon's Assistant District Attorney, David Eastling, had been made aware, and she planned to meet with him to go over her evidence.

A phone call from Patricia Earl interrupted his study.

"Something big has happened locally," she told him. "The offices of Congresswoman Agnes Pugh were attacked and three staffers were shot to death."

Jon sat forward, listening intently.

"It's on local news now," Earl continued, "should be on cable any minute now."

Pointing for Cheryl to change one monitor to news, Jon asked, "When did this happen?"

"Apparently today," she said in amazement. "Broad daylight."

Jon felt Cheryl tugging on his shirt.

"Look," she whispered. "That's the same office as those pictures from the thumb drives."

Staring at the screen shots Cheryl had taken from the news feed, he compared them to the printed photos she held up.

"Only one thing missing that I can see right away," she pointed out.

"The star picture," Jon nodded as he spoke.

"Bingo," Cheryl smiled.

~

The news from Brunswick had another viewer paying close attention. Darcy Brown, the congresswoman's chief of staff, sat in a coffee shop nervously staring at the TV on the wall. His position was low profile enough that his face wasn't readily noticed out in public. But he did know things and still held in his possession information that was dangerous to his health.

The cell phone was gone, he couldn't be traced by that, nor could any of the calls he'd made from it be used. Taking out his wallet, Darcy looked for a laminated business-card size note. On it were names and numbers.

He started to destroy it too, but something told him he might need a name on that list one day. That day looked extremely close right now.

75

Marsha burst from the elevator talking on the run, "Turn the radar on...now!" she warned. "Those Israelis have something they're going to do when we're all in here."

Jon stood and turned to her. Cheryl searched the control board until Ben reached over her shoulder.

"It's right here," he told her softly and threw a small switch.

"Whoa," Jon said, both arms extended in frustration. "What's going on?"

"Nava is in communication with the men outside," Ben interrupted. "They asked her if we were all here."

The possibilities threw Jon's mind into a spin. *What could they be up to?*

Marsha held out the note that Nava had given her.

"She told them 'no,' that we weren't all here," Marsha nearly stammered in her anger. "But they were expecting us to be." She then pointed to Colleen Dunbar, adding coarsely, "She told them 'no'...based on what that one told her."

All eyes fell on Agent Dunbar except for Director Grimes. He stared at Marsha.

"You know what she said to her, right?" Captain Hurst fumed.

Still looking only at her, Grimes told Marsha he did.

"Efforts are underway as we speak to assure their safety," he said in more a protective than informative mode.

Shaking her head as though avoiding a fly, Marsha turned and muttered a parting shot, "She's lucky she works for you and not me."

Grimes didn't appreciate the display against his agent, especially in public. He looked at Jon but spoke harshly to Marsha. "I agree with that assessment, Captain Hurst. I am lucky indeed."

"Whoa here," a voice came from the dark, "the rescue plans are top secret. How could anybody possibly know that?" It was Tim from several feet away. He and Murray were suiting up.

"I know," Grimes told him. "I've been working on this issue...Yinon Harel is a friend of mine," he spoke of the former Mossad Chief.

"So you told Dunbar, then?" Marsha demanded.

"No...I did not," the director snapped back. "But her assumption and tactic was based on information I shared with all of you." Grimes paused in a way that held everyone's attention. "It is going to happen," he added.

His next words were even more ominous. "We all need to be more careful with what we know," the director sounded as though it were a lecture. "With all the phone numbers going to Langley...that and other information we're finding on these people trying to get to us...well," he took a breath, "I'm convinced there is a mole... maybe more than one, in the CIA."

Tension and silence filled the area, then Jon sat back down and spun his chair toward Grimes who had suddenly looked again at Marsha.

Jon's question broke the silence and the director's chain of thought.

"How long?" he asked the man, "Till they get them released."

Looking back to Jon, Grimes tried to focus on an answer.

"Soon...," he said. "The hospital where they're holding Yinon is the delay. Our people have to be careful there," he rattled off and then quickly turned back to Marsha.

"By the way," he said to her very officially. "If you're interested...your tips paid off. An FBI agent in Albany got a firm ID on the one prisoner we have in your jail."

Marsha smiled slightly and managed a nod. That was good news.

"I'll plan to go down there in the morning," Jon announced. "See what I can find out about him."

"You won't need to do that," Marsha held up her finger. "The undercover officer we have in the jail...is very good. Let me talk with him. I think I have an idea."

Leaving that decision up to Grimes, Jon moved his gaze to Tim and Murray. "Where do you two think you're going?" he asked.

"There's another car out there," Tim shot back. "I'm going to find it. Murray says he wants to go with me."

"Contact your man in Charlotte, Captain," Grimes told Marsha. "See what he can do for us."

Jon looked from the Director to Murray and Tim, and then back to Marsha, each seemingly with their own agenda. He rubbed his head and asked Ben, "Do we have coffee down here?"

Shaking his head while watching the radar, Ben said simply, "No. Up in the kitchen."

He found George there sitting at the table.

"Coffee that good?" Jon asked him.

"Naw," the normally very formal DA responded. "I'm just trying to think something through."

"Your meeting with Gilbert?"

"Yeah."

"Sorry I didn't get back to you sooner." Jon offered as an apology.

George laughed, "Sorry? As busy as I've seen this place in the last couple of years...this takes the cake. No apology necessary."

"Have you figured out what the meeting is about?"

"I don't know yet," George sounded frustrated. "Travis believes they want to kill me."

"Then don't go."

"We've put them off again this afternoon and changed the location."

Jon smiled at him. "That's good strategy. Keep them guessing."

"What if they hurt Travis or his dad?"

Jon sat down, put his cup on the table, and rocked back in the chair. "If you're the target, they won't hurt their bait. If they plan to hurt them, they will anyway," he stated flatly.

"That's kinda cold isn't it?" George tilted his head for effect.

"You're the DA. You tell me."

"It's supposed to be at a diner in Marietta tomorrow afternoon."

"Stay here tonight George," Jon placed his hand on his friend's shoulder. "You and Doris can have our room and I'm going with you tomorrow."

"She's way ahead of you. Ben set up his room for us. He's staying downstairs and no...you aren't."

"We'll figure it out...in the morning, okay?"

"Yeah...sure."

~

Natalie Barrett was worried, scared, mad, and depressed all at once. Not a good state of mind for a psychopath. Her current condition, locked up in the maximum security prison at Oxford, Wisconsin, didn't help in the least. Not hearing results from her issued orders pushed her beyond self-restraints.

"I need to make a call," she screamed down the cell block.

A guard came within three feet of her cell and informed her.

"You only get so many phone calls a week," he told her. "You're already over for this week. It's just a couple more days till the weekend so calm down."

If looks could kill, as they say, but fortunately for the guard it was simply a saying.

Barrett changed the channels on her private TV, looking for news alerts on anything relevant to her orders. There was nothing. No news on Terrell, he was to have hit that Crane guy by now. No news on her lawyer, Hasbrough Fuller, he was supposed to be dead by now.

She started to throw the control at the TV screen, but thought better of it.

"Guard!" she screamed again through the bars. "Can I get some hot tea or is there a limit on that too?"

~

Doris and Colleen Dunbar sat outside Nava's room most of the night. Murray and Tim scoured the area for the Syrian's car after looking for the Israelis.

Marsha spoke with her boss and then Officer Clinton Conrad by phone. A plan was agreed to.

There was some movement of prisoners, leaving the cell block empty except for Collins and Conrad. Both would sleep, or pretend to through the night.

Jon studied what he'd heard and other notes looking for a common denominator to it all.

He was still convinced there was a massive secret being protected at all cost. Something so huge it was unspeakable. Even with that constant in his head, something else seemed to always be in the mix, Calvert Publishing. Its effect on towns or cities, where it had recently taken over the media, was always the same. When news is found to be based on an agenda, the people lose trust in it, their leaders, and eventually themselves.

The symptoms were clear around Atlanta and had been for years. Now the same conditions were underlying in Saint Simons, Brunswick, Albany, Georgia, and particularly strong in Roanoke, Virginia. Each area was part of the Calvert Publishing Empire.

That's who he wanted to justify looking at deeper. There just wasn't enough tangible evidence to back up his suspicions.

Marsha came into their room, tired and quiet. As she got ready for and climbed into the bed, she'd said hardly a word.

With the lights out, Jon spoke to a dark room.

"Something wrong?" he asked.

"No," her voice answered. "It's nothing."

Darkness approached Roanoke, Virginia, as a group meeting to discuss the re-election needs of Congressman Herschel Briar began. Led by his primary benefactor, Walter Frazier, at the offices of Frazier Plumbing Supplies and Fittings, the meeting consisted of many of the area's most influential business people.

Before that meeting would end, Roanoke would be in terror.

76

Morning sun could not directly find the small window of Jon's bedroom. It could however, bounce from the jagged outcroppings on the mountain's surface and trickle through in broken rays.

He lay awake but in no hurry to move. What bits of light that found their way into the room illuminated the form next to him. Jon enjoyed watching that form, knowing he could reach out and touch her at any time.

Two mornings in a row, he thought. *I could get used to this.*

Normal human urges welled up but he remembered, *she needs to sleep and there's much to plan ...and too much to do.* This morning, he would simply watch her sleep.

He slipped from the bed and into a soft chair. From there he continued to let his mind enjoy being with her as her breaths slowly raised and then lowered the sheet.

The wall clock finally came into view and it read 7:36 AM. Jon grimaced but held his position as the minute hand struggled on. At 7:42 he relented. It was time to get up.

He leaned forward, reaching out to wake her, when his phone rang. Its noise seemed to shake the entire room. Grabbing it, he glanced at the calling number and then to Marsha, who was now sitting up. Reflexes caused him to push answer before he looked back at the number, one which he thought he'd recognized, but wasn't sure.

"Yeah?" he answered tersely.

"Yeah... Hell," the voice barked back. "What did you do?"

Jon knew that voice, just not with that tone attached to it. Still he asked, "Who is this?"

"It's me, dad-gum it. Who'd you think it was?"

"Mr. Eagle?"

"The Eagle, damn it, you're a slow learner, huh?"

"Why are you...what's wrong, sir?" Jon tried.

"We've got a hell of a mess up here, son. Something has freaked Walter Frazier out of his mind."

"Slow down, please. Tell me what's happened."

"What triggered it, nobody knows for sure," the Eagle continued hurriedly. "But Frazier and his boys have kidnapped three young girls from their homes overnight. Business folk's kids, two of 'em I know personally."

"Kidnapped?" Jon could figure this out. "What does he want?"

"Let me back up a second. Frazier himself is not a suspect, to anyone except me that is. I know he's the one who arranged it."

"Can you explain that a little?" Jon asked.

"He has himself covered with an air-tight alibi. He was in a meeting with a ton of power brokers well into the wee hours. In fact, the news is what broke up the meeting."

"What is the ransom for these girls?" Jon asked. "You say three were taken?"

"From their homes...all under twelve years old and in two cases relatives were hurt in the abductions."

"Again...what are their demands?"

"The boys at the compound put out a statement, blaming you for the deaths of several of their friends."

"Yet Frazier himself is looking like he's not involved in any way."

"That's about right."

"What does he...or what do they expect?"

"Sounds like he wants your ass, my friend," the Eagle answered. "He doesn't know who you are, but he wants the man in black."

Jon sat for a few seconds and thought. Then he pulled the phone tight to his chin. "If you can, give this guy a message for me. Tell him I'm coming...for him."

~

Sleepless nights add up and in Charlotte, North Carolina, at the Mecklenburg County jail facility; such was the case for the still nameless prisoner from the Wake Forest shooting.

In a nearby cell was undercover officer Clinton Conrad. Armed with new information and a cleared out cell block, Conrad tried several times to engage the other man in conversation. At 1:15 AM, the undercover cop had finally given up and went to sleep himself.

It was now 7:25 AM and Conrad nearly jumped as he awoke.

Looking down to the end cell, he could see his target sitting up and again staring at the floor.

"Collins," the pretend prisoner called out in a loud whisper. "Hey, Collins, that is you. I recognize you from the pecan plant."

The other man twisted his head enough to look at his neighbor. But he did not speak.

"Collins," Conrad tried again, "Henry Collins of the security team. I went drinking with you and a few of your buds one night."

Still there was nothing in response.

"I worked the line while I was there. If you don't remember me, that's okay. Most people don't. But I know you...you're Henry Collins."

"Would you quit saying that?" the other man finally broke and barked out at the officer. "Just shut up, will you?"

"Not if you won't talk, man. Who the hell do you think you are, anyway?"

"What do want from me?" Collins asked.

"Where did you go so all of a sudden? I mean from the plant."

Collins realized the only way to silence this guy was to give him some limited information.

"Putney has a friend in Atlanta, alright?" he told his interrogator. "A very influential friend. He hooked me up with another job."

"So you worked in Atlanta, then?" Conrad pushed.

"No...no," Collins found himself spilling his guts. "The job was in Chicago." Then Collins stood and grabbed the bars on the front of the cell.

"Who the hell are you, you say?" he asked in return.

"I'm Clint, man...Clint Conrad. I've been up here working at the paper mill. We ship reams of paper to the colleges around this state."

"Yeah? Good for you." Collins was not impressed. He went back to his bunk and sat down.

"How was Chicago, man?" Conrad asked.

"It was okay, I guess. I was a...well the man I worked for cleaned up my record and my identity. He called us his ghosts."

"Huh?" Conrad nodded at the man. "So you were still in security, then?"

"You could say that, yeah. We worked for many big deals, even for the Chicago Mayor himself a year or so back."

"Man, that's cool. Who was this boss of yours? Is he still hiring?"

"His name was Pilfoy and he ain't hiring anymore cause he's dead."

Conrad thought how to get what he needed.

"I heard they got Alexander in here somewhere, too. You know him?"

Collins laughed. "Alexander...the Russian kid? That mad as a hornet shooter? Yeah...we worked with him a time or two."

That defines the type of work anyway, Conrad thought.

"So...if your boss got himself dead," he asked Collins next. "Who you working for now?"

"We got us a team thing going. There's three of us. Mostly we work for this one guy. I don't know his name, but he calls us from Washington, D.C. He's some big deal with the government, I think."

"Must pay real good, huh?"

"Well, we ain't getting paid for this last one. It went sour on us and I can't even get a lawyer or nothing. They won't let me see my guys, and I know one of them is hurt bad."

"Henry," Conrad went for the fence with one last question. "I'm out of here today sometime. You want I should call your boss or something?"

Collins stood back up and walked to the bars. He whispered almost too low to be heard.

"I don't have a name," he said, "like I told you. But call this number, 212-555-7103 and tell them the Blue Team is in lock-up down here." He waited for a response and finally asked, "Can you do that for me?"

"Count on it, Henry." Conrad told him. "Count on it."

77

Speaking only briefly to those around the kitchen table, Jon looked at Lori and asked how Nava was doing.

"She and her phone were quiet all night," Daniel's wife told him. "Doris took over for me around 6:00 am. She's still up there."

Jon nodded and poured himself a cup of coffee. He politely excused himself and went back up stairs to the elevator. He saw Doris down the hall and started to go check on her. When she waved a thumbs-up signal, he held up his hand and went on his way.

The door to the elevator seemed to open within a second of its closing. The ride down was solitary and supposed to help him think. Jon Crane stood inside the scantly lit conveyance looking out at those in the workshop, Ben's workshop.

Daniel Seay, Cheryl Duray, and Ben manned the control board. More monitors than he realized they had were all flashing with data or pictures or both. Jerome Grimes could be seen in the background, sitting in a shadow with his phone to his ear.

Jon needed to plan. Normally he needed information from which to draw that plan. This morning, it was information that was in his way, clogging his thoughts. There was simply too much of it. Not wanting to cause concern over his actions, Jon stepped out and moved slowly toward Grimes. Those at the control board noticed him but were all busy. Cheryl managed to raise one hand as he went by.

What had he gotten them all into? He asked himself. *How deep a puzzle could he figure out? Even with their help.*

He was committed to going to Roanoke, three young girls' lives were at stake and obviously he had to respond. But with George's meeting, the situation in Brunswick, and the unknown but ever growing Albany connection, he wondered which held the most importance. George's safety of course, but that could be arranged.

Jon was close enough now to hear Grimes' words.

"The Marietta Quick-Stop Diner on Highway 41," he was emphasizing to whoever was on the phone, "Total envelope from two hundred yards out and agents in the building as employees. I need this in place before 1400 hours...yes, today."

Jon sat down beside him and Grimes acknowledged his presence with a terse nod.

"You have him now?" Grimes said into the phone. "Okay, put him on." With a hand over the mouthpiece, he looked at Jon and said, "They've got the President for me."

"Do you think that's wise at this time?" Jon asked.

"He's working with us, Jon. He needs to know."

After a series of blank looks and grimaces as his call was connected, Grimes expression became serious. "Good morning to you, Sir," he said. "I need your back-up on several things. Two... that I already have in motion." He looked at Jon and shrugged his shoulders.

"Yes, Sir," Grimes confirmed, "the protective shields in Israel and one in Marietta, Georgia."

He listened for a second, then added, "Yes, Sir...our Georgia."

Though hearing only one side of the conversation, Jon still felt he knew what was happening.

"We've had that talk, Sir," Grimes said into the phone. He again looked straight at Jon before continuing. "Crane agrees and we both wonder what could be so important."

The look on Grimes face squinted as he listened.

"Ideology?" he asked softly in reply. "They would spend this much in resources...in lives and money...to protect an ideology?"

Now Jon wished he could hear the other end of the conversation. He sat up straighter and leaned in, but could not hear the President's words.

"I see," Grimes muttered. Then he looked at Jon and spoke so he too could hear. "The secret defends the ideology. Without this secret, their entire being would be at risk."

Grimes thought and then asked, "Sir, does the word 'Amber' have any significance to all this?"

Again, Jon would have loved to have heard the other side of the conversation. But he did see Grimes smile slightly. The director of the NCIS had a bit more to relay to the President.

"Jackson Terrell will not be an issue anymore ...anywhere," he said. "Yes, I'm real sure. I have his body here...Oh...and also. You already know I suspect a mole in the CIA, perhaps more than one." He stopped to listen.

"So, you're on that," he said and nodded severely at Jon. "We don't want Barrett to know any of this just yet. No, Sir," he emphasized strongly. "Her contacts, I believe, are coming unglued. Crane has a link he's working on through the Atlanta area with ties to other cities."

Again, Grimes wrinkled his face while listening.

"Yes, Sir," he confirmed. "That is indeed who we suspect."

Jon shook Grimes' arm. "Has he heard about Roanoke?" he asked softly.

Grimes waved him off and continued with his talk.

"Thank you, Sir." He said sharply. "Yes...absolutely. When this is finished we'll all get together. Thank you again. Good-bye."

Grimes turned to Jon staring at him.

"Well?" his host asked. "Has he heard about Roanoke?"

"It's Salem, actually," Grimes corrected him. "The news right now is that two teenagers, runaways, have taken up with a small time gang at their clubhouse."

"That's the news?"

"He knows what's going on," Grimes confided. "Control of information and how it's put out is a powerful thing. But we have sources of our own....Say...How do you know so fast?"

"Take a guess."

"The Eagle," Grimes smiled. "He's still on top of everything up there."

"So this news doesn't surprise the President?"

"Not in the least. His top suspect for all this, even above Barrett... is the same as yours...Carlton Calvert."

"And the secret they are protecting?" Jon wondered.

"It's their fallback lie...the comeback used every time corruption is found in their camp." The director's disgust clearly showed as he gasped deeply to shake off his anger. "It's been there...hanging over this country...hell, hanging over the entire world for years now. And they haven't hesitated to use it...every chance they get."

Jon lowered his head.

"Anyone who could think has known all along," he said quietly.

"Thinking will get you called a name," Grimes shot back.

"Still, people know. But without proof, that side always beats them back in the argument."

"It's like that 'gold ring' in the fairy tale," Grimes alluded.

"You mean, The Hobbit? That's not actually a fairy tale, it's a..."

"Whatever," Grimes snapped. "...It's their precious."

78

Cecil Magill was not having a good morning. The CIA section chief for the Middle East Covert Support Group learned that three of his Syrian hit men had been identified, posthumously. He had brought them in himself, on a C-141. They were to go to Alabama, as a diversion mainly, but to take out the SEAL who knew too much, while they were there.

"Just follow Grimes' men," he caught himself mumbling. "How hard could that be?"

How could this happen, he screamed internally. Walking down the hall in the huge Wilson Boulevard building he found nothing to lift his spirits.

Al Halbi hasn't checked in...in over fourteen hours and now Fred wants some answers. This is not good, he concluded as he knocked on the door he reached at the end of the hall.

"Cecil?" the voice within asked.

"Yeah, Fred."

"Come in... but step carefully."

Magill opened the door and immediately noticed the heavy plastic spread across the floor.

"What the hell?" he asked moving forward.

"Renovations, Cecil," the man explained, "Got to make some changes."

Cecil Magill froze in place. His face went pale as he uttered, "Oh no!"

He never saw the man who stepped up behind him. A twenty ounce, ball-peen hammer entered Magill's skull and stopped at three inches deep. There was little noticeable noise.

~

The light from the elevator door got their attention. Jon and Grimes looked at the same time as Tim and Murray emerged from the bright illumination across the room.

Their appearance was obvious.

"You've been out there all night?" Jon challenged.

"Yes... Dad," a tired cowboy shot back. "We was hunting bad guys."

Spiegel grabbed a rolling chair and sat down. He placed a small bag in front of him.

"One thing I realized right away," he said while staring at his boss. "The car we had was the Syrians'. The missing one was Terrell's."

"Did you find it?" Jon pressed.

"It was a dirt bike," Murray said for him. "Buried under some pine straw but we found it."

"There was a motel keycard taped to the front tire wheel-well," Spiegel added. He unzipped the bag he'd brought in. "This was in the room."

Money, ammunition, three burner cell phones, and a notebook were dumped out on a table top.

"You'll recognize that phone number on page two," Tim smirked.

Jon picked it up and immediately looked at Grimes.

"Fuller again," he said.

Murray shook his head. "Why are these people being so careless with these connections?" he asked out loud. "This is the top of this shit pile. I don't understand the stupidity."

"They don't normally handle this stuff directly," Jon surmised. "We're getting into their kitchen. They're running scared."

~

Israel had been quietly on edge since the no-confidence vote of six weeks earlier. The Labor Party loyalists, or Socialist Democrats, were in power, but very precariously. They had taken actions kept from the Israeli people and because of the mixed reaction to the change in government, one in particular went unnoticed.

The injuries to Yinon Harel were no accident. Teo Romach, a loyal social democrat, was named as successor in waiting to head the Mossad and its emphasis quickly changed course.

The peace movement of the newly installed government was based on pacifism. The hard lines taken by Harel and his team were considered old fashioned and harmful.

When approached by the faction of U.S. officials who had fallen from power but continued to hold similar beliefs, they were told of the need to protect certain secrets.

Amzi Reiss was taken into house arrest and care for Yinon Harel was slowed to bare life support. The fate of both men was charged to Nava Golan. She was to team up with insurgents smuggled into the U.S. to stop the threat of exposure by her friends, the associates of Jonathan Crane. She managed to wear a skirt that held a particular button. One that Yinon had issued her, having received several of them from the President of the United States.

The button was non-detectable until it came within five miles of the U.S. coast. There, it would pick-up power and begin transmitting a low frequency beacon.

The NSA was charged with immediate notification of such a signal to one agency of the federal government, the NCIS.

~

Jon stepped away from Grimes, Tim, and Murray. He leaned over Ben at the control board and whispered to him, "I want to be undisturbed in the lower level for one hour. Got it?"

Ben's slight nod was enough and he headed for the elevator.

"Where are you going?" Grimes demanded.

Jon turned as he pressed the elevator button.

"It's my house, director," he answered sharply, "I go where I wish around here."

In the third level, Jon hit a switch that lit up the entire area. He walked to a locker behind the old pick-up truck and took out a black suit. When he had it on, he walked to the hog-tied Syrian.

"Comfortable?" he asked almost sarcastically.

The Syrian looked at him with a blank stare and said nothing.

Jon waited for a full minute and then knelt down over the man's face.

"Let's get this one thing clear," he said with a much more threatening tone than before. "If you're gonna act like you don't speak English then you're no good to me... and I don't need you."

He stood, staring down at the still quiet man and reached into a leg pouch and took out a knife. The Syrian's eyes got wider.

"I've been better," he finally said. "My hands are numb and I can't really feel them."

Jon put the knife away. He looked closely at the man's hands.

"They're nearly blue, too," he said. "You ready to talk?"

"That depends," Al Halbi said defiantly. "You'll kill me none the less, right?"

412

"We don't know that yet," Jon responded. He reached down and untied most of the binding on the man's legs and then loosened the straps on his wrists. As he finished untying the hands, Jon told him, "You get the rest... now stand up if you can." He then backed away several feet.

The Syrian rubbed at his wrists until color returned and then sat up to reach his feet.

"What is it you wish to know?" he asked.

"Who brought you here?"

"It was arranged."

"Don't be cute...by who?"

"A contact from your government," he told him. "A man we worked with for years before the Sheik was killed."

"A name," Jon insisted. "I need a name."

"Maaa...gill," Al Halbi answered. "It's a hard name for me to say."

The Syrian leaned forward and tried to stand. His knees were weak so he stayed in a kneeling position.

"Why kill the two people in Georgia?" Jon asked next. He could see the man feeling around his left leg pocket with his hand.

"They knew too much," Al Halbi said as he continued to search with his hand.

Jon threw the garrote to the floor in front of him.

"Is that what you're looking for?" he challenged him.

79

A news conference was set up at Frazier Plumbing Supply. It was well known that Frazier was a "sponsor" of the Red Sharks boys "club." The initial reports of two runaways, as told by the local media, had transformed with the national cable companies rolling into town.

"Two" became three and "runaways" became kidnap victims in a seamless transition of what the public was told. This presented questions that needed to be addressed.

Walter Frazier started outside to the podium and the nest of microphones tied to it, when an aide called him back.

"What are you doing, you fool," Frazier barked at him. "They're ready for me out there."

"You need to take this call, sir."

"Who is it?"

"I don't know...but we need to."

With his eyes squinted in anger and frustration, Walt Frazier grabbed the cell phone.

"This is Frazier," he answered abruptly, "Can I help you?"

"You could help yourself, you foolish old man but I doubt you will," the voice said.

"Who is this?" Frazier commanded sternly.

"Oh...get over yourself, Walt. You're just not that impressive. Besides that, you've got a real problem and it ain't that news conference."

"I don't have time for silly threats," Frazier warned.

"Make time for this one," the old voice continued, "I have a message for you."

"What message?"

"He knows you did this to draw him to you."

"Who? Damn it."

"The one you sought," the voice was near joyful, "now seeks you."

Walter Frazier exploded in rage and had spilled several epithets before realizing the line was now dead. The Eagle had hung up.

Frazier threw the phone at his aide and stomped out toward the news conference.

~

The deployment in Ramat Hasharon, Israel, was sixteen men and women, twelve regular Mossad and four undercover NSA operatives working in the area. It was 3:00 PM there as opposed to 8:00 AM in Dalton, Georgia, but Jerome Grimes' request had taken less than an hour to pull together.

Amzi Reiss lived on a quiet street in the town of some 40,000 residents. Very few, excluding all of his neighbors, knew anything about his house arrest. It was hoped that the situation could be corrected without them ever finding out.

A power company truck set up at a pole near the Reiss home. The workman climbed to the top and appeared to be adjusting a transformer. Two women with baby carriages turned the corner as many do every day. These carriages did not carry babies, though they were loaded down.

Four other men played a pick-up game of soccer in the yard next to Reiss' home while two door-to-door salesmen approached from the other direction. All of these were involved as were seven others in hiding.

The salesmen knocked on the door at 3:12 PM. Power and phone lines were cut to the house at that exact moment. Confusion reigned inside as one armed man went to the door, and three others attempted to locate the problem with the power. They were not yet aware the phones were also out.

The soccer players met the baby carriages and pulled weapons and grenades from the strollers, the women also retrieved their weapons and the team spread across the front of the house.

The seven others hit the rear from all angles; three entering, while four waited and guarded the grounds. A smoke grenade broke through the front window, another into a side bedroom.

"Amzi!" the team leader called out as the group overpowered the men holding him and stormed inside. "Amzi Reiss," they yelled, "we are with Yinon!" It all took less than three minutes. Reiss was freed and no one was hurt.

Thirty minutes later, Amzi Reiss called the leader of the Social Democrat party and struck a deal for his silence in the matter. Yinon Harel and twelve other political "prisoners" were released quietly, and Harel was put under proper doctor's care.

One of the NSA operatives gave Reiss a global wireless phone and a number. It rang in the house in Dalton, Georgia.

"Nava," Marsha called to her. "I have a call for you down here. Come quickly."

Reiss was able to convince Nava Golan that he was alright and so was Harel. Nava broke down in tears.

"Is Marsha there?" Reiss asked her.

"Right here," she sobbed.

"Tell her to thank Grimes. He did this."

Nava looked past Marsha to Colleen Dunbar who had walked up from in the kitchen. She nodded and Nava smiled at her.

"I shall do that, my love," Nava said into the phone. She was unashamed and getting her senses back. "I shall do just that."

~

The Syrian stared at his garrote but did not pick it up.

"I was thinking something more substantial for this moment," he sneered at Jon. But Silas had taken over. He tossed a long bladed knife down next to the wire killing tool.

"Thought you might," he teased the man on his knees. "I imagine that new handle takes some time getting used to...huh?"

Al Halbi rose to one knee and took the knife in his right hand.

"It worked just fine," he offered back while standing and taking an aggressive stance.

"Yeah," Silas noted, "that was a friend of mine you used it on in Kentucky." He took one step to his right and continued, "You may want to consider that fact... before you make your next move."

The Syrian killer looked confused by that remark. The man held no weapon of his own but was clad in a strange black outfit. Al Halbi flipped the knife a single rotation and caught it.

"I'm a proficient killer with this blade as well as the garrote, my odd friend. And I don't care for your friend, whoever he was."

With those words finished, the Syrian dove toward Silas, his knife wielding hand circling and jabbing every which way. Silas did not move as the blade finally came into his body on the left side, just above his waist.

The knife glanced off without breaking, but Al Halbi's wrist was not as fortunate. The force of the blow he delivered bent his wrist inward and both bones snapped under the strain applied by his thrust.

The knife fell to the floor. Silas grabbed Al Halbi under his chin and lifted the man off the floor.

"Who was your contact in Brunswick?" he demanded.

The Syrian tried to support his injured arm with his other hand.

"What?" he asked as though the question made no sense to him.

"One more chance to answer," Silas glared into his eyes and raised him yet higher from the floor.

"Brown...Brown," the Syrian called out. "Some young one named Dar-see Brown!"

Silas dropped him to the floor and towered over him.

"Is he the one who told you the reporter knew too much?"

"He delivered the message," Al Halbi rocked in pain as he spoke.

Silas simply stared and then muttered low, "From who?"

"The man in Washington," the Syrian spit as he tried to talk more. "Magill's boss. All I know is he called him CW on 'C' Street."

Silas looked at him as though confused. The man raised his good arm up towards him, begging, "Please...that's what he said, CW on C Street."

Silas put a finger in front of his lips and made the "hush" sign to the injured man and he dialed a cell phone. Grimes answered from one floor above.

"What the hell are you doing?" the director yelled into the phone.

"What does 'CW on C Street' mean to you...if anything?"

Grimes thought a minute.

"CW?" He rolled the initials around in his head. Then an idea hit him.

"The State Department is on C Street," he speculated, "Could be someone there."

"Thanks," Silas said abruptly and hung up.

Grimes looked at his phone as if it had malfunctioned.

"Now what?" he said out loud.

80

Cheryl felt the vibration on her hip.

Who would be texting? She wondered and pulled the phone from her pocket.

"Please have your Dad call on my private line," it read. There was no signature but the caller number was clear to her. It was Jon.

She leaned into Ben and excused herself to go upstairs. As the elevator opened for her, Jon stepped out without a word and she stepped in.

"Call Gil, will you?" Jon asked while looking at George. "Our guest will need a doctor for his arm and extra security, but get him out of here."

George heard him but did not react instantly. Instead, he glanced at Ben with a concerned look and then addressed Jon.

"With Cheryl out of the room," he said, "What's happening with Westy?"

"He's fine," Jon answered in a casual tone.

"Fine? They hit his house pretty hard at the start of this and we haven't heard any more. No follow-up attacks, what's with that?"

Grimes moved forward and spoke before Jon could.

"Westy wasn't the target," he stated bluntly.

"Four men at his place?" George questioned, "Why hit there if not for him?"

Both Jon and Grimes had known without saying for some time. They looked at the young man operating the control board.

"Westy had a guest while the SEAL operation was on-going," Grimes said. "That's who they were after."

Ben swung around in his chair.

"I figured as much," he added. "Whoever is doing this has some pretty sophisticated equipment. They knew I was working from up there, helping you guys."

Daniel Seay stepped forward but stayed quiet. Murray and Tim looked on with interest but also had nothing to add.

"Does Westy know this?" George asked.

"We haven't discussed it directly," Jon told him. "But yeah, he knows. That's why he stayed up there. Once they realized Ben wasn't still around, there haven't been any more attacks on his place."

"But they're staying in Sault Ste. Marie...why's that?"

"Mainly for Cheryl and Rita," Jon answered. "He goes back to the ranch every few days to feed the livestock and look around. It's just to keep his wife and daughter calm."

Everybody looked to Ben who simply nodded and turned back to his screens.

Jon's phone rang. He looked at it and told the others as he walked away, "I need to take this."

Tim caught him and asked quietly, "You want me to bring our friend downstairs, up here?"

"Gil knows the place," Jon said somewhat reluctantly. *Too many people know this place*, he thought to himself. "Just blindfold Mr. Halbi and let them take him out the back way." He then entered the elevator and said into the phone, "You busy?"

~

The monitor screen lit up with news as Daniel sat down. A major hit, a report on the ballistics from Alexander's rifle had him read through it twice.

"Guys," he finally said loudly, "there are five confirmed matches to the weapon Alexander used in Charlotte. Four are deaths we aren't even working on, but they appear to be connected overall."

"Other 'congress' types?" Murray asked.

"Yeah," Daniel snapped as though in a hurry to move on, "aides and associates to questionable ones...but here's the big news." He looked at everyone around him. "There was enough from the slug that hit the Navy Secretary's car to match it to his rifle," he smiled though the subject wasn't funny. "Our boy Alexander has been truly busy."

Jerome Grimes grunted and nodded that he heard Daniel's news, but he also had another call. He listened intensely and then barked orders.

"Check the phone number," he nearly yelled and turned away from the others standing there. "Find out if the calls were all voice or if any were texts. Yeah...I said texts. Okay," and he hung up.

Everyone stared at Grimes and made a comment of some sort except Ben. He was transfixed to his screen, playing something over and over. The director shook them off with his head as Tim looked to Ben.

"Whatcha got?" he asked the youth, noticing his deep concentration.

"I don't know," Ben said slowly and played the digital copy over again. "It's something small and very high that went overhead about ten minutes ago."

"How small?" Grimes asked.

"I'd say a eight foot wingspan and about four feet nose to tail."

The NCIS Director leaned in as though he could see clearer. Tim stood over him and uttered two words.

"Observation drone," he said.

Grimes leaned in and agreed, "Damn right, it is."

~

The press conference had been well staged in Walter Frazier's benefit. The platform was set up between two of his buildings. In a gap wide enough to allow the rising sun to be at his back as he spoke, and in the reporter's eyes.

The speakers were large as to create a natural echo making recordings difficult. The pre-arranged questions were the best part.

"Mr. Frazier?" the first reporter asked. "How are you doing this morning? Did you get any sleep with this trying situation developing around the kids you work with so hard?"

"I did...some, yes," Frazier answered with a smile. "Thank you Martha, I appreciate your concern and that of the good folks at Channel 14."

"Do you know of any reason the Red Sharks would be charged as kidnappers?" came another question.

"I know only that Orlando was very upset at the death of his close friend, Renaldo."

"Renaldo Guiss," the reporter interrupted, "wasn't he known as 'Red Boots,' Sir?"

"He was a flashy dresser, yes," Frazier went on. "His death was a real blow to Orlando and all the boys."

"Do you think they actually took the girls who are at the compound?"

"No...no," Frazier shook his head profusely. "They called and the girls came over to talk. I'm not sure why they have chosen not to come out, but I am assured it is by their choice."

"Why don't they let the authorities in?" one reporter asked.

"The trust factor, I must assume... Miss?" Frazier stepped toward the impertinent questioner.

"Jackie Monahan, sir. I'm Gail's sister."

Frazier quickly turned from the interloper. Gail Monahan was a local reporter who had gone missing over a year ago while investigating Frazier's connection to drugs and other illegal activity in the Roanoke area. Soon after her disappearance, the local papers and TV stations were bought out by Calvert Publishing. Gail Monahan's status was not mentioned again.

"Are there any other legitimate questions from actual reporters?" Frazier laughed and the crowd laughed with him.

"Not that this is funny in the least," he stated for the record, "But a press conference should be reserved for the press, don't you think?"

There were two more staged questions about "had he heard from Orlando that morning and did the boys have enough food to last the day?" Frazier then thanked them and returned to his office.

81

Jon stopped back by the workshop on his way to the third sub-level. His conversation with Westy was private and only he and Cheryl knew it had happened. He'd left the elevator before the doors were fully open.

"Is Gil coming for our guest?" he asked the group.

"Yeah," Grimes answered and appeared almost animated with his gestures. "Look...I've heard from Charlotte, round about... anyway."

"What does that mean?" Jon's voice went into full Silas mode in only four words.

"Marsha's man inside the jail did really good," Grimes explained. "He got us verification on that name from Albany and a contact number his team was using."

Silas remembered this man spilling his guts, but not like this.

"Didn't he tell you he knew nothing about that?" he asked while calming down. "He told you one of the others handled the communications?"

"He did indeed," the director grinned. "Wouldn't be the first time I was lied to."

Jon stared at him a second, and then nodded and asked about the contact number. "CIA again, right?" he guessed.

"That's the odd part," Grimes told him. "It goes to another building, that one on 'C' Street in D.C."

Jon didn't acknowledge the information outwardly, but he understood. The others could hear a muted grunt as he sorted it out in his mind. *This was new*, he thought. Another layer he didn't really need. *How high is the top of this?* he asked himself.

Turning to the elevator he called to Murray over his shoulder, "Can you take me somewhere in about an hour?" he asked.

"Sure," the cowboy lurched forward, eager to help, "Where to?"

"I'll tell you when we're in the air." Jon's answer was short and all business. Then turning to Tim, he asked, "I need you to keep these people safe here for a while, okay?" The agent and former SEAL nodded once.

"Wait a minute," Grimes interjected angrily, "There's something flying overhead here...have you any idea what that could mean?"

Looking at Ben, Jon responded calmly, "When we're gone, go to level five on the exterior security. That should handle what they have."

Ben nodded but Grimes wasn't satisfied.

"Where are you going?" he demanded.

"I've got a meeting to attend to," was his answer. He stepped into the elevator and looked again at the cowboy.

"Murray, I'll be just a bit... in my lab," he directed at his friend. "I'll call you when I'm ready."

~

In the front guest bedroom, Nava sat with Marsha, Doris, Colleen, and Lori surrounding her. They were all concentrating on the phone Nava held, cupped in both hands.

"Still nothing?" Marsha broke the silence and walked to the window yet again, "Ben said somebody flew something overhead."

"No, there's nothing from them. I heard them speak of drones at one point," Nava shared reluctantly. "I don't want to sound alarming, but they did mention that ... once."

Colleen stood and got everyone's attention.

"Did I hear talk of an attic to this place?" she asked.

426

"Yeah," Doris said. "I can show you the access door and stairs." She looked at Marsha, who continued to stare out the window and nearly begged her, "Aren't you coming?"

"You can show her around," Marsha muttered in response. She held her spot as the two went down the hall and through an undersized door near the master bedroom.

Doris flipped a light switch at the top of the steps and Colleen Dunbar immediately noticed the T-Rex rifle leaning against one wall.

"Holy crap," she exclaimed without thinking. "I'm sorry...that's one hell of a weapon."

"I can't even pick the thing up," Doris smiled. "Don't really want to."

"So, they have shooting ports up here?"

"Yeah," Doris turned on another light and the chairs showed up. "Those three spots over there, two are for shooters and one is for a spotter... they tell me."

"How far can you see from here?" Dunbar asked while pushing a flap open.

"I don't really know. But they have used it quite successfully before."

Colleen studied the view through the spotter's hole.

"The sun doesn't seem to interfere at all," she noticed. "There's no glare on anything."

"Do you see anything...or anyone?"

"No," she answered and let the flap close on its own. "What is this above the slot?"

She pointed to a two inch thick metal panel that was held back on a hinge.

"Each hole has that," Doris pointed out. "If they need to seal the house completely, those panels slide down."

"Interesting man, this Jonathan Crane," Dunbar smiled.

~

With the lab area sealed off from the rest of the third sub-level, Jon worked on a mixture of methoxyflurane, halothane, and methyl propyl ether. He placed the mixture in three bottles with a propellant of fentanyl, for rapid onset, sealed under high pressure.

He calculated the three would cover an area of 40,000 square feet before dissipating into the air.

That should be enough, he thought as he moved to pick out masks for protection from the toxins.

Loading the thick, pressurized bottles and two masks into a duffle bag, he checked a new black suit and folded it for transport.

The seal hissed as he opened the door from the lab, but nothing escaped into the garage space. Flipping open his phone, he called Murray.

"I'm ready when you are," he said.

82

The Calvert mansion had been quiet most of the day. Carlton watched the goings on in Roanoke with some interest, but had no idea how closely they tied in with his own operation. The phone caught him off guard.

"Yeah," he answered gruffly, "Calvert here."

"You told me you could control all this," the voice said.

Calvert was stunned. He recognized the voice but couldn't believe it.

"You're being a bit brash aren't you?" he said in return. "Making a call in the middle of the day?"

"It's morning here," the man wasn't amused, "and should still be where you are. Where are Jamison and Putney?"

"At home I would expect," Calvert wasn't enjoying this call either. "Why are you calling me?"

"Too much going on out there," was the answer, "too many people are screwing up at the same time. Information is being compromised, or are you not aware of that?"

"What information?"

"Magill had to be removed. Three traces led directly to him in less than twenty-four hours. How is that possible?"

"I didn't know," the old man sounded more subdued. "Barrett has people out all over the place... and so does Magill."

"Too messy."

"Has anything come back on you...or me, for Christ's sake?"

"Not yet," the voice told him. "But get a handle on this. Back it all down. I don't even know how bad the damage is. Several of Magill's people are not checking in and a group has released Harel and his people in Israel."

"When?" Calvert couldn't believe he had not heard the news.

"It's being kept hush–hush. Neither side wants to admit it happened."

"Get Magill back in there," the publisher became adamant, "We need the Israeli democrats working this."

"Forget about Magill," the voice informed him and the old man understood immediately what that meant.

"This one damned man has us jumping through our asses," Calvert slammed a fist down.

"You should have studied your history on this guy," the voice lectured. "The Chicago cartel fell completely apart. No more girls, no more money, and Mayor Rigby is dead."

"You think he did that?"

"They did most of it to themselves, you fool. Just like what's going on now. After that audacious lawyer friend of yours tried her stunt and got nailed, it scared everybody."

The voice paused but then went on with its lambaste.

"Shannahan got herself and our highest placed political figure killed," it spewed angrily. "That's on you and Barrett."

There was quiet on the line, all except the old man's sudden heavy breathing.

"I'll see what I can do," Calvert promised.

"Yeah...whatever," the voice said and then hung up.

~

The Jaguar backed out from the upper level garage and roared down the driveway. Jon and Murray were off to get Lucy Too.

George Vincent had been quietly listening and thinking. He stepped up to Grimes and told him, "I've got a car coming to take me to Marietta."

"I've got that covered," the director explained. "Every worker, every customer when you get there will be one of ours."

George nodded without speaking and Ben walked up with a jacket, one of Jon's jackets with the Kevlar liner.

"It's business casual, right," the youth grinned at him and helped George put it on.

"Not as heavy as I expected," he said as a thank-you.

"Be careful, okay?" Ben threw in. "I know you'll want to take them alive so we can talk to 'em. But just be careful and let Grimes' people do their work."

The intercom came alive with Lori calling that Gil Gartner and two other Dalton police units were here. They would take the Syrian into the hospital ward in town, shackled and hog-tied for good measure.

Gil directed George to his car and opened the rear door.

"I'll sit up front if it's all the same to you," the DA told him with a smile.

Gartner slammed the rear shut and opened the front passenger door.

"Nice jacket, sir," he quipped and stepped around the armored patrol car. As Gil climbed in he handed the DA a .40 caliber Glock, saying, "How bout we go have lunch down in Cobb County?"

"Let's do that," Vincent answered. "I'm ready."

~

The lawyer Hasbrough Fuller was pale and could hardly sit straight as he held the phone to his ear.

"Get a grip man," Jasper Jamison chided him. "It was her that wanted you dead, not us. You just don't need to try to contact her anymore."

"I can't believe we're all talking to each other...about this shit," the nervous lawyer muttered. "How did we get to this point?"

Jamison shook his head. He agreed things were completely out of hand but didn't want to say that.

"Have you heard from Jackson Terrell?" he asked instead.

"No."

It sounded to Jamison like the response was emotionless all of a sudden.

"Why so sullen?" he asked the lawyer. "These guys are solitary types, real independents who do as they damn well please."

"He's dead, I know it." Fuller added in much the same tone.

"Well," the furniture man tried to pick up the pace of the conversation, "we simply don't know that. There's been nothing on the news and Terrell is a nationally known killer. If they got him...we'd have heard."

"What are you going to do with Barrett?" Fuller asked. "She won't give up till she gets her way, you know that."

"Not my pay grade on that one. I'll let the other two deal with her, if and when they choose to."

"What about me? She could still have me killed."

"Yeah, I guess she could," Jamison teased him viciously. "You'd best stay in touch with me...real close, right?"

"Do I stay here...in Washington?"

"I wouldn't," the furniture man nearly laughed at that. "Come down here. I'll figure somewhere you can wait this all out."

"What's in the bag?" Murray asked aggressively as the dark blue jet helicopter streaked through the sky. He had noticed the bag when Jon put it on board, but neither man had mentioned it before now.

"We're meeting Westy at the airport in Roanoke," Jon told him.

"Okay, but what's in the bag?"

"Things we'll need to do a job. There are three girls being held captive... by a gang of kids."

"That thing at the police compound," Murray had heard about it. "That's been on the news."

"Very good," Jon said sincerely. "It's my belief those young men are up past their bedtime."

"It's only 1 pm," the cowboy cracked.

"Yeah, they need their rest.. in more ways than one."

The special box he had printed came unfolded and unglued. Dawes played with the folds several times before trying to glue the flaps. It aggravated him to have to fool with this detail, but he patiently worked with it on the kitchen table of his Decatur, Georgia, home.

Should have thought about this, he scolded himself as the box finally took shape. *Would have thought they'd put the thing together.*

"Not bad," he finally said stepping back from the table. He admired his work and added, "Looks like the real deal."

The container would hold his "toys," the six canisters. Five inches in diameter and four inches in height, they were volatile, condensed mixtures of Acetyl chloride, Cyanogen, and Butane gases each separated by a thin aluminum liner.

They were a bright blue with a tiny red dot on the very top where the wireless detonator lay. The top level of each container... just under half of its overall height held a layer of C-4 explosive. The directional charge was pointed down in order to compress and accelerate the ignition of the gases. A heat surge of over 800 degrees would expand in every direction from each unit. Those not killed in the blast would find themselves surrounded by flames.

The professionally printed stickers were a nice touch, he thought.

Their appearance would cover the lethal intent.

Warren Dawes had "experimented" with a similar type weapon some years ago. The unexpected force generated by the addition of the gases threw his body into a utility pole, breaking his leg in three places. He'd been standing fifty yards from the explosion and the pole was another twenty yards behind him.

Not able to seek a doctor for days after the "hit", Dawes' leg healed but in an irregular manner. He limped profusely with it since.

With the box now complete and the canisters ready, Warren Dawes felt good about the timeline.

Three days till Tuesday, he reminded himself. *A busy first of the week... catches folks off guard, but coming ahead of schedule works even better.*

The detonator was almost ready. He would keep that with him and be sure to be out of range before he touched off the cataclysm.

83

Lucy Too was still an hour out from Roanoke when Jon reached behind him and opened the duffle bag. He pulled out a helmet with full glass face shield.

"That's new, huh?" the cowboy noticed.

"Yeah, another of Ben's finds," he answered. "The suit and all is new. They hook together for it to work," he explained while holding up the cable connector. "He found them separately and had it integrated."

"You're going to tell me, right?" his pilot begged.

"The suit measures impact of an incoming round against the material. It gauges the angle of the impact on both horizontal and vertical planes."

Murray stared at him through squinted eyes.

"It tells you where the shot came from," Jon went on, "down to the millimeter. There's a display on the inside of the face shield."

"Robo-Cop, huh?" the cowboy smiled.

"Kinda sorta, I guess. When you raise your own weapon, its aim is crossed on the screen with the location of the shooter. There's an 'X' where the two lines of direction meet."

A smile streaked across the cowboy pilot's face.

"I'm thinking I like this," he said.

"When you're 'spot on,' the center 'X' lights up and you fire. It can all happen in a couple of seconds."

"Single shot for return fire or can you hold two weapons?"

"The screen splits the target area into quads. It can project four shooters at once and keeps them on screen till you...well, remove them."

"So, that's for me then?"

"Not this time," Jon put the helmet back and pulled out a Chrome plated Desert Eagle .50 caliber pistol. "Phil gave me this after a raid in Shreveport. Hell of a gun."

"You got two of those?" Murray grinned.

"Naw, just this one," he told him. "But I have my Glock 27 and a 22 round magazine for my other hand."

"What did you bring me?" the cowboy teased him like a child.

Jon pulled out one of the heavy glass bottles.

"These are for you and Westy to be heroes with," he answered. "There are three of them."

"Lethal?"

"Shouldn't be."

"I think I get the idea," Murray acknowledged seriously. "Where are you going to be?"

"This Frazier fellow seems determined to draw me out. I guess I need to let him."

~

They were about three miles from the Dalton mansion, in a van outside a Steak -N- Shake eatery when the radio call came in.

"Assets in Alabama compromised," the transmission said. "Not sure how but communications are gone. Part two," the message continued, "Seeker Four on standby at Dobbins...can deploy at any time."

"Understood," the lead Israeli agent replied. "Test run on Seeker successful. What is importance of Alabama?"

"Former SEAL, Arnold, may have knowledge. Unconfirmed... not worth risk to leave in question."

The men in the van looked at each other before the leader asked into the radio, "Instructions for us on Alabama?"

"Take out Arnold."

"Location?" the Israeli asked.

"Animal Park... outside Gadsden, Alabama."

"Confirm home situation," the leader asked.

"Harel release is confirmed. 'C' Street says time is important now."

One of the men in the van took out his pistol and checked it, nodding to his boss.

"I have a volunteer," he said into the radio. "We'll deal with Alabama."

"Good," the voice said. "Seeker Four impact...mark... twenty-three hours and fifteen minutes."

"Wave off window?" the Israeli leader asked.

"Four minutes," was the response, "but you don't want to be that close."

The men in the van looked around at each other again. The mission had fallen apart. It was supposed to have been simple. The news from home was not good, but their resolve was still strong.

"I will rent a car," the volunteer told them. "Leave today,"

The radio voice crackled with what sounded like "Roger that," and went dead.

~

Ben Shaw played and replayed the high altitude fly over, using other angles to estimate the size of the object. Daniel Seay sat beside him, Jerome Grimes stood just behind.

"How much bigger would a payload drone have to be?" he asked the NCIS Director.

"How big do you figure that one was?" Grimes leaned in asking.

"Four feet long...maybe."

"The AGM-114 is only 100 pounds," Grimes sat down and sketched out a "Hellfire Missile" on a piece of paper. "They're about five feet long and say," he formed a circle with his hands as though he was holding a football, "maybe six inches diameter."

Daniel leaned back so he could see them both. "Just how strong is this place?" he asked.

"On paper, it can handle a small nuke." Ben's words were soft, almost a whisper. "How do you test something like that?" he added.

"I can't imagine these people using a nuke...seriously," Grimes tried to assure them. "A full strength 'Hellfire', yeah... They could sell that as a gas explosion for a cover story."

"I agree," Daniel took the information as good news compared to what he'd been hearing. Smiling, he confirmed, "So... no nukes, right?"

"The missile would still be bigger than the drone that went over, checking us out."

"So the observation drone couldn't really deliver it?" Ben surmised.

Shaking his head, Grimes told them, "The drones come in about any size you want these days. That missile could be deployed by a UVA Predator that's twice that size. But still only eight feet long."

"What altitude would it fire from?"

"20,000 feet or lower," Grimes said but his mind was turning rapidly as he spoke. "Wait a second. That small a delivery unit would be destroyed by the release of the payload." He pulled out his phone and looked up some stats. "They won't want anything found after the strike," he went on. "Ah...there we go. They would use something more like this."

He held out a picture of the MQ-9A1 Reaper Drone.

"How big is that?" Ben asked.

"That sucker is near twenty feet long with a eighteen foot wingspan."

Ben smiled at the idea.

"I can hit that," he said confidently.

~

Her cell and appearance were in complete disarray. For a day and a half, Barrett had done little more than watch the news on her private TV set. The death of a prominent lawyer, such as Hasbrough Fuller, would certainly make the national broadcast. But there was nothing.

As the afternoon of that second day dragged on, her waning patience broke down.

"I want to talk with my lawyer," she demanded in no particular direction. "Get Fuller on the phone."

The cell block guard walked down and stood in front of her cell.

"Again?" she smirked at the prisoner. "You just had him here the other day."

"I have rights," Barrett growled at her. "Tell 'em I want to speak with Fuller."

Shrugging her shoulders, the guard turned and shaking her head, walked toward the control room with the message.

84

The south end of Woodrum Field at Roanoke Regional Airport was a grassy area Murray had received clearance to land on.

"This knowing who to call at the FAA is kinda cool when you need it," he grinned as they touched down. He quickly pointed to a man standing under an overhang at a nearby hangar. "Look there, will you?"

Weston Duray had arrived less than an hour earlier. He waited, with his bag in hand till the props came to a stop.

Jon climbed down and walked toward him, "Great to see you again," he reached out his hand with a smile, "thanks so much for coming."

"How's my little girl?" Westy asked him.

"Getting to be irreplaceable," Jon said. "She's quite a young lady, kind of like her old man."

"I assume this is about the kidnapping that's all over the news."

"It is," Jon said in a matter-of-fact style. "The guy running the show is a lot deeper into the mess around here than he lets on. The congressman he props up is more of a puppet for him. You know...he enjoys staying under the radar."

Murray came jogging up.

"Hey, old man!" he grinned wide. "Good to see you still getting around."

Another handshake and the trio walked toward the terminal building.

"They said when I got here that you had a conference room set aside," Weston told them.

"Yeah...I hope it's nice," Jon admitted. "I'd like to wait a couple of hours before we go."

"Dark won't be till around 8:oo pm."

"Just before dark," Jon went on. "I think the sun going down will be to our advantage...on both ends. Let me tell you guys what I'd like to try."

~

Charles Burr climbed into the mansion's attic.

"What's going on up here?" he asked and almost immediately saw the huge rifle. "Oh...wow! Haven't ever fired one of those," he commented as he grabbed the barrel to look closer. "I prefer the Browning anyway, this thing is a butt kicker."

"I believe Colleen here wants to shoot it," Doris laughed.

Agent Dunbar smiled but in a controlled manner. "I would like to try it sometime. Hope I don't have to for any real purpose...but I would."

Burr next saw the peep holes through the angled roof.

"See anything out there?" he climbed into a chair and looked out for himself.

"Naw," Colleen responded. "Not sure where they went, but I'll bet it wasn't too far. They're not through with us yet."

"If they only knew," Doris muttered. "They would think again.

~

It was called the Quick Stop. The fifties style diner sat on the northern end of Marietta, Georgia, on Highway 41. Business had been steady but slower than decades ago, when the highway was the main route north out of Atlanta. Since the interstate system now ran parallel, customers were mostly loyal locals.

Gil Gartner pulled up outside and got out to look around. He was in uniform, which was quite normal for such an escort detail, so no one gave him much notice.

"Clear, Sir," he said as he opened the car door and George Vincent stepped out.

In a low mutter, George asked if all seemed as it should be.

"Come right this way, Sir," Gil continued in an official tone.

Inside there were three customers, a waitress and a cook seen through an oblong window behind the counter. As DA Vincent looked closer, he recognized every face there as an officer from Dalton, except for one, Travis Gilbert.

Outside, in the parked trucks, the telephone and power company linemen, a crew working on a pothole in the old road, and what appeared to be vagrants had all been replaced. One at a time, since shortly after 10:00 A.M., government agents assumed their roles.

Once they were in place, the Dalton officers were brought in for their switch with those inside. It all looked as it should, but it wasn't.

George Vincent took a seat across from Gilbert in a booth near the back and waited. Gilbert looked calm. George felt pride in the young man while realizing his own very anxious state at the moment.

"Your dad doing okay?" he asked the congressman.

"He'll be better when we're done here," was the reply. "Oh, and 'thank you,' very much."

Vincent nodded and looked toward Gartner.

The trusted officer and family friend sat in complete silence. He spoke to no one else; simply staring from his seat across the room.

The waitress refilled the other customer's coffee, but other than that, the room was inactive. Then the cars arrived outside, screeching to a stop.

Dust flew up creating a cloud while six men emerged from two vehicles and spread out in formation. They wasted no time pulling weapons from under their coats as they approached the Quick Stop's door.

Loud shouts suddenly arose from outside as workmen and truck drivers, who had been milling about, drew down on the attackers from every angle. One of the replacement road crew tossed a shovel aside and pulled his service weapon. He called for the men to stop where they were.

"Damn it to hell," their leader could be heard to say as he dove toward the restaurant doorway.

The customers inside, the waitress, the cook and Gil Gartner all stood waiting for him. He staggered into the restaurant where everyone was aiming at him.

His face going pale, the man dropped his hand gun and lifted both arms. He looked at Gilbert and snarled, "You know you've just killed your daddy, right?"

Travis Gilbert stood and in a continuous motion, walked over to him, defiant and mad as hell. He pointed toward the kitchen and said very calmly, "You mean this man?"

The hit team leader looked past the congressman's shoulder to see the elder Gilbert step out.

"I have some people here who want to ask you and your men a few questions," Congressman Gilbert informed his prisoner. "Check that," he corrected himself, "Many questions."

Gartner moved in, grabbed the man's arm at the wrist, and twisted it behind him. "You have the right," he started and looked at his boss, still sitting in the booth. "Screw that," Gil went on, "not yet you don't."

George Vincent slowly slid out from the booth and stood. Beaming with pride, he went around thanking each member of the task force.

"How did you pull this off?" he asked the 'cook' whom he recognized as the chief of detectives back home.

"Your friend in the NCIS has some kind of pull... with somebody," the man smiled back as he answered.

~

"What is that?" Daniel Seay asked. Ben was adjusting his joy stick controller for the satellite feed from Fernbank Science Center in Atlanta.

"I'm looking for a few of the old "star-wars" satellites," Ben answered without looking up. "If I can find one that still has an active laser...we're in business."

Jerome Grimes' face lit up and he took out a different phone he had with him.

"You weren't kidding about 'hitting' that drone were you?" he all but shouted as he dialed. "It's time I told the President about Terrell anyway."

The call needed to be returned and was within ten minutes. After the short conversation, Grimes handed Ben a note with a long list of numbers on it.

"Does this make sense to you?" he asked the boy.

Ben studied it for a moment and then laughed out loud.

"Does it ever?" he started typing his keys and the monitor in front of him flashed until a screen shot of space came up, except it was live.

"What is that?" Daniel leaned over to look.

"Gentlemen," Ben beamed, "you're seeing what the LAGEOS 12 satellite sees." He twisted his hand on the joy stick and the view turned bringing the earth on screen.

"Did you do that?" Daniel asked in amazement.

Ben nodded and smiled at Grimes. The view zoomed in as Ben typed in coordinates on his keyboard. North America became clear and then the state of Georgia. He twisted the joy stick once more and the view was Lookout Mountain and northern Georgia.

"The LAGEOS satellites are Laser Geodynamics Satellites, primarily for study and mapping," he told Daniel. "This one though, is the LAGEOS-Michael 1, the first of a series. They call them 'Overlook Angels,' our protectors from above."

The image on screen clarified as more and more details became evident. Interstate 75 and the City of Dalton, with moving parts, appeared as though looking out a window.

"It's a multi-directional laser armed weapon," Ben went on as he got used to the touch of the controller. "The President gave us use of it for a while."

He continued to adjust the positioning of the spacecraft. When the mansion came into focus, Ben leaned back and told the others to, "Smile."

"I'll be damned," Grimes uttered under his breath.

Ben pulled back on the controller and the view rocketed skyward above the cloud cover. Once it focused, every object below was clearly visible.

"Let 'em try now," Ben smiled.

85

Long shadows reached across the grounds of the former police academy in Roanoke. They formed dark spots against the buildings and through the practice field which now held parked cars. Beneath three of those cars, buried in fresh turned dirt, lay four bodies. But they were not the issue.

The bodies in the ground were not the reason for the complex being surrounded. Police, both local and state authorities, with a vanguard of federal officers, held siege at a safe distance. The feds were there due to the nature of the assumed crime, kidnapping.

"Do you have food in there?" the distorted megaphone voice echoed through the area. There was no response.

They tried again, in Spanish. Still, there was no response.

"Captain, we have men behind the bushes," a sergeant informed the man in charge.

"What bushes?"

"Beyond the field, sir," he tried to explain, "Where the cars are."

Oh," the officer acknowledged. "So, are we in total control of the area?"

"Except for inside that building, yes sir."

Four men in dark blue suits watched the exchange and swapped looks at each other. None said a word.

"It'll be dark in an hour," the junior officer stated, "do we go in tonight?"

"Not determined at this time, sergeant," the Captain did his best to sound official. He caught himself glancing back to the men in the blue suits. "Let's see what happens till then, okay?" he added.

~

Some five miles to the east, as the crow flies, Jon Crane prepared himself. The new suit had one other accessory, a thin light-weight Kevlar tee shirt.

It was tight and he thought it would be uncomfortable. Yet when contact was made to the upper chest portion of the outer suit, the tee shirt was fed cool air through two separate miniature tubes. The inner side became easier to tolerate than the original suit itself. The cooling air was both soothing and, in a way, lubricating for movement.

The outer tubing created a thin space between the two garments. That air pocket added to the resistance against projectiles and the tee shirt multiplied that by five times.

Fully dressed, other than the helmet, Silas drove a rental car south from the airport to an area known as Gainsboro. The former residential, now business and industrial district, housed Frazier's Plumbing Supply Company.

Structures were old, siding over frame mainly with a few brick buildings speckled in. One or two were over two stories in height.

Loudon Avenue ended at 5th Street. It was just there that Walter Frazier owned two buildings sitting side by side next to a wooden pallet storage yard.

Silas stopped on Loudon, just inside 7th, facing east and the wood pallets.

A sidewalk was to his right and a raised wall, half concrete and half cobble stones, lifted the elevation on his left side. His concentration was straight ahead.

The sun from his back picked-up even the slightest movements. Glimmers from within the windows of buildings and the grounds around them shined brightly. He counted eight trying to stay out of sight.

He saw men in plain clothes lining the avenue ahead of him. Other uniformed officers walked the street in front of the stacked pallets. Their patrol cars lined the area before 5th Street.

A one-time glare flashed from the top of one pile of wood. Silas used his own binoculars to zero in on the spot. A sniper lay mostly still, covered by a tarp. He had allowed his rifle to rock slightly causing the giveaway glare.

I was right, Silas assured himself, *he's hold up at his office.*

~

Ben Shaw received a signal from Murray. It wasn't a message or even a text, simply a tone over the phone.

With that, he switched screens to another Fernbank satellite, one with infrared technology. He had it in place over the Roanoke compound and hit "scan" on the controller.

The system could detect body heat through the buildings and indicate where humans or animals were inside and near the exterior.

"Cowboy, over," Ben said into his phone.

"Ready," Murray responded.

"Three clustered together in front room on left side from the road. Two outside that room and nine more scattered throughout the interior."

"Roger...targets in front room to left."

"You have six more bogies outside, near the structure," Ben added.

"Seventeen bogies," Murray answered. "Roger that, and thank you."

Lucy Too hung over the compound at 12,000 feet.

"You ready for this?" the pilot asked Westy.

"Strapped in and ready," Weston Duray told him. "Let's do this."

Murray checked his stability and level, and then hit the kill switch on the rotors. The engines stayed on, but the lift ceased.

Lucy Too plummeted from the sky like a rock. Murray stared at his altimeter.

Weston pulled his strap even tighter and then put his hand on the release bar. Lucy fell.

At 4,000 feet, Murray hit auto rotate on the props. They immediately turned but in the wrong direction. At 2,500 feet, Murray twisted the angle on the prop blades and Lucy Too bounced as though a parachute had deployed.

Westy pulled his release and grabbed a thick rope connected to his gear. With two of Jon's bottles in hand, he yelled, "Clear," and jumped from the open door.

Murray engaged the engines to help with lift and the big blue bird leveled and stopped her fall at barely 200 hundred feet above the ground. He continued to descend, allowing for Westy's rope until he heard the man holler out over the radio, "Contact."

Weston Duray was on the roof.

He released hold of the rope and went about his business. Lucy Too lifted straight up and roared into the sunset and out of view.

The sudden noise of the chopper directly overhead was disconcerting to everyone at the compound. The two boys guarding the captives first ran to the window to see what was happening. They heard the voice of their leader, Orlando Benitez, screaming for them to get the girls.

Benitez ran from down the hall and the two boys almost reached the door when the area was overcome with smoke. Westy had dropped one bottle into a roof air vent and another through the air conditioning tower atop the building.

The gas mixture was potent and instantaneous. Benitez, his two guards and in fact, everyone inside the building was overcome in seconds.

With his mask on tight, Westy waited for his ride to return. The boys outside the building ran toward the front door and had gathered together there when Lucy suddenly returned, swooping in low with her rope dragging under her.

Murray held out the last bottle of gas and let it drop to the front of the building. The remaining boys were quickly rendered unconscious and Westy grabbed the dangling rope. He clicked the snap ring to his harness and radioed, "Go."

The police cautiously moved in but by the time they got close, Lucy Too was gone.

86

The police compound was miles away, yet Jon / Silas knew exactly when Murray and Westy had made their move. The uniformed officers at the plumbing supplies' headquarters all jumped into their cars and streamed away toward the excitement... lights and sirens blaring.

Jon sat in the car. He checked his weapons and pulled the helmet on. When the proper contact was made the screen lit up in front of his face. He opened the car door and Silas stepped out.

With the Desert Eagle in his right hand and the Glock in the left, he began walking down the middle of the street, toward the wooden pallets.

His stride was steady and quick, but he did not run.

The sun was very low now and offered little help. His own shadow reached to the cross street at 6th, announcing his presence. But it did reflect the movements of the men who saw him coming. He was able to prepare himself for the first impact.

The chain of custody for the prisoners taken at the Quick Stop Diner had been arranged ahead of time.

Cobb County, Georgia, officials stepped aside in favor of their neighbors to the north from Whitfield County, Dalton, Georgia.

The federal agents wanted a say in the matter but were convinced by higher ups to allow the locals to handle it for now.

The men stayed quiet that afternoon but by dark, on the road back to Dalton, fingerprints had come through on all.

"CIA, huh?" Gil turned in the seat to look at the leader. The man neither spoke or flinched.

"That's fine," Gartner smiled. "When we get you to our house we'll offer you and your boys a chance to talk...before we bring him in."

The stern faced man leaned in Gartner's direction.

"Him who?" he demanded.

"Oh...I was wondering, but I think you know exactly who."

"You can't do that," the man's voice was losing strength. "You're a cop."

"You're CIA," Gil grinned at him. "We all make mistakes, don't we?"

The man leaned back and closed his eyes. He shook his head slightly while trying to remain calm.

"Four of your guys are from Albany," Gil continued to listen to his report. "How about that? We've been hearing that town a bunch lately." He turned again to stare at the man. "Don't suppose they were in the pecan business, were they?" he teased him.

The silent man's eyes gave him away. Try as he could not to, they squinted hard at the officer's suggestion.

This whole thing is blown, he thought to himself. *They know everything.*

~

Murray found an open field where he could put Westy down and then land nearby. Once back together inside the aircraft, Weston checked his weapons and nodded at the cowboy.

Murray's only words were, "Here we go."

~

The first round struck him from the right side. Silas instantly reacted by pointing that direction. He was very close by instinct as the crossed lines on the face shield showed him. A slight adjustment with the .50 caliber and he fired.

A window sill, half way down the block, exploded into splinters. A rifle fell out, and the shooter using it tumbled backwards into the room.

The next two shots came in at the same time. One hit chest high from almost straight on, the other into his left from much closer range.

Jon's left arm leveled on the visual crosshairs with his Glock and he fired a double. More breaking glass and a muffled cry went out. He also heard a round fly passed his head, a miss from somewhere.

The hit still on his screen was from down range. It indicated the shot came from over 220 yards away.

The wood stacks, he told himself, *too far yet*.

Another strike on his right side hit just above the waist. It caught an area near the end of the tee shirt. It stung.

The Desert Eagle zeroed in and he again fired two rounds into the target area. A wooden fence came apart and then a man behind it fell, pushing the remainder down with him. Another round whizzed by his head.

He looked again at the stacked pallets and saw a faint glare from a scope. Then the entire top layer of wood in that section jumped and splintered into the air. Before the dust could settle, he saw the image of Lucy Too roar over the pallets and out of sight to his right.

Men began to run from buildings in front of him, none towards him, but rather away. Another shot struck his left side, but in the multilayered protection zone. The Glock fired within two seconds and another unseen attacker yelled out.

Lucy Too came back from the other direction but did not appear to fire this time. When she was again out of view, to the left this time, Silas realized he was near the intersection with 5th street. The plumbing company headquarters was just ahead. He picked-up speed, Silas began to run.

~

The phone ringing startled them both, the lawyer Fuller and his host, Jasper Jamison. Jamison gave his guest a hard look and the man fumbled for the phone from his coat pocket.

His first look at the caller ID stopped him in his tracks.

"It's her," he more stuttered than spoke.

"Give that to me," Jamison said while grabbing the phone. He took a minute to stiffen his neck and then hit answer.

"Yeah?" he said.

"Yeah what?" Barrett immediately knew it wasn't Fuller. "Who is this?"

"You know who this is... don't play any more games, okay?"

"Jasper?" she all but screamed. "Jasper, what are you doing? Is he gone? Damn it. He'd better be gone."

"Or what, lady?" the furniture man wasn't in the mood for this.

The line became quiet for several seconds.

"What are you doing?" she tried in a different tone.

"You're done, sweetheart," Jamison told her. "We've had enough of you and your silliness."

"I still have power, Jamison. Don't threaten me."

"Use it then," he snapped and then took a breath before adding, " See where that gets you."

"Why?" Barrett was nearly crying. He'd never heard her upset to this this extent. "Why now? After all I've been through for this."

"If... we do manage to control our secret," Jamison started in on her, "It'll be years before we can use it to any degree... thanks to you."

"I've been loyal to the group," she went on. "I've always done things to strengthen the group."

"Yeah, right," he shot back, "As long as it strengthened you along with it."

Natalie Barrett was sobbing on the other end, softly but clearly sobbing.

"You pushed too damn hard, Ms. Icarus. You went too far."

The reference threw her. "What?" she mumbled.

"Never mind...Just relax and let us clean this up," Jamison told her. "You've got players involved that we never planned on."

The phone line was silent after that and then disconnected. Jamison looked over at the lawyer Fuller. He shrugged his shoulder and handed him his phone back.

"So...what now?" Fuller asked apprehensively.

"We clean this mess up, that's what," Jamison said as he moved to his desk. He pushed the intercom button and said, "Get my son for me, please."

That request would go unfulfilled. Jamey Jamison had troubles of his own.

~

His strides exceeded five yards per step and he wasn't pressing. The easy jog carried Silas through the intersection and to the edge of Frazier's property in short time. Three other shots had been fired, two missed completely and one grazed his arm. He did not return fire on those.

Once he stopped at the side doors to the building, the shots continued and became more intense. He learned that shots hitting his back did not register on the screen.

Silas turned to see four men rushing him with guns pointed forward. Two fired and struck simultaneously. Silas raised the Desert Eagle and quickly knocked two of them backwards with the impact from his gun.

The others froze in place and then jumped to the side and scrambled behind some shrubbery.

Turning back to the door, there was a man waiting inside, his face wide eyed at what he'd seen. Silas grabbed the locked door and twisted the knob. It broke off with the door still locked. Silas raised his right foot and the man inside dove to his left. The kick slammed the steel door inward and broke the upper hinge.

He moved into the building and looked around. Another round struck him on the faceguard, then another hit his mid-section. His right hand rose and fired quickly. The large rounds from his .50 caliber tore through a corner of concrete staircase and a man bounced off the wall behind him.

This must be the direction, Silas thought and started up the steps and was soon at the top. A hallway met him there.

Three doors lined the extended hallway, two on the left, and one on the right. Lights emanated from the office behind the door on the right. As he moved forward an arm with a gun came from the second door on his left. The shot missed but Silas fired through the wall and door casing and his found its mark. The man fell into the hall.

There was a commotion behind him. He turned to look back down the stairs to hear a shot and see a man fall face forward on those steps.

Westy came up quickly, jumping over the body and taking stairs three at a time. "You okay?" he asked.

"I'm fine," Silas told him and turned to go into the office.

It was empty. There were signs that folks had just been there, several of them, but they were gone now.

Silas and Duray searched the hall and the other door to the left side, it was only a closet. There were no other stairs at the other end of the hall so they went back into the office to figure how Frazier could have escaped.

Each of them went to a window, but could see only dark. The sashes were locked from the inside and didn't look like they had been raised in years.

"He didn't go out through here," Weston said, his frustration starting to build. "Something's missing here," he added while walking across the room.

Jon stared around the room through Silas' eyes trying to find a passage or trap door of some kind. A throw rug seemed too obvious, and when he pulled it to one side, it was. There was nothing but solid floor beneath it. Westy slowly rubbed his hands across the far end wall. His head was turned and his ear held close, listening closely for anything. Then they both heard it.

A noise, like a muted thump, coming from behind a built-in bookcase, grew and seemed to get closer with each added sound.

Then the bookcase swung out wide and there stood Murray with a man in his grasp. The stairs behind them were a secret passage out to the back parking area, not far from where Lucy Too rested.

"Looking for this?" the cowboy asked with a wink.

From the pictures he'd seen, Silas knew it was Walter Frazier.

"I believe he's been looking for me," Silas said and moved toward them, menacingly. He leaned into the man's face, nose to nose, and glared into his eyes.

"My name is Silas," he addressed the frightened man, "Here I am."

87

Of the three main casinos in Cherokee, North Carolina, The Eagle's Rest was always Jamey Jamison's first choice. In recent months though, his favorite establishment had lost its patience with him.

He sat in a locked room, just off the manager's office, with one guard who looked like an Indian version of a Sumo wrestler.

"You guys can't keep me here," Jamey protested. "You know I'm good for it and besides...this is kidnapping."

The large quiet man had nothing to say.

This wasn't supposed to be this way, the younger Jamison thought in anger. *It should have been done by now and this wouldn't be a problem.*

His mind had convinced him that once Dawes had done the job, all his money woes would be no more, including this current tab of some $55,000.

A huge four-by-seven foot tall door swung open and in walked Randall Swartz, known as "Three Feathers" for the adornment he wore in his hair, but with less actual Indian blood in his veins than Jamison.

He tossed an untraceable, burner cell phone to the young man sitting on his sofa.

"Call Daddy," he said quite firmly. "Tell him you need money to live on. And say it like you know it's true."

Jamey fumbled with the phone and looked up at Swartz.

"How about $ 25,000 for now and a promise I'll pay the rest next month?"

"That will not cure your illness, Jamison. I need all of it...if you expect a miracle cure for what ails you."

Jamison punched in the number for his father's private line.

~

Nava Golan stood from the bed with a start. She threw the phone from her hand across the room.

"Whoa," Marsha grabbed her shoulders, trying to calm her down. "What is it?"

"They know," she said, eyes wide and bulging with tears. "What do we do now?"

"The guys outside?" Lori seemed surprised. "They already know about the rescues?"

Nava shook her head rapidly. "What do we do?" she repeated.

"Well for one thing, we stay here and we stay calm." Marsha smiled at herself. "That's actually two things, isn't it?"

The joke was not well received.

Lori Seay attempted to help. "So what if they are?" she asked and knelt down to pick up the phone. "That's much better in the long run, isn't it?"

"Better than what?" Nava seemed confused.

"Better than your friends still being captives. That's a good... no it's a great thing."

Marsha saw a time to ask for information. Without moving from her spot, she spoke in soft moderate tones, "How many of you were sent here?"

"Didn't we talk about that?" Nava sat down and looked at her.

"No, we didn't."

"Six of them and me," the Israeli agent explained. "Two went to Louisiana right away, we came here, and then I went to find you."

"The men in Louisiana are in custody. They tried to hurt a friend of ours," Marsha told her.

Nava's look and her silence expressed her shame. Then she mumbled the team's mission, "They just wanted to draw this Silas out from the shadows. No one else was to get hurt."

Marsha looked at her friend and said nothing more. It was pointless to browbeat her with facts, and yet...*were they facts?* She wondered.

"Do you know the men outside have drones?"

Nava looked down. "It's Silas they want to find...and get rid of."

"They don't know Silas isn't here... do they?" Marsha asked.

"He was here," Nava challenged her. "I know he was."

Marsha got up and went into the hall. Dialing her cell phone, she called downstairs to Daniel.

"If there's anything you guys can do," she told him. "The next drone is going to hit us hard. They think Jon is still here."

"I wouldn't worry too much about that..." he tried to answer.

"No No...Nava just told us...it's Jon they want to kill. That damned thing will be armed."

"Slow down, Captain," Daniel raised his voice. "Ben has a cure for their drone, okay. It doesn't have a chance."

When he got off the phone with Marsha, Daniel shook Ben's arm.

"You do know what you're doing with that laser satellite, right?" he asked. "You're not just kidding around or anything."

"No...why do you ask that?"

"Marsha just confirmed...the missile coming our way will be lethal. Those guys outside... believe Jon is in here."

~

Lucy Too circled the former police compound. Her passengers were four men, one in a blindfold. A Roanoke PD Chopper closed in and called on the open frequency for them to "identify themselves."

Rather than give traditional aircraft numbers, Murray radioed that he was on special FAA clearance Bravo Tango Uniform.

"What?" the police pilot shot back.

"Just look it up," Murray told him. "It's there, I promise you."

The radio went silent for several minutes and then the same pilot's voice returned.

"BTU, you are clear to land at your discretion. Welcome to Roanoke, Cowboy."

"Roger that and thank you," Murray responded and looked over at Jon. "This really is fun sometimes," he chuckled.

With his spotlight, Murray found an old basketball court that had been cleared.

"We can fit in there," he announced and Lucy began her descent.

Walter Frazier was left tied and blindfolded inside the dark blue Sikorski.

"Try to escape, please," Silas warned him. "I'd love to hunt you down again."

Frazier grunted but offered no resistance.

"Hurt my helicopter," Murray added while leaning back, "and he'll be your second worry."

They walked across the play field, now mostly covered with vehicles, and saw officers approaching. The sound of sirens echoed everywhere, drowning out all other noise.

When face to face with the uniformed men, everyone stopped. The Captain of the police looked at Jon, Murray, and Weston in their black outfits and finally asked, "Which one is Silas?"

Murray pointed to his left and Weston pointed to his right. Jon smile and reached out with his hand.

"Sorry, we didn't have time to change," he said.

"The girls are fine," the Captain told them. "They'll have a headache for a while...everyone who was here will, but they are good. We have them being transported to Carilion Memorial for observation and to be with their parents."

Jon nodded approval and then looked over his shoulder.

"I need you to have those vehicles moved and search that ground for loose dirt," he told him.

The captain's face twisted in slight confusion by the request, but he'd heard enough about this man not to question his judgment.

"Clear those cars out of there," he commanded and waved in that direction. "Get some lights in here...big lights."

~

Jamey Jamison was literally pleading for his life.

"You've got to trust me, Dad," he slobbered into the phone. "When this is done, $50,000 won't mean a thing to either of us. It'll be chicken feed."

"What have you done?" the older Jamison demanded.

"I can't tell you," Jamey cried. "Partly because I don't know myself, but something is going to change everything...you'll see."

A strange beep came on the line and the furniture magnate didn't recognize it at first. It was 'call waiting.'

"I'll be damned," he exclaimed. "Three people have this number and two of them call at the same damn time. Hold on a second, son."

Jamey protested but the click meant his dad had changed lines.

"Yeah?" the older man answered his other line.

"My men haven't checked in." It was Dilward Putney.

"What are you talking about?" Jamison asked.

"Two agents from D.C. came here this morning and needed to borrow some muscle for the day, they said."

"To do what?"

"Hell, I don't know," Putney screamed back. "I didn't ask those guys. You know who they work for."

"They're supposed to work for us!"

"So, you don't know anything either?"

"No," Jamison told him. "But stay by the phone. I may need to talk to you again in a minute."

He clicked back over to his son and after trying for several minutes to get details from him, he finally told Jamey, "I have to figure this out, son. You've really screwed the pooch this time."

"The money, Dad, what about the money?"

"When I sort this out...unless you want to tell me now."

"I can't," Jamey told him.

The elder hung up and dialed Putney's line.

Jamey looked up at "Three Feathers" Swartz.

"It's on the way," he told him, "should be here tomorrow."

Swartz nodded at Jamison and then motioned for his man to take him away. The younger man would spend some time in a dark utility closet.

~

"We need to get to Calvert," Jamison told his partner. "Something is up."

"What are we gonna do?" Putney wondered.

"Move the secret if we need to...hell I don't know, something."

"When?"

"I can't leave here till morning. It would look too suspicious right now."

"I'll drive up in the morning too, then. Have you told Calvert we're coming?"

"No... and I don't plan to. We need to exert ourselves for once. This is all blowing up in our faces."

"See you there," Putney told him.

"Yeah, right," was all Jamison could think of in response.

~

Three huge lights and a backhoe quickly found the remains buried in the field.

"How did you know about this?" the police captain almost demanded from Silas.

He didn't need to answer, as an NCIS agent stepped forward.

"Vic Carter, NCIS out of Rockford," he identified himself. FBI Agents looked at each other and their leader grabbed Carter's arm.

"Hang on man," he said to Carter. "This is our deal, especially now."

Carter handed him some papers.

"Not this one, gentlemen. Those are from the U.S. Attorney General. We're taking this case and all its evidence," he looked at Jon and nodded. "Been a while since South Bend, huh?"

"Agent Carter," Jon smiled. "Good to see you again."

"Grimes called this afternoon. Said something about a 'Ben' giving him your note..."

"Yeah, glad you could make it."

"Make it?" Wait till you see what Grimes pulled off."

Jon didn't quite understand but nodded at the agent anyway.

"I take it you have someone for me?" Carter smiled.

"In the chopper," Jon told him.

Carter offered a slight nod and turned to the FBI agents still standing behind him. They were looking over the paperwork Carter had presented.

"Get to the part that says you work for me yet?" he asked flippantly.

The lead FBI agent looked up asking, "What the heck is this?"

"I promise you'll know everything," Carter tried to assure him. "For right now, this is how we're going to operate.

88

Phil Stone was in early that morning. He again asked to see the prisoners but this time wanted to know if they had been told the news from their homeland.

Chief Jack Merlot told him they had been.

"We felt that might help them loosen up and talk," he explained to Phil. "So far, that hasn't happened."

They allowed the retired police captain to sit in a room with the Israelis again. They had taken a tack of ignoring him, not even looking up.

Phil sat there a few short minutes, and then opened up.

"Nava Golan says 'Hi'," he told them. "She's fine. She's with some friends of mine."

One of the two looked over at him slightly.

"She says you guys forced her to help...or you would kill her and her family."

"We seek peace," one said in a muffled voice.

"Shut up," the other warned him. This caused the dissention to grow, rapidly.

"We are not killers," the first man said and then repeated, "We seek peace."

"Peace from whom?" Phil asked him.

"War mongers," the man said defiantly. "Those like in your country, who always seek to fight. We want everyone to get along and have peace."

Phil sat quietly for a couple of minutes. He watched the other man, the one who would not talk, squirm in his seat.

"You're not buying this stuff either, are you?" he directed at the second, silent man.

"Peace in our time, brother," the man offered without looking.

"Yeah, that's a noble cause for sure," Stone stood and walked closer to them. "Who helps you with that from here, in my country?"

"No one," the first man threw out.

"Magill helped get us here," the second man suddenly became the conduit for information.

"Magill? Is he an Israeli?" Phil asked, though he knew the truth.

"Magill is CIA," the man looked up and stared right at Captain Stone.

"Am I supposed to be impressed by that?" Phil asked with his head cocked to one side.

"Magill is your own," the man implored. "Yet he sees the truth."

"Truth protected by a lie, right?" Stone tempted him.

"Not a lie...an important secret," the first man muttered sounding like he didn't believe his own words.

"Secrets, lies," Phil now taunted. "If it's not based in fact, what good is it?"

"We seek peace," the second one reiterated.

"Peace through lies...yeah, I get it," Phil turned and walked toward the door. "You don't even believe this crap yourselves, do ya?"

"You talk to Magill," the first man challenged him. "Talk to him, he'll explain."

"How do I do that? How do you talk to him?"

The two men stared at each other.

"The phone number, it's stenciled on my shirt," the second one told him, "On the tail... backwards... like a laundry mark."

Phil left the room already knowing it would be Magill's number.

This would add to the evidence against him, he thought.

But Magill was no longer in the picture.

Chief Merlot's people got the shirt from the evidence bag and verified the number. The only problem was...CIA Agent Cecil Magill was dead. They just didn't know that yet.

~

Dilward Putney rang the bell after parking on the street. The butler answered and let him in.

"What's this now?" Calvert asked coming from his study. "I didn't know you were coming."

"Jasper is on his way, too," Putney told him. "Something has happened that's got him spooked. He wants us all to talk, face to face."

Calvert didn't care for surprises, especially this kind.

"Wish one of you had called me first," he said. "Since you're here and you say he's coming, let's have a drink while we wait, shall we?"

"It's 10:15 in the morning," Putney reminded him.

"Oh phooey," Calvert laughed. "You're not one of those are you?" They walked down a dark hall to the study and heard the doorbell ring.

"Maybe that's Jasper," the pecan man said and they both turned to watch while the butler answered the door.

The sharply dressed old man looked to his boss and took several steps in their direction.

"Sir, it's the county. The radon sensors they asked about bringing."

"That's not supposed to be till next week," Calvert recalled.

"They had a cancellation, sir. He was in the area."

Calvert looked aggravated but was stoic about it.

"What the hell," he sarcastically shouted, "This day is out of my hands anyway."

~

Gray. *Was that the ceiling?* He thought in Spanish. The color melted into the walls without changing at all. *What is this place?*

His head hurt inside. It throbbed and made thinking difficult. Reaching to rub it, he discovered more discomfort. He could not move.

Orlando Miguel Benitez awoke with his feet shackled to a bed as well as his right arm. A stranger sat in a chair against the wall just beyond the foot of his bed. He tried again to sit and moaned, mostly from the pain in his head.

The stranger stood up and approached him. Placing a finger in front of his nose and mouth, this stranger was telling him to stay quiet.

"Who are you?" Benitez asked in fairly good English.

"You are Orlando Benitez," Silas stated as fact but then asked, "is that correct?"

"Who are you?" he tried again.

"Your friends, the few who have come to, tell us you are their leader."

Benitez quit talking and simply stared at this stranger.

"Where is the one with the red boots?" the man asked him.

"Renaldo is dead," he heard himself say.

"So...you're the new leader, then?"

"Si."

"That's a shame," the stranger said.

Again, Benitez stared without a response.

"They dug up four bodies out in your play field," the man told him. "That's gonna come down on you now."

"I know of three," Benitez said without really thinking. "The other was there when we came here."

"Who told you to kill those people?"

"We only buried them," Benitez tried to sit up again. It still didn't work. "We did not kill anyone."

"How about red boots? Did he kill anyone?"

His head pounded harder now. Benitez could barely think.

"That, I cannot say."

"How about Frazier?" Jon asked. "Who did he kill...or have killed?"

"Mr. Walt bring us here for a new life," the youth said.

"You didn't answer me. Do you want all this charged against you?"

"Mr. Walt tell us to move them, or he tell Renaldo and Renaldo tells us."

"Now Renaldo is gone, isn't he?"

"Si," Benitez muttered.

"We'll talk more later."

~

Carlton Calvert was pouring his third two fingers of Johnny Walker Red when the doorbell rang again.

"Ah," he said to Putney, still nursing his first glass, "there he is now." The old man then looked at the county worker and asked, "Are you about done in here?"

"Yes, Sir," the man responded. Finished in the study, the workman moved into the hall to place his last sensor device.

The butler let Jamison in and directed him to the study. As he walked past, the new arrival glared hard at the man in the blue coveralls. The worker had his back to him and stayed busy with his set up.

Calvert held out a glass with whiskey as Jamison entered the study. Jasper took it and pointed back to the man working with the blue canister.

"Who's that?" he asked.

"The county is checking a radon exposure. It's been reported in this area," Calvert said while turning up his glass.

"Radon?" Jamison wrinkled his face. "That's still an issue?"

"I guess it must be... Now," the old man changed demeanor in a heartbeat. "What is this all about?"

Jasper Jamison took a sip from his glass hoping it would reorganize his thoughts. After a quick look at Putney, the concerned partner began.

"We need to move the Amber," he said straight out.

Calvert frowned but said nothing at first. He walked back to the bottle, laying his hand on its neck.

"It's been just fine where it is for years now," he mumbled softly and calmly poured as he spoke. His next question was louder and more forceful, "What's got up your backside all of a sudden?"

"Surely you know how Barrett's attempts are going," Jamison defended himself. "The whole house of cards is coming down."

"Not so fast. We may be remodeling a bit," he said as though in jest, "but we still have that which gives us control."

"I'm afraid there may be an attack on you," Jasper blurted out.

"Me? How does anyone even know about me?"

"Let's call it a hunch, okay. That's all I can tell you."

Calvert turned to open the study door where the butler now stood.

"Yes?" he asked the man.

"The county man is finished, sir."

"Do we owe anything?"

"No, sir."

"Then show him out, please."

Jasper Jamison took another sip from his glass and turned as the butler opened the main door for the worker. Something about him, his walk maybe, struck Jamison as familiar.

Carlton Calvert continued with his reasons that all should stay as it was. Putney sat in complete silence and Jamison slowly moved to a front window.

"The secrets are safe as a baby in mother's arms," Calvert said. "The amber was, and still is, a brilliant idea."

Tall hedges blocked Jamison's view for several yards, but he could see the man's truck and several feet of walkway.

"No matter how many changes in personnel we make," Calvert went on, "I see no reason to make a change in this location."

The county worker came into Jamison's view for only five steps, but there was something that registered within him. The way the man walked, that decided limp dug into his memory.

Then a strange thought came up and then out, "Whatever happened to Dawes?" Jamison asked.

"Who?" Calvert didn't like the change of topic or the distraction from his lecture. "What are you looking at?"

"Warren Dawes?" Jamison said again while his mind ran wild, adding things up.

Then as the truck pulled away, Jasper could feel all warmth and color leave his face. He turned to look at the canister left by the worker and then at Calvert, who now stared at him in silence, still confused. A small stem popped up on the canister.

"Aw, Jamey...No!" Jamison said with his mouth falling open.

They would be his last words.

89

"They gave you up," Vic Carter informed the man sitting across from him. The NCIS Agent had been given use of police facilities, including a cell block strictly for the surviving police detail from Frazier's payroll and the Mexican youth gang.

Unimpressed, Frazier appeared bored with everything. He denied being involved with any of it.

A knock on the door announced Silas' entry into the room, now in street clothes, but that meant a jacket and special right arm. His presence affected Frazier, though he tried to hide the fact.

Carter acknowledged Silas with a nod and then asked yet another question of his prisoner. "Who's the skeleton in the grave?" he pried.

"I have no idea what you're referring to," Frazier defied him.

Carter stood and went to the camera mounted high in the corner of the small room. He turned a switch under it and grabbed at his belt line.

"I need to go to the can," he said and looked at Silas. "Can you watch this guy a few minutes?"

Frazier tried to stand but could not. "You can't do that," he protested. "You're an officer of the law."

"Right now I'm an officer with an upset stomach from all the lies in this room. I need to go take a dump and I'm going to."

Carter opened the door and left. When he returned, some ten minutes later, Silas had several answers for him.

"The body we don't know about is someone named Monahan. A Gail Monahan," Silas started. "Our friend here also got his start on this empire from Carlton Calvert of Atlanta. Looks like I might need to get an appointment and go see him," he smiled at Carter. "His name has been coming up a lot lately."

Looking at the now pale Frazier, Carter smirked, "See now...that wasn't so bad was it?"

"You might want to have a Doc check his ribs on the right side," Silas told him. "He thinks he bruised them falling on some stairs or something."

Frazier had nothing to add.

When Jon called Ben to tell him about the name to expect from the skeletal remains, Ben wrote it down.

"Where'd you get that?" Daniel leaned over and asked.

"That's the skeleton," Ben told him, "Why?"

"Gail Monahan was that reporter who went missing as the Calvert gang took over the media in Roanoke."

Ben smiled, "Everything is coming together, isn't it?"

Cheryl, sitting at her monitor, yelled out, "You guys need to tune in to local TV. There's been a house blown up in Atlanta...I think you'll be interested."

~

Atlanta Fire, Police, and local FBI all descended on the scene of the house that had literally blown apart.

"What am I looking at here," the FBI lead agent asked the Fire Chief.

"First floor blew out clean," the man explained. "And I mean... clean. Like a magician's trick, you know...where they pull a tablecloth out from under dishes?"

The FBI investigator didn't quite follow.

"Then what's all that piled up?"

"That is the second floor," the Chief said shaking his head. "Beats all don't it? The thing came down almost on the foundation. Course it broke up and fell in when it got there and then the fire of course."

"Gas leak?" the fed asked.

"That would be my guess," the chief told him, "if I were a guesser." But then he went on, "You see this big hat?" The chief pointed to the front of it and though he didn't speak, the FBI agent did look.

"Does it still say 'Chief' up there? I bet it does... That means I don't guess. Get it?"

The federal agent looked back at the smoldering mass and let that slap pass.

"Find remains yet?" he tried.

"Five in bits and pieces, so to speak," he answered. "One in the kitchen... fairly intact, one near where the front door had been and three clustered like they were together, maybe in the same room."

"ID's?"

"You kidding me? Not yet, no. That could take a while."

"This is the Calvert home, isn't it? You'd have to assume..."

"Yeah," the fire chief interrupted. "That you would, But I've seen stranger things. Let's wait for the forensic folk to do their jobs, huh?"

"How about underneath?" the Fed pushed for more.

"Underneath? Oh...you mean the basement. Yeah...the plans on file show a small utility basement toward the front end... but most of it is a heavily insulated wine cellar."

"Did it survive?"

"Don't know," the chief admitted. "See that twisted steel lying there?"

The Fed looked to where the man pointed and nodded his head.

"That was an elevator shaft, top to bottom we figure. It's pretty well shut off from the basement right now. We'll get the fire out, and then move the debris. Maybe in a few days we can get down there."

~

No one was in Suite 617 at 2201 C Street in Washington, D.C. that morning. The incoming call was not answered but the silent communications alarm notified a cell phone across town. The owner of that phone was at first confused and then overwhelmingly concerned.

From a briefcase, that owner took out yet another phone. A quite odd looking device, it was a cell version of the CVAS V crypto phone developed for sensitive communications by the NSA. This one was thought to be out of service.

The first number dialed was directly to Calvert's home in Atlanta. There was no answer, none at all.

That's strange, the caller thought, *the answering machine was on fail-safe mode.* Next the caller tried a number in Albany, Georgia, Putney's private cell. Again, there was no answer.

"What the hell," the caller said aloud and dialed the office of David's Pecans in Albany.

"Put me through to Putney," the operator was told.

"I'm sorry," she said, "Mr. Putney is not available at the moment."

"What does that mean?" the caller demanded.

"I'm serious," the operator apologized. "We can't reach him. I'm sorry."

Much the same came from trying to contact Jasper Jamison. His office could not reach him either. The caller turned on a TV. The "Breaking

News" was all about the huge explosion at Atlanta publishing magnate Carlton Calvert's home.

Putting the special phone down, the caller watched with mouth agape for several minutes.

"Not possible, this can't be. They couldn't have all been together."

Looking up Jamison's son's number, the now frantic caller tried that. Randall Swartz answered at the Eagles Rest Casino in Cherokee, North Carolina.

"Yeah, Jamison?" Swartz asked.

The caller was put off. They didn't recognize the voice or understand what was happening. Normally they would have simply hung up but these were not normal circumstances.

"Who is this?" the caller demanded.

Laughing, Swartz replied, "Life support, for all you care. Where's my money?"

The caller did hang up at that point.

With no one to talk to and no one to consult, the now panicked caller dialed yet another number. This one rang in an office on Wilson Boulevard in Washington, D.C.

"Yeah?" it answered and the caller did recognize this voice.

"I need a recon and recovery team in Atlanta tomorrow. They need to be ready to search remains at Calvert's place the minute local authorities slack off."

"Slack off?" the man on Wilson Boulevard challenged. "Have you heard? They'll be on that sight till they find out what happened."

"When the numbers are in our favor, take over by any means necessary. Is that clear?"

"I understand, sure...doesn't mean it can happen."

"It better."

"I have a question about the strike," the man quickly added.

"The observers certain of the target?"

"As much as possible," he responded. "The situation over there has changed communications with the inside."

"Changed?"

"Cut-off...there are no more. But they haven't seen anyone coming or going since he was confirmed there."

"Then carry on," the voice said firmly.

~

Agent Jake Hansard's phone found him in Alabama at the wild animal park.

"Still quiet over there?" Jerome Grimes asked his lead man.

"Yeah, Boss," Hansard told him. "Looks like that team was all they had. I don't know, really. It's just been very quiet the last few days."

"Can you spare some men to go to Atlanta?" Grimes asked.

"Sure, why not? I could send Leonard, Childs, and Emerson if you like. I'll stay here just in case."

"There's been an explosion at the Calvert house. We don't know yet what all that means or who is dead."

"They found bodies?" Hansard asked.

"Five, yeah. Three could be notables...waiting for DNA because that's all we have for two anyway. The dentures were knocked out on two bodies and busted all to hell. Everything else is crispy critters from what I'm hearing."

"Ugh," Hansard half laughed. "Glad I'm staying here."

"Make it happen soon as you can, okay?"

"Roger that," Hansard assured him, "Will do... say...where's that friend of yours? This 'Son' Fellow?"

"He's on his way to Albany, Georgia. There's a chance the top three men in this syndicate might have all been in that house in Atlanta."

"Albany?" Hansard was lost for a moment. "What's Albany got to do with it?"

"The owner of a pecan business there is one of the principles we think may be dead."

Hansard hesitated to bring up his next question but did anyway. "Did he do it?" he asked.

"The hit?" Grimes was taken aback. "Hell no...we're trying to get answers. He didn't do this...least I don't think he did."

Jake Hansard didn't follow up on that. Instead he went back to the subject of men going to Atlanta.

"I'll have them leave today," he told Grimes. "They should be there later tonight."

"That works. Have them contact me at this number when they are in position."

"Sure thing, boss," Hansard said as he hung up.

Later that afternoon, a car carrying the three NCIS agents passed a rental car parked in a Gadsden, Alabama, fast food restaurant. They did not notice anything, but the Israeli in the rental car saw them.

He followed them from a distance until they reached the highway to Rome, Georgia. He figured they were leaving the area, not just going for dinner.

This is good, he thought as he turned around. *This is good.*

90

Slowly, more details were released to the public about the explosion at Carlton Calvert's Atlanta mansion. Talk of an expensive wine cellar was downplayed by the Calvert controlled media outlets, but the word did get out.

Ben advised Jon of the point as he, Murray, and Weston arrived in Albany. They changed into business suits for their visit to David's Pecans and were met at the gate by a small security team of three men.

"Homeland Security," Jon told them, holding out an ID wallet he had made for such needs. "These are my associates. Step aside please."

The other men didn't know what to do. They stared at each other for a decision and finally moved from the gate.

Jon went into the main office and presented his fake credentials once again while Murray and Westy waited on the porch of the building. One member of the gate security team walked away and pulled a cell phone.

"That could be trouble," Murray whispered. He took out his own and called Ben.

"Phone in use within forty feet of my location," he told Ben. "Can you lock on?"

There was a short pause and Ben came back on.

"Someone called a girlfriend," he said. "Telling her it might be a short day today."

"Roger that," Murray smiled. "Thank you."

"Hold on," Ben stopped him. "Are you with Jon?"

"He's inside right now."

"I need to tell him something, fairly quick."

"Hang on a second."

The cowboy went inside, smiled at the nervous receptionist, and went into the office. Jon looked up and Murray tossed him the phone.

"Ben," he said. "Something important."

Ben told Jon there was more to the news about the wine cellar.

"Okay? What's your point?" Jon asked.

"There's a certain vintage that's kept in dark green bottles," he explained. "They're so dark... they call it amber."

"I thought amber was a golden shade, like the stuff prehistoric bugs got caught in."

"Just think a minute," Ben tried to redirect him. "All the references to 'Amber... even Congressman Gilbert recalled they said something about the 'secrets in amber' when they tried to recruit him."

Staring at some notes and doddles on Putney's desk pad, Jon changed the subject on him.

"Has the name 'Jamison' come up anywhere in this?" he asked.

"Who?"

"Jamison. That's all I've got. There are some drawings...scribbles really, on this desk. Looks like a nervous hitch or something. There are wings...crashed into the ground... drawn in several places, looks like they're melting or something."

"Icarus," Ben said instinctively. "His dad gave him waxed wings."

Jon stood straight and looked down on the drawings again. "The Greek mythology story?" he said as it came to him.

"Yeah," Ben's mind was way ahead of him. "Icarus got too close to the sun."

"Huh?" Jon managed to get out. Then suddenly he changed pace again. "See if Tim can go into Atlanta to check out this wine cellar idea of yours."

Ben had not shared the drone situation with him yet. Figuring he had enough to do and that they had it covered, it didn't seem worthy of bothering him.

"There's this one thing we're dealing with here and also...the feds and locals are all over that house. They will be for several days because of the mess," he told Jon.

"What one thing?"

Ben explained in detail about the drones and the satellite. Jon's coloring went through several stages but he stayed quiet and listened.

"We need to talk when I get back, okay?" he told Ben but added nothing else.

Ben took that as approval of how he was handling everything and didn't respond with much other than, "Okay."

Jon hung up and went out to the receptionist.

"Who is Jamison?" he asked her bluntly.

Less than two minutes later, Jon emerged from the office and looked at Murray.

"Got enough gas to take us to North Carolina?" he asked.

"What part?"

"Franklin," Jon answered, "just over the Georgia line."

"I can make Dalton," Murray calculated in his head. "We'd best stop there and refuel."

~

The flight of test drones left Dobbins Air Force Base in Marietta, Georgia at 2:22 PM. At 24,000 feet, one banked away from the other four and turned north by northwest.

"Bogie incoming," Ben reported and everyone took positions at the control table. The house faced north and was imbedded into the rocky face of the mountain. That meant any attack from the south would need to fly past and turn back to make its run.

"Here's she comes," Ben said again, "Eight minutes out."

Colleen Dunbar and Charles Burr rushed up into the attic. They had discussed leaving the slots open in the roof panel. Colleen had a hunch that the Israelis might need to guide the missile in with a laser pointer.

"If so, we should be able to see them," she'd told Grimes.

Burr put on one of Jon's jackets and activated the arm. "Damn," he said, "this thing is weird."

The new strength allowed him to get into his spot with the T-Rex and take directional aim out the window. Colleen sat at a spotter position and looked over the horizon.

~

Lucy Too swooped in on Dalton's airport and touched down near the refueling station. The noise of a small engine high above caught Jon's attention. He dialed Ben's number.

"Not now, boss," Ben told him abruptly, "Kinda busy at the moment...can I call you back?"

"Are you sure you've got this?" Jon's concern came through in his voice.

"Sure as I can be...gotta go," and Ben hung up.

The noise above had flown north when Jon first heard it, now he could tell it was coming back toward his house.

~

The lawyer, Hasbrough Fuller, got word of the trouble in Atlanta after lunch that day. He had been asleep on the couch in Jamison's office for most of that morning. He woke up with a headache.

The coffee Jasper left him was strong and almost cold by the time he was up. Washing his face in the private sink didn't help much. Fuller looked out the window that faced the woods, he thought about running, but his head hurt and he was hungry.

Jamison's secretary brought him a sack from Wendy's around 1 PM and he turned on the TV as he'd finished eating.

The news took him to his knees in fear. He wasn't sure where Jamison had gone, the man didn't tell him. Maybe he'd gone to see Calvert, *certainly not to kill him*, he thought. *Jamison would not do that.*

They were to have dinner that night and discuss where the lawyer would stay for a longer period.

It's early yet, Fuller told himself. The first drops of sweat rolled down his face and he felt a chill. *He'll be along,* the lawyer told himself, *but what if this was Barrett's work?*

Calvert's home blown to shreds meant trouble any way he looked at it. The sweat was worse now. He had a pain through his upper chest that throbbed into his arm. Two attempts to stand failed and the pain grew worse.

His mind purged itself as the fear grew deeper. Breathing suddenly hurt and his joints felt like rocks rubbing against one another. Fuller rolled to his back and stared at the ceiling fan. The weight on his chest was becoming unbearable. Turning his head toward a monogramed leather briefcase, he tried, but could not reach it.

"The Amber," he mumbled with no one around to hear, "the Amber."

~

"One O'clock off the horizon," Dunbar shouted as the beam of light came on and pointed in their direction. "This was easier than I thought."

Burr shifted in his shooter's chair and reported, "Got it."

He hesitated a few seconds and Colleen asked, "What's the matter?"

"I see the light but nothing behind it. I don't have a target."

"Sight two degrees below the source and let her rip," Dunbar suggested.

"Sounds good to me," Burr responded and the attic resounded with the sound of the mighty weapon he unleashed.

There was a small explosion on the hilltop where the light had been. It was gone now.

"Hit!" Dunbar exclaimed. "You got something."

~

The craft came into Ben's view through the satellite just before it made the U-turn. He armed the weapons and focused in closer to be sure what it was.

He glanced at a chart on the table with different drones illustrated.

"Does that look like an armed drone to you?" He asked Grimes.

"Take it out," Grimes answered, "it sure as hell does."

A bright, white light released from the satellite and made contact with the drone. The explosion was huge, but at almost three miles high, it had no major impact on anything.

At the airport, some ten miles from the house, Jon looked up at the sound of the blast. The flash reverberated like a visual echo above the clouds, and then it was gone.

Jon looked at the dark blue copter, a slight smile crossed his face as Murray came running up to him.

"Damn, what was that?" the cowboy asked.

"Just remember," Jon slapped him on the back, "don't ever mess with Ben."

Weston Duray grinned and pulled open one of the copter's doors.

They loaded up and Lucy Too was again in the air, headed for Franklin, North Carolina.

~

Mayhem had found the three Israelis on the hillside approximately 275 yards from the Dalton house. The laser pointer was destroyed. One man gathered himself as best he could. Of his two cohorts, one was dead and the other seriously wounded by the shot fired from the attic.

Colleen Dunbar stared through her binoculars waiting for the dust to settle down. When it did, she could see the hole in the ground, a body and a good bit of blood scattered about.

"You got 'em," she screamed to Burr. "Nice shot!"

~

When Lucy Too set down on the open field inside the La'J Furniture grounds, guards immediately surrounded them.

Jon flashed his badge and once again convinced the man in charge that they were legitimate.

"What's this all about?" the man asked Jon.

"A friend of Mr. Jamison's, Carlton Calvert, do you know who I'm talking about?"

The man nodded he did.

"Well someone or something blew his house to shreds this morning. We're here to clear Jamison's office."

The guard stepped back and pointed the way.

Jamison's secretary was a harder nut to crack; she insisted on calling for verification.

"Fine," Jon scoffed and headed for the door. "You do that. I'll wait out here though. We don't know just what might trigger a blast.

The secretary looked at the phone in her hand and gently placed it back on the cradle.

"Mr. J has a guest staying in his office," she said meekly. "He might be asleep. I haven't heard anything out of him in about an hour."

Jon opened the door and saw a man lying on the floor, eyes open but ashen-faced. He dropped down next to the body and checked for a pulse.

Jon's eyes scanned the room finding a bag with the lingering smell of French fries on the floor and a leather case with the initials "HF," in gold on the flap. He checked for a wallet. The man's coat hung behind the door. *Must be in there*, he told himself. Nothing else was obvious to him from where he knelt. The skin on the man's neck was cool, there was no pulse.

Taking too long, he thought and turned to the partially closed door.

"You need to call 911," Jon told the secretary. "This man is dead."

"But...what about the phone?" the shaken woman recalled his warning.

"Oh," Jon stumbled for a response. "Three digits should be okay."

Limping back into his house in Decatur, Georgia, Warren Dawes washed his hands and poured himself an iced tea from the refrigerator.

The van had been washed down, inside and out, and the sparse but effective stickers labeling it a "Fulton County – Atlanta Georgia" vehicle were removed. He'd parked it at the bus garage where it was used to transport parts and tools for bus maintenance and drove his pick-up home.

Smooth, he thought as the cold tea ran down his throat, *almost too smooth*.

The TV remote lay nearby on the counter. Dawes grabbed it and brought the small box unit to life across the room.

"Local Publishing giant Carlton Calvert feared dead in massive explosion at his home," the news reader went on.

"Feared?" Dawes repeated out loud. "Guess they couldn't ID what was left." He made a mental note, *next time, less C4*.

He was tempted to call and report his success to his contractor, but professional integrity told him to wait for verification.

"It's time for dinner anyway," he said aloud.

Lucy Too was back in the air before the ambulance arrived at La' J Furniture. After convincing the secretary that Fuller had been dead for some time, he'd taken pictures of everything he could. The man's ID, front and back, because he needed to leave that with the body and other papers on and in Jamison's desk were photographed.

The leather case was another matter. He'd passed it out through a window to Murray and it was with them in the helicopter on their way to Dalton.

It would be morning before the identities of the five victims at Calvert's house were known.

~

Tim Spiegel took the armored pick-up truck and roared up Highway 71 looking for the Israelis. Ben and Cheryl monitored the area through four cameras while Daniel watched through the front room window.

Agent Burr covered him from the attic with the T-Rex rifle.

91

Jon had been quiet during the ride home from North Carolina and through the night. He sat with the materials he collected and after having a picture of the man he found in Jamison's office confirmed as Hasbrough Fuller, began sorting and putting together the details. Those details added up to a need for still more information. Without regard for the time, Jon grabbed a cell phone.

At 3:30 AM, Jerome Grimes was awakened and asked several questions. Mainly, what he'd heard from the President. Jon's first interest was other activities besides the deaths and recruitment attempts.

"Everything seems to have boiled down in the last three days," Grimes told him. "I have a list of those killed..."

"I have that," Jon interrupted him. "Fuller's briefcase has a treasure chest of information."

"You've got Fuller's case?"

"Not officially. When I officially have it, I'll need to hand it over to you, right?"

Grimes wrinkled his brow and asked, "What all is in there?"

"Like I said, it's a treasure chest. Wherever he left from and why...he took everything with him. Least it appears he tried to. The man must have been seriously spooked."

"When can I have that case?" Grimes pushed.

Jon looked down, not being evasive, just thinking.

"I'm going to my little house for a while. When I'm ready to go I'll leave the case, intact as I found it, in the trunk of my Jaguar. You'll find it there."

"Go?" Grimes stood up and got right in Jon's face. "Where are you going?"

"I have business. Meetings and visits I must take care of."

"Wait a minute...business meetings, come on," Grimes knew better.

Jon turned to leave but the other man grabbed his shoulder.

"We don't even have ID's on the victims in Atlanta yet," he protested.

"They will be Calvert, Putney and Jamison."

Grimes' face grew flush. Struck speechless for a second, he recovered with, "You know this from Fuller's papers?"

"I didn't say that," Jon answered flatly.

"You didn't deny it either."

Both men became quiet until Jon leaned into Grimes, "Don't ask me more," he scolded him. "Murray and Westy will be coming with me...for part of it."

"Do I have to arrest you to stop you?"

"I hope you don't," Jon's eyes glared directly into his friend's, "I'd hate to have to resist you."

Walking away, he could hear Grimes sit back down on his cot.

Jon climbed the stairs and went straight to the elevator. He needed to see Ben for a minute before leaving. The master apprentice lay face down on his computer table, fast asleep.

"Ben," he whispered as the boy woke up. Those mechanical bugs you were working on..."

"Yeah?"

"How many do you have?"

Ben rubbed his eyes and looked at Jon. "Three minis and four micro-minis," he told him.

"Can they carry anything?"

"Yeah, but not much."

"I'm going to the house for a while, to figure this out. Get those things ready. Remotes, visual guidance; you know what I'll want."

"Got this figured out, huh?" Ben calculated.

"I've got enough to figure it out. I'll be in touch but everything between us is secure...till this is over."

Ben leaned back. He'd seen this look on Jon before. Silas was in full command. "Yes, Sir!" he answered. "Me and you."

~

Morning reflected from the broad leafs of the Kudzu vines. Shining in through the windshield, it awakened the Israeli who had gone to Alabama.

He'd slept in his rental car about five miles from the animal park, opting to go in with daylight to look around. The lone volunteer had pulled off the road and was all but invisible in the heavy growth of weeds when owners Will and Suzanne drove past. It was groceries day.

NCIS Agent Jake Hansard had found a shady spot past the smell of the main barn to sit and eat his breakfast. The sausage and biscuit had been brought to him by one of the park's volunteers.

Cody Arnold, having finished morning chores, was working on a latch to the inner cage where Boris was kept. The lion lay just inside that gate, watching and rubbing the fence with a great head, quite contentedly.

~

Since the news first came on about the Atlanta house explosion, Natalie Barrett had not left her TV. Her state of mind had grown fragile and this pushed stability into a corner. She did not sleep, or eat, waiting for the identities of those in the house. The warden was called in to see about her.

"Barrett," he said through the bars. "What do you know about this?"

"What don't I?" she laughed and answered without looking at him. "All fall down. They wouldn't listen ...all fall down." Her eyes finally left the TV screen for a second. Staring at the floor, the warden heard her say, "The numbers and stars are gone."

"What does that mean, Barrett?" he demanded... but she ignored him.

The warden stormed away and told a guard to, "Call Doc Weinheart, we got one that just went over the top."

~

Grimes slept until 6:30 that morning and immediately went to the second level workshop. Ben Shaw was still asleep so he tried to be quiet.

The NCIS Director looked through the papers and files and organized them in chronological order. It was time to call his boss, Nelson Pharr, the Secretary of the Navy, and bring him up to speed. Walking to a far corner, he dialed his phone in the dark.

"Nelson?" he started, "We have a problem at CIA, and I'm afraid, above that."

"I'm a few steps ahead of you, Jerry," the Secretary told him. "The President had a memo walked over to me last night. He didn't trust any electronic transmission of this evidence."

"Evidence?"

"That's what it is," Pharr answered. "I've opened a case against a civilian employee at the Truman Building."

"Truman Building?" Grimes repeated him. "That's on C Street, right?"

The secretary paused before he answered with his own question, "What do you think about that? It isn't usually referred to that way."

"It's come up in conversation with a guest we have. Probably talking about the same guy you are, right?"

"When can you come in," Pharr didn't respond to the question and his words let Grimes know why. "We need to speak face to face."

"I have to see about my friend and what he's up to. Then I'll be there."

"Jerry," the secretary said and then paused, "I need you to stand down on that."

Grimes stiffened his back and considered his next words.

"Come again," he finally settled on.

"You are ordered to stand down."

"You know what I'm referring to, don't you?"

"This isn't from me, Jerry. It's higher...you are to let this scenario play itself out."

Switching to his old Marine voice, Jerome Grimes sharply responded with, "Aye, aye, Sir!"

The line went silent and Grimes closed his phone. He felt the presence behind him and turned to find Ben standing about ten feet away, holding a paper he'd printed out.

The look on the director's face caused Ben to ask, "You okay, sir?"

"Yeah...what's up?"

"The DNA is back," Ben held the report out to him. "It was two of the top guys that we know of, Calvert and Putney. There was another guy with them, somebody named Jamison."

Grimes shook his head trying to stifle the smirk he knew was displaying.

"Did you know already, Sir?" Ben was thrown by his reaction.

"Let's just say I had a hunch."

92

He'd slept an hour, maybe two. Organizing all the paperwork and information clogged his analytical process, so he chose to run. It was still dark but he knew the course by heart... jumps and all. Rounding the last turn toward home he could see the small light escaping through the basement vent.

Not to worry, he thought and smiled as one of the dogs joined him. *No one can see it except...us.*

He ran until the sun was up and bright. His escorts by then numbered three. They were disappointed when he broke off and jogged to the small house.

The information waited there for him. All lined up in an order that Fuller would be proud of. The main article was a simple spiral notebook. Charts and lists that matched up with those Jon had been able to gather through other encounters. But now with details that explained exactly who, what and why.

The breakdown within their syndicate was quite simple, much like a colony of bees. "Workers" kept things clean and orderly while the "drones" would go out seeking sustenance for the hive. Both categories broke down by rank and stature, yet all served one queen.

Natalie Barrett, Jon thought. It all fit...except the chart did not show her at the top. She was under a tirade led by Carlton Calvert and even he reported to a higher authority.

The last page in the notebook was a hand-drawn version of the numbered star picture. A prototype, Jon assumed. The image itself was mesmerizing, but that was because he knew what it meant to others.

A small flashing light finally caught his attention. There were three missed calls on his cell phone but he decided to take a shower first.

The decision was a good one. He felt renewed as the water poured over him and the facts of what he was dealing with fell into the place. It was beginning to make sense now. The run, the air, and now the hot water had cleared his mind. He was ready to study and prepare for a mission.

I had rules once, he remembered. Strict rules that somehow seemed like long ago. *What's done is done*, he thought and almost said aloud.

In clean, fresh clothes he returned to the basement of the small house and pulled out the freezer. His small, dug out safe room brought a smile to him. It felt like home.

The coffee maker had turned itself off but the pot still felt warm. Jon poured a cup and put it in the microwave. His phone rang yet again.

"Jon," the voice said excitedly.

"Yes, Ben," he replied.

"The DNA came back. Have you heard?"

~

Spiegel had returned with a body, but nothing else. Nava identified the man as the group's leader, Leon Urgig. Urgig was one of Ted Romach's top lieutenants when he had taken over the Mossad. With him dead, the job here was over without completion.

"He was a good fighter," Nava explained, "but then his wife died in an attack on their village. He turned off on war and fighting."

"Yet he came here to kill Jon?" Marsha said with more than a touch of sarcasm. "Just a bit hypocritical, don't you think?"

"They only thought of ending the big strife," she countered. "I didn't say it made any sense."

"What will the others do now?" Colleen asked of the remaining team members.

Nava caught a disapproving glare from Marsha at the other woman's question, but answered her anyway.

"They will try to get home, I suppose."

Grimes walked into the area and looked at Dunbar and Burr.

"It's time for me to head back," he announced. "You want to go or stay here for a while?"

"There's an option, Sir?" Burr asked him.

"You might be more useful here, frankly," the boss answered. "This may not be over." He looked at Spiegel directing his next words at him.

"I need a ride to the local airport," he suggested, "I've got a jet coming to get me."

"Yes, Sir," Spiegel nodded.

Grimes then looked at Marsha.

"George is still in town handling interrogations," he told. "Till he gets back you're in charge around here."

Marsha nodded but said nothing.

"You need to call somebody and get these bodies out of here," Grimes continued quite officially. "They're starting to stack up."

~

Warren Dawes sat staring at his small TV. The news had him fixated and more than a little concerned. He had already tried to call "Jamie" several times since the story of the three main bodies in the house in Atlanta broke.

I thought I knew that guy, he said internally, while remembering the man who came into Calvert house. *What the hell was he doing there?*

He dialed the contact phone again and this time a strange voice answered.

"What?" it barked. "I'm getting tired of this. Where's my money?"

Dawes stood from his chair.

"Who the 'Sam-Hell' is this," he demanded.

Randall Swartz still held the phone as he screamed at a man near him, "That's it. Take this SOB out and lose him."

Dawes listened closely and heard another voice.

"You sure Randy?" it asked.

"Do it," the angry man shouted again. "Get him out of here."

As a door opened more sounds came through to Dawes. The faint chiming of slot machines was familiar to the hit man. He could make them out before the man yelled into the phone, "Your boy is dead," and hung up.

Dawes sat back down and leaned against his chair's back. His eyes focused on a pencil he'd left on the table. Fumbling through his shirt pockets, he found a slip of paper and sat back up reaching for the pencil.

He wrote two words on the paper, <u>Randy</u> ...and then after several minutes of thinking, <u>Cherokee.</u>

~

Following a family in their van, the Israeli parked next to them and then walked up to the admissions window and bought his ticket. He waited for the group to assemble and stayed close as they headed into the park.

Agent Jake Hansard watched the group approach the entrance as his cell phone rang out.

"Jake, it's Leonard," Agent Monroe began. "We're here, looking at the mess. Carter is here from Chicago...Grimes put him in charge."

"Everything on the up and up?" Hansard asked while the family group disbursed into the park. That was pretty normal and didn't bother him. "No funny business from other departments?" he continued with Monroe.

"Locals haven't cleared the area yet." His partner told him. "Remains of a second floor are still smoldering and the access to the lower level is really questionable right now."

"Stay with it, back up Carter unless Grimes says different and...." Agent Hansard stopped mid-sentence when he heard a sound he'd been told about. It was a lion's roar.

"I gotta go," the agent told Monroe. He hung up as he jumped to his feet.

93

A young man entered the building at 2201 C Street through a back door. The security guard stopped him there and called up to Suite 617. After a brief conversation the uniformed man pointed him to a chair.

"Wait right here," the guard ordered. "Someone will be right down."

The visitor tried to straighten his disheveled clothes. Having been on the run and hiding for the past three days showed on him. He ran his fingers through his hair with little helpful result.

Bright light filled the area as the elevator doors opened. A man looked out and then stepped toward the visitor with the guard.

"No need to sign him in, Patrick," the man explained to the guard. "He's family."

"Yes, Sir," the uniformed man nodded in uncertainty. Still, he waved his arm for the young man to go ahead and watched them walk away.

The two didn't speak until they were on the elevator.

"Not a word in here," the man ordered. The young visitor complied.

It was several paces down the hall in total silence until the man pushed his door open and gestured to his guest. Once inside, the door closed firmly, yet softly. It was there the man's demeanor changed.

With a move surprisingly quick for a man of his age, he pinned the guest against the wall with a forearm under his chin.

"What are you doing here?" the older man glared at him.

"You don't know?" the visitor squirmed. "They tried to kill..."

The aggressor stepped back, releasing the visitor. The young man rubbed his neck and finished, "Or they would have. They took out my office," he coughed trying to speak. "If I had been there...I'd be dead."

"But you weren't there, were you?" the other man said angrily. "You think that was by accident?"

Those words stunned the young guest. His momentary confusion quickly added up and made sense. It also made him angry.

"You were watching?" he growled from deep in his gut.

The older man turned calmly and walked across the room.

Leaning away from the wall in a threatening posture, the guest followed him demanding, "Why didn't you call me?"

"I don't do that," the man said opening his inner office door. "Get in here," he pulled the younger man inside and continued. "The company wanted your place shut down after those phony agents got into Styles' office. We couldn't be sure about any links to that Syrian or to your office they may have found."

The guest shook his head. He looked at the numeral star picture on the wall and all but laughed. "Fat lotta good that does us now," he spat.

~

Boris had sensed something was wrong as the man approached. Springing to his feet, he looked past Cody Arnold and bellowed a mighty warning.

The roar both stopped the approaching man and got the ex-SEAL's attention. Cody turned and saw the Israeli with a gun in his hand. He turned and threw his hammer. The tool struck the crook of the man's arm. His gun flew to the side and into some tall grass.

The Israeli hesitated and then moved toward the grass but in that length of time, Cody was on him. With one good arm, the SEAL gripped and threw the man toward Boris' enclosure. He fell over the first fence and rolled into the second layer where Boris tried to bite through the chain link to get to him.

The Israeli jumped away from the fence and turned back to Cody, hitting him in the face with a left hook. The former SEAL turned slightly with the blow and swung his good right arm in an upper cut motion. It caught the attacker square in the chest and lifted him off his feet. When he landed against the inner fence gate, the one Cody had been working on; its unattached hinge gave way.

Twenty minutes out from Dalton airport, Director Grimes was called to the cockpit of the LearJet taking him to Quantico.

"Radio call for you, Sir," the pilot explained and handed him a headset.

"Sir?" a voice said through the speaker. It was clearly Ben Shaw.

"Yeah, Ben. What's wrong?"

"Your aircraft began emitting a beacon the second you got to 18,000 feet. You're being tracked."

~

The older man walked to the picture on his wall, the one his guest had just made light of and pulled it down. Holding it in both hands, he smiled for a moment, and then turned to that guest without the smile.

"You shouldn't have come here," he said.

"Where was I supposed to go?" was the reply. "Why is all this happening, Uncle Chester? I haven't heard from Agnes or anything."

"And you won't," the man countered in a stern tone. "That district needs a new representative." The older man paused for a deep breath.

"She was in a wreck this morning," he added and turned his head away.

Darcy Brown walked around to face his Uncle. "She didn't know anything... Why her?" he demanded.

"She knew who I was," Chester Weiss answered coldly. "It could have come up in an interview or, or something." He slowly went to his desk and sat down. "I'm sorry, Darcy," he mumbled. "It just had to be."

"Did Magill do this?" the still angry nephew begged.

"Magill is gone," Weiss looked up and spit out. "Too much pointed at him."

Darcy Brown took a minute to compose himself. His anger now pure rage on his face, he threw out another question. "Who is this 'Son' dude, anyway?"

"Some damned guy from Georgia," his uncle answered. "We planned everything... so that nothing like this could ever happen...and then he comes along."

"You're not supposed to be...out...actively exposed like this. Where's Calvert? Where's Fuller?"

"You haven't heard, huh? Calvert, Putney, and Jamison are all dead. Fuller, I can't find. Barrett put a contract on him and he's gone underground."

"Fuller has everything, doesn't he?" Brown asked.

"Everything except the Amber," Weiss muttered. "This ain't good."

The younger man felt his way into a seat on the couch. He grew pale and slumped over before he asked, "What now? What about us?"

"We get out of here," Chester Weiss told his nephew. "As soon as my team gets the Amber out of that house...we're gone."

~

Agent Jake Hansard ran down the trail to Boris' enclosure. He heard the struggle unfolding and arrived as the Israeli went through the gate and onto his back inside the lion's den.

The big cat's eyes grew to twice their normal size as the man struck the dirt. Boris leapt faster than the human mind could consider it. He landed with front paws to either side of the man, one seven inch wide pad next to his ear, the other just outside his shoulder. Boris scratched at the ground beside the man's ear and tilted his large head down. He exhaled with a grunting sound and the putrid breath circled the man's face and chest while the shaggy head stared down at him.

Pure, complete, and total fear blocked the attacker's ability to scream as he stared into the jaws of the angry lion.

Staff members appeared but held back. Several groups and families units, having heard the commotion, came from different directions. Each stopped, gawking at the scene before them. Senior staff moved into position off the trails and prepared to take action.

Hansard had his service weapon out and aimed as he ran. He also moved off the trail to see around Arnold. His body had become an obstacle as he moved cautiously toward the clash. Before Hansard could pull the trigger to stop the beast, he and everyone there heard Cody Arnold call out, "No, Boris...No!"

The huge head lifted and turned to the sound of the voice. Boris grunted yet again and looked at his friend as Cody moved closer still.

A child screamed but her father quickly covered her mouth and quieted her down. Boris glanced in that direction for a moment.

Prudently, but diligently, Cody stepped closer to the man and the lion standing over him.

"I've got him, Boris," Cody said calmly, his hand outstretched, "good boy."

Hansard stopped, still thirty feet back. Raising his gun with both hands, he held his breath and felt the trigger.

"Back, Boris," Cody Arnold commanded while moving nearer still.

Boris rolled his head in the air and everyone watched as the lion stepped away from the downed man. With head down, the big cat walked to a far corner of the enclosure and huffed twice before turning around.

Cody now stood over the man and smiled at Boris. He was showing him he now had control of the situation. Pulling the Israeli up with his good arm, the ex-SEAL looked him square in the face.

"Are you going to behave or do I need to call him back over here?" he asked.

With hands held chest high, the man walked out from the enclosure where Hansard grabbed him. The agent handcuffed the attacker while Cody lifted the gate back into its position. Boris sauntered over gingerly and rubbed against the ex-SEAL's leg with his large head.

"Thank you, Boris," Hansard heard Cody say to the cat.

Cody Arnold re-pinned the hinge and knelt down. He and the great lion looked eye to eye and Cody nodded with a smile saying, "Good boy."

Boris yawned a huge, silent yawn and rubbed the gate with his head.

94

"Agency Flight 926 requesting deviation to flight plan, over," the pilot spoke into his radio. Director Grimes had advised him of the warning from Ben and he climbed in altitude while asking for authority to do so.

"33,000 and rising," his co-pilot read off the meter, "ceiling 51,000."

"What's that mean?" Grimes asked impatiently.

"That's high as we can go, sir."

"Well, how about changing course?" Grimes inquired.

"Not till we clear 45,000, Sir. This sky is full of airplanes and we're not supposed to be here."

As the craft began to shake, Grimes sat down behind the pilot and strapped in.

"Agency Flight 926, requesting alternate flight path north and east," the pilot tried again.

The radio finally responded.

"Agency 926, are you declaring an emergency?" the voice asked.

"Roger that, tower. We need clearance around our original plan, over."

There was a short delay in the answer, then the voice calmly stated, "Agency 926, cleared to General Route 9 at 40,000. Take Heading 332.4 and hold for Columbus tower."

"Roger, control," the pilot responded, "332.4 at 40,000 engaging now."

"Have a good trip 926, Columbus should pick you up in 40 minutes."

Three men sat on a mountain top south of Charlottesville, Virginia. They waited until long past the time their target was to have come overhead.

The leader shook his head and motioned for another man to lower the SAM launcher they had set up. The leader called in by phone.

"Target no show," he said, "repeat...target no show."

"Get off the damned phone," the other voice ordered and hung up.

In the second floor workshop of the mansion in Dalton, Georgia, Cheryl Duray looked at Ben in frustration.

"Dad gum it," she exclaimed. "They weren't on the line very long."

Ben finished typing and smiled at her.

"It's okay," he spoke softly but with confidence. "I got 'em."

~

Jon's materials formed what amounted to a pyramid. He was amazed at the detail of the notes and records kept by the lawyer Fuller. What was even more amazing was that he recognized links in the organizational chart.

He paused with a paper that referenced "The Sponsors" and groups under them for fund raising. The east Texas motorcycle gang that he and Murray had run into was not listed specifically, but one phone number stood out to him. It was on his list, the one he'd found in the gang's hideout.

Sherry Shanahan was predominately marked out, after having been moved in the chart from a "legal support" role to her assumed position of "king maker." That didn't work out for her.

The Chicago mayor tied to the white slavery ring was also there. His organization had been responsible for large dollar amounts to finance the operation of the syndicate. His was but one of many.

Out of curiosity, Jon flipped through everything searching for a reference to the Argus Group. Though they were not mentioned, a connection to Shreveport was clearly there.

The Russian Drug Cartel had paid a tariff to the syndicate until Torbof's fall from his tower. The link appeared to end at that point.

Connecticut Congressman Ted Beale was listed, though his name had been crossed out with a black "X." That same section mentioned the Sheik in Yemen.

Evidence of the recent purge and attempt to rebuild with new blood was there. Many of the names under "remove" had already been confirmed as casualties. Congressman Travis Gilbert and Senator Wallace Edgett were listed under "prospects," along with two dozen others.

Barrett's name and those of Calvert and his Lieutenants, Putney and Jamison were near the top of the chart.

As he read further about Carlton Calvert, the name Walter Frazier appeared with a small note, <u>useful,</u> written beside it.

But the mystery held true at the very top of the chart. There were no names, only references to "C Street" and "Wilson Boulevard."

A hand written note, in the margin next to "C Street" looked like a phone number. "9125552910."

That's not a D.C. area code, Jon thought, *that's south and east Georgia.*

He dug out an unused burner phone and dialed the number. A recorded, "The number you've dialed is no longer in service," message answered.

That could be Albany, he told himself. Then it hit him and he spoke out loud, "It could be Saint Simon's Island or Brunswick, too."

He immediately called the Earl home on the island.

~

The prison psychiatric staff had tried to interview Natalie Barrett but she would not co-operate. In their report to the warden, they suggested her return to Alderson. Perhaps her stay at the maximum facility had been more than she could handle mentally.

That was all the warden needed to hear. Any excuse to rid his community of this cancer did not require repeating. Barrett's return to West Virginia was signed and processed that day.

~

"Sir," Ben reported to Director Grimes, "the call went to a phone in the building on Wilson Boulevard in Washington, D.C."

Through the cockpit noise, Grimes heard what he needed.

"Thank you, Ben...Great job... as always."

Changing phones, Grimes called the office of the president. He was put on hold.

"Yes, Director," the voice came on within two minutes.

"Sir, I have confirmation on Wilson Boulevard."

"Thank you, Director." The President replied.

"Shall I have my people move in?"

"Hold on that, Director. Let me get back to you, okay?"

Grimes didn't want to understand, but he was afraid he did.

"Yes, Sir," he told the Chief Executive. "Waiting to hear back."

Within five minutes, Jon Crane heard a phone ringing on his table. It was one used for one purpose only. He put his other call on hold and slid down the ringing phone.

"Hello," he answered.

"Please hold for the president," a voice told him.

Jon went briefly back to his other call.

"Patty," he said. "Thanks again, I need to go."

Warren Dawes pulled into Cherokee, North Carolina, and went to Harrah's first. Not finding what he sought, he drove down the street and parked in front of Eagles Rest Casino.

He smiled and leaned back against the truck's seat. The big sign right out front answered his question.

It read, Welcome to Eagle's Rest – Randall Swartz Proprietor.

Hello, Randy, Dawes thought as he stared at the sign. *You have my money, I presume.*

He climbed down and entered the casino to look around and plan his assault.

95

What remained of the second floor of Carlton Calvert's home now smoldered atop its foundation and that which lay beneath the surface.

Agent Carter placed an urgent call to his boss.

"Where are you, Sir?" he asked Grimes.

"In my office," he responded excitedly. "Is it clear to get in there yet?"

"Not quite, but that's not my issue."

Grimes frowned. He didn't need any more issues right now.

"About twenty guys in khakis just showed up. They claim to be Homeland Security."

"Did you explain you were in charge of the scene?" Grimes asked.

"Didn't impress them at all, Sir. They told me to 'go take a hike', I believe were the words."

Grimes shook his head. "Look," he told Carter. "Hang on and hold your ground. I'll have a platoon of Marines there in twenty minutes. Don't let those guys in that basement...you got me?"

Carter looked at his Glock service pistol and smiled. "Sure...I got it."

Grimes called Dalton, Georgia, and got Ben on the line.

"Kid," he said almost disrespectfully, "if Jon wants in that basement he'd best get over there. I expect a huge stand-off within the hour and that might give him a diversion to get in."

~

Chester Weiss knew people. His thirty years as a civil servant piled up many notable contacts, some who were fellow travelers, politically, and others who knew nothing of his beliefs.

He had been at the State Department since the Clifton days. It was during that period, and her lack of attention to detail, that Weiss was able to institute his plan. Based on information he had obtained while in Foreign Service with the CIA in Syria, he convinced and recruited people to help protect what he told them was "the" secret. Knowledge that if used correctly, would forever keep the other side off balance and the public dead set against them.

His vast network began with an attorney and fellow believer, Hasbrough Fuller. They worked nights on the structure of this syndicate. Layers to provide political cover, layers to provide armed protection and overt actions. And most importantly, still many more to provide funding to pay for all this. Fuller's idea for what they called themselves led to his creative logo, the star formed with numbers.

Carlton Calvert proved himself beyond his perceived value. His ability to sway public opinion through his news services was unheard of. The joke was, "if Calvert doesn't publish it – it didn't happen." They learned that many things could be accomplished under the cover of misinformation.

As his power grew, so did his control and desire to be the keeper of the secret. That privilege was given him to assure his loyalty.

As Weiss now packed what he could, he waited to hear from his ally across town. The link to their secret was now in jeopardy. That link must be secured.

He could not reach Fuller, and that was bad. Reports through other trusted sources advised that the main cartel was falling apart rapidly.

Mid and lower level "Celestial Enumerates" had cut ties to the organization. Something none would dare to do before this. The star of numbers pictures were down from office walls and in trash bins.

With his power base collapsing, there was little else he could do. It was time to go.

His arrangements were made long in advance. An open ticket on a flight to Venezuela, under the name Albert Frost was in his briefcase. All the forged IDs necessary were there with it.

He looked at his nephew sitting across the room.

It would have been easier if he'd been in his office that day, Weiss thought. *Oh, well...he'll know soon enough. There's only room for me.*

~

Jon put aside his planning and dressed in the uniform he had brought from the mansion. He walked to the back door, stared for a moment into the woods and then skyward waiting for the sound.

When he heard it coming, Jon grabbed the end of an inflatable balloon and tied it to the harness on his suit. Stepping into the backyard, he straightened the line from the balloon to his harness and pulled the cord.

Continuing to walk away from the house, he watched the balloon soar into the sky until Lucy Too roared over and grabbed it.

Jon was lifted into the air and hoisted quickly. He was aboard the dark blue machine, talking to Ben within two minutes.

"I still wonder about that green suit," he teased the boy.

"You're just jealous."

Murray looked over his shoulder and called out, "Atlanta in fifteen minutes... Calvert's house... in five after that."

Jon and Ben prepared for their descent, which would also be fast and hopefully surprising.

~

Agent Carter heard the huge trucks before he saw them. Two military deuce and a halves, two and one-half ton vehicles, turned the corner and twenty six armed Marines exited into a formation around the foundation of the destroyed building.

The khaki clad team from Homeland Security stepped back but then moved closer with weapons drawn.

Carter looked at Childs and Everson then leaned over to Agent Monroe.

"Watch this," he said grinning broadly, "this should be good."

The noise and excitement of the diesel trucks obscured the blue helicopter's approach. Add to that noise the now more than forty men squaring off at each other and Lucy Too came in unnoticed.

One block over, two figures lowered themselves from thirty feet to the ground in three seconds and the chopper was gone.

Ben, who had studied the plans for the house, led Jon through the heavy shrubbery to a coal chute door. Jon burned through the lock with a hand held laser, and they went inside.

Darkness everywhere was what they'd hoped for, and they got it. Any intrusion of light from above could betray their presence. They hit the headgear lights on their suits and moved forward.

The shaft had not been used for coal in over fifty years, but a few blocks remained and made walking difficult. They entered a short hallway and then everything was heavy gauge metal.

"You said there was a door," Jon reminded Ben.

"Follow me," the younger man said and gingerly went deeper into the void.

"It's not here," Ben finally admitted.

"How old were those plans you had?" Jon asked.

"Nearly eight years."

"Do you remember where the elevator shaft is?"

"Should be just down here," Ben told him, "but it's walled off."

Jon felt the wall surrounding the elevator and said it was not as thick as the others. "Maybe half-inch," he said.

His laser tool was also a plasma cutter. He looked at Ben and advised him, "Turn your head."

Hot radiant light burned through the metal and Jon fashioned a three-sided cut in the shaft's side wall. The incisions at the top, bottom and one edge allowed that section to be pushed inward, with the strength of Jon's suit, creating a path into the elevator shaft.

The elevator car was wedged in just above their location, but pushing the wall material inward served as a brace.

Opening the shaft's doors into the wine cellar was simple compared to everything else. Once inside, they stood and stared at the vastness of the space.

"This is incredible," Ben said out loud.

"Yeah," Jon said with a touch of Silas coming through, "Now...if you were 'Amber', where would you be?"

96

Marsha came to Nava Golan with news from Director Grimes.

"One of your team was caught in Alabama," she told her. "He was trying to kill that young SEAL."

Looking angered and confused, Nava shook her head slowly.

"The SEAL was not our responsibility," She complained. "We were told Syrians would handle that."

"How could you work with Muslims?" Marsha asked bluntly.

Nava lowered her head. "It was not the fight," she offered, "It was the cause."

"Is that what you believed?"

"I believed my friends...my lover, were in danger. I did not say it was my cause...Can't you understand this?"

Marsha stared at her without a response. Colleen Dunbar stepped in to alter the conversation.

"So there are three alive...plus you," she said. "Is that everyone?"

"That I know of...yes."

"Grimes has talked with Yinon Harel," Dunbar added.

"How is he?" the Mossad fighter sat straighter and became much more attentive.

"Better every day, according to him," Marsha assured her. "He asked the director about you. He wants you to come home as soon as possible." She then smiled slightly, adding, "He says Reiss is waiting."

Once again Nava's head lowered as she thought of the trouble she was in. "My going home," she muttered, "That will be up to you."

"It will be up to Grimes," Marsha corrected her. "I see no problem with you going home," her tone was harsh. "This mess is about over."

~

With his head resting on his open palm, a man sat silently at his desk on Wilson Boulevard in Washington, D.C..

All the planning, he kept thinking, *down the drain. Weiss is cutting out...so should I. But to where?*

The fireplace in his office was consuming papers. It wasn't the season for a fire but he didn't care. Destroying what he could was all that mattered now.

A cell phone rang within a desk drawer.

"I thought I got them all," he half mumbled and pulled the drawer out roughly. Looking at the phone, he saw it was a call from overseas. Many contacts had been attempting to find him, to get a situation report. He had nothing more to tell them.

Standing up and leaving the still ringing phone closed, he walked to the fireplace and threw it in the fire with everything else. Turning back to his desk, he glanced out a window and froze in place.

Two black SUVs sat in the courtyard across the street. He moved closer to the window and looked to one side then the other. More black SUVs.

Damn, he thought and inhaled deeply. *If they know, why just sit there?*

~

"Red wine is more likely to be in dark green bottles," Ben suddenly announced as he looked down the rows of bottles.

"What?" Jon asked. "You said special vintages, before. Which is it?"

"I've been studying what I could," Ben explained as his flashlight panned the area. "Amber could be a reference to dark green bottles, right?"

"That's why we're here," Jon answered in a singsong-style sarcastic tone.

"I'm just saying there's a bunch of bottles down here. Let's find the 'red' section and look through them first. That's where the dark green bottles will be."

"How do you know so much about wines all of a sudden?"

"I told you... I looked it up," Ben grinned at him. "You should try it sometime." He continued to smile broadly at Jon as he moved forward shining his light on the tops of the racks. "They say the reds are more protected by the dark green glass."

Ben took the lead and they both moved forward until a rack in front of them was marked, <u>Red.</u>

"Here we are," Ben announced.

Jon looked down the row at lines upon lines of dark bottle bottoms. He shined his light across them slowly and them Ben called out,

"Hold it...right there. Did you see that?"

He grabbed a bottle and pulled it out from the rack.

It was empty.

"I thought it looked different," Ben said while comparing the bottle to others nearby. "The light reflected oddly. There's nothing in it."

"Evaporated, maybe?" Jon offered. "Check the seal."

Ben rolled the bottle around, check the cork and then the label.

"The cork is fine. But this looks funny to me," he said holding it out. "These others don't have numbers like this on the labels."

"What is it?"

"I don't know. A lot number, maybe," Ben guessed. "But these others don't have anything like it."

"You said you studied this stuff," Jon reminded him.

"Well, it didn't say anything about this."

Jon took out a camera and snapped pictures of the bottle and the label. The long string of mixed Arabic and roman numerals was in the same font as the rest of the label. It had been printed professionally and with great care.

"Make sure you get the numbers," Ben insisted.

A disgusted Jon stopped and stared back at him for a moment.

"This is why you normally stay at the mansion," he growled.

"What?"

"Just put the bottle back, and let's look some more."

As Ben gently returned the bottle, Jon took a lipstick camera from his pouch and placed it on an adjacent rack. The lens would capture the area around the mysterious bottle.

"I thought I was doing pretty good," Ben complained.

Jon shined his light down another row and walked away.

"Just keep looking, will ya," he grumbled.

~

The gray walls and even grayer trim gave the room a dim and dark feel. Scratches in the one-way glass gave its purpose away, but no one seemed to mind.

Two detectives settled down across from Walter Frazier in the interrogation room of Roanoke's police station. The three men sat, two on one side and Frazier on the other. That's how it was, unsettlingly quiet.

For several minutes they all simply stared at one another until Frazier started shaking his head almost violently.

"Who the hell is that guy anyway?" he whined.

"Who? The man in the black suit?" one officer smiled and put his hands on the table between them. "He's just the instrument, the tool that rooted you out. The man who gave you up lives here...and has for some time."

"What are you talking about? That freak in the black outfit, the one that can't be killed...he's my problem."

"No, Mr. Frazier," the detective taunted him. "A tip from a stranger and the bodies in that grave, besides your little boys club, have done you in."

"I know nothing about what those kids were up to...nothing! I just tried to help... and this is what I get for it."

"Really? So they killed the congressman we've identified, all by themselves? And then brought his body down here from D.C.?"

"I already told you," Frazier insisted. "I don't know nothing about that."

"They say different."

"I don't have a care about what they think or say. I'm a respected man in this community, and my word will stand above theirs."

"One little problem with all that," the officer leaned over the table. "You see, we also found Gail Monahan in that hole...with the others."

"Who?" Frazier tried and looked away.

"Yeah... who?" his interrogator mocked him and then paused for a moment. "Your problem is this..." the man leaned in closer to Frazier, scowling at him now, "she disappeared before you ever brought those kids up here. And the records will show she was on to you and your use of influence through Congressman Brian."

"You're crazy," Frazier insisted. "You can't prove any of that."

"Herschel Brian is in custody in Washington," the officer leaned back and grinned. "They already have his statement about the reporter."

The detective stood up and went to the door. The silent partner stayed quiet and followed him. With a hand on the doorknob he looked back at Walt Frazier. The man's color had faded a great deal.

"Seems the congressman didn't like having to ID his son's body that way," the officer told him. "Oh, and one more thing...The Eagle says to tell you, 'Hi'."

~

Murray circled over the bombed out house in Atlanta. Finding a vacant lot two blocks over, he radioed Jon for that and one other reason.

"Yeah," Jon answered him, "go ahead."

"Two blocks to your left as you come out, there's a bare lot I can set down in...call me as you get to daylight."

"Good," Jon agreed, "that would be easier than the rope."

"One other thing," Murray spoke quickly. "Cheryl called...she has info on that phone number and what Patricia over at the island told you."

"Well...what is it?" Jon asked.

"Sounded pretty detailed," the cowboy answered. "You just need to call her when you're done in there. How's it going anyway?"

"You know anything about wine?" Jon asked.

"Girls like it," Murray shot back.

"Thanks...that's a big help."

97

Agent Carter stood with the other NCIS agents watching the standoff. Marines in full battle gear staring down the Homeland Security agents. Carter suddenly spoke without directing it at anyone in particular.

"Notice anything missing here?" he asked.

The others looked around and then Everson wrinkled his brow and said, "Yeah, where's the media?"

"Exactly," Carter pointed at the other agent. "Old agendas and practices die hard, huh?"

"They don't want folks knowing too much about this," Everson added.

"You saying they aren't covering this... because of politics?" Monroe challenged with a skeptical glare in his eyes.

"You tell me?" Carter responded.

His colleague stood in silence. He had no answer.

Playing the slots for a couple of hours had afforded Warren Dawes the time he needed to get the feel of this new target.

The main room was large, as one would expect, surrounded by smaller rooms for private games or other activities. Dawes had only brought "so much" material with him. He calculated location, amount, and effect as he pulled the big lever on the machine.

Randall Swartz had come to the floor twice while he played and figured. Once to greet what had to be a dignitary or politician, and once to throw a card counter out of his casino. The latter was done with great fanfare and noise, to make an obvious example of the man.

There was no sign of Jamie Jamison but that really didn't matter.

Jon and Ben left the wine cellar as they had come in. The only sign of their presence would be the elevator shaft but that wouldn't be noticed for several hours.

"Why don't we take the bottle?" Ben asked of the only oddity they'd found.

"Naw," Jon told him. "If that is it, they'd know we have it and things could change. It's best to let them think the secret is intact."

"Yeah, well...it still could be," Ben shrugged. "You got good pictures of that label, right?"

"I hope so," Jon gave him a look. "And I left a camera so we can see if anyone else is interested in that particular bottle."

Once outside, Jon told him of the call from Cheryl.

"You want to talk to her about it?" he offered.

"You go ahead," Ben decided, "it's stuff you'll need to hear anyway."

They called Murray first and then Jon got Cheryl on the line as he and Ben walked to the vacant lot. The call took the entire time.

She told Jon the number matched the office that Patricia Earl had told him about, Agnes Pugh's congressional office in Brunswick, Georgia. There were two things new about that, the congresswoman had been killed that very morning in a D.C. traffic accident. Her car was hit from behind at a red light and shoved into the path of an oncoming cement truck.

"And," Cheryl went on, "when the office was ambushed and the staff killed in that apparent robbery, everyone was dead except the chief of staff. He is still not accounted for."

"What's this guy's name?" Jon asked.

"Darcy Brown," Cheryl read from her notes.

"That name rings a bell," Jon muttered. "That Syrian at the house said something about a 'Dar-see.' That's not even a coincidence. That's dead on."

"There's more," Cheryl spoke up. "This Darcy Brown has an uncle who's a life-time employee at the State Department."

"Now you're joking," Jon smiled. "Do you have a name on this guy?"

"Chester Weiss," Cheryl stated.

Jon looked at Ben who was wondering what all was being said.

"CW on C Street," Jon muttered and shook his head. "I'll be damned."

~

An anxious phone call between the office on C Street and one on Wilson Boulevard got testy real quick.

"Why haven't they gotten in there yet?" Weiss demanded.

"Because you got in too big a damned hurry, that's why."

"I don't understand."

"Of course you don't," the frustrated voice answered. "You sent your storm troopers in there before it was physically possible to enter the building. You scared somebody and they called in the military."

"Who would do that?" Weiss trembled as he asked.

"I'm not sure... but we need some cover story as to why those DHS troops are there."

"I'll take care of that," Weiss told him. "I have contacts in...."

"Whoa," the other voice stopped him, "hang on a second."

Weiss waited patiently while the man in the CIA office took another call.

"Forget about it," the voice returned and said. "Don't know why, but the military has just pulled back and your guys are going in."

~

It was near dark when Dawes finished his tour of the outside of Eagle's Rest Casino. He found it very promising for his intents.

Things were a bit too active and alert right now, he thought. And will be until around 4:00 AM, when blurry eyes feed information to inebriated minds. He would wait to do his work then.

~

Jon, Murray, and Ben got back to the mansion and found a large gathering leaning over the workshop table. They were all studying the pictures Jon had sent of the wine bottle.

The long string of mixed style numerals was a mystery.

XXXVLIII20.58-37XXVIXVII199

"If it's a code there must be a key," Daniel advised.

"It's not a serial number," Colleen added. "Vineyards don't do that."

Cheryl spoke up as Ben leaned over her, "Those numbers look like roman numerals, but that's not how they did large numbers," she told them. "3553 would be shown as MMMDLIII, what's here is really sets of numbers all pushed together."

"She's right," Lori piped in. "XXXV is thirty-five and LIII is fifty-three."

"The same with the later numbers," Lori went on, "XXVI would be twenty-six, and XVII is seventeen."

Jon then noted the dash between the two sets of numbers.

"Separate them," he suggested. "That would give us 35, 53, 20.58 and 37, 26, 17.199. What is that?"

Ben jumped to another screen and keyboard nearby and began furiously typing. "The first numbers should be 'north' and the second set should be 'east', " he said. "They're global coordinates."

"Latitude and longitude!" Daniel said out loud as he caught on, "But where?"

"Southeast of Aleppo, Syria," Ben informed them with his map on screen. "It's a desert outside the city."

"So we have a location but what's the big secret?" Marsha asked.

"Weapons," a meek voice said from across the room. Everyone turned to see Nava standing there with Doris.

"How did she get down here?" Lori asked.

"I brought her," Doris answered defiantly. "I believe she has and can still help us."

Jon stood wide-eyed but remained silent. He watched the discussion and viewed a link on his phone to the small camera he'd left in the wine cellar.

"What weapons are you referring to?" Daniel asked skeptically.

"The lost...the missing weapons." Nava answered.

The room became quiet as a church except for the fan motors of the computers. No one spoke, some became pale, and several mouths dropped open at thought of the potential.

"You mean they've been there all along?" Ben asked Nava. She nodded.

Jon took one step closer to the group and held his phone up. It showed a film playing from the wine cellar.

"She may well be right," he said. "This Homeland Security guy went straight for that bottle you found," he looked at Ben as he finished. "Nava could be quite right. The question is...what do we do about it?"

98

The early morning hour was much as Dawes had predicted. People were still moving about, from buildings to cars and then back into the casinos, but their movements were not nearly as steady as they had been.

He carried his payloads one at a time, having found spots inside the foundation of the main building and under one very large propane tank that sat in the rear, between the building and the parking lot.

In all he placed six, it was all he had left. Some were more potent than others but each placed with a purpose in mind.

Warren Dawes then drove back to his motel room on the outskirts of the town, to wait for the right time to make his move. He fell asleep the minute his head touched the pillow.

~

Daylight broke and the man in his office on Wilson Boulevard went straight to the window. They were still there, five in all, black SUVs. The dark tinted glass made it impossible to see who was inside, or even "if" anyone was inside them. But he ventured they had occupants.

He called a friend at Secret Service just to chat. The call was normal, no information about anything going on and the other man acted the same as he usually did. Yet the vehicles were there.

A call to Weiss didn't help. He could tell the man did not like the current pressure, much more preferring to put that on others as they always had.

"Keep your wits, will you," he warned while again looking out his own window. "I received word that our men got into the cellar. They have the bottle."

Weiss nearly cried with relief. He steadied himself against his desk and then caught Darcy staring at him.

"Yeah, great," he said into the phone. "I knew it would all work out. We just need to re-group...that's all."

"I'm gonna sit tight for a while yet and I suggest you do the same...do you hear me?"

"Of course," Weiss put on a smile he didn't mean, "talk to you later."

The State Department official hung up and turned to his nephew.

"The secret is safe," he said. "We're good."

"So we can leave then?"

"In a bit," Weiss said. "I need to pack a few things from around here."

~

Harold Foster called from the Dalton airport at 9:25 that morning.

"I'm ready when he is," he told Ben.

Jon was asleep, but had only been for an hour or so. He had spent most of the night in his lab preparing and making last minute plans. Ben knew to wake him when Harold called.

The passenger list for the flight to Washington was lengthier than usual.

It included Jon, the NCIS agents Dunbar and Burr, and Nava Golan on her first leg back home. Jon had arranged her trip through the president, who agreed after Grimes signed off on it.

Riding with Nava was Marsha. This was to keep peace more than anything. Not with Nava, but because of Marsha's growing attitude toward Colleen Dunbar. Jon had heard about it and now he'd seen it. Not knowing just what to do, he decided having Marsha along might hold down her imagination.

They all got to the airport at 10:30 AM and loaded everything on the G5. As she stepped toward the plane, Jon went to Nava and whispered in her ear. With no one else watching, he handed her a small piece of paper and nodded. The Mossad agent nodded back.

Harold enjoyed getting to give his departure announcement. It had been a while since he'd had a nearly full aircraft.

"Ladies and gentlemen our flying time to Reagan International this morning should be just under two hours." He ended with, "please keep your seat belts on and once again, thank you for flying Foster Airlines."

The levity was a welcome break from the stress they'd all been living under, and the look the others saw on Jon told them it might not be over.

Agent Dunbar swung her seat around to see Nava.

"Can I ask you something?" she said leaning her way.

Nava nodded and looked into the agent's eyes.

"You apparently knew the secret all along, I mean, the way that group acted you all had to know. Why did you not tell us earlier?"

The Israeli agent sat slowly shaking her head for several seconds before answering. Jon heard the question and turned his seat quietly to watch and listen.

"You're thinking the wrong way," Nava began. "We knew those weapons existed, yes. Many people did, they had to have." She looked at the faces around her, all riveted to every word. "Hussein, the butcher," she went on, "used them many times... before he was forced to hide them in 2003. Your politicians have argued for many years now about an 'unjust' war you started...because the weapons we all knew were there could not be found."

"But they were there, they did exist," Dunbar spoke up. "Why not just tell the world you knew."

"The knowledge was not the proof, agent," Nava sat straighter and stretched her neck in near anger. "The secret was not the knowledge. Everyone knew that. The secret was the proof."

"By keeping the argument alive," Jon entered the conversation, "those who pushed for peace above all else could hold the other side at bay."

"Peace is not a bad thing," Nava added.

"No," Jon agreed. "But the idea of it can be naive and self-serving, if not based in fact."

"So...the secret was the location," Dunbar surmised, "that no one knew."

"It's still just a theory," Jon cautioned. "It could all be a trap, too. Or...we could simply be wrong about this."

It got very quiet on the plane after Jon said that. Nava said nothing to dispute him, but her eyes disagreed.

~

The gaming establishments in Cherokee, North Carolina, were open twenty-four hours. Serious gamblers came in late in the afternoon and stayed till dawn the next day. The morning traffic was mainly tourists and vacationers. They started to arrive around 10:00 AM.

Warren Dawes blended in well with the vacationing crowd, and this fit his plan. He arrived at 11:40 AM.

"Welcome to Eagle's Rest," the two scantily clad greeters smiled and pulled the doors open for him. "What's your pleasure today, sir?"

"Slots," Dawes answered and was promptly pointed to the ten dollar machines. He walked through the rows and found some fifty-cent units mixed in. After a trip to the change window, he returned with a large cup of tokens and sat down.

He added one coin of similar size from his coat pocket to the cup. It was bent slightly and had a notch gouged in the edge.

He worked around that one for a while.

The group split up at the airport in D.C. Marsha took Nava by taxi to Andrews Air Force Base where her ride home awaited.

Dunbar and Burr exchanged handshakes and hugs before the driver sent by Director Grimes found them.

Jon grabbed his bag and hailed a cab. He had an appointment at the White House at 2:00 PM. A quick look at his watch told him he needed to hurry. There was only an hour and a half for his unspoken mission.

99

Chester Weiss was packed and ready to go. Darcy Brown was nervous and getting worse as time went by.

"Where are we going?" he asked his uncle.

"Go see if the guard is in place downstairs."

The younger man looked puzzled by the request but obeyed.

As the elevator doors closed, Weiss dialed three numbers on his phone, laid the receiver down, and left his office. He went to a back stair case. Slipping through a utility area, Weiss shouldered open a rusty door into the alley and cautiously went outside.

Darcy walked close enough to see the guard and then stepped back into the elevator. The guard saw him and hollered out, "Hold it!"

The uniformed man ran toward the elevator asking, "What's wrong up there?"

The confused Darcy Brown could only shake his head and asked what the man meant.

"The phone rang from up there and no one was on the line," he told him, "The lines still wide open."

The guard hit button number six and the two rode back up together.

Ten feet from the main street, Weiss froze as a cab stopped at the opening of the alley. A man with long grey hair and glasses climbed from the cab. He had one hand inside a jacket pocket and a paper or photo in the other.

The expression on the stranger's face changed and he raised his head as he looked at a paper and then Weiss.

The stranger immediately walked toward Weiss.

The State Department official turned to run, but realized he was in a dead end. When he turned back the stranger was standing right there.

"Who are you?" Weiss demanded.

"I could ask you the same," the stranger smiled, "but that's not necessary...is it?"

"I don't know you," the now frightened man trembled, "how could you know me?"

"You're Icarus, aren't you?" the stranger said oddly.

Weiss' mind spun nearly out of control. He recalled hearing of Jamison referring to the Greek tale with his concerns. The reference went through him like an icy blade.

"No," he cried out and turned to try to run again. The stranger grabbed him with a handkerchief over his mouth. It smelled sweet.

As he walked around the corner after laying the man's body out, the stranger found another cab and waved it down. *That was too easy*, he thought as he opened the door and climbed in.

"1600 Pennsylvania, please," he told the driver.

Chester Weiss would be found within the hour. A note on his chest read, <u>Daedalus Was Right.</u>

~

Dawes played into the early afternoon, when things got busy with the tourist crowd. He reached into the cup and found the bent coin.

Pulling the lever hard as he could the machine promptly locked up and the dials froze in place.

"What the hell is this," he shouted out loudly. "This thing was due to hit a jackpot and now it sticks?"

A floor walker, "bull", came to him quickly and asked what the trouble was.

"You fixed this game so I couldn't win," Dawes yelled even louder. "That's what's wrong. Where's the manager?"

"He's busy right now, sir. Let me get you to another machine, please."

"No," Dawes complained even louder. "He's too busy to see a customer that's been wronged in his house? What kind of place is this?"

"Look," the bull tried, "come with me to the office and I'll get him."

"Hell no, I ain't going nowhere. This is my machine and it was hot...fixing to hit big any time till you guys did something to it. You have him come here!"

The floor walker keyed in his radio, "Tell Randy I've got a situation out here. There's a crowd of onlookers gathering...he needs to come out quick."

~

Jon was kept waiting outside the Oval Office for about ten minutes.

"I'm sorry Mr. Crane," the president said, coming out to greet him personally. "I just had a rather disturbing phone message about one of our State Department employees. A long time employee at that."

"I'm sorry, sir," Jon stood and took the president's extended hand. "If this is bad time..."

"No...no, of course not, come in please."

As he opened the door to the Oval Office, the President spoke softly with a question.

"I trust you received my message about Barrett's move?" he said.

Jon nodded, "I did. I understand she should arrive in West Virginia later this afternoon."

"Hmm," the president grunted as he led Jon into the ornate room.

They sat on opposing sofas and the leader of the free world paused in deep thought before he started what he had to say.

"Daedalus is an odd reference, don't you think?"

"What are we talking about, sir?" Jon smiled and answered. "I'm familiar with the Icarus tale of course, if that's what you mean."

"Interesting," the president said softly. "You had mentioned before that one of the underlings had used that Greek tale as a warning."

"I have no first-hand knowledge of that, Sir, just what I've heard through others."

The President rested an arm outstretched across the top of the sofa. Looking down for but a moment, he considered his next approach.

"It seems to me that this pyramid has all but been scaled, do you agree?"

"The very top is still sharp, Sir. But what we've found out may be of more interest than the personalities involved."

The President leaned back and pulled his arm down. Jon drew a piece of notebook paper from a pocket and handed it to the man. First simply staring at it, then unfolding it, the president looked at him as though confused.

"What do we have here?" he asked.

"We believe it may be co-ordinates detailing the location of some things thought never to have existed."

"I understand latitude and longitude," the President said looking at the paper. "But I don't recognize where this is."

"Syria, Sir," Jon answered.

"Oh...I see."

The President stood and walked behind his desk.

"How sure are you of this information?" he asked.

"Reasonably so," Jon told him, "Enough to bring it to you."

Picking up a phone, the president hit two numbers.

"You don't mind if I call in my expert on these things, do you?"

"Not at all, Sir."

One of the President's most trusted advisors on Middle Eastern affairs came into the office. He and the President spoke near the door quietly for several minutes. Jon noticed the man in a thoughtful pose, before he shook his head, no.

The President let the man out and returned to the seat across from Jon. His expression was dire.

"There's no guarantee that this is accurate...is there?" he asked.

"No, Sir," Jon responded, "Just very good authority and the manner in which it was kept."

The man across from him looked at Jon in silence for nearly a full minute.

"I can't take the chance," he finally said. "I believe you and I trust you, but I can't risk this might be a hoax."

Jon did not react. He had already considered that possibility.

"If we went public with this," the president said as he slid up to the edge of the sofa, "and it wasn't there. I mean, they could even move the damned stuff before we got there to look, do you understand?"

"Absolutely, I do," Jon assured him. "But I had to let you make the determination."

Sitting back, the president asked him what he planned to do now.

"There are a few things I'd like to clean up," he answered. "You mentioned a man who works on Wilson Boulevard. Do you have a name?"

"Would I be signing a death warrant by telling you?"

"Not at all," Jon told him, "Simply confirming a bad guy."

"I've had him watched for two days." The president paused and then asked his guest, "I assume Grimes knows about this?"

"He does, sir."

"I'll have the watch stand down immediately."

"Thank you, sir..." Jon started to add how honored he was to help, but the president thought he might try to explain his next steps and cut him off.

"No...no...I'll hear no more about this...okay?" The Chief Executive stood and walked behind his desk.

Silas smiled and looked down to the plush carpet. "No, sir," he agreed as he pushed on the arms of the chair to stand. "I wouldn't think of doing that."

Moving to the door, Jon turned back respectfully. "Again," he said. "Thank you, sir."

100

His eyes scowled from under scrunched brows as he stomped toward the slot machines. Randall Swartz didn't like to be ordered around, not even a little bit.

The area floor walker shrugged shoulders at him and stepped aside when the boss arrived on the scene.

"What seems to be the problem here?" he demanded.

"Well, hello Randy," Warren offered with a smile, "I've been looking forward to meeting you."

The greeting threw Swartz off his stride. He looked around as though he'd come to the wrong place.

"You the one who demanded to see me?" he asked in a lower and much more subdued tone.

"I am," Dawes pulled out a stool next to his own and pointed, "Have a seat."

"You need to tell me what this is about before I have you tossed old man. I don't care for jokes, and I'm really busy."

"Busy, huh? Busy with Jamie?"

Swartz grabbed the stool and spun it to him. Sitting down within six inches of Dawes' face he leaned in even further.

"What is this?" he all but whispered.

"Young Jamison owes me money," Dawes said and shrugged at him, "Simple as that."

"Then why are you bothering me?"

"You either have him...or you have assumed his debts."

"You're either bold as brass or you're nuts," Swartz figured as he spoke. "I'm through screwing with ya." And he stood from the stool.

Dawes showed him a small box with a red button he held in his hand and said two words, "Sit...down."

"What is that?" the manager of the casino asked with more than a touch of concern coming over him.

Warren waited, then looked at the stool he had told the man to sit on and fiddled with the red button.

Swartz sat and leaned in again. "Are you kidding me?" he said. "That creep owes me fifty large."

"He owes me 150... large... as you say."

"Well he ain't here no more and he ain't coming back."

"That's fine. But you have assumed his debt to me...and I want my money."

"Or what?"

The old man grinned. "Or things get real exciting around here. It might even cause damage to your neighbors next door...I'm not real sure."

"You want to come with me?" Swartz asked him.

"Call ahead...if there's anybody else in that office, we all go bye-bye."

Swartz did as asked and the two walked to his private office and the safe. He pulled a stack of bills from the safe and Dawes looked at it and said, "That looks like it'll do nicely."

"This is over a quarter mill," the man protested. "You said 150."

"Now I got time, travel and aggravation expenses mixed in. That stack will do just fine." He pulled a bag from inside his pants and had Swartz put the money inside.

"I'm going to walk out of here now and you're going to sit there like a good boy...right?"

"I'll find you," Swartz threatened.

"Two things about that," the old man's face got red for the first time. "You come near me and the feds will hear about Jamison. Where ever you've put him, they'll find something."

As Dawes headed for the door, Swartz asked, "What's the other thing?"

"Oh yeah," Warren walked back and stared him right in the eyes. "I'll kill you...dead."

With the last bit of color he'd had now drained from him. Randall Swartz watched as the old man, and his money, left the Eagle's Rest.

~

Once Nava's plane was in the air, Marsha headed to NCIS Headquarters to wait for Jon. She found Dunbar and Burr there, waiting to meet with their boss.

"Is she okay?" Colleen tried to ask.

"Yeah..." Marsha responded in short snappy words, "She's fine. I don't think she saw them, but agents from Louisiana were on board with the other rogue Israelis caught in Shreveport."

"How do you know that?" Burr questioned.

"I talked to the agents. They are to turn those guys over to Mossad directly when they get to Israel."

"Who made that decision?" Colleen asked bluntly.

"I guess," Marsha pointed at Grimes' office, " he wanted them sent back. I don't really know," Marsha again was short with her response.

Agent Burr lifted his forehead but said nothing.

They all sat around in awkward silence after that.

~

Jon's phone rang the minute he cleared the White House. It was Ben.

"I've been monitoring those DHS guys that were at the house in Atlanta," he started.

"Good, where are they?"

"They're in D.C.. They went by Wilson Boulevard but the place was walled off by SUVs."

"Those should be gone now."

"They are now," Ben confirmed. "And the minute they left our guy left too."

"Do you have a bead on him?"

"Looks like he's headed for Quantico, he may be going to see Grimes."

Jon looked desperately for a cab and tried to call Grimes. He wasn't answering.

~

The car pulled up outside the NCIS building and the Director of the CIA walked to the guard.

"Wilson Farley to see Jerome Grimes," he stated.

"Is he expecting you, Sir?" the young man asked.

"He'll see me, son," Farley answered while flashing his ID.

"Yes, Sir," the guard opened the door and stood aside.

On the elevator the man checked his pocket and what was in it. He took a deep breath as the doors opened.

"Director?" Colleen called to him as he approached the stairs. "What brings you to Quantico?"

"Is he up there?" Farley asked. "I'm in a hurry."

It was then the CIA chief saw Marsha Hurst sitting by an assignment desk.

"You're her aren't you?" he asked, his face flushing. "You're his girlfriend."

Marsha stood and turned to him.

Frustration and anger poured through Farley. He reacted to Marsha's presence as though it were a sign. Fumbling for and then pulling a gun, he aimed at Marsha.

"Crane will finally pay for what he's done," he screamed out and pulled the trigger.

Marsha flinched but Colleen Dunbar dove across a desk in front of her. The shot meant for Marsha hit Dunbar in the side.

"Farley!" the voice bellowed from the top of the staircase. "It's me you want." Jerome Grimes stood with both arms flailing above his head, "I'm coming down."

Farley waved his gun around the room in a panic, keeping Burr and Marsha from aiding the downed woman. He pointed at the other teams in the room, screaming at them.

"Out...now," he ordered and the eight people backed away.

Jerome Grimes came down the steps two at a time, his hands lightly touching the railing.

The men met at the base of the stairs, some five feet apart.

"Why, Wilson?" Grimes asked him. "You helped us with this investigation more than once."

"Can you think of a better way to keep tabs... than to be a part?"

"But you almost got killed in Texas."

Farley twisted his head as he remembered. "Shit happens," he said.

"You know it's over, right? Grimes asked.

"It shouldn't be...this really can't be happening. We planned it down to the most minuscule detail."

The man was clearly coming unhinged. He had been in complete control for years and now his wheels were falling off.

"You and that Jon Crane," he shook the gun at Grimes. This is your doing. You two broke more laws than we did. It wasn't right."

With his hands up, Grimes stepped closer. "Just give me the gun, Wilson," he pleaded.

"At least I'll take you out before I go," Farley muttered and fired two shots into Grimes chest.

The NCIS director spun and fell to the floor.

Burr reached for a gun on one desk, but Farley pointed at him and motioned to back off.

Marsha Hurst took the opportunity to attend to Colleen, rolling her over and applying pressure to the wound.

"Why?" A mystified Marsha asked her. "Why did you do that?"

Looking confused by the question, Dunbar struggled to breathe and answer. "You're important to Silas," she blinked, "he saved me twice...I had to try..."

Marsha's expression softened and she mumbled, "Thank you."

There was no response that time. The agent was unconscious.

Farley stepped quickly toward Grimes and stood over his prey. He reached for a shoulder to turn him and Grimes suddenly flipped over, his own Glock in hand.

The Director fired into Farley's neck and blood flew from both sides of the gash. The man staggered backward and sat down against a chair.

Burr was on him in an instant, kicking his gun away but then Grimes yelled for him to leave the man be. The agent stepped back as his boss got to his feet.

Grimes straightened himself and looked down at the still breathing Farley.

"I borrowed one of Jon's jackets for today," he said, "Thought I might have company."

Wilson Farley grimaced, his hand tight at his throat. He tried to say something but only blood came from his mouth. His eyes grew large and then blinked. His body slumped and slid down the side of the chair.

Grimes ran across the room.

"How is she?" he asked of Dunbar.

"Call 911, quick," Marsha yelled back. "She's hurt bad."

~

As Jon jumped from the cab at the NCIS building his phone rang yet again.

"Harold called," Ben said. "He said to tell you he was on his way back to D.C.. That the delivery you wanted in West Virginia was done."

Jon had all but forgotten the mission he'd sent his trusted pilot on.

"Thanks, Ben...tell him I'll call in a bit."

101

Natalie Barrett did not recognize where she was at first. Her mind had unglued to the point that time and place meant little to her.

They signed her in and gave her a new number and cell assignment. During the change of uniforms, a guard approached her with a long white box.

"Someone is glad you're here, it seems," she said.

"What is that?" Barrett managed to ask.

"Flowers we assume," the smiling guard told her, "It's been X-rayed, and MRI'd up and down. Just flowers and a card in there," the woman continued. "A courier delivered them this morning."

Barrett carried the box with her, under one arm, through the remainder of her check in.

Her cell had not been swept for bugs or other devices, a normal part of a new prisoner's arrival, so she was walked out to the garden area. It was there she began to remember.

"Have a seat," her escort told her and placed her on a concrete bench at a concrete table. The hedge next to her felt familiar and she smiled at it briefly. The box sat on the table in front of her for several minutes. She did not move.

They brought her a Styrofoam cup of water and that directed her attention to the white box. Reaching past the water, Barrett pulled the ribbon on the box and lifted the lid. It was indeed roses, red ones. A small insect flew out as though just awakening. It circled behind her head.

She picked up the card and her face turned the color of her flowers. But it was too late.

The insect was one of Ben's electronic devices. The light caused it to come to life and its facial recognition programing set the bug into motion. Following Ben's preprogramed instructions; the bug flew around her and then released Jon's toxic payload right under her nose.

Barrett was found lying across the concrete table holding the card. It read, "For all you've done." There was no signature.

~

Jon's arrival at NCIS Headquarters was blocked by emergency vehicles. He jumped from the cab and ran. Getting closer, he watched as they brought Dunbar out on a stretcher, with Marsha close to her side.

Another gurney right behind them was fully covered and Jerome Grimes walked head down, following it.

Jon made sure Marsha saw him but neither said a word. Seeing the heavy dent marks on Grimes' jacket told the tale.

The NCIS Director came up to Jon as Colleen was loaded in the ambulance. The director stood next to him and grabbed his arm.

"She saved Marsha," he told Jon. "Dunbar is hurt...bad, but her chances are good."

"Farley?" Jon asked and looked at the covered gurney.

Grimes simply nodded.

"It's over," he said. "I do believe this is finally done."

Jon looked at his friend and patted his chest where the impacts had been stopped.

"Almost," he told him. "Almost."

~

The next seven weeks would be long for Colleen Dunbar and those around her. Besides her parents, others were constantly at her side or available. Grimes came by every day, as did Agent Charles Burr.

The recently retired ex-Captain of the Charlotte Police Department took an apartment in D.C. to be nearby. Marsha hardly missed a day.

She never said much about her change of heart, but her contrition was slowly replaced with her natural compassion and real admiration for the injured agent. She and Colleen's parents became good friends over time.

One other frequent visitor was Murray Bilstock. With his hat held tightly in his hands, he would stand in one corner, quietly. Marsha would later recall a tear she saw early on. His never-give-up spirit was on hold through her recovery, but he was there for her and she understood why.

~

Jon made several trips during that time. "Missions" as he would refer to them. He spoke to no one other than Ben about the travels and what motivated them.

He attended a lavish retirement ceremony for old friend Sharon Swanson. The colonel had decided it was time, and she was pleased to see Jon there. His admiration for her ran deep, but the trip was also timely.

Shortly after Jon left Kentucky, Reino Petteri was found dead in his cell. A heart attack had claimed him. No foul play was suspected.

A week later, Alex "Alexander" Raffini, the man who tried to kill Marsha in Charlotte, swallowed his tongue during an apparent seizure. An unknown allergy was listed as the cause.

While in Charlotte, Silas looked into the hit team from Wake Forest. One had developed a blood clot and died unexpectedly, the other two were then transferred to Guantanamo under a loosely interrupted application of Homeland Security's terrorism act.

That will have to do, for now, John told himself.

Darcy Brown had been held for a short while and questioned about his uncle's death. Evidence showed he knew more than he tried to let on about his uncle's business. But nothing could be proven. A month after his release, he was found at the bottom of a pool in the condo complex where he lived near Brunswick, Georgia. Many beer bottles were found where Brown's effects had been left. It was listed as a tragic accident.

Varkey Al Halbi, the Syrian assassin, being held in Atlanta at the Federal holding facility, had apparently tried to escape through a storm drain. It didn't work out for him. Witnesses claim a man in a black suit appeared to be an accomplice in the escape attempt. That man was never found.

The Israeli caught in Boris' enclosure had been sent to Washington for extradition on a later flight. That decision saved his life.

Last on Silas' unwritten list, was the name Walter Frazier. It took some time, but several of Ben's electronic bugs were sent up through the plumbing system at the Roanoke jail. They managed to eat into a gas line running through Frazier's cell block. The leak was directed into Frazier's glass lined cell. Cause of the ensuing spark was never known.

The fire burned for some time. The helpless authorities had to wait for the gas company to shut off the supply line before they could get to his charred body.

~

Meanwhile in Decatur, Georgia, Warren Dawes had bought a new pick-up truck with money he had "saved" from his retirement. He drove it to his favorite Italian restaurant, which sat behind a former large shopping mall called Northlake, to celebrate.

Warren wore his best new shirt and sat alone. He sipped his wine while he waited for his pizza, a medium Bambi, with no mushrooms.

He never heard from Randy Swartz again.

102

Miss "Lucky," as Colleen Dunbar became known, was released from the hospital after the seventh week. She and Marsha Hurst had enjoyed many hours sharing tales of law enforcement and of course, talking about Marsha's favorite subject, Jon.

Murray's visits continued, but he remained mostly quiet and as he could be, helpful.

Her parents wanted her to come home with them, but she insisted on staying at her own place in Washington, near her job, until ready to return to it.

"I'll be around," Murray told the parents. "I assure you, she'll be fine."

The old Colleen would have bristled at such a remark, this time she smiled and nodded to her Dad and hugged her Mom. Murray cautiously took her hand as the Dunbars left her apartment.

"Dinner whenever you're up to it, okay?" he offered.

"You got it, cowboy," Colleen grinned and squeezed his hand.

Murray became serious, or it seemed to start that way.

"I've never dated a woman braver than me before," he said with a straight face. "So...be patient with me, okay?"

Colleen's grin stretched and became a full blown laugh. Her hold on his hand tightened and she leaned in to offer him a kiss.

"I don't believe that's the case," she whispered, "But I'm proud you think so."

~

Marsha returned to Dalton shortly after Colleen's release from the hospital. It was time she reassumed her place in the mansion. Ben had already straightened the maple tree and replaced the blackened window glass on the front. *The house looked good*, she thought, *like new.*

Ben and Cheryl picked Marsha and Harold up at the airport and told them of their news, an official engagement. That was no real surprise, but what was were the plans they would wait until they had completed college. Both would study on-line through a new opportunity set up by Berry College in Rome, Georgia.

Tim Spiegel left New Orleans to head up a special NCIS Taskforce out of Quantico. It would report directly to Grimes and the president. Known internally as "The Sons of Liberty," the group would take on missions in a rapid response mode, with the help of Jon Crane and when needed, Silas.

The first new member of this group was the former Navy SEAL, Cody Arnold. Agents Leonard Monroe and Walt Everson also signed on.

~

Negotiations between the U.S. and Israel had fallen apart over the last month. Threats from Iran and Syria were becoming more serious. Behind closed doors, Israel claimed knowledge of a massive weapons stockpile, perhaps even those of the long dead Saddam Hussein.

The U.S. offered sympathies and promises of support should an attack occur on Israel, but the tiny nation was not appeased by that.

With information supplied to them by Mossad Chief Yinon Harel, the Israeli government had watched from satellites as the weapons were moved from the desert outside Aleppo to an even more remote location on the Khabur River.

The news broke early that morning when Israeli missiles hit the area setting off massive explosions that altered the terrain between two cities, Al Hasakah and Fadham.

The destruction was so complete that talk of Saddam's weapons surfaced after years of being ridiculed by many.

The President went on TV to talk of the country's disapproval of the rogue actions taken by Israel. "Yet," he made abundantly clear, "we stand ready to defend our ally against any retaliation launched at her."

On his desk, in clear view through the entire telecast, was a dark green wine bottle. It was not mentioned or explained.

Jon smiled as he watched the reports and thought to himself, *she did it. She told Harel.*

~

The mansion was decorated for another wedding when he got home that day. George and Doris were finally tying the knot.

Marsha met Jon in the lower level as he parked the Mercury.

"That thing is about dated," she smiled and told him.

"I know," he said softly. "Guess I'll need to look for something else."

They walked past the green Jaguar and Marsha reached out to touch it.

"Ben is really proud you gave him this thing," she smiled.

"He deserves it," Jon sighed, "and besides, it matches his suit."

"Phil and Sara are coming for the wedding," she went on. "They want us to come back to their lake house with them for a while. Phil says you owe him some stories."

"I guess I do," Jon smiled again. "That sounds good." He then looked at Marsha asking, "Daniel and Lori...and Westy and Rita?"

"They're coming. Oh, and Murray is bringing Colleen. In fact we'll have an entire NCIS entourage here, with Grimes, Tim, and his new team."

Stepping into the elevator, Marsha continued with her news.

"Sharon is coming," she said.

"Colonel Swanson?" Jon was surprised.

"She said she was looking forward to getting dressed up and it not be in uniform."

Jon laughed slightly, "That's great," he said.

On the ride up she told him, "Cheryl made a neat discovery about the star picture."

"Really?"

Gesturing with her hands to help explain, Marsha told of the revelation.

"If you start at the right side," she told, "from the one that points east if it were laying on a map, and work counter clockwise around the edge...it's the numbers from the bottle... in order."

"You're kidding?"

"Nope," she confirmed as they stepped from the lift into their room. "They don't make any sense until you know what to look for, but they're right there, have been all along."

Their room looked different to him. He saw the warmth and care in the way she had everything arranged. Jon realized that Silas was at ease finally. The tensions were gone and he could relax and appreciate what he had.

"Do you regret giving up that new job?" He asked her and immediately headed for his favorite chair.

"Not at all," she replied then jumped and sat on his lap in the big leather chair. "This is where I belong."

He closed his eyes and said, "Indeed."

Marsha stared at him for more than a minute, eyes still closed and not moving except to breathe. She watched him and felt herself smile.

He hardly ever just rested like this, she thought. Then Marsha felt compelled to say something else, something private. She said it within the silence of her mind.

Silas, I know you're in there. Thank you for protecting him.

Jon stirred just a little, adjusting one leg under her.

"Are you alright?" she asked.

"Yeah, finally... I think so." He put his arms around her and sighed, "I'm just tired."

Jon pushed back in the recliner pulling her close. They and the chair formed a growing shadow behind them. Lamp light pushed the dark silhouette high on the wall, topping it against the ceiling with the shape of a tri-corner hat. Across the chest of this shadow, extending from unseen hands loomed the trace of a long-barreled musket.

Government is instituted for the common good; for the protection, safety, prosperity, and happiness of the people; and not for profit, honor, or private interest of any one man, family, or class of men; therefore, the people alone have an incontestable, unalienable, and indefeasible right to institute government; and to reform, alter, or totally change the same, when their protection, safety, prosperity, and happiness require it.
John Adams

Doug Dahlgren

Other Books by

Doug Dahlgren

The SON Series...

The Son Silas Rising	Book One
The Only Constant	Book Two
The Basics of Fundamentals	Book Three
The Four Samaritans	Book Four
Eight of Six	Book Five

www.dougdahlgren.com

also available :

It Was Thursday

And coming soon....

The Eagle

Doug Dahlgren